Praise for Yvonne Navarro and *deadrush*

"Navarro does the near impossible of reviving one of the oldest themes—the curse of the undead—by making it fresh, frightening, and uncomfortably relevant to the nineties."

—*Stanley Wiater,*
author of *Dark Dreamers*

"*deadrush* is the *Pulp Fiction* of dark suspense, and Yvonne Navarro is who comes after Clive Barker. From page one, *deadrush* had a death grip on me. I loved it."

—*Nancy Holder,*
author of *Dead in the Water*

"The voice of horror has a new cutting edge. Yvonne Navarro places a fresh blood-wet shine on tarnished and familiar themes. Things still do go bump in the night, and there just may be a monster under the bed after all. . . ."

—*Kevin J. Anderson,*
author of *Darksaber*

"From the horrifying birth in the beginning to its dark echo at the end, Navarro never lets the reader draw an easy breath. Solid, believable characters—alive and dead—make *deadrush* a roller coaster ride from beginning to end. Not for the squeamish, *deadrush* is the work of a writer we'll be seeing lots more of."

—*Gary Brandner,*
author of The Howling series

Bantam Books by
Yvonne Navarro

AfterAge
Species

Bantam Books

New York
Toronto
London
Sydney
Auckland

dead rush

Yvonne Navarro

DEADRUSH

A Bantam Book/October 1995

ISBN 0-553-56359-9

Published simultaneously in the United States and Canada

Bantam Books are published by Bantam Books, a division of Bantam Doubleday Dell Publishing Group, Inc. Its trademark, consisting of the words "Bantam Books" and the portrayal of a rooster, is Registered in U.S. Patent and Trademark Office and in other countries. Marca Registrada. Bantam Books, 1540 Broadway, New York, New York 10036.

PRINTED IN THE UNITED STATES OF AMERICA

RAD 0 9 8 7 6 5 4 3 2 1

To Don
unexpected magic
in my life . . .

He who most
resembles the dead is
the most reluctant to die.
—La Fontaine

The Thank-Yous:

(in no particular order)

For Information:

Officer "No Acknowledgment's Necessary" Spencer
of the Chicago Police Department
Melissa Vrdolyak
Charles C. Lin, M.D.
Elliot M. Levine, M.D.
Steven Rasmussen, R.N., CEN, TNS

For Morale Support and Brainstorming, too:

Tammy Thompson
Jeffrey Osier
H. Andrew Lynch
Marty Cochran
Janna Silverstein
Howard Morhaim
Don VanderSluis
Elizabeth Massie

Amy and Kurt Wimberger
Wayne Allen Sallee
Brian Hodge and Dolly Nickel
Joan vander Putten
Diana Gallardo and Harry Fassl
Dave and Jo Wilson
Kathleen Jurgens and Rodger Gerberding
and Joan, an extra time

For Computer Support:

H. Andrew Lynch
Don VanderSluis
Linda Schroyer

**And, of course, for
Love and Life Support:**

Don VanderSluis

Prologue

Harmony, Georgia
Fifteen Years Ago

"God help us," the old woman whispered.

"What is it?" her granddaughter-in-law demanded. "What's wrong?" The blood of her son's birth still stained the linens beneath her hips but her voice was strong, rising as her question went unanswered. "Why doesn't he *cry*?" She clawed at the sodden sheets, struggling to sit upright.

Grandmother Nokomis turned her back to the bed. "He's fine, Miriam," she said hastily. "Just a quiet little boy, that's all. I've seen plenty of newborns who didn't so much as whimper. I'll clean him up a bit—"

"Let me have him. *Now*." It was strangely cold for an early June night and Grandmother Nokomis had built a fire when Miriam felt her first labor pains at sunset, then fed the flames steadily as the hours crept past. Now the firelight sparkled in the rivulets of cold sweat on either side of Miriam's face, flicking across the darkness of her eyes and making the crescent-shaped shadows above her cheeks look more like charcoal slashes. When the old woman had seen the boy's head emerge—and of course it would be a boy—her first panicked hope was that the infant would be dead, perhaps strangled on his own life cord, ending—finally—the Spiro family forever. But that was not to be, and so she offered her gnarled and age-beaten hands to catch the dark child of her grandson's seed and show him into the world. And she accepted him, despite the blight he brought to her family's legacy. She had thought to at least temporarily hide his mark before—

"Grandmother! Give him here!"

Old plaster walls, clean wooden floors that dipped in places from the wear of two centuries, windows that creaked and let in more air than they kept out. Familiar, the same sights she'd been seeing for eighty-five years, all moving in a slow spin to her left as she turned to face the pale young woman waiting on the bed against the right wall. Now, more than any other time in the past, Nokomis Spiro thought she could feel the spirits of her ancestors from her father's side, this time clamoring in alarm.

She tried to think of something comforting to say as she turned and handed the silent, bloody infant to his mother. She failed.

Smiling at first, Miriam accepted the child. Then her face went rigid with shock. "This c-can't be," she stuttered. She looked at the elderly woman imploringly. "Grandmother? Please?" Within the cradle of her arms, the boy's still-slippery body trembled slightly as his chest rose and fell rhythmically. Miriam's left hand spasmed, then her fingers curled into claws and she began ripping at the baby's face. "God, we've got to get it *off*!"

"Be careful!" Nokomis snapped. She batted Miriam's hands aside and lifted the now struggling baby clear. "You might hurt him if you tear it. It should be cut." She carried the newborn to the changing table and placed him atop the clean sheet she had folded in anticipation of his birth. He calmed instantly, but he looked *wrong* there, amid the sweet plastic rattles and a small, soft stuffed bunny.

Why doesn't he cry?

The old woman swallowed as she pulled the sewing scissors from her apron pocket and began to snip at the hideous black caul covering her great-grandson's face.

"I'm going to name him Jason," Miriam announced. "I read that it means 'healer.' " It was her first day out of bed, and settled on the family's antique rocker, she looked recovered from the birth.

Nokomis nodded but said nothing, thinking that the boy's name could mean "Jesus Christ" and it still wouldn't help him. The three-day-old suckled calmly at Miriam's breast, his blue eyes unnervingly piercing. All babies have blue eyes when they're born, she reminded herself. Odd that his eyes had lightened so soon. She rose unsteadily from the couch and went to the kitchen to make a cup of tea, nearly scalding herself halfway through pouring the boiling water into her cup when Miriam was suddenly behind her.

"No one is to know about the caul, Grandmother." Nokomis knew without turning that her granddaughter-in-law's eyes would be fierce, could *feel* the presence of her great-grandson where Miriam had placed him in the wicker bassinet a few feet away. "I won't have Axel's son marked in the eyes of our neighbors."

Axel. Her only grandson, dead now six months. What would he have said to see his newborn child, its face obscured by the evil of a black birthing membrane? A foolish question: no Spiro man had ever lived to set eyes upon the next male issue of his seed. Except for her, the female descendants had died out, too. Dear God, she thought in sudden terror, what evil history would this child create as he passed to adulthood?

"He's a baby, that's all. A *normal* baby. No one's to be told any different."

Normal now, Nokomis wanted to say. *But what about when he grows up?* "Would you like a cup of tea?" she asked instead. "There's more hot water." The cold weather was gone and she had cut a pile of wild daisies from next to the barn early this morning. Bathed in the high-noon sunlight, they sat in a quart Mason jar on the windowsill like a sparkling lie. Her pulse was a reedy spasm through the tired old heart within her chest.

"No, I don't want *tea*," Miriam said. Her voice was showing strain. "What I want is some indication that you heard what I just said."

The elderly woman turned with her cup and stepped past her granddaughter-in-law and the child, careful to touch neither. She waited to say her piece until she was fully settled on a kitchen chair.

"The neighbors have a right to be warned," she said evenly.

"*No!*" Miriam lifted Jason and held him in the crook of her arm, then slammed her other hand down on the table in front of the old woman hard enough to make the table's Formica top rock on the metal legs. Nokomis didn't jump, though the tea sloshed over her cup's rim; the baby's eyes widened, then narrowed, as though he were aware not of his mother's anger but of his great-grandmother's statement, and disapproved. Still, he didn't make a sound. Miriam yanked out the other chair and dropped onto it. "Listen to me—no, don't turn away, damn it! Please!" She leaned forward, her expression earnest. "It's almost 1980, Grandmother. All the old talk about cauls, white ones, red ones, black ones—that's all it is. *Old talk*. No one believes—"

"You may fool yourself into thinking that, girl," Nokomis interrupted, "but you won't fool me. I know better."

"This is an old town full of superstitious fools," Miriam snapped. "If you tell any one of those idiots Jason was born with a black caul, you'll damn him for life. He'll be an outcast, shunned by everyone. The children will taunt him and he'll spend his life lonely and without friends, without anyone. Is that what you want, old woman?" She lowered her face to the soft brownish fuzz covering Jason's scalp and rubbed one cheek against it. "He's a little *baby*, for God's sake. He doesn't deserve to be tortured all his life because of a stupid belief that no one can justify."

Grandmother Nokomis stared at her, then took a sip of tea while she considered her next words. "You're not from around here," she finally said. "I thought my grandson explained our history, at least as much as he could and still talk you into marrying him. None of the townswomen would have him, you see. They all knew he'd die if they got pregnant with a son."

It was Miriam's turn to stare. "Crazy talk, that's all."

Nokomis shrugged, her bony shoulders stiff under her housedress despite the climbing temperature in the farmhouse. "You can think whatever you like, Miriam, and it's obvious you didn't believe him. But didn't you wonder why a handsome, healthy man like Axel was still a bachelor at thirty-five?" She dropped her gaze to her cup, studying the cooling liquid. "I prayed you'd have a girl," she whispered. "At least then there was a hope that I could keep my grandson for a couple more years—sometimes that happens, you know. I buried my son the month before Axel was born. I wanted to be the one to die first."

"I'm not going to listen to this." Miriam started to rise.

"Sit!" Nokomis commanded. Despite the sun-filled room, Miriam's face was dark, hostile. "My father was Olin Spiro," Nokomis went on. "He died a year after I was born, in 1895. At the time, my mother was three months' pregnant. She lost the baby, a boychild, when she got kicked by a plow horse doing morning chores." Her eyes, an ancient, seawater-blue version of the eyes of her great-grandson across the table, started to fill with tears but she blinked them away. "My mother—the whole town—knew that my father was . . . *touched*. He could see things, do things, *predict* things, that a man had no way or right to know. It was an accepted thing—he never misused his 'talent' and it'd been happening for so long, since the Spiro clan first came to be, that no one thought twice about it—"

"What do you mean 'it'd been happening for so long'?" Jason had fallen asleep and Miriam rocked him gently, hating her reluctant fascination with the elderly woman's tale.

"A male child touched in some way is born every fourth generation in the Spiro family. The last time it was my father," Nokomis explained. Her gaze dropped to the sleeping infant. "Now it's . . . Jason."

Miriam leaned forward. "If you believe that," she pointed out, "then that makes Jason special, not . . ." She frowned as she tried to think of the right word.

"Jason is tainted." Nokomis kept her voice steady. "I spent my youth in shame by bearing a son out of wedlock to maintain the family name, and that son was Axel's father.

Now Axel's son—*your* son—has turned the history of the Spiro family in the direction of darkness."

Miriam snorted. "Very poetic, and completely ridiculous. Crazy superstition building on itself, like a nasty, uncontrolled infection." She turned her face toward the open window with its jar of spring daisies; birdsong filtered through, then a dog's faint bark, carried on the summer breeze from another farm a quarter mile away. After a moment she again faced her dead husband's grandmother. "I won't have any of this," Miriam said quietly. "You're right in saying that I'm not from here, but that doesn't mean I don't know how small-town people hang on to small thoughts, and it doesn't take a high-school education to know they'll use those beliefs to destroy another person. Axel's dead and this baby is all I have left. This is my *son*, Grandmother. I'll do anything to protect him, anything to see he gets a fair shot at living a happy, *normal* life. I won't let you or anyone take that away from him. I loved you once."

Nokomis sat quietly across the table from the strong young woman who had suddenly become a dangerous stranger.

"But I'll kill you if I have to."

Today . . .

Miriam could see her son, fifteen years old today, stride across the half acre of disused field north of the farmhouse, on his way to Saturday-afternoon services at that awful church. He was so tall for fifteen! By the time he turned eighteen, she was sure he'd be as tall as his father had been, maybe taller, and he'd fill out by then, too. She watched his light brown hair gleam in the sunlight until he reached the road and bounded out of sight, then she turned and went inside. Had Axel really been tall? The truth was, she couldn't remember; too many years of hardship and harder work, with no one to keep her company but Jason, and for that she would damn Axel Spiro with her last breath. While Jason was popular and well liked and the townsfolk were unfailingly polite, Miriam had no close friends, and none of the men from town would date the widow of a Spiro. Even Grandmother Nokomis's superstitious conversation would have been welcome. All those doomsday stories about Jason and singsong tales about raising an illegitimate son in the poverty of the south in the 1920s—at least they'd been interesting. But the old woman's heart had given out before Jason could be baptized—no fault of Miriam's, but her bitter words had left her with unresolved guilt all these years.

There's nothing wrong with Jason.

How many times had she thought that over the last decade and a half? Thousands—*tens* of thousands—a comforting psalm to be whispered at every opportunity. And it had been true . . . until the construction of the church two years ago that housed the preacher Abel Scanlon and his Pentecostal Serpent Handlers. Before that, she'd taken Jason to Sunday services at the Baptist church in downtown Harmony every week, and if she didn't sing or clap or say "amen" along with everyone else, at least she was *there* for her son's sake, grimly offering him the opportunity to learn about a God in which she no longer believed. Hoping that he would find the faith she had lost somewhere in the pain of her husband's long-ago death.

A lot of good it had done; here it was the boy's fifteenth birthday and Miriam couldn't keep him away from a church and religion so far removed from the placid little Baptists that it was ludicrous. Over the past six months she'd tried *everything*, even complaining to the sheriff—

"I'm sorry, Miz Spiro, there's nothing we can do. It's that First Amendment thing, freedom of religion and all that."

"But Jason's only a boy and these people are handling dangerous animals and doing who knows what else!"

"Reptiles, Miz Spiro, not animals. And Jason is almost fifteen. If the courts in this county'll let a boy that age decide which parent to live with in a divorce, you know darn well they won't stop him from going to the church of his choice."

"First Amendment or not," she'd replied heatedly. "These snake-handling churches are banned in most states. People die because of them, for God's sake!"

"Well, they ain't banned here, and ain't no one died."

"Yet," she interjected in an icy voice.

"Like I said, there's nothing I can do. Besides, most of the *people who show up in that place go just to watch—they don't want anything to do with those snakes. Boy's only curious, like any red-blooded American kid would be. It'll pass."*

So here she was, a forty-year-old single parent with a "curious" teenager who spent every free moment at a white-washed shack on Blue Highway, a structure this "Preacher" Scanlon had topped with a rusted tin roof and dubbed a place of worship. At fifteen Jason ought to be discovering girls, not becoming obsessed with Holy Rollers. Each time he attended services, Miriam's skin crawled and she went nearly crazy with fear, her imagination supplying feverish pictures of long-fanged snakes and Jason twisting in death throes beneath the stares of the other worshipers. She'd done everything but outright forbid him to go, but she knew instinctively a move like that would be disastrous. Still, there was one more option: her mother, who had died several years ago, had a sister named Theora who lived in Chicago with whom Miriam had exchanged obligatory yearly cards at Christmas, on birthdays, and at Easter, plus an occasional short letter with a hazy, home-shot photo of Jason as he grew. Miriam was not a pushy woman, but desperation sometimes forced a woman to ask for things she otherwise might never have the nerve to voice.

She retrieved her purse and stepped to the counter, glancing out the window as her fingers touched the single Greyhound bus ticket inside. The barn door was already coming loose at one hinge and she could see a dozen half-inch fissures in the wood at the base of the old building's southwest corner, where the sun beat the hardest in the heat. The pane of glass she stared through was cracked at the lower corner and needed replacing. It would be an exhausting summer without Jason to help, and while she had scratched together the money for the ticket north, she'd have to beg and borrow to bring him back. He would be so angry . . . still, she couldn't help but think the boy might enjoy a summer stay in the city.

And please God, Miriam thought, *let him outgrow his infatuation with that deadly religion.*

Sweet, hot southern day, the sun bright and fierce outside the church as the grasshoppers sang, the birds screeched, and the gnats and mosquitoes dive-bombed the miserable farm animals. Inside, a different kind of singing, voices raised in adulation, floating on the humid air along with the cloying scent of the bundles of lilacs, clover, and wildflowers brought to adorn the room by members of the congregation. Unheard beneath the music—the battering of the old drum set in the corner and the strum of an older guitar—was the darker sound of smooth reptilian bodies sliding over each other in close quarters, soft hisses and angry rattles masked beneath the joyous clamor of worship.

Jason Spiro, sky-blue eyes shining, nearly catapulted into the church. He was *early*, for Pete's sake, and folks were already dancing up front, clapping their hands and stomping their feet. A few were already speaking in tongues, their twisted sounds hanging on the moist air within the church until they found Jason's knowing ears. He heard every one of them, *understood* every word, even if his mother didn't believe him. He didn't know what else he could do to convince her that he belonged in this church as much as possible. He couldn't find the words to describe how he felt when he was here, and how he felt when he was away—incomplete . . . *hungry*. He thought the answer might be admitting he'd found Grandmother Nokomis's journal at the bottom of the cedar chest in the attic five years ago, the mildewed pages filled with spiky, eloquent swirls that said everything. The ravings of a madwoman? Jason didn't think so, nor was he convinced that his mother should know he'd read all the things Grandmother had written about him.

Axel's son was born with a terrible black caul.

More details, much more, and he drank in every bit—the things Grandmother'd thought he might do or say or cause in his lifetime. Obscure accusations and predictions—speculations—all things that hinted at what he was inside and showed him what *not* to do, enabling him to build a careful wall of normalcy. Jason didn't think he was at all the evil creature Grandmother Nokomis had believed he would become—he'd never done an intentionally mean thing to anyone. He'd been through that book so often over the last half decade that he'd worn the corners of some of the water-spotted pages translucent. Reading and rereading, waiting and listening to the whispers in his head that had grown steadily since the first time he'd struggled to decipher Grandmother's ancient flowing script.

Jason *was* different, and he'd have to be blind not to see that difference in the uneasy gazes of his schoolmates. He had only one friend, a husky teen named Duwayne Unwin who was, for different reasons, as avoided in the normal circles of Harmony as Jason. Duwayne's family farmed pigs, and Duwayne's clothes always smelled like pig droppings. The aroma permeated the boy's hair, skin and clothes so thoroughly it would probably never come out, and how could it? The Unwin house bordered the sties and was itself steeped in the smell. Duwayne was a strapping boy, bigger than Jason, with thick dark hair and black eyes, a sure sign of Cajun blood somewhere in the line. Being handsome didn't matter; the way Duwayne's father made a living made him an outcast forever.

Pigsmell or not, Jason had started hanging around Duwayne Unwin after Scanlon's church was built. Mr. Unwin was a regular member, a *real* one who didn't hesitate to thrust his hand into the crate and pull up a rattler or two in a scar-studded fist. The elder Unwin allowed his family to attend services with him, but wouldn't hear of letting Duwayne or his eleven-year-old sister handle snakes. Duwayne's mother never missed a service, singing along in an unreliable voice but with no desire to pick up a snake or drink from the jar of strychnine water sitting on the front railing. Duwayne hadn't hesitated to repeat her words to Jason earlier.

"Duwayne, I know I'm living right and I know the good Lord sees me. He don't need for me to pick up no filthy snake to prove it. Now, your father . . . well, I guess he feels he got to show the Lord how good he is. Maybe he thinks God can't see him when he's in town, in that bar. Or maybe your father knows that's exactly when God's been watchin'."

Duwayne had been quick to add that his daddy told things differently, and Jason could hear in his friend's voice which parent he believed. "My daddy says only a man's faith will keep the serpents from bitin'," Duwayne had said proudly. "He says that's why you don't see no boys our age up front. Once I told him I wanted to do it and he liked to slapped my face right off."

"Why?"

Duwayne had looked at him impatiently. "For thinking I had the balls of a man, of course."

Jason's eyebrows raised. "Yeah? Well, what about the women who go up and handle the snakes? What's he say about them?"

"He says they're whores." Duwayne's hands were shoved deep into the pockets of overalls washed to a faded faint blue. Frayed spots at the cuffs and knees were nearly white from the bleach Duwayne's mother used constantly. Underneath the smell of chlorine, the fabric still smelled like pigs.

Jason couldn't help sniggering. "No way. Scanlon would never let anyone touch his snakes if he thought they had a dirty spirit. Plus they'd be sure to get bit."

Duwayne shrugged. "Maybe, but I ain't gonna argue the point with my daddy, if you get my meaning. You coming to services tonight?"

Jason's grin was wide. "I wouldn't miss it. It's my birthday—"

"I didn't know that!"

"—and I got a thing or two to show Scanlon. *And* your daddy."

And finally, an end to all that waiting, the rising of raw instinct that gifted him with the feeling that his moment had arrived . . .

Tonight.

How many times had he heard the words *You are the Chosen One* uttered to him among the tongues and music and the holy fervor in this room over the past two years? Thousands, literally. These people, some from the shabbier outskirts of Harmony, some forest squatters, others truck farmers who drove in from the deeper hollows and more remote swamps—they *needed* him. To lead them, to teach them God's ways, to show them that their message—*You are the Chosen One*—though misunderstood by those who uttered it, stood true to life before them. He had no written instructions or calendar or specific scripture to quote. He just *knew* that tonight was it. When he burst through the door, Jason could tell by the escalation of the singing and speaking in tongues that they knew as well, deep in their souls, that tonight was *the* night:

Jason's birthday, his initiation . . .

His coming to *be*.

It was the same every time, that spreading sense of . . . *welcome* that he couldn't make his mother fully comprehend—a certainty that he'd finally found the piece of his life puzzle missing all this time. It wasn't the people, or the snakes twisting sluggishly in their dirty wooden crates while sweat-slick folks swayed around them. It was . . . *fulfillment*. A sense of something sliding into his soul, slipping in and swelling until it shut out all the emptiness he'd kept secret so long. It filled him and grew bigger, and heavier, and ultimately all-encompassing.

Scanlon was up front, kneeling by a husky, middle-aged woman in a pink dress who sprawled on her back on the floor, twitching and mumbling while her eyes rolled in her head and her mouth yawned in a nearly toothless circle. As Jason weaved among the brothers and sisters swaying in the center aisle, the preacher pressed one hand on the woman's streaming forehead.

"And they shall lay hands on the sick, and they shall recover!" he bellowed. His flushed, chubby cheeks quivered with effort and heat. "Come out of this woman, devil! Begone and free this woman to *Jesus*!" His fingers grabbed a tuft of her greasy bangs and he thumped her head twice against the floor. "Begone, I command thee!" The thinning strands of grayish hair stuck across the crown of Scanlon's head fell forward and bobbed with each motion of his head.

Suddenly the woman grasped his wrist and grinned jaggedly. "Yes!" she screamed. She jerked Scanlon's arm up and down in a parody of a handshake and clutched at his jacket. "Glory be, I'm healed! I'm *healed*!" She scrambled to her feet and she and the preacher whirled past Jason and down the center aisle, until Scanlon kissed her resoundingly on one cheek and propelled her into the last row of chairs.

"A hard one, brothers and sisters," he called out to the swaying and clapping people as he strode back to the pulpit. The knees of his light gray slacks were dusty and his pink sport shirt was open at the collar, already sodden with perspiration under the arms and down the middle of his back. "But the Lord wins for the faithful, because the Lord protects His own, and the Lord is moving in this building tonight!" Cries of *"Hallelujah!"* and *"Amen!"* burst from the parishioners.

Scanlon reached Jason and grinned at the boy, then pulled him up to the pulpit with him. "Brothers and sisters," he shouted. "Are you holy?" There was a spattering of affirmative shouts from his audience. "I said, *ARE YOU HOLY?*"

The response was a medley of righteous screams of agreement. Jason beamed happily next to the preacher, tapping his feet and waiting for the right moment. Scanlon was practically vibrating with excitement. "Then let us show each other the faith of God within ourselves, and tonight, in celebration of the date of his birth fifteen years ago this very day, brother Jason Spiro will join us in that holy display for the first time!"

An expectant hush fell over the worshipers and Jason filled the void with the familiar words, not shouting as Scanlon had done, but doing much more than merely speaking . . . *mesmerizing*, his gaze finding and paralyzing the people who waited.

"They shall take up serpents, and if they drink any deadly thing, it shall not hurt them. They shall lay hands on the sick, and they shall recover!"

"Who will join us?" the preacher demanded suddenly. He thrust one meaty arm above his head; clutched in his sweating fist was a pint jar of cloudy, vile-looking liquid. The handwritten words on the jar's label had long since smeared away. "We will drink in defiance of Satan, and he shall not harm us!"

"Amen!" a woman cried from the back of the church.

"Praise God!" came the hoarser cry of an older man.

The preacher swung the jar at his audience again. "Who will—"

"*I* will." Jason snatched the jar from Scanlon's outstretched hand before the man could blink. The preacher grinned and clapped with the onlookers, urging his parishioners on while he swung an arm around Jason's shoulders and hugged him. The men and women in the church applauded and danced to the beat of the band as the heat and the music and the moment enfolded them. Scanlon's eyes were big and soft as a doe's as they locked with Jason's, the kind of gaze a God-fearing person knew in their bones could be trusted. Still, his whispered, heavily accented words were forced through his teeth in the midst of a wide, unfaltering smile.

"Boy, for the last time, I sure hope that God's a'moving on you to do these things t'night, 'cause they's death in 'em otherwise. Many's the man who's died of weak faith."

"Don't you worry, preacher man," Jason shot back. Something in the teenager's voice made Scanlon's hearty smile slip for an instant. "I've been waiting all my life for to-night. Like Jesus, I would die for you." He laughed abruptly and skipped away from the older man as he unscrewed the jar's lid, following the music and weaving among the five or six people crying in tongues and jumping to their own rhythms on the carpeted floor in front of the pulpit's vibrating railing. More than anyone else in this room—more than even the preacher who still followed him across the front of the church—Jason knew he was *supposed* to be here, moving among these simple folks, showing them the way of *true* faith.

He'd show them something, all right.

"Praise the Lord!" Jason cried as he raised the jar of strychnine-poisoned water to his lips. His own fear made the first taste flowing over the crusted rim of the glass nasty, like caustic, gritty metallic water; then the flavor changed as it touched his tongue, *sweetened* and slid like warm honey down his throat as he drank deeply. When the jar's contents dropped to the halfway mark, the shock that rolled from the preacher was palpable and the older man wrested the jar from Jason's grip.

"That's enough, boy. You *aiming* to die tonight?"

"Oh ye of little faith," Jason hissed into Scanlon's face, careful to let no one else hear. "The piddling sips that you and your *faithful* take prove nothing. Tonight you'll see what true belief *really* means."

The concern on the preacher's face switched to indignation and his cheeks went dusky red as he said something back, but Jason neither heard his words nor cared what they were. Head spinning, Jason jerked away from the useless old churchman and headed for the serpent crates, his stiffening feet and arms twisting and flailing from the effects of the strychnine. He could feel his tongue and lips thickening and his lungs hitching for air, as though he'd downed a half-pint of Jack Daniel's on his way here. No matter; he had much, *much* more in mind for the gazes of his fellow worshipers than a simple death by poisoning, and the best was yet to come.

Behind the pulpit a few men already had a snake or two in hand and the reptiles, carefully rotated and fed before each service by the honorable Scanlon, did little besides hang and bob within the sweaty, jouncing grips of the gyrating faithful. More serpents twined over each other inside a crate placed on a table, tongues flicking in and out monotonously. The table was placed behind a speaker's platform to minimize the danger of being kicked over, and in his blurring line of sight Jason saw a woman grab a double handful of snakes and hold them aloft, terror etched in every line of her face before she flung them back into the crate and whirled away. He was going on intuition and adrenaline now, obeying a dark, silent force within himself that had always been present, just waiting for its time of birth. The time was *now*.

There was fear in Jason's brain, but he disregarded it, knew it was too late for surrender. His legs and hands were shaking, yet when he moved to stand in front of the crate, Jason's heart wasn't at all afraid and his hands were rock steady when he plunged them into the midst of the snakes. He came up with two in each fist, a fair selection of fat diamondbacks and a single cottonmouth, as many as he could wrap his fingers around, then staggered back to the carpeted floor in front of the pulpit.

"Look, brothers and sisters!" he cried. His words came out mangled, sounding like *Loo', blutherth an' sthlisthers!* but it didn't matter. Jason waved the snakes over his head, feeling their sinewy bodies start to struggle. The voices raised in worship and the singing around the church stuttered, then faded altogether as those people within range of the snakes he held tried to back away without seeming obvious. At the edge of his vision, he caught a glimpse of Duwayne and his family in a front row, their expressions ranging from Duwayne's slack-jawed incredulity to Mr. Unwin's deep scowl. No matter.

"Glory!" *Glo'ee!* He was nearly past the point of communicating; if he didn't move fast, the convulsions would take him before he gave Scanlon's "faithful" his show of true belief. His arms were heavy and jittery, the muscles beginning to contract, and he swiped the air again with the snakes to create at least the illusion of control as he fought the sudden urge to heave up his bellyful of poisoned water. Only the preacher had the courage to stay anywhere near him.

"Boy," he growled, "you gettin' carried away, ain'tcha? Anybody can see you ain't feeling right smart. Whyn't you save the serpents for another service."

Jason stopped then, stopped *entirely*. No more jitters, nausea, or preconvulsions. No more *movement*. When he raised his face to meet the stunned gazes of his fellow churchgoers, his eyes were open and sharp, his voice inexplicably clear.

"This is the *New* Word:

"*I* shall take up serpents, and *I* shall not be harmed; *I* shall drink any deadly thing, and *I* shall recover. And *I* shall raise them up and heal them." He thrust his hands forward and shook them; the snakes trapped within his grip hissed in angry response, trying to squirm free.

A mutter ran through the crowd, culminating in a cry of "Blasphemy!" from a woman in the back.

"*Behold!*" Jason suddenly roared. He crushed the rattlers and the cottonmouth against his chest then, in a deadly embrace of furious fangs and lethal venom.

All the snakes were caught and crated away, the plain little church almost empty now. The boy's body was certainly not a pretty thing to see, Abel Scanlon thought as he and the handful of parishioners who hadn't beat a quick retreat when Jason collapsed rolled the corpse onto a sheet. Six bites against skin gone pale gray, although three of the bites had been weak, repeat strikes and one of the rattlers had somehow been killed in Jason's grip before it'd had an opportunity to attack its tormentor. It was the first three strikes that counted the most, and from the look of the puckered flesh swelling beneath the collar of the dead boy's T-shirt, he'd taken two of those on the left side of the chest, right above the heart. There was another bite higher up at the bend of his neck, and two more—one clearly the last of the heavily dosed first strikes—along the line of his right jaw. The final bite was a deep puncture in one forearm, more than enough to kill a man twice the size of this skinny farm boy. There were a number of men and women who'd been snakebit and lived through it, and about half of those never took ill from the strychnine. One older man who'd been handling snakes most of his life had been bit over a hundred times—but at least the man was responsible for himself. Why Jason Spiro, of all people? Scanlon knew Miriam Spiro complained about the church to the sheriff at least every two weeks. He was going to have a mess of explaining to do, all right, not to mention the sheer waste of it. All because the boy'd been in too much of a hurry to let God come on him naturally. Right now Scanlon wished he could go home and shut himself up until the hell that was coming just went away. Well, his old easy chair and laboring air conditioner weren't going anywhere, and he had a bunch of dirty work to do before he'd be seeing either one.

"Fold it over and hoist him up," Scanlon ordered as he swabbed at his grime-covered face with a handkerchief. "We'll put him in the back room. Can't leave the boy out here for folks to wander in and see."

The four men who'd remained bent to the task as Scanlon pushed open the door to the rear office. "You gonna call his mother first, or the sheriff?" one of them asked.

"Boy's own fault," another said. Then he shook his head and whistled. "Still, I wouldn't want to be in your shoes." He grunted as they started to lift the body; Jason had been healthy and heavier than he looked.

Scanlon looked thoughtful. "Well, I reckon I'll call the sheriff first. Miz Spiro might bring me the business end of her shotgun otherwise."

"No need to call anyone, Preacher Scanlon."

One of the men yelped and dropped his corner of the bedsheet, backing away as Jason's feet thumped awkwardly to the floor and the boy righted himself while the other three still stood, stupidly holding corners of the empty sheet. Scanlon froze, then released the doorknob and let it swing shut.

"Jason." Scanlon couldn't imagine how he kept his voice so calm, and he was more than a little surprised that he could hear himself say the boy's name over the doubled rate of blood pulsing through his arteries.

"I have to get home to the wife and kids, Abel," one of the men, the elder of the Unwin family, said suddenly. His voice was full of forced cheer and he aimed a carefully averted gaze toward Jason's shoes. "Glad to see you're all right, son." He was gone before Scanlon could protest or ask him to stay. The man who'd been the first to drop the sheet hadn't bothered explaining as he headed for the door.

"Then there were three," Jason said softly. He swallowed and Scanlon's gaze went to the wounds on Jason's jaw and neck, masses of ugly, mottled swellings encircling the suppurating puncture marks. Jason smiled and touched the bloated flesh along his neck. Then held up his arm, with its twin black-and-blue punctures nearly to the bone, offering it for closer examination by the three men frozen before him. His voice dropped to an intimate whisper and his eyes glowed with bluish fire.

"And I shall recover."

Something . . . *rippled* along Jason's arm and the wounds, so black and gray, softened suddenly to pink and started to close.

"I'll be going home now." Myer, the biggest of the men and another hog farmer who always smelled like his animals, jammed his cap tighter on his head. He turned and simply walked out, not bothering with excuses.

"One down, two to go. What about you?" Jason grinned devilishly and there was a burning in his eyes, an intensity nearly too painful to see; Myer's companion, a thin middle-aged man whose name Scanlon couldn't remember, was a first-time visitor and had only stayed because of Myer. Now, with the ravaged skin of Jason's face starting that same writhing dance as his arm, the man held up his hands and stumbled backward, nearly babbling in terror. He tripped and fell on his backside, and Jason laughed and raised both hands in mock claws. "Should I *chase* you?" The man hauled himself up and fled to the sound of Jason's shrieking laughter.

"Jason, son—"

"Are you still here?" Jason stared at the preacher, the fire in his irises turned suddenly cold.

"I—"

"And still talking, too," Jason marveled. "Still trying to yammer on about your so-called faith. Look at me, *preacher*." He pushed his face close to Scanlon's. "See what real faith can do. What *my* faith can do."

Paralyzed by the sight and terrified by this fifteen-year-old anomaly, Scanlon could only stare and sink to his knees while the remainder of Jason's hideous wounds shrank and healed in front of his disbelieving eyes.

Beneath the faded, frayed wall hanging of a wise-looking Jesus at his Last Supper, the Pentecostal Serpent Handlers' Church was, finally, silent.

1

Summer in the city and a different, bigger kind of heat, a different *soul* to the soaring mercury: the never-silent sounds of traffic a few blocks away, a horn's sharp blaring, the abrupt hissing of air brakes cutting through the sticky air as a CTA bus stops for a solitary night traveler. The same stars shine in the midwestern sky, of course, as are suspended over a small Georgia church nearly a thousand miles east, yet here they seem more remote, purposely distanced from this swarming, dirty knot of humanity. In the night hours, voices rise in anger above the blare of a television from an open window, while soft laughter floats from another in the same building along with the sound of silverware scraping against a plate. Here and there the thick layer of heat battles the hum of old air conditioners and window fans. In the alley behind a small, shabby house on Newport Street, a pocket of darkness waits for daylight or the shine of headlights to reveal its brutal secret.

"Definitely number four." Detective Jude Ewing grimaced and turned away from the woman's corpse, the skin of his face lightening then darkening in the revolving blue lights of the police cars crowded into the alley. He jabbed a finger at the uniformed officer closest to him. "Why isn't Amasa here yet? Get the ME's office on the radio and find out. I want to get this over with and get the body out of here." He raised his head and scanned the backs of the houses and small apartment buildings lining the alley; he could see at least two dozen people leaning out of windows and gathering on back porches, drawn by the lights and the noise and the presence of the police. Farther down where the alley met the street, a patrol car had parked lengthwise to block access and the two cops were already arguing with an ensemble of reporters who'd picked up the call on their scanners. "And for Christ's sake, will someone *please* cover her up before one of those photographers manages a picture?"

"We've got her purse." Jude turned at the sound of his partner's voice and Detective Sandra Wilfred held up her forefinger; from it dangled a small canvas tote. The zipper along the top of the cream-colored bag was still closed. "Never opened, so we can forget robbery—but we knew that anyway. Might as well dig in and find out who gets the bad news." A few moments later she pulled out a vinyl wallet and flipped it open; as expected, the victim's cash and credit cards were still inside. Sandra peered at the driver's license. "Delta Arvel," she read. Her gaze met Jude's and she answered his unspoken question. "She was twenty-eight. Youngest yet."

"Shit," Jude muttered.

"Here we go. This says to notify her mother." Jude dutifully reached for the card, but Sandra held up a hand. "You did the last one, and this is only a block away. I'll take a uniform with me while you stay here and wait for Amasa."

Jude glanced back toward the body and almost gave in to the urge to bellow at the nearest uniformed cop; still no one had covered the woman and Delta Arvel's bared legs were twisted up against her torso at an impossible angle. Her driver's license had shown a lovely young woman with dark, shoulder-length hair. Now her battered face, bruised neck and one outflung arm rested outside the shadows of a gangway between a ratty wooden garage and an apartment building; perhaps her rapist murderer had decided that finishing the job of hiding his victim's body had been too much trouble. The blaring stereo of a car on Newport flung the words of an old Harry Belafonte song through the spaces between the houses as it passed, something about women being smarter than men. Detective Ewing shook his head; not this time.

Only a block away.

Sandra slipped the wallet back into the purse and walked off, leaving Jude to again scan the people milling around the crime scene and sneaking horrified peeks at the body. Cops mostly, though there were two paramedics from some independent service who had seen the blue bubble lights and edged their way in. They'd probably hoped for someone to save, a bill to send tomorrow and a few more bucks in the company till. Again: not this time.

Twenty-eight years old, and a single block had made all the difference in her life.

Ewing cussed angrily under his breath, then let his temper go for a moment. The crash of the trash bin as he kicked it still didn't get him a fucking sheet to cover the body.

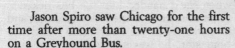

2

Jason Spiro saw Chicago for the first time after more than twenty-one hours on a Greyhound Bus.

He'd never been to an actual city before—never been out of Georgia, for that matter. Thus the cities and towns that the bus passed all seemed unreal, far removed from his tangible flesh-and-blood family. Make-believe, like the movie sets in the old films that the tiny theater in Wenona, the closest town to Harmony, was always showing. He'd been both excited and angry when his mother had waved the ninety-dollar bus ticket at him and announced he was on his way north for the next two months, but the anger was short-lived, gone by the time he'd loaded up an ancient suitcase. Somehow, the simple act of jamming his sneakers between his clothes and the side of the bag had put a new light on the trip. Above everything, it was staring at those grimy, rubber-soled shoes that made him realize that there was a *world* out there, an entire country beyond the peanut, cotton, and tobacco farms surrounding Harmony and the never-experienced promise of Macon to the north. All those spreads of earth covered in concrete and waiting to feel the weight of Jason Spiro carried in those shoes.

Harmony hadn't been good for him lately anyway, not since he'd walked out of the pitiful Church of the Pentecostal Serpent Handlers two days ago and left Reverend Abel Scanlon kneeling in the dust. Since then he had . . . *wanted*, burned inside for something as unnameable as it was elusive in the physical world, and of one thing Jason was absolutely certain: Harmony did not have whatever it was that called to him. The townspeople, in fact, had shunned him even more since the incident in the church. His mother, bless her foolish heart, had unwittingly placed the means to free him right into his hands, never knowing he was already through with the snake church when she'd handed him the bus ticket.

Jason became more awestruck as the miles sped past and the sizes of the cities grew. When the Greyhound rolled into Atlanta for a half-hour stop, he was nearly afraid to disembark. Still, how could he resist exploring a bus station that at any given moment had more men and women in it than his entire hometown? There were people here the likes of which he'd never seen—young men dressed in ridiculously bright leather suits, teenage girls wearing scraps of material that barely passed as shorts and blouses. Old men argued and chugged from paper-covered bottles in alcoves while wrinkled elderly women with rouged cheeks and scarlet lipstick plastered across their faces like out-of-focus clown mouths checked the trash cans. Wrung out, Jason climbed back aboard the bus and foolishly thought he'd seen it all before he'd left the state of his birth.

Now, almost a full day and fourteen stops later—which had included the larger cities of Chattanooga, Louisville, and Indianapolis—Jason was still unprepared for the bus station at 95th and the Dan Ryan Expressway at the south end of Chicago. He felt a physical swell of relief when the driver told him to stay on the bus because his ticket was good until the main station on Harrison Street outside of downtown. The cityscape was already so crowded—how could it take nearly ninety more blocks to get to its heart? He was scared and bone-tired, as exhausted as he might've been after a full day's work at home, but it didn't matter. This city terrified and *filled* him at the same time, pumped him up and sent his heart racing and his pulse screaming anew for that mysterious *thing* that he couldn't identify. He *needed* it, as much as he'd ever needed anything or anyone in his life. More than that, he knew:

It needed him.

The Greyhound bus station on West Harrison was surprisingly clean, still fairly new and equipped with dozens of vending machines, food stands and gift kiosks. Jason couldn't afford to buy anything, but he wanted to examine and learn about everything—including the sprinkling of pimps, hookers, drug dealers and runaway teens. Everything was new, and he wanted to test it *all*, see if any of it—or *all* of it—had something to do with the maddening craving that itched at the borders of his mind like poison ivy. The feeling had intensified since the bus disgorged its final load of passengers and disappeared, merging with a hundred others like it and mocking Jason's tired and slap-happy belief that he'd have the sight of that particular vehicle branded into memory for the rest of his life. Old feelings tried to intertwine with the new ones: a bittersweet, diluted homesickness fraught with childhood memories of never quite fitting in and leaving behind his only friend, leftover shame at the avoidance by others as he grew into a teen. There was nothing concrete to which he could point and say, *That's it, that's the thing that pushed me out.* He truly believed that only he and his dead grandmother had read the damning words in her old journal—Jason would bet his next breath his mother didn't even know the book existed—but there was something instinctive in Harmony's townsfolk, and whatever that elusive sensitivity was, it made them unconsciously strive to keep their distance. At home, the result was a constant, tiring masquerade of popularity Jason learned to wear for his mother's sake, simply to halt the ongoing inquiries about how people treated him at school and in town. At least Duwayne and his smelly clothes had helped him maintain the illusion that kept his mother's suspicions at bay. Facing it, Chicago was a monster and Jason should have felt insecure, adrift . . . instead he felt only elation and a growing sense of adventure.

Nine-thirty in the morning and it seemed like midnight. While he'd been an early riser all his life, Jason was also used to bedding down by nine P.M., ten at the very latest. This bus trip had rearranged everything in his body clock, and he no longer knew or cared which hour was the right one for sleeping. That had been impossible on the highway anyway; he'd spent most of the time keeping a nervous eye on the thin-faced man sitting next to him who kept "accidentally" rubbing against Jason's leg. While Jason was ready to explore this new city and be damned to his country-bred fear, a woman who looked uncomfortably like his mother was already waiting when he hauled his suitcase through the glass doors and into the chaos of the station.

"Jason? Jason Spiro?"

He had the sudden, devilish urge to say, *No, ma'am, my name's Tom. I think the boy you're looking for died on the way here.* It took everything he had to imprison the words behind his teeth. Instead Jason put on his best farmer-boy smile. "You must be Aunt Theora."

"You certainly have grown. The last time I saw you was . . . well, I guess I don't know *when*. Just pictures, all these years." Theora Waite, his maternal grandmother's sister, stared frankly at him, as if unable to believe that this strapping teenager had come from the belly of her sister's child a decade and a half earlier. She was not what Jason had expected either; back in Harmony old people *looked* old, but in Chicago apparently it took them a lot longer to get that way—at least it had this woman. He didn't know exactly, but if he remembered his family tree correctly, his great-aunt had to be fast approaching seventy. Yet he could swear she looked no older than fifty-five, and the smartly tailored summer suit and nylons she wore dispelled any sense of fragility her snowy hair might have implied. Her eyes, though, gave her away: faded blue and small, despite Theora's ruler-straight posture, they darted in every direction, watching and weighing everything with that fearful, unique sense of self-preservation only the elderly possess. "Well," she finally said, "shall we go? If you're hungry we can stop and get you breakfast somewhere by the apartment before you settle in."

Jason considered this as he picked up his bag and followed her through the terminal and onto Harrison. The street was another prime example of how small Harmony was: cars sped by with people dodging between them and not bothering with crosswalks or traffic lights; Jason could hear the roar of trucks and automobiles on the Dan Ryan all the way from here. Harmony's one tiny restaurant was open for breakfast and lunch. What were restaurants like here?

Before he could puzzle out the answer, Aunt Theora—as his mother had insisted he call her—made the decision for him. "I know you're probably exhausted, but I can imagine what you've been eating during all this time on the bus. There's a sandwich shop close to the apartment. We'll grab something there."

Jason watched with interest as she raised one arm over her head and waved briskly at the oncoming cars; a garish Yellow Cab instantly weaved out of the traffic and slid to a stop at the curb in front of them. The older woman opened the rear door and motioned to Jason, then climbed in after him. The driver glanced at them expectantly in the rearview mirror, his face dark and Mediterranean. "Lincoln and Oakdale," Theora said simply. The driver nodded and pulled back into the flow of traffic.

"I don't think I want a sandwich this early," Jason said. His eyes tracked their progress, drinking in the sights and sounds as the taxi took them steadily north. It was almost too much to take in, the noise, the people, trains thundering on tracks overhead and six-lane streets in the midst of crowded neighborhoods. And everywhere, something Jason had never expected: *trees*, bending and rustling in an afternoon breeze that smelled faintly of water—Lake Michigan. "Are we close to the lake? Can we see it?" Jason suddenly felt the weight of the driver's stare again, but his aunt spoke first.

"Where we're going will serve breakfast," she assured him. "Actually, we'll be heading away from Lake Michigan, but you've got all summer to see it."

Although he had no desire to eat anything, Jason nodded and turned his attention back to the window as the traffic slowed appreciably. The taxi inched along, coming almost to a standstill as the driver edged around a Chicago Police squad car double-parked at the intersection of Halsted and Division; in front of it sat two civilian cars, the back bumper of one and the front of the other smashed together like demolition-derby contestants. Next to two cops stood the drivers, the angrier of whom boasted a faceful of blood from a busted eye—no doubt a beltless encounter with the steering wheel. Although Aunt Theora appeared not to notice and sat staring patiently ahead and over the driver's shoulder, Jason leaned forward as his gaze fastened on the blood winding down the side of the young man's jaw. For a while he'd been able to push his strange craving from his mind as Chicago's complexities seemingly drowned him; now it all returned in a dark, eager rush and he swiveled his head as the cab passed, let his eyes hurriedly trace the delicate weaving of bloody lines along the victim's face before the taxi pulled them out of sight.

He had all summer.

3

"Listen to me—"

"Don't you tell me *anything*, you high-nosed bitch! You're not in my life anymore, remember? You opted out, if I recall. So you just keep your opinions *and* your orders to yourself—or aim them at hubby dearest, since you've decided you prefer his company to mine."

"Cecil, you don't understand. There are a lot of considerations here—"

"This is not a fucking accounting problem, Lillith!" Cecil Gideon screamed into the phone. "I thought you *loved* me!"

"I *do*—"

"You know what?" he interrupted her again. His voice had gone suddenly cold, curiously emotionless. "I think I'm tired of this conversation."

"Well, I'm not, and if you haven't listened to anything I've said, Cecil, you better listen now." Despite his rage, Cecil couldn't help but grin at the heat in Lillith's voice. He could picture her, standing

somewhere—perhaps a library or den—in that fine Wilmette
mini-mansion, fingers white-knuckled around the telephone
receiver while her chunky, precious husband snored blissfully in the master bedroom upstairs. She'd be wearing some
sort of expensive lingerie thing from Saks with lots of lace
and her hair would be down, spilling around her porcelain-
skinned face and onto her shoulders like thick, silken ropes.
And those jade-colored eyes . . . God. They always sparkled
like jewels when she was angry. Ah, he knew Lillith so well.

"*I know what you've done, Cecil.*"

Or at least he'd thought he did.

His expression went blank. Enough of this.

"You don't know shit," he said, and hung up. Then he
took the telephone off the hook so he wouldn't be tempted
to answer it when she called back, which he knew she
would—she always did. There was only one kind of callback
Cecil wanted, and Lillith seemed disinclined to give in, so he
had no choice but to turn his attention elsewhere.

Methodically, Cecil shed his clothes, tossing his shirt,
socks and underwear into the dirty-clothes hamper and carefully folding his slacks over the valet. Despite the soothing
classical music playing on the stereo, his thoughts, slightly
off focus since Lillith's last comment, didn't tilt back until
he'd donned a clean jock, muscleman tee and running shorts.
By the time he sat on the edge of his bed and pulled on a
pair of socks, he was, once again, starting to get pissed off at
his ex-lover.

He couldn't shake the tenseness during his twenty-
minute stretch, and it was easy to see the tightness reflected
in the mirror by the way his muscles jerked instead of
flowed as he went through his routine. He had so *much* on
his mind, a huge workload, bills, trying to juggle all those as-
inine details of day-to-day life. Hell, he couldn't even find
time to walk over to the DMV on his lunch hour and register his car, and the Thompson State Building was right across
the street from his office. Why did Lillith have to call him
anyway? When it came right down to it, if she didn't want
to see him again, then she should leave him alone, stop calling him, get the hell out of his head. Bad enough her memory haunted him all the time and everywhere, occasionally
ghosting the faces of women he saw on the street. Taunting

him, tormenting him, using him, no matter what he did to
put a stop to it. She had to double—no triple—his pain by
subjecting him to the cultured, sugary sound of that North
Shore voice nearly every fucking day. Bitch.

Cecil was perspiring freely by the end of his stretching
exercises. He studied himself in the full-length mirror on his
bedroom wall, watching morosely as sweat ran down one
side of his face until it dropped off the edge of his jaw and
landed on a well-shaped shoulder. His image wasn't a bad
one: he was a nice-looking guy with neatly trimmed light
brown hair and brown eyes, and it wasn't an exaggeration to
point out that he had a better-than-average body for a man
forty-two years old and over six feet tall. The Sports and Fitness Center in the R. R. Donnelley Building a block away
from where he worked kept him pumped up and healthy
during the week and he jogged consistently on weekends.
Dressed in a suit he looked like an ex-linebacker, but his
running outfit showed a burly, solidly muscled man with not
a hint of a flabby doughnut circling his waist.

Cecil's face reddened as he stared at his reflection. He
was single and eligible and seldom lacked for attention from
the women in his office, despite a too quiet personality.
What the hell was wrong with him that Lillith would pick
that guy instead? While she and Isman Jerusha had been
married a long time and had a son in a fancy Michigan law
school, what difference did that make when it was obvious
her day-to-day existence was so miserable she'd had to
search for affection and compassion somewhere else? Maybe
it was simply that he didn't make as much money as her Mr.
Banker husband. Involuntarily, Cecil's big hands curled and
he began to flex and unflex his fists. Wouldn't that be the
kicker? he thought bitterly. He made a decent living too, better than most, though a junior partner's salary at Coppers &
Lybrand was a long way off from senior VP at First Chicago
Bank.

Christ, he couldn't believe it. Here he was, younger than
her husband—younger than *her*—and she was dumping him.
And absolutely *nothing* he could say or do would change her
mind. Just thinking about it made him feel a bit . . . crazy.

Time to go out for a run.

4

Staggering into their bedroom, balancing an overfilled basket of clean laundry, Evelyn Pelagi couldn't help but laugh at the sight of her husband. Warren looked almost as loaded down as she was—legs splayed atop their king-size water bed, he had two insurance binders and a proposal packet balanced on his thighs. Two more piles of computer printouts were fanned open beside him, along with what had to be every piece of paper he'd maintained in the Falconer & Dixon Law Offices file. On its stand at the foot of the bed, the little Zenith portable showed an attractive newswoman speaking earnestly to the camera while a mini-box with the words 4TH VICTIM! displayed in red floated above her left shoulder. Evelyn had no idea what the woman was saying since Warren had the sound muted and his scratchy old Carole King *Tapestry* album playing softly on the stereo. He glanced up at the sound of her chuckling, then slid everything off his lap and came over to help her.

"Hey, it's okay," she protested as he reached for the basket. "Don't interrupt your—ohmigod. Where did you get *those*? A comics shop?"

Warren gave her a mock scowl as she stared, pulled the laundry basket from her arms and set it on one end of the dresser. "I'll have you know I bought these boxer shorts yesterday at Marshall Field's."

"Field's? I don't believe you. They have *cartoon* characters on them."

Warren sighed. "Superheroes, Evie. Wolverine and Psylocke, from the Uncanny X-Men. Get your facts straight." She giggled again, louder this time, and he raised his chin. "You have some nerve laughing at my underwear considering some of the ridiculous T-shirts I've seen you wear in public."

"But—" Evelyn clapped a hand over her mouth.

"What?"

"*This* one, Warren—" She poked at the front of his shorts and he jumped and looked down guiltily.

"Hey, cut it out!"

"But look where her *boobs* are."

"Where?" He scrunched his chin against his chest and tried to see.

"Here," Evelyn said congenially, "let me help." She stepped toward him and smiled.

"Help with what?" Warren smiled back, his eyes behind his glasses so dark and brown and framed by smile lines, and she had to laugh out loud this time, because this man whom she loved and who was so damned smart most of the time was such an outright *victim* at others.

Eye to eye with him, almost taller in fact, she grinned widely, right before she grabbed.

"Help you check if her boobs are *real*!"

Carole King still sang in the background, volume turned low, the turntable set on repeat. Warren knew the words by heart, had listened to them on and off for so many years he could hear every nuance of the singer's voice in his mind on any cue he wanted. Over thirty years old, yet the song— "Will You Love Me Tomorrow?"—remained one of his favorites. It was a lovely little touch, one of those far-off, barely acknowledged things that add to the moment and combine to make perfection.

Evelyn moved beneath him, her soft, tanned skin sliding exquisitely against his in all the right places. Her face glowed from the sun she'd gotten earlier in the afternoon, freckles deepening outrageously as they did every summer. Even her hazel eyes seemed to sun-fade, as if the season had turned her inside out and created a negative image just to surprise him. Her black hair tangled on the pillow and around his fingers, silken and slightly oily from the day's labors. She still smelled of grass and soil and sun, and laundry, too, like clean, steamy cotton pulled from a hot dryer, an irresistible combination that was homey and dusty and sexy all rolled into one. He kept moving, carefully riding the same crest of hot electricity that had shot through him the instant his body had joined with hers, fighting to control the physical urge to simply explode.

Her eyes glistened as she lifted her head and strained to find his mouth; his wide lips covered hers, tongue exploring and teasing as she shifted beneath him, then gasped.

"Top?" he breathed into her ear. He nipped lightly at her earlobe, her neck. "We can switch if you like."

Evelyn's arms tightened around him, her smooth hips pressing harder against his as her face flushed. "No." Her voice was barely above a murmur, rising and falling with their movements on the water mattress. "You know I like the feel of your body . . . your . . . weight . . . on me." Warren rocked again, back and forth, more insistently now, and she sucked in her breath sharply, once, twice. "Oh—you feel so *good*. . . ." She began to shudder, breasts trembling against his chest, and he felt her fingernails dig into his back, not painful, just a little *stingy*, tiny, hot jabs of pleasure on a line straight to his insides, making him clench his teeth as her whole body *tightened* under and around him.

A breathless, endless moment later and Evelyn slid her legs up, one foot intentionally trailing the back of his left leg until her knees and the insides of her thighs—God, she was so *supple*—pressed warm against the sides of his ribs. Then her hands were loose, free, starting more fires on his skin, everywhere, until one long-fingered hand snaked between the warm flesh of their bellies and touched him.

"Don't!" Warren gasped. "Not yet, you—"

"Oh, no," she purred. "I feel *so* fine." Her hand turned somehow and she stroked him, twisting her fingertips in his body hair and suddenly flexing her hips up. He groaned and felt control slide away as she rubbed her face against his, then licked the line of his jaw playfully. Her voice was a whisper of warmth in his ear as her other hand cupped the back of his head, tugging at his thick, coarse hair until their mouths met.

"Your turn, lover boy."

Evelyn studied her face in the bathroom mirror as she toweled her hair dry. Warren was right about her eyes fading in the summer—they always had, all the way to a yellow green by the beginning of September if she spent a lot of time outside. Bad for the skin though, and as if to prove it, she could swear she had twice as many freckles as she'd had last week. A few more years and maybe her face would turn into one big freckle and she'd have a permanent tan. Like Karla Bryant, her upstairs neighbor and best friend, though Karla's creamed-coffee complexion had nothing to do with a tan. A light touch of makeup, then she pulled a brush through her shoulder-length hair and worked it expertly into a loose French braid, finally slipping on her white ER uniform.

A peek outside the bathroom door told her Warren had fallen asleep over his Falconer & Dixon proposal, and Evelyn debated whether or not to let him sleep. It was almost ten-thirty and he'd set the alarm clock for five in the morning. She still couldn't believe those lawyers and how they'd insisted on a Saturday presentation at their offices. Didn't they have lives? Families? She'd be so glad when tomorrow and his Falconer & Dixon proposal were over; he'd been working on this project so heavily for the last three weeks he practically talked about the law firm in his sleep. Still, he had said he wanted to walk her to work while that murderer was on the loose. Dressed and standing by the bed, Evelyn found herself inexplicably unable to decide as she gazed down at her husband. He looked like a sleeping boy, his dark brown hair rumpled into a dozen cowlicks by the pillowcase, the worry lines between his eyebrows smoothed out for a while. It would be such a shame to disturb him, to bother him with the ridiculous chore of walking her eight blocks to Illinois Masonic. At the same time Evelyn was filled with the urge to touch him, stroke his hair and see the sweet smile that always appeared when he opened his eyes from a nap or first thing in the morning.

A glance at the clock—ten-forty—decided the issue. What on earth was the matter with her? She'd spent nearly ten minutes standing here watching Warren sleep; if she woke him now she'd have to wait while he dressed and splashed enough water on his face to make him coherent. She'd end up clocking in late, and that was a no-no. He'd sleep through the worst thunderstorms as far as noise went, but the lightest touch, her tiniest kiss, would wake him. She opted for a note instead, scribbling a few words on one of the notepads that had gotten pushed off the side of the bed in favor of their lovemaking.

> *Sweetheart,*
> *Didn't want to wake you—you look so cute while you're sleeping. I'll call you in the morning before you leave.*
>
> > *Love you,*
> > *Evelyn*

She set the notepad on top of the television but left the page still attached so it wouldn't get buried in his papers, knowing Warren would wake in a couple of hours to turn off the television and the light on the nightstand. A quick touch of lipstick at the hall mirror and she picked up her purse and stepped outside, quietly locking the door behind her. Warren would undoubtedly be a little ticked off at her tomorrow for not waking him, but he'd get over it. Barry Street stretched to the east until it was bisected by Lakewood; quiet and empty, well lit by the evenly spaced streetlights. It wasn't at all scary and Evelyn set off for work at a brisk pace.

Insisting on walking her to the hospital when he was already so tired and overworked was absurd, and really, in a city the size of Chicago, what were the odds she'd be the next casualty anyway?

• • •

Warren twisted in his sleep, then sat up abruptly. It was quiet in the apartment despite the Carole King record still playing—too quiet. Where was his wife?

"Evelyn?" What time was it? He glanced at the alarm clock, then cursed under his breath. Five to eleven—she'd probably left a half hour ago, walking alone in the dark with that maniac out there somewhere and the cops chasing their tails without so much as a description of the guy. Warren swung his legs over the side of the bed and sat there for a minute, studying the colors of his new boxer shorts, grinning when he remembered Evelyn's reaction to them—exactly what he'd expected, right down to the comical expression on her pretty face. He ought to be tired—it was amazing he'd woken before midnight—but he was completely alert, feeling downright *sharp*, in fact. Fidgeting, he got up and started pulling the Falconer & Dixon file back together, one less thing he'd have to do in the morning, when he'd no doubt pay for this bout of energy. It took only a few seconds to find the pad of paper on top of the television and read Evelyn's note. He was going to chew her out good when she called during her last break in the morning. He tore it off the pad, crumpled it into a ball and tossed it in the bedroom wastebasket. The basket was empty and the paper wad made an odd *thump* when it hit bottom, a perfect beat in time to a line from the song "Tapestry," whispering from the stereo speakers.

"*. . . he's come to take me back.*"

He couldn't for the life of him explain why that old line suddenly made him tremble.

5

"Well, well. What do we have here?"

Jason Spiro, sequestered behind the questionable privacy of the bathroom door in the apartment, held his fingers up to one of the four naked lightbulbs above his Aunt Theora's medicine cabinet. Clad only in his briefs, he looked like he was sweating freely. He wasn't. Rather, some stupid former tenant had nailed the window shut in this box of a room and Jason had been closed in here since he'd finished his bath forty-five minutes ago. All that heat and steam with no ventilation, cooking away under two hundred watts of blazing electric light.

The tips of his fingers were thin and sunken; hard, too, like cured leather. He carefully inspected the ends, then tapped them sharply against the mirror's wet, dripping surface and grinned at his reflection. "Can't feel a thing, no sir."

But it didn't matter that his hands were numb, Jason realized—his toes, too.

As a matter of fact, hardly anything fazed him anymore: not the condensation pouring off his skin or the hot, damp air so heavy around him that it made moisture slide down the shiny, ancient paint on the walls. Not even the overwhelming fear of the city, its *hugeness*, that had seemed so threatening. Sometimes he tried to reach for those old sensations and emotions, but . . . nothing. His aunt's feelings certainly made no difference, though he could hear her pacing back and forth in the hall—probably needing to use the pot but too timid . . . too *afraid*, to ask. As well she should be.

What would she—and everyone else—say if they could see the snakebite wounds that still punctured and bruised his skin after nearly two weeks? They couldn't; only he had that special sight, that unique ability. It logically followed that *he* was the most important, and only *he* mattered. Jason—him and what was happening to him. What he *wanted*.

The dried out fingertips of Jason's hands folded slowly into fists at his sides.

If only he knew *what* that was.

"I like this city," Jason told Theora around a mouthful of bran flakes. "It's so *big*, so full of needy people."

Theora Waite eyed her great-nephew warily, wondering again how the boy could eat that tasteless cereal, especially so late at night. He was a strange one all right, and a problem better suited for someone younger and stronger than her. Whatever had Miriam been thinking when she'd shipped her son up here? There might not be a Snake Handlers' church around for the boy to get involved with, but Chicago had a whole lot more—a whole lot *worse*—to offer this curious teenager. "Needy?" she repeated. Lord, how'd she let herself get talked into this one? He's so *strange*—

"Well, sure." Jason's smile was wide around his soft, southern accent, his teeth spotted with brown mush. Unexpectedly, he leaned forward and spat his huge mouthful of chewed cereal back into the bowl. "Don't have to look too far to see it," he continued without explanation. "That big church right down the street on the corner—"

"St. Alphonsus." Should she say something about his atrocious table manners? What? The jerky way his neck and head had moved made her think of a large, dangerous bird, regurgitating half-digested prey. She tried to remember the last time she'd seen him swallow food or water and couldn't, decided to let it pass for now.

"Yeah, that one." He pushed the bowl aside and wiped his mouth with the back of his hand. "Lookit how people flock to it, like sheep to the Holy Shepherd."

"So," Theora said carefully, "you're going to . . . join the parish there?"

Jason laughed. "Catholics? You're kidding, right? I was over there this morning, at the eleven o'clock mass. Those folks're so wrapped up in old habits and themselves that the Savior Himself could be passing out that little wafer and they'd never notice. They're past feeling *anything*, like religious robots. And I don't think the priests are any better."

Theora rose and carried the bowl of soggy flakes and dirtied flatware to the sink, feeling Jason's gaze track her slow movements. There was a palpable feeling of anticipation rolling off the boy, as if he couldn't wait for her to comment on his behavior, as if he were *daring* her to do so. Well, let him wait; she wasn't going to say a word. Having him here for the past week had made her suddenly *feel* her age, more so than she ever had before, made the coming summer months stretch painfully ahead like a truckload of boxes looming over a worker with an aching back. She couldn't figure out why the boy made her so uncomfortable, but he did. One day at a time, she thought stoically. The days'll turn into weeks, and so forth, and then he'll take his return ticket—I'll buy him one, if I have to—and head back home to be his mother's problem. *That* thought added to her general confusion; a month ago she'd been repeating the same complaint to her lady friends about how lonely she was for company, real company like family. Well here it was, and all she could do was wish it gone. How fickle could an old woman get? Jason was still talking at the table, and Theora blinked as some of the words registered. "What?" she asked. "I'm sorry, what did you say?"

"I said, as soon as I find the right partner, I'm going to stay in the city and start my *own* church. Right here in Chicago."

• • •

Poor Aunt Theora. He hadn't meant her any harm, but she sure had taken a spell at his announcement, hadn't she? Well, she'd be all right in the morning, and in the meantime he needed some fresh air. Her apartment was okay, small and dark and probably the standard thing for the neighborhood and her income, and she worked at keeping it clean and trying to keep the roaches out. But Jason was used to the Georgia countryside, dense with greenery and the nightsongs of crickets and frogs, the smells and sounds all carried along on a sweet, heated breeze. That's what was needed here, Jason thought, a clean wind, a fresh point of view. All these people, with their habits and their skepticism, their downright *disbelief*—what would they say to see the miracles such as had been wrought on Jason's body? He aimed to show them those things, too, and more. He would be their leader, their new Messiah. He could feel untapped power squirming within him, searching and straining for release, growing bigger every day that had passed since he'd risen from the dead in that pitiful tin-topped shack in Harmony. Growing outright *huge*.

First, a partner. Someone to share in the building of a congregation and pick up the slack where Jason failed in the knowledge of Chicago and its people, its streets, its life. It was a solution that had taken some long, hard thought, but Jason finally realized that he needed something, some*one* to fill the emptiness inside him which had started clamoring right along with the sense of unnameable power after his resurrection in Harmony. Jason could think of no other answer, and when it came right down to it, what else could it be? God had begotten Himself a partner, in the form of His Son, Jesus Christ. Man, woman, child—Jason didn't have any idea, and he didn't care. He'd trust in his intuition when the time came, let his soul do the job of recognizing his mate.

When he found that person, why . . .

Let the miracles begin.

6

Evelyn was already regretting her decision to walk to work alone by the time she turned north onto Lakewood. Stubbornness was her biggest fault, and sometimes she took it to ridiculous lengths. Like now—reasoning her way out of letting Warren walk her to work, and for what? Because on principle she didn't like being told what to do. Silly—at the very least, she could've called a cab. Lakewood was wide and empty despite the lovely new town houses and decorative paving poured over almost all of the old train rails sunk into its surface, with few bright streetlights. Dark fronts of town houses and small buildings stretched along its western side to Wellington a full two blocks away, with occasional postage-stamp-size yards and groups of trash cans stacked in front of the older structures and the sides of buildings on the other side. Behind her was a construction zone, more expensive town houses popping up while the remaining older buildings underwent detailed renovation. Adding to the darkness were the industrial-sized Dumpsters and the bulky paving equipment waiting to spill loads of asphalt and cover the rest of the old silver rails forever. Overhead, the sky was an unrelieved black. The sliver of moon and thin city stars were blotted out completely by the overhanging clouds, which had promised rain and a break in the unseasonable heat for the last three days but not delivered. The oppressive silence was almost eerie, overwhelming and out of place for a Friday night. Suddenly the seven blocks remaining on her walk to work might as well have been seven *miles*, because something wasn't right, her pulse was barreling inexplicably and Evelyn thought she could hear someone or something breathing behind her, following her—

She spun and backstepped, almost tripped, one hand spiraling in front of her, mouth opening wide as she sucked in air for a scream.

The response to her graceless movements was a snuffling and the tinny clatter of a pop can rolling down the alley she'd just passed on her left, making her release her breath with a squeak. *Jesus, a dog. That's all. A stray.*

Cars were parked here and there along Lakewood's east side and Evelyn slid her purse strap off her shoulder with trembling hands, then looped it over her head and across her chest as she decided to walk in the middle of the street. Breathing raggedly, she glanced quickly back at the little dog that had startled her so badly, a spotted, ratty-looking mongrel. It met her eyes and went instantly into a defensive crouch, lips pulling back to reveal tiny, sharp teeth. Frozen on shaking twiglike legs, the mutt's gaze suddenly shifted, as if it were looking behind her, and it gave a frightened *yip* and leaped away.

Evelyn frowned. *Now why would it—*

The weight of the man who hit her from behind answered the question she never had a chance to finish in her thoughts. Propelled by his bulk, Evelyn crashed to the ground face-first and the streetlight-washed sidewalk exploded into red fragments behind her eyelids as her right cheekbone shattered. She could have lain there and let the luxury of unconsciousness take her, but her attacker had more work to do and he was pulling her by one arm and the back collar of her dress, dragging her along the pitted cement toward that same alley where she'd seen the starving dog. One eye swelled shut immediately and the pain in her face was monstrous compared to anything else she'd ever experienced; pieces of bone ground together when she tried to open her mouth to scream and once again she nearly passed out, instead barely managing a low gurgle around the blood pooling inside her mouth. She tried to kick her way free and clawed at the rock-hard hand clenching her uniform, the only thing she could reach. In return her assailant released her arm then punched her in the face, and whether he struck the damaged or undamaged side didn't matter, because this time Evelyn did lose it for a while, battered body and shocked mind seeking solace in warm, muggy blackness.

She came to a minute or a year later and realized instantly that she couldn't see, something—her dress, perhaps—was pulled over her head and wound tight around her throat. The attacker was on top of her, heavy, doing something—*raping her*. But his movements against her lower body were a nagging, faraway bumping, as unimportant as a mosquito bite in the face of the agony that blossomed across her head when she tried to move. Her hands were limp, nearly strengthless, slapping uselessly atop the sidewalk in disgustingly perfect time to the grunts next to her left ear.

I'm going to die. The thought was in Evelyn's mind with sudden, brutal clarity. *It's not fair! I'm not ready! Warren*—Tears then, salty water blazing across the smashed terrain of her skin and soaking into the bloodied expanse of once-white cotton plastered across her face. Warm water dripped onto her bared chest and belly, the sweat of her killer, the smell of him sliding up her nose despite the scent of her blood and the starch of her uniform. But she would not lie here and die quietly, *cooperatively*, while this thief of the worst kind enjoyed himself during her last moments. She would do *something*, some little thing so that someone, somewhere, would know about him, would know what he was.

It took every bit of will she had to force her slack left hand into a fist and thrust it up and toward the man's face—but she couldn't hold it, she simply didn't have the strength and God, she was in so much *pain*. Two of her fingernails, strong and carefully manicured, still found their mark, laying a neat double stripe across the rapist's cheek and the bridge of his nose. His retaliation was immediate.

And permanent.

7

" 'Jason, don't you think it's too late?' " the teenager mimicked under his breath as he descended the dimly lit hallway stairs from his aunt's apartment. " 'Jason, be careful.' " She acted like he was a four-year-old playing with a chain saw, for crying out loud. Not that it was her fault; probably more his mother's doing than anything else. Well, Aunt Theora would see, in time, as would his mother . . . and a whole lot of other folks, too. Speaking of seeing, she'd squeaked out a comment about his face, had asked him if those shadows beneath his jawline were bruises. This was a new twist—apparently the damage from the snakes was starting to show up, slowly but surely. What, he wondered absently, would it take to once again make it invisible to the eyes of others? True, his fingers were as numb as balsa wood, but with Aunt Theora's question had come the realization that the snakebite punctures were starting to hurt, small stings now and then but ripe with the promise of more to come.

At street level Jason stepped outside and made sure the door closed and locked behind him—this *was* Chicago, after all, and he had taken in quite a bit of visual knowledge on the couple of neighborhood tours Aunt Theora had given him. He glanced at his watch, a cheap plastic thing from his aunt, then at the quiet expanse of Southport Street. Theora's building was next door to another housing an old-fashioned German bakery on the corner of Southport and Fletcher, and though it'd been closed since yesterday after-noon Jason could still smell sugar and flour as he passed the darkened entrance. Chocolate, too, like the pies with sweet cracker crusts that his mom made. He used to love those when he was younger, but he'd lost his taste for their flavor not long after he'd started going to Scanlon's church; now he couldn't stand food period, much less anything sugary.

There was nothing at all cool about the air tonight, and Jason wiped his forehead on the back of his arm. Heat in the city was more smothering than in the countryside; too many buildings blocking the pitiful, dirty breezes and not enough shade trees. Still, there were more trees than he would've thought, though they weren't nearly as tall and lush as the ones in the Georgia farm country. He turned east on Nelson for no other reason than doing so made him head into the slight movement of the wind, though it wasn't enough to do any good. Even the streetlights twenty feet above the side-walk seemed to add to the heat, and Jason could have sworn that each time he passed below one the temperature in-creased a good five degrees. As he reached the intersection of Nelson and Lakewood, a man jogged smoothly past, clad in running shorts and a muscleman T-shirt. Jason paused and watched him for a moment, envious of the way the jogger appeared to be unaffected by the sweltering weather and vis-ibly increased his pace when he became aware of Jason. A few seconds and the man disappeared around a corner, leav-ing Jason to puzzle over a glimpse of what he thought were dark stripes painted diagonally across the guy's face.

After a minute of indecision Jason turned north, with the vague idea that he might find an all-night diner on Belmont and buy a cup of ice cubes to roll across the skin of his face. He was surprised at the way the heat was bothering him tonight, more than usual, pressing across his back like a damp bale of hay. Maybe it wasn't the heat at all, but that pervasive restlessness that wouldn't leave him alone and made him constantly click his strange, flattened fingertips together as he walked. Now the scant breeze from the east was gone entirely, obstructed by the low, dark buildings on his right. Three blocks away, Belmont's more plentiful lighting hardly seemed worth the energy it would take to walk there, and the street and the scene reminded him of the old black-and-white movies on late-night television. Still, the thought of returning to his aunt's dreary apartment—cooler at night but still filled with stale, humid air—spurred him on, made his feet continue their stubborn, unnameable search.

A sound, small but startling, made Jason jump and he turned toward a small dog rooting amid a haphazard group of trash cans at the mouth of the alley on his right. The mutt froze at the sight of Jason, oversized liquid eyes locking on his for an instant before it snarled fiercely, a ridiculous sound completely out of proportion to its size. Jason had been good with the few animals on the farm in Harmony—only a couple of pigs and a milk cow—at least before his dealings with Scanlon's church. Dogs had especially liked him, although he and his mother had never bothered to get one of their own. After his resurrection, the same pair of dogs from the neighboring farm had turned vicious toward him, but when he'd met their slobbering growls and showing of teeth without fear, both had turned tail and run. Standing here on this bleak street in Chicago, the teenager felt nothing but a sudden contempt for this stupid little mongrel's instinctive protection of some tidbit of street garbage.

"Go on!" Jason snapped. He stomped one foot in the dog's direction and it snarled again and leaped sideways, spraying saliva as its spindly legs leaned and sprang it away like a jackrabbit. "Scat!" The stray skittered into the alley a few feet away and darted out of sight. "Idiot animal," Jason muttered. He turned his back toward Belmont and then it was his turn to freeze as he glimpsed a foot, encased in a white work shoe, jammed between two of the rusted trash bins.

Something changed then: his perception, the street

around him, the *world*. When Jason stepped forward and leaned into the black space amid the cans, he could have sworn he was making his way underwater, way down deep, where the pressure was so immense that the water pushed its way into his body through each and every one of his pores. Why else would it take so long to actually *see* that the foot led to a leg, and the leg to a dead woman?

"Oh my," Jason whispered. There wasn't enough space for him to squat and barely enough for him to be next to her between the cans to begin with. Surely she couldn't be dead . . . could she? Terror, stark and unexpected, tried to clog his throat. "Miss?" he finally managed. "Can you . . . hear me?" He took a half step back as vague thoughts of going for help entered his head, then were overruled as he thought of her lying here, helpless and unprotected. How long would it take to find a phone or get someone to answer a stranger's knock at their door late on a Friday night? Pulse hammering, instead Jason reached into the darkness and quickly felt around until he found her hand, still warm but unnervingly limp.

He could think of nothing to say except, "I'll help you up." When she didn't respond, the teenager clasped her hand with both of his and pulled on her arm experimentally, then almost dropped it as he felt the drag of her full weight. When he instinctively let go, her arm fell against one of the trash cans with a nasty clanging noise that clearly meant she hadn't felt the impact. Then . . .

Silence.

Dismayed, Jason leaned over the cramped opening, grabbed the handles of the can in front of him, and rolled it aside. Streetlight the shade of dirty water spilled into the space and for a moment Jason couldn't breathe, couldn't move, or think, or do *anything*. Never had he seen firsthand a victim of such unspeakable violence, splayed blamelessly before the world and at the mercy of anyone who passed by. The seconds ticked by: five, ten, twenty, and finally his brain kicked him, guiding his movements as he twisted and pushed the can out of the way, ignoring the horrendous noise the container made, bumping and scraping the concrete when he shoved it aside and knelt next to the woman's body.

Her white dress was yanked up around her neck, under-things and stockings mauled to expose what might have been a lovely body had it not been for the black marks smudged across her skin—dirt? Bruises? But her hand when he had clasped it had been *warm*. Jason fumbled furiously with her clothes, tearing and pulling at them until he got them down and found her face, freed the space around her mouth so she could breathe, despite the common-sense thought in his head that knew he was far too late to help. Her head was turned away from him, dark hair tangled and sticky with a tar-colored liquid that was ugly upon her skin beneath the sodium light; it didn't take a college degree to know what it was. Still, he slid a hand beneath her neck and lifted her shoulders, staring wordlessly when her face, disfig-ured in a way he'd never considered beyond lurid movie makeup, swung in his direction. Then it lolled backward, dis-playing a perfect imprint of black fingerprints around a crushed and misshapen throat.

"But you're still warm," Jason said dumbly, as though she could hear him. "How can you be dead when you're still *warm*?" He could feel the heat of her body against the bare skin of his arm, burning and burning and burning. He hugged her close, wanting to feel it more, feeding a nearly scandalous need that instantly rose inside his soul. Had this happened to him in Scanlon's church, to his corpse as it was surrounded by the faithful and perhaps held by Scanlon? Had his body been to them the heat, the *power*, just as hers seemed to be now, blazing against the flesh of his suddenly frigid hold?

Her eye . . . he could see the one that wasn't swollen shut, sparkling with moisture—with *tears*—from beneath the almost closed eyelid. What color was it, when it was seen in the clarity of God's sunlight? Jason leaned closer, trying to see, *needing* to know, shivering then, violently, the air around him gone inexplicably arctic as it sucked the heat from his body and left the dead woman cradled within his arms his only source of warmth.

Beckoning too, her mouth: lips swollen and purpled from brutality and suffocation, still calling out for him, beg-ging him to be her savior. As his head bent and his cheek brushed hers, matted and wet with tears and blood, the thought tumbled in his head, end over end. An incredible question, an all-consuming *demand:* could he do just that? Could he *save* her? Him, a fifteen-year-old student of CPR like all the rest of the kids in Harmony township, so many farm accidents in the hot Georgia harvest season—

Could he bring her back from the dead?

Mouth over hers then, breathing for her, the routine rising from memory then shattering as reality interfered. He was supposed to breathe, in and out, twice, right? Or three? Then stop, change to chest depressions, one-one-thousand, two-one thousand, three—

Futile panic then, incapable of escaping his own dark act as his hand involuntarily pulled her closer, embraced her while his lips and tongue defiled her dead mouth in an obscene kiss. His brain screamed at him to stop but was overruled by the deep, rampaging rush that exploded inside his head and chest and hands and heart with roller-coaster speed, dragging him along, drugging his senses, hurling his *essence* on a midnight ride hands free and the hell with the seat belt besides. One clear sentence comprehensible in his mass of boiling thoughts—

SHE is the one I need!

The darkness exploded then, disintegrated under the power of halogen light and for an instant Jason thought he had died and finally gone on to Glory. A moment later the true realization set in as somewhere above the teenager and his dark, dead bride the painful spotlight was split by flashing blue and a harsh demand that he release her. He had no choice but to comply.

And sit back, smile, and watch, as she rose from what should have been her death.

8

"Face down on the ground and lock your fingers behind your neck!" The squad car's speaker sent Lucita Vilmos's voice hammering through the heat-drenched air, but the teenager she and her partner had spotlighted made no move to obey. In fact, the perp simply sat there, his mouth hanging open around a stupid, nearly *smug* smile he directed at the woman on the ground next to him.

Correction, Vilmos thought grimly. The *dead* woman on the ground—she'd been a cop for five years and had never seen a victim this bad off who'd made it to the hospital.

"What the hell is he doing?" Rod Fremont muttered. He was a rookie and still on the nervous side, a potentially dangerous mix. His revolver was already out of its holster, aimed at the kid's midsection. "Fucking weirdo."

Suddenly the boy glanced their way, finally seemed to realize who they were.

He waved at the body and Rod's fingers tightened visibly on the grip of his gun as the teenager spit out a few words, some nonsense about the woman being hurt and him doing CPR.

Then he looked at them, one cheek smeared with blood where it'd been pressed against the victim's face, and his mouth widened in a horrible liquid slash of a smile.

"I think it worked."

"I've had enough of this shit." Knowing Vilmos would cover him, Fremont holstered his gun and strode forward, one large hand reaching for the boy's arm. "Get up—*shit!*" Both her partner and the boy froze, their eyes nearly bulging as they stared at the corpse.

"What?" Vilmos demanded. "*What*, damn it?"

"Oh, Lord," the boy whispered.

"Lucita, get over here. You—you've got to see this. *Quick!*"

She stepped forward warily, revolver leading the way and trained on the perp in case he had something planned, a setup to divert their attention. For all they knew, the woman was wearing stage makeup and she and the teenager were working together. She'd seen things that were a lot more farfetched during her duty. "What?" she repeated. Vilmos followed her partner's pointing finger, then stared.

The woman was bad off, all right. The right side of her face was a pulpy mass of lumps and blood, and from where she stood, Vilmos could see the irreparable damage to her throat. She knew instantly that this slender boy hadn't had anything to do with this crime. But he'd done something, all right, because this woman, who should've died when her windpipe had been crushed, was groaning and pulling herself to a sitting position, clawing at the ground and her shredded clothes as her hands sought leverage. The teenager's fingers were tightly clenched in a gesture that absurdly reminded Vilmos of fervent prayer as he urged her on, saying something so very odd:

"Yes, *do it*. Do it for *me!*"

Sitting upright now, wobbling before her paralyzed trio of an audience. Fremont made a low sound in his throat, a sort of sick whine as the woman lifted her disfigured face toward the streetlight and raised her fingers to her throat, digging at it and trying to breathe, struggling to pull air through her savaged windpipe.

Instinctively Vilmos started to extend a hand, opening her mouth to speak. The words stalled before they could be formed, shifted into more of a gasp. Her face, she thought in horror. It's . . . *moving*.

Rippling, twisting, re*shaping*, right in front of them, as if the skin had become a separate creature that was determined to mend and refused to be bound by the laws of death and decay. Cratered flesh and splintered bone, shifting and glowing with a dark luminescence that spilled through the woman's fingers like liquid light as she raised her hands from her throat and cupped her face. A form of dirty gold *bleeding* that spun from her face and spread down her arms, crawling over and upon itself as it searched out the rest of her battered body, enveloping her in a foul halo that had nothing to do with holiness.

Then it was gone.

Just

       like

           that.

The teenager was still on the ground but as proud as if he were standing upright and gesturing to his own newborn child; when he spoke, his voice was soft and sweet and inexplicably evil:

"And Jesus said, 'Raise the dead.' "

Something, the boy's words perhaps, snapped both Vilmos and Fremont from their trancelike state. "Get up," Fremont ordered, and if he hadn't been listening before, this time it was clear to the teenager that the cop meant what he said. The young man rose immediately, stiff, like an old and brittle plastic doll, struggling within the narrow space for balance. When he finally found his footing, Fremont grabbed his arm and hauled him out; Vilmos's turn then, crouching next to the victim as her thoughts tumbled madly and tried to explain what her eyes had witnessed. Behind her, the boy started to say something, only to be cut off by Fremont's barked "Shut up!"

A sound from the woman then, which should have been impossible given the condition of her throat moments earlier. "Ma'am, please stay where you are. We'll radio for an ambulance." Vilmos's voice was shaking, she couldn't help it. *What the hell had they seen?* There was a sharp *crack*, the familiar noise all that was needed for her to know that Fremont had handcuffed the boy and was calling their situation into the dispatcher. Vilmos thought the cuffs might be overkill; the young man seemed as shocked as the police officers, standing and staring at the woman at Vilmos's side with an odd mixture of longing and awe on his face.

"*No.*" Vilmos nearly shrieked aloud when the woman actually spoke to her. "No ambulance. I'm all right." Her eyes were open and clear, and now it was her turn to work her way upright. "I must have fallen. Would you help me up?" The victim's voice was calm and cool . . . *cold.*

Vilmos shook her head. "I don't think you should move," she began carefully. "You've been hurt—"

"Nonsense, I'm fine." The woman's gaze in the washed-out light was unreadable, strange. "Are you going to help me or not?" Mute, Vilmos offered a hand and braced herself; a weighty tug and the woman was standing. She swayed for a second, then stepped out of the cramped space between the garbage cans. Then there they were all over again, a repeat of the scene where the four simply stared at each other, except this time all four were upright.

And unharmed.

"I guess I fell," the woman said again.

"I don't think so." Vilmos's voice was flat, slipping into the "don't bullshit me" tone that was so often a part of her job. "Look at yourself, lady. Look at your *clothes.*" This is all wrong, Vilmos thought hazily, wrong procedure, wrong collar, wrong results. What had happened to the black and white of crime and victim? Out loud, at least, experience took over. "What's your name?"

The woman glanced down at her dress—a nurse's uniform, Vilmos suddenly realized, and frowned. "I . . ." Her voice faded.

"Your name." Vilmos's tone had become a demand. If the woman couldn't tell her at *least* that much, Fremont would call for an ambulance whether the victim wanted it or not; as if to confirm her thoughts, Fremont's radio squawked and she heard him mumble something into it.

"Evelyn," the victim said. "My name is Evelyn Pelagi."

Her gaze darted over Vilmos's shoulder and stopped on the teenager, then swept back to the front of her own dress. With abstract amusement Vilmos saw that Fremont had handcuffed the teen to the handle of the squad's passenger door; too many fake cop movies. Abruptly Vilmos blinked, fighting the sudden impulse to rub at her eyes; while the Pelagi woman's dress was rumpled and torn in more than a dozen places, nothing but the dirt and grime of the alley marred the otherwise white material. She was sure that the collar and shoulder of the uniform had been splattered with blood, in big dots, like the careless splatters of a surrealist artist. Now, not a speck of it remained.

"Ms. Pelagi," Fremont said, "we have to get you to the hospital. You should be checked—"

"Of course," the woman replied. "I've been a victim of something, haven't I? An attack, I suppose." She looked over at the teenager again, her expression bewildered. "But I don't think he did it." She took a tentative step forward. "I was . . . on my way to work," she explained. "Illinois Masonic. You can take me there. An ambulance—that's not necessary."

"All right. It's only a few blocks," Vilmos said. There was the hum of a powerful engine and the crunch of gravel, more flashing blue lights as another squad car pulled up, the backup Fremont had requested. "Please, Ms. Pelagi." Vilmos gestured toward the car. "Climb in the back, please, and we'll drive you to the ER. The other officers will take the young man to the station."

"Why?" The woman's eyes were dark, eerily deep, and Vilmos looked away uncomfortably. "He hasn't done anything. I'm sure of it."

"Nevertheless, he'll be questioned. Routine, that's all—he might have seen something, or heard something. You're positive this kid is not the person who attacked you? Absolutely sure?" The Pelagi woman nodded mutely and Vilmos saw her partner roll his eyes as he stepped around to the passenger side of the patrol car. For a second Vilmos felt the hair on the back of her neck rise, like a swift, gentle charge of static electricity; she turned and realized the teenager was staring at her and the woman, his gaze vacant. Fremont had to snap his fingers in front of the kid's nose before he could pull his attention back to the real world. "What's your name, son?"

"Jason Spiro. I'm staying with my aunt over on Southport."

"What happened here?" one of the officers from the backup car asked. "Is he the perp?"

"I don't think so." Fremont came up with a key and unlocked the handcuffs circling the boy's wrists; he would have expected the young man to rub at his skin—they usually did—but his hands dropped to his sides and hung, limp. "Take him over to the station anyway. He's got a lot of questions to answer." Fremont turned to his partner and inclined his head at the victim. "Illinois Masonic?"

Vilmos shrugged. "We'll drive her in. That's what she wants, and it's a couple of blocks away. She's not bleeding or anything, so . . ."

They looked at each other for a long moment, fear mirrored in each gaze, then quickly masked. *Did we see what we think we saw?* Abruptly Fremont turned back to Spiro and the moment was gone, like shutting the hood hard on a squad car: you can close it but not hide the fact that the engine is still there, still running. The boy had already been hustled into the other patrol car.

"Let's roll," Vilmos said. "For all we know, this woman has internal injuries. We're making this shit worse by waiting around. You drive." Fremont nodded and moved to the driver's side, settling onto the seat and shifting to drive. His partner's next words were quiet but clear.

"Keep your mouth shut about . . . what we saw—until we see who gets assigned to this case. Your career'll last longer that way."

9

Late Friday—Early Saturday

The ER on a Friday night:

Two doctors, three residents, all juggling patients as though they were sharp-edged knives rather than human flesh, decisions of life and death and who gets treated first and why, made so often that no one thinks in terms of emotions anymore, only efficiency. Police officers roamed freely and carried paper cups of coffee, watching over perps being treated for injuries and waiting for the doctors to finish so they could do their paperwork and head out. In one curtained cubicle, a man groaned and clutched at his abdomen while a nurse quickly set an IV into one of his arms. In another, a young girl sat upright on the examining table, cradling a hand wrapped in a blood-soaked bandage. Tears coursed down her face as she banged one foot against the table's metal leg. Her mother stood next to her, stunned expression disintegrating into her own tears when a doctor hurried over.

Two more occupants with trivial wounds, dabbed with anti-
septic then turned loose. All in all, a relatively quiet load for
a weekend night that would be short-staffed unless the nursing supervisor managed to get hold of one of the on-call
trauma nurses to replace the woman who hadn't shown up.
The emergency room still functioned quite capably, not
swamped despite the missing staff member. A few light conversations floated here and there despite the bustle and the
blood, an occasional joke to take the edge off reality. No
strain, not yet.

Until, accompanied by two police officers, in walked
one of their own, the missing piece of their Friday-night
work puzzle.

Maurilla Levin looked up from the notes she was scribbling
and her face registered surprise at the sight of Evelyn, then
went gray as her coworker's torn clothes made her realize
why Evelyn had a double escort of cops. She snatched up
the wall-phone receiver without taking her gaze from Evelyn
and punched a single button; her words were instantly transferred to the PA system. "Dr. Thieu to the emergency room,
stat. Code one-oh-one. Dr. Thieu to the emergency room."

It took a mere thirty seconds for trauma personnel to
appear.

"Evelyn, can you hear me? Evelyn?"

"Of course." She seemed to be floating, treading water in
some great void, suspended and weightless, spiraling with no
urgency at all, as though she were living in real time the
dream of drowning she'd once had as a girl. A sharp crack,
a sudden excruciating light, and the sounds of snapping fingers and voices. Why did she think abruptly of amniotic
fluid before she finally opened her eyes?

"Don't move your arm, Evelyn. We're starting an IV."
Fingers gripped her forearm, cold and a little shaky, the
shock of having to treat a coworker showing in the faint
wobble. Evelyn pulled away before the needle could pene-
trate her skin.

"Don't," she said. "I'm—I don't need an IV. I'm fine."

The light surrounded her, surgery lights for some reason,
washed her and the small crowd in a harsh, unnatural glow

that made everything seem icy, brittle. She had the absurd thought that if she smacked one of the gaping faces hovering over her, the features would shatter, explode like a sparkling icicle hit with a hammer.

"Just put the damned IV in her arm," someone said impatiently. "Can't you see she's in shock? Here, give it to me."

Fingers fumbled at her arm again, still without her permission, and this time she slapped them away, heard a surprised intake of breath. "Stop it," Evelyn said harshly. "I said I don't want it." She rubbed at her eyelids to stall for time, feeling grit on her face, tiny cement pebbles from the surface of the street. She should let them treat her—she knew better than to act like this or to refuse treatment. Didn't she? But what would they find? Something ugly? Something that would make them all stare at her with horror and loathing? A strange thought, but she couldn't shake it.

The fingers she ran across her skin felt numb, as though they'd been shot through with Novocain. She slid her fingertips beneath the mat of hair hanging across the back of her neck *(what happened to my braid?)* and pulled hard but without being obvious. The pain sensors in her neck responded immediately and her eyes watered as the sharp tugging cleared her mind enough for her to think again. Her gaze focused abruptly: seven or eight people surrounded the cart upon which she was sitting, the tools of their trade held comfortably in their hands as each presumably waited for a turn at her. Their expressions seemed to better match those of the patients and victims they were so accustomed to treating. Evelyn could easily imagine the questions bouncing in the minds of her fellow employees as if they were clearly tattooed across their foreheads:

What's the matter with her? Drugs?
Shock, of course, isn't it obvious?
She should let us treat her—
Shock, of course, isn't it
She knows better—
Shock, of course
We're all trained—
Shock

"I'm fine," Evelyn repeated, using the sound of her own voice to bring her fragmenting thoughts back to ground.

She'd been victim enough tonight; they had no right to assume—as had her attacker—that they could do whatever they wanted without asking. This was *her*, not some nameless patient on a cart. No one should be able to do what had been done to her—no one should take away her right to simply say no. Not even her coworkers.

Most of all, not her coworkers.

She slid forward to the edge of the metal cart, paused until her dangling feet found the floor and let them hang for a moment, as though she were a child again and too short for her feet to reach. Another disjointed moment of hesitation, then she let them go the rest of the way and felt the automatic balance adjustment that allowed her to stand. A flicker of uneasiness as it registered that she couldn't *feel* her toes—was the circulation impaired? Was it temporary? A chorus of voices distracted her from the thought, babbling on about procedure and caution and tests that should be run. Evelyn ignored them all.

"Evelyn, sit back down."

She recognized Juan's voice and her body involuntarily obeyed. Juan was an EMT she'd been working successfully with for years—more than successfully. The two of them had a working relationship and routine that many of the other trauma nurses and techs considered nearly telepathic. She could feel the breezes on her skin from all the people gathered around her—nurses, techs, EMTs, both of the ER residents and one of the ER doctors. Surely there must be other patients in the ER tonight who needed tending. Had the entire staff come to her rescue? For some reason she found the idea blackly humorous and she quelled the sudden urge to giggle by biting her tongue hard. "Don't you guys have patients?" she managed at last.

"They are not your concern, not this time." Juan again, all business, and she felt movement against her chest, his fingers placing the cool metal of a stethoscope between the ripped folds of her uniform. The touch made her shiver. "Come on," he chided. "Let us do our jobs. We'll check you out, run the standard tests, and let you go home in the morning. Think of it as an overnighter in a hotel, with the best of service and the shittiest food." Something encircled the flesh of one arm and Evelyn looked down to see a blood-pressure cuff being pressed into place; the Velcro gave off a tearing sound as it was adjusted that made her wince. She felt oddly disconnected from the whole emergency room scene, as though she were floating above it all. Juan's voice, coupled with that of Dr. Thieu's, yanked her back.

"Run a chem seven, urinalysis, amylase. Blood alcohol, too." Following the sound of the Vietnamese woman's voice, Evelyn's eyes found and locked with those of Dr. Helen Thieu, a career ER physician who seemed to thrive on stress and high efficiency. The doctor frowned. "I don't like her color, either. Do a full set of head and chest X rays."

"No," Evelyn said again. Irritation, finally, put some strength in her voice. "Isn't anyone listening to me? I said I don't want any tests." Silence then, and for an instant Evelyn wondered exactly *who* was in shock, the others in the room or her. That's it, she thought suddenly. They're right: I am in shock. I should let them run their tests, their chemical checks, their—

X rays

No.

That old obstinance again, like a hardheaded dog pulling against a leash only because its owner is mean, fed by an undercurrent of irrational fear.

The person at her side—a nurse Evelyn didn't know and who had probably been pulled in on call when Evelyn was late—moved and the black nylon ringing her arm loosened and fell away. "BP's low," the woman said sharply. "Abnormally so, seventy over forty."

"That settles it," Juan said. "You're staying."

"That settles nothing." Evelyn aimed a severe look at the nurse who'd spouted that ridiculous blood pressure, but the woman ignored her. "Besides, low BPs run in the women of my family. Check my records—it's nothing new."

"You could be bleeding!" Juan's voice, usually so calm, was starting to rise and Evelyn felt a pang of sympathy. Her behavior was inexcusable, irrational, full of classic symptoms for post-traumatic shock. These people were too logical, too *medical*, to accept that she could not allow herself to be bullied into something she didn't want.

"I'm not," she said aloud. "I'd know the signs."

"You don't know shit," someone else said. One of the

other EMTs, Maurilla, scowled back at her. "If you did, you'd know to keep your ass in here. I don't think we should let her go, especially with a blood-pressure reading like that. Something's wrong." Maurilla turned back to Evelyn and used one gloved finger to flip up a scrap of Evelyn's uniform. "So what actually *happened* to you, Pelagi? Care to tell us? I know the cops're mighty interested in what you have to say. They seem to think you escaped the Ravenswood Strangler. So let's hear the details."

Details? Evelyn stared at her blankly. There *were* no details—just a smudgy black sense of pain, and then spinning, down and into the comfortable arms of that same old breathless and water-filled dream. All those questioning faces around her, and she couldn't answer.

"Oh, for God's sake," Dr. Thieu said irritably, "I can't believe it's taking the police that long to get from Barry to here. I need to talk to them."

There was a slight prick on the back of her hand, another needle. Alan, the trauma tech, gasped when Evelyn yanked it out, blood welling to fill the small puncture, then trickling across the pale, freckled expanse of skin. Not her fault, not really: he'd done a bad job of setting the needle to begin with, too harried and too freaked out by her, a botched attempt at stealth. She almost snorted. Had he really expected to stick her without her noticing? An unexpected shift in her mood then, a swift and uncharacteristic change to angry exasperation. "Jesus," Evelyn said. "Am I talking to the *air* here? Or are you all fucking deaf? I said I'm *not staying*! I don't *want* to."

"As you wish," Dr. Thieu replied stiffly. "Then you'll go out against medical advice and you may explain your actions to the Review Board before returning to work. Is that what you want?"

"If that's what it takes!" Evelyn snapped back.

"Very well then." Dr. Thieu spun with a sharp click of one heel, addressing no one in particular. "Get her an AMA form."

Juan looked stunned. "But—"

The physician dismissed him with a wave of a long-fingered hand. "There are other patients and I don't have time to argue further. You," she fixed Evelyn with a withering stare, "are not free to leave the hospital until you explain to the satisfaction of the police detective in charge of this case—who is not yet here, I might add—what happened to you tonight. I understand he has gone to your home to pick up your husband. You may leave the ER, but *not* the building." She turned again to Juan. "Make *sure* she's taken somewhere—one of the private staff offices maybe—and kept there. I refuse to catch grief from the police because of her foolishness, and I want to talk to her husband when he gets here." Evelyn shot her a pained glance, but was ignored. "Her behavior is erratic. He needs to know this." She peered at her watch. "If I'm not in the ER, have me paged. I'm on shift all night." She flung Evelyn's incomplete chart on a countertop and stalked out.

Another silence, this one more uncomfortable. Finally, Juan cleared his throat. "Well, I—"

"My locker," Evelyn interrupted. "I have an extra uniform in it. I'll change and go on duty."

Someone gave an impatient sigh from behind her left shoulder and Evelyn turned her head to see Phia Holey, the night nurse supervisor, with her arms folded across her chest and one black eyebrow arched. "Not a chance, Evelyn. You're off the schedule and you know it. Dr. Thieu will have to approve your return to work and you sure haven't helped your position by telling her you're going out AMA. You'll be lucky to be working by Monday."

"I'll talk to her," Evelyn said. She rubbed at her temples. "Tomorrow night when I come in."

"Don't bother showing up unless you talk to her *first*," Phia retorted. "I'll just send you right back out." She shrugged. "Sorry, but that's procedure. She'll have my head if I don't follow her orders."

Juan studied Evelyn. "Sure you won't reconsider? It's a few stupid tests."

Evelyn shook her head stubbornly. "No. I don't want them."

With Dr. Thieu's departure, most of the remaining people had gone as well, hurrying off to waiting patients and duties. With a quick glance around, Juan touched her arm. "Listen, I've known you a long time. I know you can be stubborn, but this . . ." He hesitated, then plunged on. "Is there a problem with running the tests? You know, like drugs? Is that it?"

"Of course not. You know I don't do chemicals." She glared at him.

"Then you might as well head to the one of the offices and wait. You won't get out of here until Thieu has a chance to talk to Warren and the cops have a turn at you." His gaze momentarily dropped to the shredded uniform. "I think Phia's got an extra sweater at the desk. You can at least get covered up."

Juan strode away and Evelyn let her head fall forward wearily, then saw the focus of Juan's pointed glance. A more than generous expanse of her chest was visible, the ruined uniform and bra all but useless. Her hand, the fingernails rimmed with dirt—and was that blood under several of them?—went automatically to pull the material together, then dropped away. Always a modest person, she could find nothing right now, no shame, embarrassment, no *sensation*, that made her care.

She looked at her fingernails again and thought they should be cleaned now, before her mind took the thought and tossed it down that same faraway pit that had claimed the vital memory of her attacker's face. A realization sparked inside her brain, the connection tenuous and nearly missed, like jumper cables on a badly corroded battery post: the police would want samples of whatever it was under her nails, would need it for evidence in this crime she could not swear had been committed.

Before she could forget, Evelyn went to get a plastic bag and a sterile nail file.

10

At twelve-fifteen in the morning, the two-flat on Barry Street was unremarkable. Identical to the hundreds of other two- and three-bedroom apartment buildings that made up the neighborhood, this one had only two levels but stretched far enough back on its lot to be a three-bedroom layout. That its first floor sat at ground level rather than eight or ten feet above a basement or garden apartment fell a little out of the normal design, but not that far: as they did today, contractors had cut corners a hundred years ago when these had been built. What did set this particular building apart was that in about three minutes Detective Jude Ewing was going to wake up and shake up the man who lived there, and Ewing's mouth turned down at the thought. While he didn't much care if his job made him any friends, he'd never gotten used to the chore of passing along bad news, even to the luckier ones like Warren Pelagi.

Ewing's gaze flicked over the building front and sidewalk again, automatically scanning the shadows for movement: dog, cat, human, it didn't matter. There was a soft fluttering at one of the windows on the top floor but no sound; muted light bled through the gauzy curtains. Perhaps a pet peeking out, drawn by the sound of the car pulling to a stop in front. Then again, it was still early on what he considered to be Friday night—to him the day didn't change to Saturday until he went off duty in the morning. A lot more people would be awake than if it'd been a weeknight, and Belmont, a few blocks over, had the noise, people, and gridlocked traffic to bear that out. The movement at the window didn't come again and Ewing ignored it; the Pelagis lived on the first floor anyway.

Ewing got out of the unmarked Ford and patted his pocket, making sure his notepad and an ink pen were in place. The holster underneath his left arm didn't need checking; it fit like a familiar companion after eleven years as a cop, the last six as a detective in Area Three. He stretched for a moment as he stood by the driver's door, trying to yank out the kinks that always settled in his shoulders when he was on his way somewhere with shitty news, especially in the middle of the night—the most startling time to ring someone's doorbell. He'd always thought the telephone was worse: nothing but an emotionless, disembodied voice in the darkness, a faceless stranger on the line, existing only to make a life darker. If at all feasible, he preferred to grit his teeth and deliver bad news in person, where he could at least offer a hand or an expression of sympathy.

The Pelagis' front door was hardwood, cheap but strong, and no doorbell. Ewing bruised his knuckles knocking on it; still, the windows at his left showed him that a light came on immediately and the detective felt a sick twist in his stomach when he heard the rush of footsteps toward the door. Sometimes, and more than most folks imagined, the people—though they had no reason at all to worry—were waiting and had been for hours, kept from sleep by some nagging sense they couldn't identify.

"Who is it?" A man's voice, clear and sharp. If this guy had been asleep, it hadn't been for very long.

"Warren Pelagi?" Ewing began. "My name is Detective—"

The door was yanked open from the inside but Ewing was prepared for it and didn't flinch. Even so, the nearly wild-eyed expression never failed to sting. "Evelyn—my wife—is she all right?" The man's hands reached for Ewing and the detective let Warren Pelagi pull him inside. He was still tugging on Ewing's sleeve as the police officer used his toe to nudge the door shut behind them. No sense rousing the nosy neighbors.

"Your wife is at Illinois Masonic, Mr. Pelagi. She—"

"—works there. She's a trauma nurse." Pelagi looked at him expectantly for a second, then his face sagged. "You know that, of course. What am I saying? What's happened?"

Ewing led the smaller man to a chair and motioned for him to sit, then bent his knees so he wouldn't be looming over him. "Your wife has been the victim of an attack. As I said, she's at Illinois Masonic, in the emergency room."

"How badly is she hurt?" Pelagi's complexion had gone white, the difference between his dark hair and skin nearly ghoulish.

"I'm afraid I can't answer that," Ewing admitted. "The dispatcher didn't fill me in, and I haven't been to the hospital yet. I thought it was a better idea to pick you up on the way." He inclined his head toward Pelagi, who was dressed in a T-shirt and boxer shorts with some sort of cartoon characters on them. "If you'll throw on some clothes . . ."

"Yes, sure. I'll get dressed." Pelagi jerked around and grabbed at a pile of what Ewing called "pocket things" on an end table, thrusting his hand beneath an overhanging lamp shade to get at his wallet and keys. The key chain promptly slid away from his fumbling fingers and Pelagi's spasming attempt to keep them from falling succeeded in sending the lamp, a heavy china thing with a blue-and-white country design, spinning off the table. The carpet was not wall-to-wall, and the base of the lamp landed hard on the strip of wooden flooring beyond the rug with a crash loud enough to make Ewing's ears ring and Pelagi cry out in surprise. As Pelagi flailed helplessly at the loose lamp shade, Ewing's reflexes took over and he snatched at the lamp before it went rolling.

"Leave it for later, Mr. Pelagi. Go get dressed." Pelagi

needed no further urging, and he sped down the hall and through a door leading to one of the bedrooms; thirty seconds later he charged out of that room and into another, clothes flapping in one hand. A minute ticked by, then two, and Ewing drifted toward the hall. On his right he glimpsed the bedroom and quickly looked away; he had a cop's healthy curiosity but still had no desire to see the truly private belongings of this couple. The kitchen was directly in front of him and he headed toward it, thinking vaguely of a glass of water when he heard a sound. For a moment he turned back to the living room, then realized he'd been going in the right direction to begin with—toward the back door. The knocking was too soft for Warren Pelagi to hear over the hurried rush of water now coming from what Ewing guessed was the bathroom. Although the hallway was long, he could easily see all the way into the kitchen, a large, homey room that carried that same cornflower-blue-and-white country theme. Backlit by the glow of a porch light, a faint shadow moved across the pane of frosted window glass in the upper half of the dead-bolted back door. The knock came again, more insistent.

"Warren? Warren, it's Karla," came a woman's voice, muffled by the glass-and-wood barrier. "Is everything all right? I heard something fall."

Ewing's glance found the key to the dead bolt hanging on a nail to the right of the door and he plucked it free and shook his head. What good was a dead bolt if an intruder could break the glass and grab the key? He slipped it in and turned it—wrong way—then tried again. This time the tumblers released and the door swung open.

"What was that noise—oh!" Gray eyes widened in surprise and Warren's visitor, a lovely young black woman, skittered backward. "Who are you?"

Ewing reached into his jacket pocket and pulled out his badge, offering it and waiting patiently while she studied it. "Detective Jude Ewing, Nineteenth District. You live upstairs?" She was fully dressed in a long-sleeved lightweight sweatsuit, but her feet were comfortably encased in oversized red felt slippers.

She seemed satisfied with the badge, though she still frowned at him as she nodded. "I'm Karla Bryant. Why are you here? Where's Warren?" Her gazed skipped over his shoulder and it was obvious that she was a good friend of Evelyn and Warren Pelagi's; he stepped to the side and motioned her into the kitchen. "Please, come in: Mr. Pelagi is getting dressed."

Karla's eyes narrowed, a connection suddenly made. "Evelyn—what's happened to her?" Her hand, long-fingered and impeccably manicured, snatched at his wrist with impressive speed. Her skin tone, a dusky golden tan, deepened perceptibly.

"We're on our way to the hospital," Ewing said as gently as he could. "We'll know more when we get there."

She didn't hesitate. "I'll get my shoes. Don't leave without me." She turned and was out the door, speeding up the stairs with her footsteps making hollow slapping sounds on the painted wood.

Ewing looked back as he heard Warren Pelagi come into the kitchen. The look on the man's face was terrible, his mouth twisted into a cross between dread and agony. Clutched in his fingers was a small, crumpled piece of paper. "Did I tell you she left me a note?" he asked the detective in a strangled voice. He offered it and Ewing accepted it, though there was really no use in him reading it.

> *Sweetheart,*
> *Didn't want to wake you—you look so cute while you're sleeping. I'll call you in the morning before you leave.*
>
> > *Love you,*
> > *Evelyn*

Ouch, Ewing thought. He started to give it back but the man had already turned away; instead, the detective tucked it inside the breast pocket of his jacket. "Please, Mr. Pelagi," he said. "Don't jump to conclusions. Let's take it one step at a time. We'll start by getting over to Illinois Masonic." He pointed at the open back door. "Your neighbor—"

"Karla."

The detective nodded. "Right, Karla. She wants to go with us." Confirming his words, they heard a rush of footsteps across the floorboards over their heads and a small thump followed by Karla talking to someone. Finally there was a slam of a door and the sound of a lock engaging. "She has a roommate?" Ewing asked casually.

Pelagi shook his head but didn't bother to elaborate, leaving Ewing with the strange impression that the woman who lived above them talked to herself. A moment later Karla joined them, slightly breathless. She had replaced the felt slippers with a beat-up pair of white-and-purple Nikes and slung a frayed canvas purse over one shoulder. She came in without waiting for an invitation, then twisted and as a matter of habit locked the door behind her. When she started to put the key back onto the nail, Ewing couldn't keep silent any longer.

"Don't," he ordered. When she paused, he reached and took the key from her, then dropped it on the countertop along the opposite wall of the kitchen. "It's not safe," he explained, "especially in a ground-floor apartment like this where someone can break a window on the back porch and reach through." He glanced at Warren Pelagi. "I know you've got other things on your mind right now, but later on try to remember to hang it out of reach of the window." Warren nodded absently and Jude figured he would need reminding. Maybe Karla would take care of that; the way she was eyeing the door made him think she, at least, had heard his words.

The walk to Ewing's car was wordless, hurried, their shoes quiet on a street steeped in heat and darkness. A faint, useless air current ruffled the leaves, barely enough to split the stillness. Certainly nothing to cool the perspiration beading among the thick dark blond curls already plastered on Ewing's forehead. Karla Bryant looked wired, ready to explode but at the same time competent, as if she were used to dealing with pressure situations and could jump right into the fray and take charge; Warren Pelagi just looked miserable. At least the ride was mercifully brief.

When they arrived, the emergency room was bedlam and it didn't take long for another cop to rattle off a story about a drunk losing control of his car at the intersection of Clark and Diversey. He'd hit six pedestrians before planting the boat-sized 1976 Impala through the plate-glass window of a mom-and-pop video store, killing two customers and nearly crushing another man in the process. The injured were starting to arrive, but a quick question to a nurse as she rushed past got them started in the direction of a block of private offices down the hall, where Pelagi's wife had been ordered to wait before the ER had turned chaotic. Ewing wondered how badly she could be hurt that they would park her off to the side rather than admit her, but still not allow her to help out with the injured people stacked up in the ER cubicles. That notion fell apart when the detective pushed open the door to an office labeled E. M. LEVINE, M.D. and got his first look at Evelyn Pelagi.

Dark hair, matted and still dotted with gravel and bits of dirt, floated above a face that at first glance appeared utterly bloodless but oddly speckled. A second look showed the faint spots to be freckles nearly washed out by the rude fluorescent lights evenly spaced in the ceiling. Her eyes were an off-color hazel, sun-washed and light above the smudges of shadow beneath them. And her clothes—what a mess and not at all concealed by the sweater that someone had drawn over her shoulders and buttoned at the throat. She sat totally still, motionless, didn't even bother to raise her head as her husband and neighbor rushed to her side.

"Evelyn, honey, what happened? Are you okay? Are you hurt?" Warren Pelagi's hands were trembling as he reached to brush aside the wisps of blue-black hair stuck to his wife's cheeks. "I can't believe they just stuck you in here—"

"Hey," Karla said softly. She stepped around Ewing and knelt next to Evelyn. "You want to fill us in? Jesus, we were so scared!"

Something in Karla's voice, finally, cut through some of the haze clouding Evelyn Pelagi's mind and she blinked and managed to focus on her friend. "No." Her whisper was barely audible. "I don't think I'm hurt. I—I don't know." Warren and Karla exchanged looks and Warren crouched next to his wife's other side.

"What happened, honey?" He waved toward Ewing. "The officer—I mean detective—he couldn't tell us hardly anything."

A pause then, a shade short of Ewing opening his mouth to urge her on. "I suppose I was attacked." Evelyn fingered a piece of torn material dangling from between the folds of the sweater. "It sure looks that way."

Timing was everything, startling a victim was not. Ewing took a double step forward, letting his feet make enough noise to draw her attention, then presented his badge. He kept his voice carefully modulated and bent his knees so that his six-foot height wouldn't seem so imposing over the seated woman—it seemed he was always having to do that—when he introduced himself. "My name is Detective Jude Ewing, Mrs. Pelagi. I've been put in charge of investigating this matter." He stopped for a second, giving the husband a chance to protest his questions if he was so inclined; better to learn early what kind of a battle the family would give him. Warren Pelagi and the neighbor woman surprised him by waiting politely for him to continue, and Ewing saw no reason to pass up the opportunity. "Did you see your attacker, ma'am? Can you tell me anything about him?"

Evelyn shook her head. "No, I didn't see anything. I know you must've heard this a thousand times, but it was so dark . . ." Her words faded.

Ewing dropped to his haunches along with the others, completing a triangle in front of Evelyn. "I want you to close your eyes and think," he ordered firmly. "Now, while it's very fresh, I'm going to have to ask you to *relive* the attack, if you can." Warren's face darkened ominously and Karla opened her mouth to object, then closed it when the detective held up a warning finger. "I know the thing you want most to do in the world is to forget, Evelyn—may I call you that? But right now, before the details become too blurred, we need to hear everything you can remember, the most minor piece of trivia. Sights, sounds, it doesn't matter how inconsequential it seems to you. Close your eyes and *think back*, then tell me what you remember. Maybe," he said very softly, "we can stop this from happening to anyone else." Evelyn stared at Ewing for a moment, long enough to make him uncomfortable under that odd-colored gaze. Next to him, Ewing sensed Karla fidgeting before Evelyn's eyes flickered and closed. Ten seconds, twenty, then a full minute: right before she spoke, Ewing saw her fingers twist together so tightly he thought she'd probably have bruises in the morning. He slipped his hand into his pocket and flipped the on switch of a small pocket recorder that was sensitive enough to pick up the conversation despite the fabric of his jacket, then habitually pulled out his small notebook and ink pen.

"I was stupid," she said quietly. "I should have woke Warren up and I didn't." From the corner of his eye, Ewing saw Warren Pelagi wince outright. "It was so dark, and so very . . . empty."

"Yes?" Ewing prompted. Sometimes it was best to keep the words going.

"He got me from behind," Evelyn said suddenly. "I think he was big, like a football player maybe. He was so *heavy*." Karla's fist went to her mouth and Ewing saw her sink her teeth into the side of her forefinger to keep from crying out. Warren's complexion had gone stone gray. "I know he knocked me down, and I hit the ground face-first. It hurt a lot, and I don't remember much after that." She hesitated. "I—I think he hit me, and then I passed out, but . . ." Evelyn's fingers came up and touched her cheekbone tentatively.

"He hit you?" Warren asked, bewildered. "In the *face*?"

Evelyn nodded and it took an immense effort for Ewing not to show his disbelief. If her attacker had been the size of a football player, how the hell could he have struck her yet left no damage? His next question, Ewing knew, would not be a welcome one. Still, it had to be asked and this small, private office was as good as almost anywhere else.

"Did he rape you, ma'am?"

Warren's head jerked, and Karla, who had done such a fine job of keeping a calm, quiet front, couldn't stop a small moan from escaping. Evelyn's answer didn't help matters.

"I don't think so." She raised her face and Ewing met her gaze, still vaguely emotionless. "Maybe. I can't remember."

"Yet she refuses an examination or tests," came a clipped voice. Standing in the doorway was a Vietnamese woman in doctor's garb. "Perhaps you can convince her otherwise." The physician strode forward and offered her hand, the skin so scrubbed it was rough and chapped, first to Warren, then to Karla, and finally to the detective. "I am Dr. Thieu."

"A concussion?" Ewing eyed Evelyn speculatively.

"I don't have a concussion," Evelyn snapped, turning abruptly alert. "Post-traumatic amnesia is common and not necessarily indicative of a concussion."

"But it *is* an indication of shock, as you well know." Dr. Thieu folded her arms in front of her.

"Evelyn, honey, you should stay overnight, do the tests—"

"No."

"Why not?" Karla's tone made the two words more than a simple question; to Ewing, who had immediately recognized a long-standing friendship, the simple inquiry implied unreasonableness on Evelyn's part and demanded a truthful response.

"I—" An instant of delay, then Evelyn found the words. "I just don't want to, I guess. Haven't I been forced enough tonight? I just want to go home, to my own house and my own bed." She looked at her husband imploringly. "Is that so bad?"

Warren Pelagi stared at her wordlessly and Ewing wanted desperately to jump in and say something like *Yeah, if it costs you your life because of something we can't see right now!* But he couldn't, not when there were no discernible signs of injury. If the doctors were willing to discharge Evelyn Pelagi, against medical advice or not, who was he to run his mouth? Just a cop.

Karla cleared her throat. "You should be examined to see if you were assaulted, especially since you can't remember." She leaned forward, her face sincere. "I know you hate to be told what to do, but let's be candid here, Evie. What if you *were* raped, and what if your attacker was HIV positive? You need to be checked, given medication, just to be safe. You can't take a chance with something like that."

"I don't *feel* like I was raped," Evelyn insisted stubbornly. "I don't need any medication, or any tests. I'm not even *sore*, for God's sake. *Please*, just let me go home."

Dr. Thieu gave a snort. "Lack of symptoms at this early stage means nothing and you know it."

"Well," Ewing interrupted before the argument could escalate, "why don't you tell me what else you can recall. As I said before, any detail, anything at all—"

"I have no more time to waste here," Dr. Thieu cut in. "The ER staff knows where to reach me if necessary. If you prefer, you may choose another doctor. Good evening." The doctor left the small office with a purposeful slam of the door.

"Evelyn—" Warren began.

"I'm *tired*," his wife said slowly, "of defending and explaining myself. I am a grown woman, damn it." Her expression was as close to anger as Ewing had seen in the short time he'd spent with her. "Why can't anyone respect my wishes?"

Warren seemed hurt for a moment, then his mouth set into a determined line. "You're right. I suppose we aren't being very considerate, although in our defense it's out of concern for you." Karla nodded reluctantly and Warren straightened, then held out a hand to his neighbor and inclined his head toward Ewing. "We're going home, Detective. And my wife is going with us."

Karla touched Ewing's arm. "Why don't you stop by tomorrow?" she suggested. "Evelyn will be rested, things will be . . . calmer." When Ewing's forehead sank into a frown, Karla lowered her voice. "I'm afraid it's the best you'll get. I know her—she won't talk now, and Warren's getting angry. Pushing things tonight won't be productive, but tomorrow . . ." She let her voice trail away.

Ewing closed his notebook with a small snap and slid it into the inside pocket of his jacket, then remembered to turn off his recorder. It was impossible to miss Evelyn Pelagi's look of relief. "I'll take you all home," he offered. "It'll save you the aggravation of a cab. No more questions, I promise." Warren smiled thinly as Evelyn rose. It was the first any of them had actually *seen* the damage to Evelyn's clothes. Warren hissed, and Ewing had to grind his jaw against the next half dozen or so questions that popped into his mind at the sight of the destroyed dress. All he could allow himself was a tight, "By the way, please don't dispose of or wash your uniform, ma'am. If you don't mind, I'd like to take it as evidence." Evelyn nodded her agreement, an absent move that seemed more to humor the policeman than anything else. Karla, in a motherly gesture, adjusted the sweater draped across Evelyn's shoulders and led her to the door.

The ride back to the two-flat was as silent as the initial trip to Illinois Masonic, with each of the car's occupants lost in his or her own dark reverie. When Ewing pulled to a stop in front of the apartment building in which the Pelagis and Karla Bryant lived, he could have sworn he heard a sigh of relief from Evelyn's shadowed corner in the backseat. "Here we are," Ewing said with as much cheer as he could manage. Not a whole lot, considering he could almost *see* the clues flying away on the dreams of a night's sleep, one probably augmented by a strong sleeping pill. But you couldn't force someone to cooperate, and chances were if she'd stayed overnight at Illinois Masonic, the medical staff wouldn't have let him near her until the next day anyway. "I'll be in touch tomorrow." He stood next to the Ford and watched as they all climbed out and moved slowly toward the front door of the Pelagi apartment. Suddenly Evelyn stopped and came back, motioning for Warren and Karla to wait. Puzzled, Ewing leaned down as she held up her fingers and looked puzzled, then put her mouth close to his ear.

"I scratched him, Detective"—as she had done earlier, she paused, as though she was having a difficult time remembering his name—"Ewing. Across the *face*. I'm sorry—I forgot to tell you earlier. If you check with Juan back at the ER, I left a sample of the material that was under my fingernails in a plastic bag at the trauma nurses' station. It has my name on it. He'll know where it is." She turned and strode away.

Shocked, Ewing couldn't help himself. "Hey, wait—"

"You promised," Evelyn reminded him over her shoulder. "No more until tomorrow."

Then the door closed behind her, leaving the perplexed detective to stand on the empty sidewalk with nothing but a hundred more questions.

11

Saturday

The Nineteenth District Police Station on Foster Avenue was constructed of pale concrete blocks, a squat, single-story box of a building that was anything but welcoming, especially in the middle of the night. Ewing wondered how the boy Sandra had told him about, Jason Spiro, had felt upon being brought here, then pretty much left in one of the locked interrogation rooms to wait for Ewing to finish at Illinois Masonic. From Sandra's report, she'd gathered the boy's presence at the scene of Evelyn Pelagi's attack had been accidental. The two uniforms who'd discovered him with the victim hadn't witnessed any actual assault on Spiro's part, but something in Sandra's tone of voice suggested a situation out of the norm, and that coupled with her decision to wait for him before talking to Spiro made Ewing even more curious. Sandra had mentioned Evelyn's insistence that the boy only tried to help her, yet despite the time Ewing had spent with Evelyn, the woman never spoke a word about this teenager to him, her husband, or her friend Karla. None of it made any more sense now as Ewing pushed through the entrance than it had a half hour earlier, when Evelyn Pelagi had dropped the biggest clue on him, then basically shut her door in his face.

The front desk was running about average for a Saturday at two in the morning: a couple of drunks, a few prostitutes arguing as they were led back to holding—holdouts who refused to accept the new Alderman's crackdown. One teenager with a beaten face would've been in the hospital had he not been so belligerent, plus the usual run of minor complaints: fights, domestics, fenderbenders. In one of the interrogation rooms in the rear, Jason Spiro waited. From the background information Sandra had left before going as backup on another call, the boy was from Georgia and had been up here about a week or so, although that didn't mean much. Ewing hoped to God the boy could shed some light on this case. The detective couldn't help but be excited—whether the teenager knew it or not, he and Evelyn Pelagi were, as far as they could tell, the only two people who had thus far survived an encounter with the man police believed to be the Ravenswood Strangler.

Jason had been sitting in this room for a good two hours and they'd let him out only once, escorting him to the men's room after he'd banged on the two-way glass for at least ten minutes before getting anyone's attention. That was over forty-five minutes ago, and he was starting to wonder if whoever was supposed to be keeping track of him, or questioning him or whatever, had simply forgotten and gone home for the night. He couldn't get out, but they had no concrete reason to hold him—he was just a witness, after all—and the police probably didn't want to risk putting him in an actual cell. What better way to sidestep the situation than to "forget" him in a room somewhere?

He was giving serious consideration to beating on the window again when the door finally opened. The man who stepped through was undeniably a cop, and Jason didn't need the badge pinned carelessly on the guy's lapel to tell him that. A detective, of course, dressed in a pair of black

denims and a light gray T-shirt under a darker gray tweed
sport jacket. Despite the casual clothes, the man had a sense
of power that preceded him to the table where Jason waited,
and while his interrogator was about six feet tall—not that
large compared with Jason's five-foot-ten—he gave the impression that he was much, much bigger. Although a shaggy
crown of dark blond curls tried to soften the cop's hard face,
Jason couldn't find anything at all chummy in the depth of
the policeman's clear blue eyes. To be fair, though, neither
was there anything outright hostile.

"I'm Detective Ewing," the cop said without wasting any
time. "I'm going to ask you some questions about the woman
you were found with tonight."

Jason folded his hands in his lap. "All right." He was facing the detective, who had chosen a chair directly in front of
the two-way glass. Somewhere behind it, Jason presumed
others watched and recorded his answers. How amusing. For
a short while after that woman's resurrection, Jason had
been filled with terror and amazement. Had he really done
that? Brought her back from the dead? His thoughts over
the past couple of hours had been frantic, bouncing around
in search of an explanation like the centipede in the arcade
game of the same name. Finally, he had succeeded in
squelching his own fright and replacing it with self-
confidence. Pride, too. Yes, he *had* resurrected her.

Now Detective Ewing pulled a small notebook from one
pocket and flipped it open, revealing several pages of
cramped, tiny handwriting. The officer started to say something, then sat back and dug in a different pocket instead,
producing a small tape recorder. He set it on the table and
turned it on. "Tell you what," he suggested as he gave Jason
a frank once-over. "I'm tired of asking questions—I've been
doing it all night. Why don't you tell me instead, in your
own words, how you met the woman and what happened after that, all the way up to when the police car pulled up
next to the two of you in the alley."

"All right," Jason said again. He was more than amused
now, he was downright *tickled*, as his mother would say. Oh,
it was going to be so interesting to test this strapping cop's
tolerance with the plain old truth! To make the situation
more fulfilling, Jason was submerged in this feeling of . . .

completeness. He knew what it was, oh sure. Or at least what had *caused* this physical sensation of being sated, of a deep, primal hunger having been satisfied.

The woman, of course.

Too bad he didn't know her name.

"Let's begin," Jason said abruptly. He wasn't the only one ready to get down to business. "I was out for a walk, it was late."

"Which way were you going?"

"I was, uh, headed toward the lake."

"All right. Where were you coming from?"

So much for not asking questions, Jason thought with a silent smirk. Aloud he said, "My aunt's apartment. So I was going to the lake, and while I was still on Nelson, a man ran past me—"

"Ran?"

"I suppose jogged would be more accurate. He was a big guy, athletic, wearing shorts and a T-shirt. Heavily built. Oh—and there was something wrong with his face."

Ewing leaned forward. "What?"

For the first time Jason's expression showed some effort as he tried to concentrate. "Well, I'm not sure," he finally admitted. "It had some kind of stripes across it, maybe paint. It was really dark, we were between streetlights. I didn't get a good look. A glance, that's all. To be honest, I doubt I could identify him again—unless, of course, those marks were some kind of tattoo or birthmark."

Ewing picked up his pen and scribbled in his notebook. "What color were his clothes?" he asked. "Was he wearing glasses?"

"No glasses," Jason responded. "The clothes, I couldn't say other than they weren't bright. Under the streetlights, they just looked different shades of gray."

Ewing nodded; not much help there. Green, tan, gray—it all looked the same under sodium lights. Still, he let himself feel a tingle of elation at the prospect of, *finally,* having an idea of what the Ravenswood Strangler—provided it was the same man, of course—might look like. So far, it jibed with what Evelyn Pelagi had told him. "Okay. What else?"

"Well, then I turned on that stretch of Lakewood be-

tween, which is it? Oakdale and Belmont, I think, the part
that's been all fancied up with those new town houses.
When my aunt showed me around the neighborhood, she
told me there used to be train tracks running down the middle of the street. It's kind of cool—you can still see some of
them. I can't tell you which way I was heading. I don't have
any sense of direction in this city."

"North," the detective said. "Go on."

"So I was going toward Belmont, and I saw this dog." Jason flicked his hand dismissively. "A nothing stray, that's all.
It was rooting around some garbage cans, and it snarled at
me. I stomped my foot at it, it ran. Then I saw a woman's
shoe poking out from between the cans. I'll spare you any
description right now, detective—unless, of course, you require it, but she was obviously dead."

Ewing looked up from where he'd been ticking off
points in his notebook, his face carefully blank despite his
excitement of a moment ago. "Excuse me? The woman is
very much alive, young man. You must be aware of that after being at the scene. She's not even injured. And yes, I will
require a full description of everything."

Jason nodded sagely. "Of course, I'll tell you everything
I saw. I know she's alive and unhurt *now*. But she wasn't
then. I healed her." He sat back, pleased with himself.

Ewing put down his ink pen, his fingers lining it up next
to his notebook with exaggerated care. "You mean you used
CPR techniques to resuscitate her."

Jason smiled widely; although the boy had a handsome
and healthy farm-boy face, it was not a pleasant thing to see.
"Not at all, Detective Ewing. I mean I healed her.
I brought her back to life."

The sunlight damn near blinded Ewing when he left the station house. Squinting and rubbing at one eye with his knuckles, he dodged around the other squads and unmarked cars
parked in the side lot until he found his black Ford, then sat
for a blissful three minutes of hot quiet inside the car with
the windows still rolled up. It was like being in an isolated
sauna with his eyes closed before he rolled down the window, turned on the scanner and started the engine. Ewing's
shift had ended an hour ago and the boy had certainly told

a wild tale, but the detective wondered if the teenager had realized when he'd made it all up that his fantasy would keep him at the police station all night.

To hear Jason Spiro tell it, he had literally brought Evelyn Pelagi back from the dead. It didn't matter that the woman exhibited no visible injuries; Jason insisted he'd healed a whole slew of them: crushed face, caved-in throat, whatever injuries were sustained as a result of the rape—which Jason also matter-of-factly confirmed. If that hadn't been hard enough for Ewing to swallow, the teenager had started asking *him* questions about Evelyn: what was her name, where did she live, and so on. None of which Ewing answered, of course, although he was careful not to alienate the boy as he avoided giving out the information. The boy had kept talking and Ewing had kept listening and writing, and somewhere around five-thirty in the morning things had started to get even weirder. Jason Spiro had said a lot of things, but a couple of sentences in particular stuck in Ewing's mind. They had sounded rehearsed, pulled straight from a bad movie about evil religion:

"By bringing her back to life, I have made her the vessel of my holiness, and in turn, she has become holy. As Eve was born of Adam, this woman is born of me, and together she and I carry the seeds of a new mankind."

The teen's eyes had glazed and focused on someplace faraway and at that point Ewing had been pissed enough to check off the box in his mental tally labeled QUESTIONABLE WITNESS. A bullshit fabrication like that shouldn't have warranted a second thought, and normally Ewing's temper would have made him bounce the kid out on his butt—after being satisfied he'd gotten as much information as possible about the jogger who was witnessed close to the scene of the attack. However, there *was* the matter of Rod Fremont's retelling of the crime scene as he and his partner had first pulled up, and Ewing tapped his fingers on the steering wheel in frustration. Jason Spiro's story matched the rookie uniform's account almost exactly, with the notable exception being that Jason claimed to have been the cause of a miraculous healing and Fremont reported only that such a thing had happened, much to the consternation of his seasoned partner. Ewing knew Lucita Vilmos well enough to know she had a solid head on her shoulders and a strong reputation; no doubt she was not pleased at her partner's rash wording on his paperwork. Ewing hadn't talked to Vilmos or Fremont—Sandra had—and maybe that was something he'd have to do to put the kinks in this case in more of a straight line. On its face, Freemont's report appeared to be level-headed and written by a sane man who was thinking clearly.

Except for the part that read, *The dead victim was resurrected*.

Ewing checked his watch: a few minutes after eight. Still, he wasn't writing Jason Spiro off, not by a long shot. The boy's appearance bothered him, but Ewing wasn't sure whether the strange shadows on the teen's face were the result of his own weary eyes or an odd reflection caused by the interrogation room's dark two-way glass and glaring fluorescent lights. A couple years ago he'd been dating an artist and had gone to a Halloween party with her. He still remembered the dark circles and blue-bruised sunken-cheekbone effect she'd managed for her costume by using pastels. Jason Spiro's face had looked like that—but not all the time. Rather, it had been filled with vague, odd colors that shifted with every turn of his head. Added to that was the impression—and it was only an impression, because now that Ewing thought about it, the boy had taken care to keep them out of sight most of the time—that the teenager's fingertips were somehow deformed, *flat*. Yeah, he'd be talking to that kid again, and probably soon.

Right now, it was time to head back to see Evelyn Pelagi and find out if a night's rest had done anything for her memory.

12

At seven-thirty in the morning, the heat outside was already stifling enough to wilt plants and make the gardener cranky. Too hot for June, and even Lillith Jerusha, protectively encased in the cool air of the house, longed for the return of the lower temperatures that were normal for mid-June in Chicago. She wanted to go outside and help Chuck make depressions in the soil for the annuals he was going to plant around the toolhouse, bright yellow and orange marigolds. Better yet, she could fill the newest wheelbarrow with the purple, red and white petunia seedlings and line the walkway that led to their stretch of private beach, and be damned to the gloves, too. Dig her fingers deep into the earth, brush aside the earthworms and snails and honest-to-God dirty her French-manicured fingernails, feel the sunlight on her face and get away from the constant murmur of the television in the background. But damn it again; she couldn't stand this heat.

If you can't stand the heat, get out of the kitchen.

Or stay in, she thought morosely. She'd gotten out of a few things lately, hadn't she? Coward.

She poured a cup of chocolate-laced coffee, Godiva's special blend, and chose a glazed almond croissant from the glass-covered plate that Ami had set out for her. As recently as six months ago their housekeeper had still been getting up at five-thirty in the morning to bake fresh pastries. Lillith had finally made her stop; with Davis two states away at the University of Michigan Law School and Isman constantly fighting to control his weight and blood pressure, Lillith was left to stare at a dozen or more assorted sweets each morning. Predictably, her waistline had swelled drastically. Now Ami, bless her heart, drove over to the bakery each morning and hand picked two of the freshly made pastries; whichever one Lillith didn't eat, Ami would include in her own lunch.

Sitting at the table in front of the huge window at the back corner of the kitchen, Lillith drank her coffee and munched on her breakfast, staring blankly through the glass. The lawn was meticulously cut and shapely bushes stretched to the east, finally ending in a wall of greenery that separated the lake area from the actual rear grounds. The bite of croissant in her mouth was tasteless but she chewed and swallowed anyway, knowing the problem was hers and not the fault of the excellent Swedish bakery in downtown Evanston. Sun rays dappled the verdant trees, the heavy leaves rippling gently in the occasional breeze. The whole effect was quite beautiful, quite restful, but totally unsuccessful at giving Lillith any peace of mind.

Cecil.

She could not quite believe he was a murderer, no matter what every instinct in her mind screamed every time she heard some plastic newscaster gleefully announce another killing. The Cecil Gideon she knew—or had known before their nasty breakup—was a quiet man, generous beyond his means, strong and compassionate. A considerate listener, an ardent lover, thoroughly devastated by her announcement a month ago that their relationship was over. What had he expected? They were attracted to each other, yes, intensely so.

But she was so many things that he was not—chief among them married. And don't forget to include older, richer, more social, more *greedy*. That, above all else, was her downfall. It was greed that had driven her into Cecil's arms, pure but not at all simple. The things she wanted were not so simple—if they had been, she would simply buy them. Money was no object, not anymore. After twenty years in the upper echelons of First Chicago Bank, her husband, Isman, practically exhaled the stuff. The problem was that Lillith had yet to find a way to *buy* Isman himself—his time, his attention, his affection. He seemed to be encased in a sort of unbreakable see-through bubble, a biosphere all his own, and she could look but not touch. How she envied David and Janet, their closest friends and the couple with whom they socialized the most. Twenty-five years of marriage for them, too—they'd been wed the same year as Isman and Lillith—yet they still doted on one another, still took trips together, still did little, inconsequential things for no purpose but to please the other. Lillith wanted *that*, more than anything else in the world.

She had met Cecil Gideon when she and Isman had attended a black-tie dance at the Palmer House Hilton downtown, given by the bank as a cosponsor to honor Samuel Harris, a billionaire and long-standing advocate of children's education. Isman, of course, was a keynote speaker at the affair, and also, of course, had left her to flounder among the gossipy, shrewish women who made up the circle of senior-VP wives—also abandoned by their spouses but apparently none the worse for it. Lillith had gritted her teeth until she could grit no longer, then escaped the entire tiring hoopla and fled the Grand Ballroom for the quiet of the main lobby of the hotel. There, beneath forty-eight-foot mural-painted ceilings surrounded by elegant carved borders, she sat amid the plush antique furniture and gazed at a huge floral arrangement on the center table, waiting for midnight and the close of the festivities like an aging Cinderella who'd never been found by her prince.

Off to the right of the scarlet brocade settee on which she perched was another pair of charming velvet wing chairs. In one sat a husky man, chin on hand, quite asleep. Amused, Lillith had watched him for a while, unaware of how

soundly he slept until he began to snore. The noise was ungodly loud in the softly lit room and more than a match for
the gentle notes filtering in from the piano bar. As patrons of
the hotel started to stare, Lillith's charitable nature took
over. If the positions had been reversed, she certainly hoped
someone would wake her before she humiliated herself too
badly.

"Pardon me," she said in a pseudo-whisper as she shook
his shoulder lightly, "but you're snoring rather loudly."

His eyes opened. "Am I?"

Lillith smiled. "I'm afraid so."

"Sorry." He sat up, straightened his tie and looked sheepish. Then, in an obviously impulsive move, he stuck out his
hand. "My name is Cecil, Cecil Gideon. May I buy you a
cup of coffee?"

And just as impulsively, Lillith had accepted. They
walked, not touching, down granite stairs that bore the gentle slope worn by hundreds of thousands of footsteps, de-
scending into a peach-wallpapered lower level to Palmer's
Coffee Shop. With her husband of nearly a quarter century
five floors above, a well-built stranger with a quiet, attentive
personality had worked his way solidly into Lillith's mind.
She'd had no specific desire to sleep with anyone else or
have some lurid affair with a younger man—through the
years she'd had plenty of chances, dismissing them all without serious thought. But Cecil Gideon had awakened something within her, bringing it to the surface with a fury. Lust?
Not really, at least not in the beginning. A hunger instead,
one that had nothing at all to do with sex but with her
heart—her *empty* heart.

That had been a year ago.

What, Lillith wondered now, had she awakened in Cecil
Gideon in return?

One telephone call to the police would end all this, she
thought. One call . . . but no, they would want to know her
name, and why she thought Cecil was the so-called
Ravenswood Strangler. What could she really tell them?
That the timing was right, and that he had changed since
Lillith told him their affair was over. That something was in
his voice now, something that hadn't existed four weeks ago

and that made her heart stutter with terror and robbed her of sleep. She could well imagine the response.

Hands suddenly shaking, Lillith rose and carried her breakfast dishes to the sink. She was contemplating washing them—Ami would fuss at her for doing it, though—when the crisp, professional voice of the newscaster cut through some of the cobwebs in her mind.

"—become the fifth victim of the Ravenswood Strangler, according to police—"

Struggling to turn then, to face the sound of the television, her movements slow and painful in the sunlit room, like a fly caught in golden molasses.

"—the woman was assaulted on Lakewood Avenue slightly before midnight last night, making this incident the second attack this week. Police—"

Lillith gripped the edge of the wide Corian countertop that fanned out of the kitchen and separated it from the family room, not remembering when she had taken the steps that had gotten her across the room. She focused on the man's voice, Bill Kurtis, as he gazed into the camera and simultaneously smiled and looked concerned. How, she wondered disjointedly, does he do that?

"Superintendent Matt Rodriguez had these words to say about the case." Kurtis looked off to his right expectantly and a smaller box opened over his shoulder then spread to fill the television screen, showing a dark-haired Latino man standing next to a squad car with pulsing blue lights, his eyes swollen from interrupted sleep. Still, he talked earnestly to the reporters, chopping the air with his hands to emphasize his statement.

"I'd say this woman narrowly escaped death. Had it not been for the coincidental appearance of another person at the scene, she probably would have been the next murder victim."

Stumbling backward, hand at her throat in relief, Lillith found the bamboo stool Ami used when she sat at the island and made up the grocery list. She settled on it gratefully, let the relief slide over her, that feeling of restored well-being after a bad fright.

"Unfortunately, as it stands now we are still without a concrete lead. Neither the woman nor the young man who quite

possibly saved her life saw the attacker. They can't tell us a thing."

So no one was hurt, a harmless encounter with someone who was probably a neighborhood mugger. Not good, but certainly not deadly. No new murders this past weekend, a chance for her to think on it awhile longer. Make sure she hadn't jumped to any conclusions about her former lover and the deaths that had started almost immediately after their breakup. If it were Cecil, wouldn't he simply stalk her? She could wait—

"This woman was lucky," the Superintendent continued. He looked puffy and unhealthy in the throbbing lights. *"We are certain that the man who attacked her, then presumably fled when a witness showed up at the scene of the crime, was the Ravenswood Strangler. She is the only woman to survive so far, and the odds are high that the next victim—and until this killer is apprehended we must assume there will be more—isn't likely to have the same opportunity. Please, ladies, always drive or take a cab to your destination, or if you can't, at the very least travel with a companion. We don't want any more bodies."*

The bamboo seat was pinching the bare skin on the backs of her thighs below her shorts, like needles accompanying the snapshots Lillith was suddenly seeing in her mind. Four of them, every one fuzzy family shots, every one with long dark hair like hers, high cheekbones and thick, shapely eyebrows. If she called the Chicago police station right now, she would bet the white Mercedes 350SL in the circular drive out front that all the victims had had green or hazel eyes.

And what would she tell Isman when the questions were all over? How would she go upstairs and wake her blissfully snoring husband and the father of her son, look him in the face and say . . .

Forgive me, dear, but I've been sleeping with a murderer.

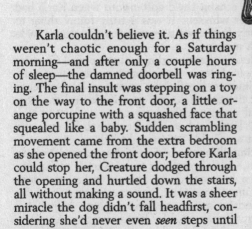

13

Karla couldn't believe it. As if things weren't chaotic enough for a Saturday morning—and after only a couple hours of sleep—the damned doorbell was ringing. The final insult was stepping on a toy on the way to the front door, a little orange porcupine with a squashed face that squealed like a baby. Sudden scrambling movement came from the extra bedroom as she opened the front door; before Karla could stop her, Creature dodged through the opening and hurtled down the stairs, all without making a sound. It was a sheer miracle the dog didn't fall headfirst, considering she'd never even *seen* steps until a year ago.

"Get back up here," Karla commanded, knowing it wouldn't do a bit of good. Well, she had to go down to see who was ringing the bell anyway; she'd sworn at least a dozen times since she'd moved in four years ago that she was going to get a cheap intercom system installed. So much for good intentions. "Heel!" But how could she be angry at the red-and-gold striped greyhound bouncing at the bottom of the stairs like some kind of wound-up stuffed animal? Tongue lolling, eyes rolling, tail lashing the walls as her toenails slipped on the small squares of ceramic tile: she was just too comical for words.

Coming down the stairs did give Karla a security glimpse through the door's three triangular windows of the man waiting outside. She made sure she got a tight grip on Creature's collar before she pulled open the door, and figured she might as well forget getting to work today at the time she'd planned. At least she was fully dressed.

"Detective Ewing," she greeted him. "Please come in."

He looked surprised that she remembered his name—how could she not? she wondered wryly—but he stopped in midstep at the sight of the lanky dog at Karla's side. Creature was grinning, a habit she'd gotten into when Karla had started tickling her whiskers. It was a truly funny thing to see, but apparently Ewing wasn't sure what Creature's wide showing of teeth meant.

"She's harmless," Karla assured him as she pulled Creature aside to make room. "Doesn't bark, growl or bite. Trust me."

"Said the spider to the fly," he muttered. Nevertheless he stepped over the threshold and past Karla and the dog, giving the animal a wary sidelong glance.

"Go on up," Karla said as she checked to be sure the door lock caught and held. "We're right behind you."

"Great." Ewing climbed obediently but paused outside the open door to Karla's apartment to let Karla and the dog go in first. When he entered, he politely pulled the door closed behind him. "Nice place," he commented, and his tone of voice said he meant it. Karla couldn't help being pleased; not many people cared for her decorating. A unique blend of African masks and knickknacks accompanied furniture upholstered in mixed black-and-white geometric patterns. Nearly floor-to-ceiling black-and-white sheer curtains bracketed the windows. It was a rather startling effect, and most of the time her guests seemed to have difficulty relaxing under the fierce tribal faces hung on the walls. The detective, however, appeared right at home.

Karla waited patiently as he gazed around the living

room for a few moments, but when he didn't say anything else, she let go of Creature's collar and headed for the kitchen. "Coffee?" she called over her shoulder. The dog was already making a beeline for the big, blond-headed cop, who was still staring up at one of the higher masks. Well, if he wanted to stay in the front room, he was on his own.

"Okay," she heard him answer. Three more seconds, then *"Oh!"*

Karla thought about letting him fend for himself against Creature's affections, then decided to take pity on him. Her mug in one hand, Karla stuck her head into the hallway so she could see, then laughed out loud. Creature was leaning against Ewing, almost knocking him over in an attempt to coax him into petting her. She had succeeded in wedging the poor guy between her body and the couch and it looked like Ewing was maintaining his balance out of grim force of will. He seemed utterly perplexed. "Creature! Stop that!" she admonished. "Go in the other room—now!" Finally, her dog obeyed the "I mean business" inflection in Karla's voice and scrambled away, but not before giving Ewing a final, companionable push from her long head.

Ewing steadied his footing and raised his eyebrows. "Interesting pet."

Karla laughed again. "She's always entertaining." She tilted her chin toward the other end of the apartment. "Follow me. Coffee's in the kitchen." This time he didn't need another invitation. "Cream and sugar?" she asked as he emerged from the hallway. She chose the biggest mug from the cabinet and set it on the counter.

"Black's fine."

She poured for them both, then set the two cups on the table, and pulled out a chair, motioning for him to take the one across from her. "Please, make yourself comfortable."

"Thanks."

She took a sip of the strong brew and waited while he tasted his and gave a smile of approval. "Good stuff." A small noise made them both glance back toward the living room, where Creature cautiously peeked around the doorjamb. Karla looked at the dog severely and snapped her fingers; Creature promptly lowered her body to the floor and put her head on her paws. "Entertaining—and well behaved, too. Was she trained when you got her?"

"No. As a matter of fact, she wasn't trained for the real world at all. She was a racer at the dog track, and I got her from an organization called REGAP, which means Retired Greyhounds As Pets. Most people don't realize that trainers consider racing greyhounds to have reached their peak at three or four years old, and a lot of them never see that ripe old age. After that, they're usually destroyed or used as lab animals. Unless they're adopted." She glanced in Creature's direction and the dog's tail thumped against the floor twice. "Although they do need a fair amount of exercise, they're gentle with kids, have sweet dispositions—they make great pets. And they're colorful." She met his eyes and the blush across her cheeks suddenly deepened. "But you didn't come her to listen to a lecture about animal rights, did you?"

The detective set down his cup, the attentive expression on his face going suddenly serious. "No, I didn't, Ms. Bryant."

"Karla, please."

"Of course not . . . Karla. I—" He hesitated. "You seem to be good friends with the Pelagis. To be honest, I thought I would stop here first to see if there's anything you thought I should know before I talked to Evelyn again this morning. Anything that might be helpful." His fingers tapped lightly against the side of his mug. "I wondered in particular if she'd told you that she scratched the man who attacked her."

Karla's mouth dropped open momentarily. "No. I had no idea."

Ewing nodded. "She dropped that bomb on me last night, after—of course—I'd agreed not to ask her any more questions until today. She'd even taken fingernail scrapings and left them for me at the hospital, though again, she didn't tell me that until right before she went into her apartment. I thought maybe the three of you had talked more after I left."

Karla shook her head. "Not at all. I would have if Evelyn had wanted to, of course, but they basically said good-night and went inside. I was a bit surprised, but . . ." She shrugged. "I can't tell you anything you didn't already learn last night."

Ewing drained his mug, then stood and took it over to the sink. Above the double bowl was a small window covered by open white mini-blinds. Not much of a view from the second floor; the kitchen window downstairs probably offered a dismal look at the bricks on the side of the building next door. "Then I guess I'll go on down," he said.

"No way." Karla turned her wrist so that the face of her watch showed the time. "Unless Warren stayed home—and if I know Evelyn, she wouldn't have let him since he had a huge presentation this morning—he's been gone for at least an hour. If you remember, Evelyn works third shift in the ER. That means she's used to sleeping in until four or five o'clock. If last night had been normal, she'd be in bed for less than an hour."

Ewing couldn't help but scowl. "I was under the distinct impression I could talk to her this morning."

"No way," Karla said again. "She's sound asleep. How many witnesses actually have something worthwhile to say when you wake them up in the middle of the night, anyway?"

"You'd be surprised," he retorted. "For me, this *is* the middle of the night."

Her eyebrows raised. "They always say the job makes the man."

"Only if you let it." For a second Ewing looked unaccountably awkward, then he tapped his fingers against the countertop absently. "I hate stereotypes. The more I see in my line of work, the more I'm convinced they're a handy act people hide behind so you can't find the real thing."

Karla smiled. "An interesting opinion, coming from a cop."

Ewing crossed his arms and gazed at her solidly. "Cops are always opinionated, about everything. I'll tell you more if you let me treat you to breakfast."

It was an unexpected offer and she couldn't help grinning. "Very tempting, Detective—"

"Jude."

"Jude, then. Especially since I'm an atrocious cook. But I already ate and I do have to get to work."

"What do you do?"

It must have been his line of work that made him able to ask without seeming to pry, and Karla didn't mind answering. "I'm an account executive at an advertising firm. Leo Burnett." He said nothing, his gaze never leaving hers. She slapped herself mentally for giving in, but she explained anyway. "My team and I are gearing up for a major pitch on Tuesday." Karla brought her mug over and reached around Ewing to get it into the sink. She could smell the faint odor of aftershave on his jacket and, oddly, cigarettes. "Do you smoke?" she asked, startled. "I could have gotten you an ashtray."

He shook his head. "My partner does. My clothes pick it up in the car, unfortunately. Hey, we're straying from the subject here. If not breakfast, then dinner. Watch me really blow my sleep schedule to hell."

"Can't do it," Karla said as she stuck her hands into the back pockets of her jeans. "It's nice of you to offer, but I'm going to be tied up until this pitch is over."

"Wednesday night, then. I'm off and you'll be through with your project by then. You pick the place."

"My, you are persistent."

"You'll be hungry by then," he pointed out.

"Ravenous," she agreed.

"Six o'clock?"

"Too early. Eight."

He smiled then, and for the first time Karla realized how outright handsome the oversized guy was. Not tall, but still husky, dark blond hair, light blue eyes; Jesus, he was positively Aryan. "I'll be here. On time."

Karla ran her tongue around the inside of her cheek. Handsome—and smug, too. There were lots of things that could take a person's sense of superiority down a peg or two, one of which was right here at home. "Speaking of being on time," she said casually, "you have made me late." He looked instantly contrite and Karla fought the telltale smile that wanted to play over her mouth as she opened a drawer to his right and pulled out Creature's fifteen-foot leash. The dog was at their side in an instant. "Would you mind taking Creature for a walk? Spare key's on the top shelf of the bookcase by the lamp in the living room." Karla snatched her patchwork denim jacket and purse from the back of one of the chairs as she hightailed it out the back door before he could protest. She could have let it go at that—after all, Ewing was in for a real romp with Creature—but she couldn't resist the final warning.

"Hang on, Detective. Creature likes to *run*!"

14

When Ewing again pulled up in front of the two-flat on Barry Street, he felt his teeth grind in frustration at the sight of the darkened windows. He didn't expect Karla to get home for perhaps another hour and wouldn't have bothered her if she had been there; after all, the woman needed to sleep sometime. It was past nine o'clock now and she'd left for work nearly twelve hours earlier. What about Creature? he wondered. Shouldn't she be walked again? His fingers went to his pocket absently, and he touched the key there. Belatedly he realized he should have put it back on her bookcase and pulled the door shut so it locked behind him. Putting it in his pocket had been unintentional but would still seem questionable. In the meantime . . . should he or should he not walk the dog for her? Maybe she wouldn't appreciate his prowling around the place in her absence, despite that excuse. She certainly hadn't asked him to do it, though he grinned at the memory of this morning. Karla hadn't asked him then, either. She'd *insisted*.

Lady Luck, however, was apparently noticing him tonight, sparing him further deliberation on an idea that was an invasion of Karla's privacy and bound to land him in hot water anyway. As Ewing watched, a light came on in one of the front-room windows downstairs, glowing a soft blue behind the cotton-print drapes. The Pelagis were home, finally, and they must have parked their car in one of the spaces in the back. Before Ewing could slide out of the car, the door on the first floor opened and Evelyn Pelagi stepped outside. Expressionless, she pulled the door closed behind her and walked over to the entrance for the second floor, pulling a key from the pocket of her slacks. When she went in and hit the switch, light shone through the triangular windows and the door frame. She didn't bother to pull the door completely shut—something uncharacteristic for a recent violent crime victim—and the detective got a glimpse of her through the mini-windows as she climbed the stairs. Of course, Ewing thought, Karla would have made some sort of arrangement with her downstairs neighbors to make sure Creature was taken out if her mistress was stuck at the office. Confirming his theory, a light, bright and not at all like the soft glow Ewing remembered from Friday night, snapped on behind the black-and-white curtains lining the second-story windows. Immediately a frenzy of sharp barks split the hot, quiet air hanging along the street.

The seconds ticked by and the barking continued. At the count of five, Ewing began to frown. At the quarter-minute mark he was on his way up the stairwell. He found Evelyn Pelagi standing in Karla's well-lit kitchen, Creature's leash in hand and a blank expression on her face. The dog was cowering by the door, growling and snapping and trying to jam her whip-thin body into the small space between the white-tiled table and the wall. Her gold-and-red-striped fur was standing high along her neck and back, and the show of teeth in her elongated muzzle was anything but friendly. Evelyn, however, didn't seem at all afraid, just . . . *bland*, as if the startling change in the personality of the once amiable dog were nothing more than another annoying snag in her daily routine.

The dog kept barking. And snarling.

Evelyn just kept staring.

Ewing could stand it no longer. "Creature!" The animal's head jerked in his direction, then she was out from behind the table in a flash, her supple body twisting nearly sideways as she propelled herself toward him. He braced for the impact, but it never came; instead, Creature skidded to a halt, then twined between his legs and hid, going unexpectedly silent as she pressed against the backs of his calves. He felt the dog shudder and a piece fell into place in Ewing's mind. He blinked as he faced Evelyn. Creature hadn't turned mean, not at all.

She was terrified of Evelyn Pelagi.

"What's going on?" he asked mildly.

Evelyn gazed at him, her mouth strangely slack. She waited long enough for Ewing to think she wasn't going to answer, then gave herself a visible shake. There was something about her that wasn't right, though, something he couldn't quite catch. Her eyes maybe. Hazel-colored, light, but . . . *off*, somehow *wrong* as her sight tilted toward the dog, then came back up to Ewing.

"I don't know," she answered finally. Evelyn raised the hand clutching the leash for emphasis. "I came up to walk her. Maybe she's having a bad day."

Karla had never asked—hell, she hadn't known him long enough to find out—but Ewing wasn't particularly fond of animals. Dogs, especially: he had the usual list of things that seem to bother people who didn't own pets, such as the dirt and the mess. He had also clashed with the canine variety of life twice, once as a child and once as a cop. The situation on the work shift had been short and brutal, and he had felt no remorse for shooting the pit bull that a drunken assailant had turned on him. The run-in with a German shepherd when he'd been a young boy had left a more lasting imprint. Ewing clearly remembered the paralyzing fear he'd felt as the loose and vicious full-grown male dog had snapped and snarled at his ankles in front of the house where its careless owner had left a gate open. He sensed that same hot emotion here, in Karla's bright and cheerful kitchen. Except his intuition told him it wasn't Evelyn who was afraid.

Now Ewing held out his hand. "How about if I walk her?"

Evenly looked at him, then at the leash in her closed fist. When she offered it, her arm seemed to float upward, as if it were hollow and weighed next to nothing. Her knuckles were pale, bloodless. "All right."

Ewing took the strip of leather and bent, snapping it onto the hook dangling from the red collar encircling Creature's neck. Karla's pet gave him a scared little lick on the side of his wrist. "You'll be home when we get back, say in about fifteen or twenty minutes?" he asked casually. "I've been trying to catch you all day. There's still paperwork and a report to finish, you know." She nodded but didn't move; after an awkward fifteen seconds of staring at each other, Ewing led the cowering dog to the front of the apartment and down the stairs, wondering at the relief both he and the dog seemed to feel once they were out of Evelyn Pelagi's presence.

Ewing seldom had trouble questioning victims anymore. It never got easy, but he had learned to distance himself out of necessity. Sure, there was the occasional mind-blown suspect who had to be talked to carefully for a whole host of reasons, or the hinky witness who wanted to play blind man, but a victim wasn't the same as a witness or a suspect. While it was true that sometimes a victim wouldn't talk, most of the time that was out of fear—they knew the attacker and were betting on big-time retaliation. With Evelyn Pelagi, Ewing felt like a green detective again, back when he'd been yanked out of uniform and thrust into an unmarked car almost overnight, all on the basis of an absurdly high test score. But there were lots of things you couldn't learn from a book. It'd be great if he could look up the answers in the index of the *Police Operations* chapters of the Chicago Municipal Code.

"Let's got over this again, Mrs. Pelagi." She nodded. There was no protest, only that dull patience, never-ending cooperation. She reminded him, in fact, of the teenage boy who'd supposedly resuscitated her, Jason Spiro. Both of them seemed to exude a sort of *emptiness*. "You left the house to walk to work alone and decided it had been a poor decision. You left your husband this note." Here, Ewing held up the small piece of note paper that he'd transferred to his current jacket.

"Yes. I was attacked by a man on my way to the hospital."

She said the words with all the emotional enthusiasm of *Your shoe is untied.* No wonder he'd lost the feeling that he could call her by her first name. "All right, you were attacked. You scratched the man who attacked you, presumably across the face. But you didn't see him."

"No. I didn't see him. It was too dark."

"Did he bleed when you scratched him, Mrs. Pelagi? Did his blood get on your uniform?"

For a second Evelyn seemed nonplussed. "I—I don't know if he did or not. There . . . was no blood on me or my uniform, but it was ripped, so I threw it out."

Ewing sat up. "You what? *Threw* it out? I know I told you not to do that!"

Evelyn dropped her gaze to her hands and wouldn't look back up. "I'm sorry. I suppose I forgot."

"Is it in the garbage cans out back?" he demanded. "Or did you take it somewhere else?"

She was still looking at her hands, more closely. "What? Oh—the uniform. Well, I guess it is. It should be; Streets and Sanitation doesn't pick up until Wednesday."

He was so angry he wanted to reach over and shake her. What kind of shape would her clothing be in tonight, after nearly a full day in the cans? *If* it was still there. Christ—and now he was going to have to pick through whatever crap was thrown on top of it. Ewing started to say something, then followed her line of vision to her hands and the words stuttered away unvoiced. What was wrong with the tips of her fingers? Before he could put a name to it, Evelyn saw the direction of his gaze; her fingers folded in on themselves like closing petals and she dropped her hands to her lap. For a second, he was again reminded of Jason Spiro.

Ewing cleared his throat. "You said you were at a . . . what? A meeting or something tonight?"

"Yes, a Review Board meeting. They said I can go back to work on Tuesday night."

"What about Dr. Thieu? What did she have to say?"

"She was there. If she hadn't attended, I could have

probably started tomorrow." Despite the topic, there was *still* no charge in Evelyn's voice, no resentment, no anger, nothing.

"I see." Ewing stood. He was finished here anyway; she had nothing more to say to him, and after all, the trash cans beckoned. "Why did they insist on waiting that long?"

"Because of the bruises, of course."

That made him pause. "Bruises? I thought you said you had no visible injuries." He peered at her, but he'd been right about the light in the first-floor apartment's kitchen being pretty dim and she'd made no move to flick on the lights.

She turned toward him. "There are a few showing up now, which is to be expected." She touched the line of one cheekbone and jaw. "Here, especially, and a few other places if the lighting's right."

There *was* the faintest trace of yellowish blue, but not much. Still, if it showed up already, tomorrow Evelyn might really be a rainbow. He decided not to comment on it, although for the third time he had a disturbing memory of the Spiro boy. Evelyn Pelagi and Jason Spiro seemed to be running on parallel tracks in his mind. "Do you have any paper towels?" he asked instead. "I've got to go look for that uniform."

"Certainly." She stood jerkily, like a marionette being hauled upright on bad strings. From the cabinet next to the stove, she pulled out a fresh roll. "Help yourself." Then she wasted no more time as she indicated the back door. "Call me if you need anything else."

"Yes, ma'am. I will." He stepped out and the door closed before he could turn and offer a final farewell. Warren Pelagi, Ewing had learned, was still not home, working diligently in an office somewhere putting the final touches on Saturday's postponed insurance proposal, getting it ready for Monday. "At least he doesn't have to go through the garbage in the dark," Ewing muttered. Why didn't people listen?

The smell as he pulled the top off of the first can was enough to make a normal person lose both lunch and dinner, but Ewing had bagged enough corpses—the ones in the dead of summer were the worst—to close off his nostrils instinctively. Fifteen minutes of grubbing around inside the filthy trio of cans gave him nothing: whether or not the uniform had been covered with blood, some street person had decided it was a worthwhile find. Still, Ewing kept at it, and he'd just used a wadded paper towel to sweep aside the last of the garbage in the final can when he heard a noise behind him. He couldn't help but groan at the familiar female voice.

"Out for a night on the town, Detective?" Her tone was half-amused, half-sarcastic.

Screw it, he thought. Might as well jump in with both feet. He turned to look at Karla as she held a grinning and obviously docile Creature at her side; the two looked very svelte standing there: the dog, lean and long, and Karla, her denim outfit still crisp after the long day. "Just looking for something to eat," he remarked, keeping his face utterly straight.

"Really? I certainly hope we do better Wednesday night."

Ewing winced. "Touché."

She chuckled, all trace of the smart-ass disappearing. "Evelyn told me I'd find you out here, and that you also walked Creature. Thanks." The small smile disappeared. "She said there was a problem with the dog?"

"Nothing major," Ewing said smoothly, glad he'd remembered to replace her house key this time. He reached out a hand and the dog practically fell against it in her eagerness to be petted. "Just an attack of nerves."

"Nerves?" Karla looked at him, disbelieving. "This silly animal hasn't been nervous since I picked her up from REGAP. She knew she had it made the minute I spotted her."

"We all have our moments." They stared at each other, mute.

"Yes," Karla finally said in a soft voice. "I guess we do."

She turned her head and stared wordlessly at the darkened windows of her friend's first-floor apartment.

15

Sunbeams leaked through the fabric between the tiny white-and-cornflower-blue daisies printed on the draperies, striping the floor and creating a false fluid in which dust motes turned slowly. The hot light cut through unaccountably cold shadows and bathed the small living room on the ground floor with moody, uncomfortable light.

On the carpet, facedown: Evelyn Pelagi.

Not really breathing, more like an occasional sigh: cold skin, lips blue and eyes open, staring sightless at something she couldn't see in the real world—

Blackness:

The vague knowledge of death and its taste in her mouth and mind in all its fleeting forms but gauzy, like viewing life through a veil of hospital bandages wrapped loosely around her eyes. There was a rush in her ears, a dark, screaming wind pounding its way inside her head and swirling, spinning

*until it exploded into a feeling like being squeezed out into
something—rebirth, and she wondered disjointedly if this was
what a baby felt when it came spilling from between its mother's
legs. On the heels of that, a queer sense of triumph borne
on the feeling of having been born—born and healed at the
same time, and of instant hunger unrecognized.*

*Someone was bending over her, touching her, not the same
person as earlier but it didn't matter. Breath in her lungs, a force
fit, air pumped in, feeding that dull, dead rush in her ears, her
body a resistant balloon, in and out, in and out, and she wished
from far away that she could simply stop this intrusion of oxygen into the cold of her body cavities. In and out again, a heav-
iness in her chest as if she had an infection in her lungs, thick
congestion hanging on every sucked-out inhalation, a wheeze
riding every exhalation, heard only by her.*

*She felt the inside of her mouth move as it opened according
to the will of her savior, numb but still so pliable, accepting. A
deep tickle in her belly, and confusion. A singing in her depths,
a chorus of need, and her cracked thoughts managed to coalesce
into enough form to ask herself silently* Why Am I Still Alive?
*The tickle turned into a sweet, hot fluttering, the fluttering into
a desperate cry of need, and the cry into—*

She woke screaming, her dry mouth against the carpet
in the brittle light of late afternoon. But in the empty apartment, the empty *building*, who was there to hear?

Two eggs over hard—she couldn't stand runny yolks—and a
couple of maple-flavored Brown 'N Serve sausages, wheat
toast with tart passion-fruit jam. A great late-morning breakfast and Evelyn couldn't swallow the first forkful in her
mouth.

Physically couldn't do it.

She finally had to spit it out.

She left the plate, now dotted with the mashed remains
of her attempt to eat, sitting on the table. There was no
compulsion to *do* anything anymore, not eat, or drink—
when was the last time she'd taken in liquid? She found herself staring blankly at a closet as she tried but couldn't
remember the last time she'd urinated. Did it matter? She
couldn't answer that either, only wander aimlessly from
room to room, her mind an empty hole.

At least she was alone now, away from Warren and Karla and that police detective whose name she periodically forgot, all those people who kept asking her questions she didn't want to answer. In reality, she *couldn't* answer a lot of those queries, but that didn't explain her reluctance to talk to them, especially . . . there: Detective *Ewing*. Of course she remembered his instructions not to get rid of her mangled uniform—common sense would tell anyone that. How could she explain what it was like to see the fabric, so soaked in the splashes of blood that no one else could see? It had something to do with that teenager—they'd said his name was Jason—who had brought her back to life, she was sure of it. She knew the cops, even the ones who'd been there when she'd regained consciousness and seen it with their own eyes, didn't believe that was what had happened. She knew better, felt deep inside her brain that it was so.

None of which, of course, made any sense, even to her.

She was better now, alone, and she didn't need to explain anything to anyone. Thoughts of her resuscitation, her *resurrection*, brought others to the forefront, a sweet, primal need, so much like the elusive rush of birth three days ago when she'd returned from the dead—a *deadrush*. The sensation a shadow, like the hot, liquid feeling of new lust buried in the stomach before its richness fades with time and familiarity. This new thing not fading but growing, ravenous and huge, pounding against the walls of her insides and howling to be free. Blotting out so much of her life, her routine, thoughts, logic. All those fragile things that fled from its grasping fingers, left it unsatisfied with the rape of herself and dismissed the need to eat or drink or do those things that pertained to her everyday existence. And still, this overwhelming feeling, this *addiction*, sliding so smoothly to the back in the presence of others, steeped in the primeval instinct of self-preservation, but whose? Hers? Or that of the addiction itself, the . . . *deadrush's*? Content but not sated: willing, for now, to retreat and wait.

But for how long?

Evelyn blinked again, and the closet was gone, overtaken by the bathroom mirror, the light above it sour and fluorescent and something Warren had always intended to replace. Harsh, high-intensity brightness, spilling onto her pasty skin and showing its injuries in all their lurid glory. She had seen her reflection in a mirror at the hospital the night the police had brought her in, after her healing, seen how her skin was unblemished and clean, utterly free of pain and blood. Now, thirty-six hours later, Evelyn was finally beginning to see herself as had the boy and the two policemen, and presumably her killer. Not clearly, though. To her eyes, the likeness of herself had a fuzzy overlay, like a layer of watery tracing paper on the surface of which floated the ghostly truth, spreading like a monstrous bruise caused by the puncture in a vein after the poor insertion of a needle. Taking a course of days as it spread its visual poison across her pale, cracking flesh.

I see me, Evelyn thought. *I see—*

Skin, beaten and purple blue beneath a wash of red blood . . . how can it still look wet after three days? The right cheekbone was a pulped mass of crushed bones, the eye closed yet still impossibly clear-visioned.

Her gaze dropped away from the mirror to linger on her fingertips, comparing them to the sight of a child in a coffin so many years ago, a coworker's infant stolen in sleep by SIDS. What Evelyn remembered most was the baby girl's tiny fingers and tinier fingertips: dead only two days and already dried to flat little boards at the end as if they'd been pressed between the pages of a telephone book like an old and cherished rose. Hers were the same, her toes too, perhaps as lifeless as those of that long-lost baby, yet her body refused to acknowledge it. Suddenly Evelyn was furious with her own stupidity—

You stupid, stupid woman, you're dead, aren't you, damn you!

—and she beat her fingers against the wall, searching for sensations that were no longer felt. Whirling rage—

Don't you have the fucking sense to lie down, die and be done with it!

—nearly out of control, and she snatched up a razor, one of those ridiculous perky-pink Lady Schick things, found it nearly useless when she forced it against the emery-board roughness of the skin at the end of her fingers. She pushed harder, not caring if she cut the fucking ends *off;* finally she bled, a thin, dirty-looking red fluid that looked as if it were days past usefulness but couldn't escape the circular prisons inside her skin.

Still, complete and total numbness.

She threw the razor aside, ignoring the smear of her body's pitiful fluid it left inside the basin. That was wrong, she realized. She wasn't *quite* numb, and growing less so by the hour. There were tinges of pain, trickles along the over-lay of damage on her face and throat. And of course there was the *need*, that pulling toward something unknown, dark and foul, searching for that same teeth-vibrating feeling of orgasmic flight that she'd felt when she'd come back to her-self Friday night. Inexplicably she thought of the young man again, and sharp, hellish instinct kicked in, bringing her flash images of him and her. His mouth on hers and a pulling, yet nothing at all to do with sex, a foul, taunting promise that fulfillment was only a dead kiss away.

She gasped and tripped, her thoughts sending her reel-ing in the bathroom, bouncing from wall to wall like one of those cheap superballs the kids got from the quarter gumball machines. Full pain, at last, but not from the slash on her finger, oh no: that would be much too simple, too predict-able. Poker hot and startling across the planes of her face—

Jesus!

—speeding down the newly convoluted lines of her jawbone to blast into the tendons and hollow of her throat, twisting and tightening until it cut off her breath. Evelyn couldn't help it, she clawed at her throat, digging her fingers in and trying to create a new opening through which to breathe, deep suffocation a thousand times worse than drowning by reason of its damned impossibility—

Gone, just as quickly.

Leaving Evelyn to shudder on the floor in the cold space between the toilet and bathtub. She would have cried—

But she couldn't remember how.

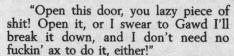

16

"Open this door, you lazy piece of shit! Open it, or I swear to Gawd I'll break it down, and I don't need no fuckin' ax to do it, either!"

More pounding; if the place had been built like one of the newer and cheaper townhouses the contractors were putting up all over the neighborhood, the door would have probably splintered and given way by now.

"I know you're in there, Izquierdo." Outside the door, Butch Neilson's voice dropped, and if his screaming was an annoyance to Hernando before, the newly ominous tone guaranteed the door was going to stay firmly shut. "You and that whore you live with are four months behind on the rent. I know you got more people in there. You pay up, fuckface, or I'm going to put you all out on your asses."

Damn it, Hernando thought, how much was a guy supposed to take? His fists bunched uselessly against the inside of the door. He could picture Neilson in the hallway, his spiky blond hair flat-topped at an inch, two prissy gold loops dangling from his left earlobe. Hernando leaned against the wood, feeling the coolness of the old oak through his T-shirt, wishing he could reach through the grain and strangle the jerk. He was so *sick* of this—

To hammer the feeling home, Neilson started slamming his fist against the door panels again. "I'm coming in there, boy. I swear to Gawd—"

"Get an eviction notice!" Hernando screaming suddenly. "You come in here without one and I'll cut you in pieces. Just try it!"

"I don't *need* no fuckin' eviction notice!"

Neilson was howling now, sounding like an enraged wolfman. The Russian family downstairs might be having a good time listening, but screw 'em; one peep and Hernando would pick up the phone and call Immigration and they knew it, just as both he and Neilson knew they didn't dare complain. Which brought him back to the stalemate with Neilson: the day Neilson put Hernando and his friends out, Hernando would make the phone call and Neilson would lose his first-floor tenants, too. Still, four months was a lot; if he pushed it too far, his landlord might decide an empty building available for rent to all new tenants was more profitable. Hernando couldn't let that happen; his girlfriend Carissa was seven months' pregnant, and his best friend Tho, and Hernando's younger brother and teenage wife, lived there, too.

"I'll get you some money, okay?" Hernando shouted. "By the end of the week."

"You get it to me tonight or I'll take a pry bar to this fucking door and put all your crap outside on the sidewalk. I'll teach you to change the damned lock!" Neilson's voice had dropped once more, this time to a growl. That wolfman impression hit Hernando again, squashing the reckless impulse to tell his burly landlord to stuff it up his ass. "I ain't afraid of you, kid. You come at me with a knife and I'll cut my name in your forehead. You just try me." The man beat on the door a couple more times for emphasis, then stomped away, footsteps so hard that Hernando could feel their vibration through the second level's floorboards. He leaned against the wall in relief, sweat trickling down the side of his face and neck, soaking into the shoulder of his sleeveless T-shirt. *I oughta go to the window and spit on his damned head when he comes out the front,* he thought bitterly. But he wouldn't, because he and Carissa and the others needed this apartment and besides, Neilson was an ex-marine and a weight lifter and would probably beat him bloody for the rent, much less a little added saliva.

"Fine," Hernando muttered instead. "You want money, you prick, you'll get it." He went to the bedroom he and Carissa shared and dug his way into the tiny, junk-filled closet, stepping over old shoeboxes that should have been thrown out, dirty clothes forgotten on the floor for months, worn-out shoes and God knew what else. Fumbling deep within the back corner on the floor rather than the overhead shelf, he pulled out a wooden box, splintered and stained with mold from years of the same kind of hiding places. When he opened it, however, the Rossi .38 Special inside was fairly new. Its grip was still smooth, and it shone with careful cleaning. Hernando picked it up reverently, letting the light from the dirty windows play along its chrome barrel. It was a new piece for him, but the dude he'd purchased it from three weeks ago had already used it and Hernando had no doubt it'd been stolen to begin with. The serial number had been obliterated, and the seller, showing a gleam in his eye that had made Hernando nervous, had strongly suggested that Hernando try to disguise the rifling in the barrel by scraping it out with a rounded steel file. Hernando wasn't sure doing that would change anything, but he'd come up with a piece of iron rod small enough to fit into the gun barrel and done it anyway, just in case.

The Rossi felt good and heavy in his palm, a solid solution to this mess with Neilson. With some careful timing later tonight, he could pick up more than enough cash to appease the building's owner and get some food in the place as well. If he was lucky, there might be a little left over to score some coke if he felt like it, though if he did, he'd have to hide the blow or Carissa would suck it all up in a day or so. Damn, but the woman was a greedy thing, and Hernando grimaced when he thought of a future that promised him

Carissa and a kid—who'd probably grow up just like her—
and more of the same way his life was going.

Right down the shithole.

He purposely thrust the thought away and instead
found a rag to wipe down the .38, get his sweaty fingerprints
off it and anyone else's, too, to be positive. He found one last
beer in the refrigerator, lukewarm but better than nothing,
the glass lip of the bottle stinking of the wet vegetables that
rotted somewhere in the crisper no one had bothered to
open for weeks. No big deal: he could hold his nose and still
drink. Setting the gun aside, he sat down and gave some serious thought to the options available around the neighborhood. A liquor store would carry more cash than a grocery
or video store, especially near closing time; banks were big
time and he didn't want some trigger-happy security guard
waving a company-issued gun at him, whether or not the
fool fired it. A lot of the places had signs that warned of
money drops into safes, but he didn't believe that for a minute, and neither did any of his friends—though he'd pull this
one alone anyway. Daylight was starting to fade from the
street outside, but there were still a couple good hours left,
plenty of time to take a long cool shower and bring down
the body temperature—the only way possible in this top-
floor sauna of an apartment. He didn't know where Carissa
was and didn't particularly care; if she walked in now, she'd
likely demand money, like that damned Neilson.

Not to worry. He'd satisfy them both tonight.

Special Choice Liquors had been robbed three times in three
months, and when the lean and dark-headed young man
came into the store precisely five minutes before he
would've closed up, Felix Kramer knew it was going to happen again. It wasn't a premonition or a sixth sense or some
silly religious notion of his wife's that God was looking out
for him; it was more like radar picking up a missile, then telling you it was there not with a stupid *bleep* but with a sudden nasty jolt of electricity. He wished to God he knew what
it was about his place that drew the criminals. True, he had
a good, busy location, but you'd think they'd look for out-of-
the-way joints, not a store fronting on bustling Halsted

Street with the intersection of Diversey a quarter block away.

Still, there he was, the next would-be robber: tall and slender, with thick dark hair that wasn't all that long but spiked out with hair gel anyway. A nice-looking boy, as his wife would have said, with a chiseled Latino face and deep-set, bottomless black eyes. Of course, it was in those same black eyes that Kramer could see a glint of red that was aimed straight at him and his cash register. In addition, nothing made his visitor's intentions more clear than the fact that the boy was wearing a leather jacket, for crying out loud, in sticky ninety-degree heat. Kramer's palms dampened when his so-called customer scoped out the aisles for other customers then craned his face toward the ceiling, checking to see if the store had a security system. Kramer had thought about it and decided against it. ADE, the least expensive security outfit around, still wanted nearly a thousand dollars for the buy-only equipment plus a start-up fee and monthly service charge. Monitoring, they called it. Kramer called it another form of robbery. He elected to spend his security budget on something other than a plastic case and lens that would simply watch as someone stole his next mortgage payment, maybe take pictures as he was blown away by some young punk. Big help there; he'd never been shot, but he had a friend who had, and the guy had told him the wound felt like it was on fire, all the time, and hardly any kind of drug succeeded in stopping the pain. How many times could Special Choice be hit before it happened? The odds weren't good, and perhaps each time gave his store more of an easy-target reputation in the 'hood.

Kramer moved quietly behind the counter and slid the lock in place on the half door behind him, knowing a good kick would bring the whole thing down anyway. Two aisles over, the dark-haired youth bent and inspected something on the bottom shelf, and Kramer watched him in the curve of the theft mirror at the far back of the store, the only one in which the movements were visible. It was a long-range view from his position at the front, but the shopkeeper easily made out the silver flash as the guy pulled something from inside his jacket and thrust it into the outside pocket.

"On my mother," Kramer muttered. "You'd think these

boys would learn, but they never do." He'd been through this all too many times; he could do nothing until they pulled a weapon or tried to take the money. The police would hang him for calling in a "suspicion" that a robbery was about to occur—as well they should. He would be on the telephone to them eight or ten times a day if he dialed 911 every time someone unsavory came into the shop. After all, it *was* a liquor store—what did he expect? Society ladies? Well, he got a goodly number of those, too.

Now, at last, the man who was supposed to be a customer was moving up the aisle toward the front.

"Did you find what you were looking for?" Kramer called helpfully. He wondered if a criminal had second thoughts about firing on someone who'd been nice to him a moment before, then pressed his lips together in disgust. How ridiculous—the prisons and the streets, were filled with people who did just that and took pleasure in the acts. Still, he had to give this young man that chance; it was his nature to at least try. "Is there something I can find for you?"

"Yeah." His gaze darted from Kramer to the door of the shop, daring someone else to come in. "There is."

And it happened, so fast, like it always did. The robber's gun was out and aimed, waving loosely in a gloved hand, at the juncture of Kramer's jaw and throat. Kramer was looking down the moving barrel of a silver .38 and its owner's stance was far enough away to keep his victim from slapping it out of the way. The young man looked quite comfortable with the weapon in his hand, as if he'd done this before and knew the routine.

"The cash," the youth hissed. "Hand it over, old man. *Now!*"

"Sure, anything you say." Kramer tried to sound calm, but he knew his voice was wobbling: Robbery Number Four, as he thought of it, and the fear was still there. It was the unpredictability that did it, the inability to tell what someone would do, robber or victim. The victims were always scared shitless and the criminals were always nervous. The register, a fairly new model that always seemed quiet when the store was crowded, opened with a *clang* that made them both jump. The .38 twitched dangerously in the young man's hand and again Felix Kramer knew, as he had known when the youth came in, that it was going to go off. Maybe not right this second, but soon.

He dug into the register drawer and offered all the cash it held, maybe about a hundred and forty dollars. He knew it wouldn't be enough; hell, it didn't even *look* big to him, much less this money-hungry thief.

A stinging in his fingers and the youth snatched the money away. "Where's the rest? I know fucking well there's more!" Face flushed with anger, the youth swept the counter clear with his left arm, beef jerky, candy and a jar of garlic pickles all crashing to the floor. The sharp tang of garlic and dill instantly filled the air and the teenager glanced quickly down, then kicked his feet. With a sort of slow, abstract terror, Kramer thought that up close the 'teenager' actually looked more like he was in his early twenties. "Shit—got that crap on my shoes, man." The younger man's eyes flicked back toward the shopkeeper, still frozen behind the counter. "You deaf or what, mister? I said, get me the rest of the fucking money! Where is it?"

Kramer nodded downward. He could feel moisture trickling down the back of his neck and into the fine hair that grew along the ridges of his shoulder blades, and never mind the frigid air-conditioning. His hairline was receding at forty-eight—not so soon, compared to other men—and his chest and back hair was thickening by the day. His wife didn't mind the balding and liked the body hair, and he felt like he was going to die today. "Lockbox," he managed. "Under the counter."

"Bring it out," the guy said. "No, wait—I'll get it. You just back away—not so fast!" He hurried toward the half door at the counter's end.

Kramer had five seconds, six at the most before the robber came around the counter and put a hand into the recesses of the shelf beneath the NCI register. The lockbox was there, all right, but it was *behind* the "security system" Kramer had opted for instead of the all but useless video cameras: a Winchester twelve-gauge Defender pump shotgun. The small shotgun was fully loaded and had a double-ought buckshot shell in the chamber; one squeeze of the trigger and it would fire. He'd learned how to use it at a shooting range in the suburbs, but had never pointed it—or any other weapon, for that matter—at another human being. Still, the young man fumbling with the lock at the end of the counter meant to kill him after taking whatever money was in the lockbox, shotgun or not.

The shopkeeper pulled it out, brought it up and pointed the barrel, praying that his voice would work when he needed it. "Hold it," he rasped. "Stop right there. Drop the gun."

The youth froze, his face blank with shock. His .38 was held loosely in his right fist, which rested on the edge of the half door while he pulled at the latch with his other hand. His mouth dropped open, and if his face had turned red at the discovery of the thin till in the register, it went absolutely scarlet now. "Why you dirty cocksucker," he said wonderingly. "I'll be *damned*!" He brought his pistol up and fired without aiming.

Kramer was facing the robber, his back to the window that fronted on Halsted. For one, horrifying instant he was caught within the incredibly *huge* report of the .38 firing, the shattering of the glass behind him, and the sudden scream of a passerby. He thought, quite calmly, that he had died, and that his last, incredibly stupid thought would be that he should have stuck with the surveillance cameras, because at least then they would be able to identify his murderer.

Then the youth was cussing and finally throwing open the latch on the half door, bringing up the silver pistol for another crack at it. Kramer squeezed the trigger of the Defender without making the conscious decision to do it.

If he'd thought the noise the .38 Special had made was loud, he was completely unprepared for the booming of the Winchester. He distinctly remembered reading somewhere in the papers that came with the shotgun that the stock was padded for extra comfort; nevertheless, he was unbraced and the recoil whacked him a good one on the right side of his ribs, nearly knocking the breath out of him. The slug caught the young man on the right side of the chest and would have lifted him clear off his feet if he hadn't already come around the half door and entered the space behind the counter with Kramer. Instead of being thrown backward, the robber slammed against the edge of the counter where the left and right corners junctioned. He spun, a complete one-eighty turn, then flopped backward with his spine at an awful angle. Finally, he stayed there, never making a sound throughout the entire ordeal.

Kramer was paralyzed. Mouth dry, heart pounding—what do to now? He couldn't see any blood, yet his aim had obviously been successful. He let the barrel of his weapon drop slightly and stepped forward; when he did, his feet crunched on glass and he realized that pieces of the destroyed window were under his shoes. Had they cut him? He had no idea. Ten feet away, gun still dangling from one limp-fingered hand, the dark-haired young man groaned and suddenly pawed at his jacket with his empty fingers; they came away glistening and covered with red. The youth's eyes were closed, and he could be dying, right there in front of him. It didn't matter right now to Kramer that the guy had tried to kill him; the shopkeeper didn't want the guilt of having taken another man's life hanging over him in the years to come, and it certainly wasn't something he looked forward to having to mention in the confessional this Saturday. The thought of the sadness that would show in the eyes of the kindly old priest who ran his parish was finally what pushed him to action, and Kramer turned and reached for the handset of the telephone on the wall. Considering the circumstances, he thought his fingers were remarkably steady as they punched 911. But when he opened his mouth to relate his situation to the mechanical-sounding voice on the other end, he heard instead a *click* from behind, a sound louder than anything he'd heard so far that evening, easily surpassing the blast from his Winchester.

The sound of the .38 being cocked.

He spun and raised the Defender, pumping the next round into the chamber automatically, as if he'd been professionally trained to handle an occasion like this one. The young man was still working to raise the pistol toward him, the effort of cocking it almost too much and the only thing that saved Felix Kramer's life. Though he meant to kill the shopkeeper, the robber was clearly not familiar with his gun, or he'd have known that it wasn't necessary to cock the .38 to fire again, and that wasted movement gave Kramer the warning he needed. Self-preservation ruled: the would-be robber was still struggling to pull up the weight of the pistol when Kramer shot him in the chest again.

This time the youth's jacket flew open and the older man had a chance to see, at last, the damage the Winchester had done. Beneath the biker's leather, the boy's white T-shirt was a hideous crimson collage of light and dark holes, the worst of which spilled blood like a stepped-on tube of painter's color. The silver .38 went sailing over the counter to land somewhere within the small stock of potato chips Kramer kept on a rack up front, and outside, standing amid the ruins of the window, someone looked in—Kramer felt the person's movement rather than saw it—and screamed again. On his left the handset still dangled where he'd let it go and he could hear the dispatcher's voice, full of alarm and actually sounding human. The place smelled like gunpowder, a smell he'd always believed was only something they claimed on television in western movies and detective shows. It also had a *feel* to it, as if the humidity had climbed eighty percent and the air had gotten somehow salty.

He picked up the handset. "There's been a robbery, and there's been a shooting," he told the disembodied voice on the phone. "There's a man here who needs an ambulance very badly. To be honest, I can't tell if he's alive. The address is Special Choice Liquors on Halsted." Kramer hung up without bothering to give any more information. If the cops in the area didn't know the building number at his store by now, there was something seriously wrong with this precinct.

They did, obviously, because a blue-and-white police cruiser came screaming to a stop outside in less than two minutes, and the ambulance was there before the heavyset cop or his partner could think about deciding to administer CPR. Kramer surrendered the shotgun to one of the cops and went to find his FOID card and gun permit; his mind was numb, his heartbeat still chunky and painful underneath the bones of his chest. The shopkeeper couldn't look at the young man he'd shot without cringing, though the efforts of the two paramedics working on him made it obvious he was still alive. There was so much blood! He'd never thought about the quantity in the human body or had reason to think he would have it splattered across the countertops of Special Choice Liquors. It was even smeared on the floor under his feet, mixing with a thousand fragments of glass to make a sharp, soupy mess that was digging into the crevices on the bottoms of his athletic shoes.

The youth and the paramedics disappeared, but not the cops. Hours of questions, witnesses and cleanup, and he learned, finally, that he was okay with the law because a woman outside had heard the boy shoot first and had seen the window blown out, even had a few nicks from flying glass to prove it. The commotion had brought others with varying points of view, and it seemed he was pretty much in the clear. His weapon was legal and his gun permit was up-to-date, and on and on, until he thought all the questions and the answers and the speculation would never stop. But it did, at last, and he was left with an empty liquor store and a floor splashed in scarlet. The words of one of the uniformed cops rang in his brain, the judgment that it was all right to shoot that young man, whether or not he died, because as far as they were concerned it was clear that the robber had intended to kill him all along.

So it was time to go home, and tell more to his wife than the sketchy *I'm all right and I'll explain everything later* that he'd given her over the telephone hours ago.

And, at the next Saturday-morning confession, it would be just him and his priest and his God.

17

"I think you should see a doctor," Aunt Theora said unexpectedly. "You might have some sort of skin disease. Your mother might not have mentioned it, but skin cancer runs in our family."

Jason blinked, then scowled at her. "There's nothing wrong with me." The older woman said nothing, just stared at him, and he had to fight against the automatic urge to obey. He couldn't help but admire her for this sudden burst of courage. Normally she wouldn't meet his eyes.

"Yes, there is," she finally said. "You've had those sores on your neck and your face for two days, and I see you're getting another one on your arm. The swelling—"

"I am not blind," he said defensively. "I can see what's on my face when I look in the mirror. It's acne, that's all. If I think I need a doctor, I'll go to one."

"You're only fifteen," she said stubbornly. She'd gone from a semiparental authority figure to being unable to look him in the face. Now, apparently, she was trying to regain her position. He couldn't let that happen. "You don't make the rules here, young man," she continued. "I won't have your mother hold me responsible if you get sick."

"My mother is not here."

"But I am!"

"And you are *not* my mother." Jason stood abruptly, feeling the kitchen chair tip backward behind him. He could have grabbed it, but he didn't bother, preferring to see his aunt jump when it crashed to the floor. "If you don't mind, *Aunt* Theora, I'll go to bed now. I'm sure the quiet will do me good." He strode out of the kitchen and into the extra bedroom that he'd occupied since his arrival. Previously it'd been a junk room, but his aunt's life wasn't very cluttered and its meager contents had been easily crammed into her storage locker in the basement. Now the bedroom was a small, bare box, nothing on the walls, mismatched linens on the twin bed, an old and faded sheet hung on nails at each side of the tiny window. Aunt Theora had suggested he decorate it, but Jason had refused; she probably believed—ridiculously—that it had something to do with his religious convictions. She couldn't be more wrong—the truth was, the blandness of the room suited him perfectly. With the slamming of the door behind him, Jason's icy expression went slack; his anger at her was a ruse, designed solely to keep his aunt at bay and provide a little entertainment to break the monotony.

He stretched out on the bed and stared at the ceiling. He had believed that he was the only one who could see the original injuries, but as time went by that camouflage ability was deteriorating, as was his physical condition. People on the street were starting to give him puzzled glances as they passed, and he could hear them whispering among themselves, speculating on the injuries that seemed bent on reappearing in all their original, opulent glory. He was starting to get a bit frightened. See a doctor? Out of the question. What was he supposed to do? March into some med-school graduate's office and say *Hey, doc. I got these six oozing holes from a bunch of snakebites about three weeks ago and can you fix them? Oh, and by the way, they killed me when I got them, but I came back to life.*

Jason started to turn over and was rewarded by a blast of pain in his upper left chest, courtesy of the two black-and-purple puncture wounds there. Gasping, he rolled carefully back; with his head propped against the pillow and his face tilted, he could look down and see a faint stain spreading across the white of his T-shirt at the location of each bite. What was so incredibly weird was that no one—not Aunt Theora or anyone he'd seen in public—was able to see the nasty yellow smudges . . . yet. As he tried to pluck at the stain with his fingers, he wondered briefly if the woman he'd resurrected was going through the same thing. Picking at it gave him a nasty jolt from the area of the final snakebite that felt very much like someone had run a sewing machine needle across the width of his forearm. Immediately following that he got a stomach-roiling chain reaction of jitters that grew until they bordered on convulsions—fond memories of death by strychnine poisoning. The room grayed out and he welcomed sleep, again, deep and forgiving as only it had been since his death and resurrection. He reached for it.

Maybe he'd wake with some new answers.

18

When Warren knocked on her door at eleven-thirty at night, Karla expected to see Jude; after all, his day was just beginning and if he'd seen the lights shining from her living room windows . . . he seemed as unpredictable as she was sometimes. She was not, however, prepared for the way her downstairs neighbor and longtime friend looked: she supposed disheveled was the proper word, but never would she have attributed it to Warren. His hair stuck up in tufts, his clothes were wrinkled, his eyes were puffed. He couldn't seem to make up his mind about coming in, simply stood on the back porch and shuffled his feet until she finally tugged on his sleeve.

"May I get you something?" she asked when he settled himself on a chair. "Decaf tea, milk, or I can make a pot of coffee if you like."

"No coffee," Warren said hoarsely. "I'll be up all night." Suddenly he gave a short, raw laugh that made Creature left her head from her spot in the dining room and look their way. "Who am I kidding? I won't sleep anyway. Sure, let's have coffee."

"On second thought, let's not," Karla said firmly. "You look like you could use some good sleep, not a bunch of caffeine-riddled catnaps. We'll have warm milk, like my mom used to make me drink when I woke up in the middle of the night."

"I can't stand warm milk."

"Too bad. Drink it anyway." Karla busied herself around the kitchen, dragging out a small pan and setting it on the stove, getting the milk, a couple of mugs.

"I'll just have water."

"Huh-uh. When was the last time you sat at my table empty-handed? Besides, the milk'll go down fast and help you in the long run." She looked thoughtful for a moment, then smiled. "I know—I'll put a touch of hot-chocolate mix in it, just enough to flavor it." Karla lit the burner under the pot, adjusted it carefully, then moved to sit across from him. "What's going on, Warren?" she asked softly. "I've certainly seen you look better."

Again that short, raspy laugh, a sound like verbal sandpaper. "Me? What's to see? I'm tired, that's all, ever since that business Friday night." Karla nodded gravely. "You think I've looked better, you ought to take a close look at Evelyn."

Karla's eyebrows raised. "What's wrong with her?"

Warren leaned forward, hands gripping the edge of the table. "When was the last time you talked to her in the daylight?"

Her brow furrowed. "Well, I—"

"It's been since before she was attacked, hasn't it? You remember how good she looked, all tan and freckles? How healthy?"

"Of course I do. Are you telling me she's sick?"

"I—" His hands lifted momentarily, then dropped back to the tabletop. "I don't know. I mean, if she were sick . . . she's a *nurse*, for God's sake. She knows to get help if she needs it."

Karla rose and retrieved the pan before its contents started to boil, carefully pouring the milk into the two mugs after adding a spoonful of Swiss Miss. When she set one in front of Warren, his hands wrapped around it immediately, seeking warmth; she doubted he was aware of the movement. She took a slow sip of her milk to give him a chance to keep going, but he had lapsed into silence, staring at nothing. "You still haven't told me what's wrong with Evelyn," Karla finally said. "Is it a problem between the two of you? Because of the rape?"

Warren jerked. "Rape? I don't know if there *was* a rape. Evelyn still says there wasn't, but refuses an examination. That kid swears that's exactly what happened, while the detective—"

"Ewing."

"Yeah, Ewing. He isn't saying anything—except chewing my ear off over the telephone because Evelyn threw the uniform away after he told her to keep it."

Karla nodded. "I know. I saw him going through the trash on Sunday trying to find it, but it was gone."

"I'm telling you, something's wrong with her. She *looks* sick. Her skin is so pale it's like Japanese pancake makeup. Plus she walks around with her head down all the time, looking at her feet and her fingers. And all that's what I see from a distance, because she won't let me get anywhere near her."

"She needs counseling," Karla said. "She should—"

"Of course she should—*we* should! We all know that. *She* knows that. But she won't talk about it—hell, she won't talk, period. I called her today probably six or seven times. All I got was the machine—she refuses to pick up the phone, and ignores me when I gripe about it." He hunched over his cup, his face miserable. "When I got home this afternoon she was in bed. I tried to take her by the hand and I thought she was going to slap me. I went into the bathroom and found a bloody disposable shaver in the sink, and you know what I found in the kitchen?"

"What?"

"Her lunch, or dinner, or whatever she would've called it." Warren's fingers were wrapped so tightly around the mug that his fingernails were bright spots of pink. "Untouched.

"Karla, I'm sure that Evelyn hasn't eaten or drunk *any-thing* in three days!"

• • •

"Trauma team to the emergency room, stat! Trauma team to the emergency room, stat!"

Autopilot kicked in, Evelyn's years of training propelling her out of her seat in the hospital cafeteria and toward the ER. She wasn't sure how long she'd been sitting with a cup of coffee in front of her, but the coffee was cold and no one in the group she'd come down with was around anymore. Of course, she hadn't been very sociable with the others, and at one point her attitude had gotten nearly surly; no wonder she'd ended up at a table alone.

"Trauma team to the emergency room, stat! Trauma team to the emergency room, stat!"

"All right, all right," she muttered. "I'm coming!" She willed her feet to move faster, concentrating fiercely on forcing them to obey her mental commands. Instead they plodded along, each one seeking careful balance on the linoleum before allowing the other to follow suit. She supposed that was a good thing, since she could feel absolutely *nothing* from the ankle down; she wished that whatever primitive part of her brain was acting as her body's vertical guide would shift into gear before somebody recognized her as a trauma-team nurse who seemed to be ignoring the page. She dug into one of the pockets of her uniform and pulled out a pair of pale plastic gloves into which she first sprinkled a liberal dose of baby powder to deepen their milky coloring. By the time the third command blared over the PA system, the gloves were on and her stupidly flat fingertips were well hidden.

She stepped into the ER and into the midst of a whirlwind of personnel bent over a young, dark-haired man on the cart, shot twice in the chest and a "scoop and run" by the paramedics. She had a second to be relieved that the trauma surgeon on duty wasn't Dr. Thieu, then she moved into position and let routine take over. She eyed the thoracotomy tray to make sure it was complete and slipped between staff to check the patient's incubation and IVs, one eye on the cardiac monitor and the other carefully watching the autofusers coming out of his chest.

"We're losing him," she said matter-of-factly. "Pressure's down to thirty and dropping . . . gone. No pulse."

"Son of a bitch," snarled the physician. He was new to

Illinois Masonic and to Evelyn, a middle-aged man with salt-and-pepper hair and a stubborn set to his jaw that said he wouldn't give up his man without a fight. His movements jerked his name tag far too much for Evelyn to read it. "The heart must be hit. Give me the—"

Evelyn's gloved hand offered him the chest splitter before he finished his sentence. More hands, all plastic-encased and bloody like hers and the doctor's, positioning and pulling. Thirty more seconds saw the young man's chest open to the wash of white light in the ER, revealing the lungs and muscle tissue swimming in blood. The motionless heart was ragged, with tears *everywhere*, pieces of lead shot embedded all over the aorta and both pulmonary arteries. It was a damned miracle the guy had still been alive when they rolled him in.

"No way he's gonna make it," someone—Juan—said next to Evelyn's ear.

Anger flashed on the doctor's face—*You're not getting away so easy!*—and he reached into the chest cavity, working fast but efficiently, no wasted movements. Turning, lifting, and finally, grudging surrender. He pulled his hands free, scarlet moisture coating his fingers. "Forget it—we can't fix this," he said. "There's a tear in the rear right ventricle that's probably half a centimeter long, and a solid chunk of the left atrium is just *gone*. Everything we pump into him spills into the body cavity. Guy's totally exsanguinated. Wrap it up." He turned away, pulled his gloves off and scribbled his signature on the code sheet. Then he was gone, presumably to wash up and attend to the next patient.

"Cleanup time," Juan said with false cheer. For a moment his face softened. "Jesus, what a waste. This guy can't be more than twenty-five. Any info on him?"

"Nothing yet." The rest of the trauma team had already slipped out of the curtained cubicle and Juan and Evelyn looked up to see a cop neither recognized. Her name tag said VELASQUEZ. She held up a plastic bag containing a silver gun and a crumpled wad of money. "Just the thirty-eight and the money from the register at the liquor store. Want to bet the gun's stolen?" Her mouth turned up. "Fourth time the guy at the store'd been robbed. Guess he got tired of it."

"I see," Juan said. The officer turned and walked away

and he reached around Evelyn to flip off the heart monitor and oxygen, then reached for the chart.

"You go ahead," she said. "I'll do the paperwork."

He looked at her quizzically as he signed off. "It's my turn, you know."

She shrugged. "That's all right. I could use some time out. If you don't mind, that is."

"Hey, no problem." Juan motioned to his blood-splattered smock. "Got it pretty good when he first came in. I should change before I scare the next mommy who comes in with little Billy's sprained ankle." He rolled his eyes. "I'll put in the call to the coroner. You sure you feel like dealing with this?"

Evelyn waved him on without bothering to reply and had already started filling in the information on the chart by the time he ducked out of the curtained cubicle, recording the time, the IVs, and the amount of blood that had been used. Gathering paper strips from the monitors, she eyed the corpse critically, noting the heavy leather jacket and blue jeans. Besides checking the pockets of his denims for identification, there was probably an inside pocket in the jacket that she'd have to explore. It was doubtful the cops had opted for a thorough ID search amid the wet tangle of flesh and ruined clothes, and the paramedics would've been too busy trying to slow the bleeding. Even Evelyn's experience didn't make it easy to manhandle a body that was still warm and pliable, especially with the chest splitter gleaming in place between the ribs.

Looking for an emergency card or not, Evelyn always felt like a grave robber when she went through the pockets, and her damnably numb fingers made the chore harder than normal. A careful pat was all she needed to tell there was nothing in the pockets of the denim jeans, but the black leather jacket required a closer look.

Uncertainty suddenly gripped her and she stumbled and had to grab at the edge of the cart for balance. She didn't feel well, didn't feel *right*. For no apparent reason her head had filled with a thundering sound and her face was hurting again, really *hurting*. It was an effort to keep her hands from digging at it, knowing that because her gloves were covered with the young man's blood it would be unsanitary to touch herself, and how would she explain it anyway? Her lungs hitched and she had to clamp her mouth shut hard to keep the sound from coming out and being heard beyond the flimsy curtains surrounding the cubicle.

What on earth was the matter with her? Knees bent, hanging on to the side of the stainless-steel cart for dear life, so much *effort*, especially since she could hardly feel anything in her fingers anymore. With a quiet grunt Evelyn stood again, wobbling and staring directly at the dead man's face. Her sense of balance swung wildly and his eyes, dark and slightly open, looped in and out of her vision. She blinked furiously, trying for Christ's sake to make it *stop*. Still, the rocking kept going, back and forth, his nose and fine cheekbones swaying as though the entire cadaver were suspended in a hammock, and finally his mouth—

Abruptly, it stopped. Her sense of balance returned suddenly, along with an explosion within her, fierce and bright, a blasting return of that dark craving. But for *what*? Her fingers moved unwillingly to the dead man's mouth, flat tips prying his lips apart to remove the respirator tube and toss it carelessly, unprofessionally, aside. His lips were rimmed in red, bloody evidence of his last breaths before the rude intrusion of a plastic tube. He was so *pale*, this young man, but still so *warm*, so much more so than her own suddenly shuddering form. She glanced around desperately; the curtains cut them off from the rest of the ER, held her in a wash of suddenly frigid air. She felt *blue*, she was so cold, but when she brushed a tentative hand against the dead man's forehead, he was like a furnace, beckoning with irresistible warmth.

Helpless, control sliding away, Evelyn bent until she could rest her cheek against his, felt the skin of his face vibrate from her chattering teeth. *Stop it!* A wailing in her mind—*What are you doing!*—but unable to prevent the turning of her head, the *stretching* of some unknown offering smothering the cry in her mind for common sense. A rush of white noise, escalating to a howl when her mouth met that of the cadaver's.

Speed, then: a full bodyrush, like hurtling through hot darkness after leaping from seventy stories up but without the terror of destruction. Spreading her arms like wings and soaring but not knowing if she did it in realtime or only in the sweet, twisted ecstasy that blasted through her psyche as she pulled the death-filled air of the corpse's lungs into her own and kept it there. Held it and absorbed it, deep into herself and whirling, faster and faster—

"Ah!" Evelyn yanked her head free and gagged, the taste of the dead man's blood heavy in her mouth, circling her lips like some kind of obscene lipstick. She stumbled and went down on one knee, scrubbing at her face with the back of her forearm and getting a fresh smear of blood across her sleeve as the final proof of her unspeakable act. *"Jesus!"* She heard a noise then, and couldn't tell where it was coming from because she'd lost her footing, whacked her kneecaps good while she was at it. She was up immediately, terrified that one of her coworkers or worse, a cop, would find her like this. Again, the noise, and she gasped and spun, trying to pinpoint the source beyond the instant realization that her feet and fingers were *hers* again, sensation finally returned—

The dead man was getting up.

She would have screamed had her throat not locked on her. The best she could offer was to reach a hand out in a futile gesture at him to stay down—*Dear God, the chest splitter is still IN there!*—but he kept going as she backed away. If he saw her, he gave no sign. She couldn't believe her eyes when he struggled and stood, the hole in his ribs an open, dribbling horror. Still searching for her voice, she watched him rip the splitter free and fling it aside, saw his other hand wrap around the drainage tubes in his chest and the monitor wires and *pull*, no thought to pain or the mixture of dark and clear liquids that gushed from deep lacerations in his skin. He turned and his gaze caught hers, dark eyes utterly devoid of feeling as they swept over her. Evelyn's hands tangled in the curtain behind her and she felt the bump of equipment on the other side, leaned against it to keep from crumbing beneath the force of his dark and hungry grin.

His eyes were . . . *glowing.* Her brain was a mess, but even in her nearly hysterical state the word fit perfectly. Like fire, but green, some kind of bizarre liquid Halloween paint overflowing from his eyes and down his cheeks, pouring down the front of his chin to sink into the pit of his chest. More and more, filling him up and backlighting his insides like a flashlight under a nauseatingly green sheet. The edges of the chest crater *writhed*, scrolling together like twisting lips—

She shook her head then, hard, side to side. When she looked again any trace of light was gone and she couldn't believe it had existed in the first place. Still, he was *dead*, he shouldn't be upright and taking that single, deadly step in her direction—

Finally Evelyn found her breath and screamed, as long and loud as she could. She squeezed her eyes shut before the crash came, but they flew open when something hard and cold careened into her. The cart—slamming painfully into her side and showering her with sharp, soiled instruments from the thoracotomy tray. Voices swelled behind her as people responded to the scream, strong arms in CPD blue lifted her to her feet as more uniforms thundered past in pursuit of the walking dead man.

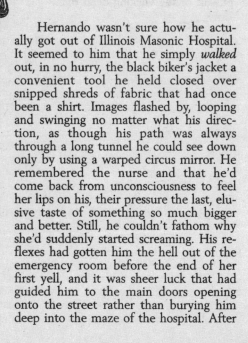

19   Tuesday—Early A.M.

    Hernando wasn't sure how he actually got out of Illinois Masonic Hospital. It seemed to him that he simply *walked* out, in no hurry, the black biker's jacket a convenient tool he held closed over snipped shreds of fabric that had once been a shirt. Images flashed by, looping and swinging no matter what his direction, as though his path was always through a long tunnel he could see down only by using a warped circus mirror. He remembered the nurse and that he'd come back from unconsciousness to feel her lips on his, their pressure the last, elusive taste of something so much bigger and better. Still, he couldn't fathom why she'd suddenly started screaming. His reflexes had gotten him the hell out of the emergency room before the end of her first yell, and it was sheer luck that had guided him to the main doors opening onto the street rather than burying him deep into the maze of the hospital. After that, he couldn't say; he'd sort of *blended* into the street, and the shadows, and the night, seen but not seen as he walked nonchalantly back to the apartment.

His memory was full of holes, a useless piece of Swiss cheese. He remembered being in the liquor store all the way up to when he'd pulled out the Rossi; after that, he could find only fragments—the sound of the register opening, something about a stupid latch-type lock, his snarl of rage, though he didn't know why. Still, he wasn't a fool and it was pretty easy to guess that the owner of the store had pounded him good with a heavy dose of lead. Yet . . . he distinctly remembered yanking a big silver piece of metal out of his chest, a medical instrument that reminded him of a robotic crab. It had come away covered with blood and had left the skin of his chest and his ribs splayed open like something in a butcher shop. Why wasn't he dead?

The walk to his apartment took a good half hour, maybe longer. Hernando kept waiting for someone on the street to say something about his chest and the bloodied shirt. Once, nerves jittering, he walked right past a cop car with the idiot standing there sipping a cup of coffee. He was almost three quarters of the way home before he finally came to believe that no one could really *see* the blood, himself included. Try as he might, every time he looked down at his chest, all he caught was a faint, unreliable shadow of colored splatters amid the pieces of torn fabric brushing the smooth, muscular skin. He was starting to believe he'd never really been shot.

Lights blazed in the upstairs windows, a full house tonight. Carissa would be there, plus his brother and sister-in-law, and the guy with whom they shared the three-bedroom place. Too bad—all Hernando could think about right now was sleep, something the Russian people on the first floor had become experts at pretending to do.

He was on the second step of the front landing when Neilson called his name from the curb.

"Izquierdo! Where the fuck's my rent?" Hernando heard a car door groan as it opened and a squeal of springs from the front seat. Looking back, he saw Neilson climbing out of an impossibly ratty old Volvo sedan, its rust-eaten body sitting at the curb like some spotted, predatory beetle. "Been waiting for you for a damned hour, you asshole. Fuckin' whore of yours slammed the door in my face!"

Hernando stopped on the third riser and turned back toward the street. "She's not very sociable," he said agreeably. He felt disconnected from his body, or more specifically from his hands and feet. They seemed to be as numb as if he'd slept on them wrong for hours, and for a crazy instant he had a mental impression of beating on a set of drums with his bare fingers, using them as a perfectly workable substitute for wooden sticks. The thought made him giggle out loud.

"What the fuck's so funny?" Neilson growled. He stopped at the bottom of the stairs and glared at Hernando. "Where's—"

"Afraid you're out of luck tonight," Hernando said. "My . . . ah, deal didn't come through."

"I got your *deal*!" Neilson exploded. "You and the rest of your fucked-up group can get the hell *out* of my building!" He shook a fist at Hernando. "And do it *tonight*!"

Again that odd sensation of separation, of not caring what happened or why, his dead fish hands hanging loosely at his sides. "I'm afraid that's not going to happen." His voice sounded warped and strangely lilting, as though someone were inside his head and playing with the volume control, turning it up and down, over and over.

Neilson's face turned absurdly purple in the streetlight's grayish glow. "Afraid, afraid, afraid! I'll *show* you the meaning of that fuckin' word!" Neilson leaped up the three steps between them like a top-heavy cat, both gnarly-knuckled hands latching onto the worn lapels of Hernando's coat and yanking him forward. "I'll beat you until you turn inside out, you piece of—"

There was a sudden drop in the tunnel of Hernando's sight, like stepping over a hole and falling straight down, mimicking a thousand moves by cartoon characters on television. A jolting landing made his teeth jitter and Hernando bit his tongue. He felt the skin split but didn't care about the sting, tasted the thick, unique flavor of blood as it laced through his teeth and made him automatically lick his lips. His weight-lifter landlord was no longer standing in front of him and Hernando raised his deadened fingertips and pulled them across his eyes, trying to shake his vision straight.

At his feet, unmoving, was Neilson.

Hernando circled him speculatively, thinking he didn't look so tough now that his overly loud mouth was shut. There was no blood, and no sense in Hernando trying to search for a pulse using fingers that felt nothing—he didn't care anyway, beyond the fact that it was going to look pretty fucking bad to have a dead landlord on his front steps. He prodded the man in the ribs experimentally a few times with the toe of his shoe. Neilson finally groaned and turned his head, showing a nice hearty lump on his right cheekbone, high enough to swell his eye nearly shut.

Hernando grinned down at him. "Cool. Next time you come knocking, remember who put you there." He half expected the older man to get up and jump him from behind as he climbed the outside steps, but it didn't happen. By the time Hernando was on the second-floor landing, he heard Neilson fire up his beater and take off, the old junker's engine coughing in protest at the hard acceleration. *Cool*, he thought again. He'd laid the ex-marine out flat; too bad he couldn't remember a damned thing about it.

"Carissa!" He had to yell to be heard above the pounding of Metallica on the stereo—and a fine piece of electronic crap it was, too—and the laughter of Adelpho and Maralina in the living room. He ignored them, much as it seemed Carissa was ignoring him, and turned down the long hallway leading to the kitchen. He found his other roommate and best friend, Tho Pham, seated at the table and smoking a joint with a new girl, Vietnamese like him and just as sunken-cheeked and dangerous looking. Hernando didn't bother asking what her name was or what had happened to the last one; he hadn't known her name, either. "Where's Carissa?"

Tho snorted, then choked and let out the pungent smoke. "Where else, man? Bathroom." He offered the joint but Hernando shook his head.

"I'm right here."

Hernando turned at the sound of Carissa's sultry voice, still amazed that she could sound like that when she looked like such a cow—though he had to admit pregnancy had not affected that dark and beautiful face. Being knocked up hadn't done anything for her disposition, either: she was as bitchy as ever, maybe more so. Still, if he kept his gaze at tit level and above, the view made it almost bearable. He got that now: large black eyes stared at him from the picture-perfect skin of an oval-shaped face, while long, blue-black curls sprang in every direction. As usual, her carefully shaped eyebrows raised derisively when she saw him. "Do you *have* to scream?"

"To be heard over this racket, yeah. Come in the bedroom with me. I want to tell you what happened tonight."

"Hey man, don't go," Tho said. "Share it with us. We're interested too."

Hernando's eyes cut to his friend's new—and probably temporary—woman. "Maybe later."

The Vietnamese woman's lip curled up at that and she looked at Tho for defense; he shrugged. "Sure, man."

"You got money?" Carissa asked as she followed him into their room. "I need some coke."

"You always need coke," Hernando retorted. "It ain't good for the baby."

"Like you care," she sneered. "You just don't want to give me the bread." She pushed the door shut, muffling the pounding music.

"Hey, I got nothing, okay? You want to check my pockets, go ahead." He shrugged off the jacket and it hit him that it was probably eighty-five degrees in the apartment tonight and it didn't bother him, with or without the leather coat. "Look at this."

Her cool gaze swept him. "Your shirt's ripped open. So what."

"I got shot tonight," he said softly.

She straightened; finally, some reaction out of the coldhearted bitch. "Shot? Where?"

Carissa came toward him, reaching, and he batted her hands away. "What's the matter, baby? Afraid your meal ticket's gonna stop?"

"You're an asshole, you know that? My mother told me I should stay away from you."

He laughed, then darted out a hand and snagged her by the hair. She hissed but didn't fight as he pulled her to him.

"Well, we both know what you think of that old bag." He gave her a quick kiss, pressing hard against the fullness of her mouth, then pushed her away and pointed to his jacket. "Look."

She picked up the biker's leather and peered at it, then studied his shirt. "Jesus, I think you're telling me the truth." She scrutinized him carefully. "But you're—"

"Not hurt," he finished for her. "Not a single scratch. Carissa, I came to in the *hospital*, I swear, with this nurse giving me that CPR stuff. I had this metal . . . I don't know what the hell it was, clamp thing, stuck into my chest. I pulled it out myself, and then I was *healed*!"

"You're bullshitting me."

"I *swear*, Carissa! On the church, God, whatever you want—but I came back from the *dead* tonight!"

He would be the first to admit that he despised this woman, but that he loved her too, as best he could. Why?

Because at times like now, as she stood there and stared at him, shining deep in her coal-black, almond-shaped eyes he saw the first glimmer of acceptance when he knew no one else on this earth would ever believe him.

20

"Mrs. Pelagi, please. We don't want to be here all night, and I'm sure you'd like to go on back to work or home or whatever. So let's start from the beginning, and you think about everything very carefully. Who took the body from the cubicle?"

"I already *told* you, no one *stole* that man's body. He was alive. He got up, pulled out all the medical apparatus and insertions, and *left*. There's nothing more to tell. Jesus, weren't you listening to anything I said? I've been telling you the same damned thing for two hours!"

The uniformed policeman's expression didn't change. "Yes, ma'am. I've heard every word, and so has my partner, and so has the hospital's administrator. I've sure you understand our problem, though." He inclined his head toward the huddle of doctors and EMTs waiting at the other end of the cafeteria, quite comfortable to stand and gawk at her as long as the emergency room was quiet. "According to the doctor in charge, Dr. uh—"

"Penrod," Evelyn snapped.

"Right. According to Dr. Penrod, the young man was dead, so dead that it would have been impossible for him to be resuscitated. Also according to Dr. Penrod, the cadaver's chest had been split and his insides were open to the world." For a second it looked like the man's cool demeanor was finally going to slip, but training must have taken over where his patience was wearing thin. "There's an obvious disparity between what you're telling us and what the good doctor says is medically and physically possible." He gave the clipboard in his hands a sharp tap with his ink pen. "I have to find a way to make those two ends meet, or I can't go home. I'm sure you can appreciate that, Mrs. Pelagi."

"I can appreciate a lot of things," she shot back. "Like the fact that in your line of work you must see a lot of different sides to a lot of different stories. Count this as another one of those and be done with it. I've got to get back on shift." She started to stand.

"According to your supervisor, you were involved in an attack this past Friday evening. Is that so?"

Teeth grinding, Evelyn sank back onto the hard plastic chair and swore under her breath. "Yes, I was. Which has nothing to do with tonight. Why do you ask?"

"Has the man who attacked you been caught yet? Your supervisor doesn't know."

"No, he hasn't. As a matter of fact, I don't even know what he looks like."

Her examiner's eyebrows shot up. "Really? So this man could have been him?"

Evelyn nearly choked, then recovered. "Look, Officer Leggitt," she said, reading the name from the tag pinned to his pocket, "I may not know what the man who attacked me looks like, but I clearly remember his build. The young man who left here tonight was definitely not that person."

The policeman sighed. "You're sure you won't reconsider your statement, Mrs. Pelagi? This isn't going to sit well with a lot of people at the station house, not to mention your supervisor and that Dr. Penrod. They don't look too happy right now."

"I'm not here to make anyone happy." She had shed her bloodstained smock earlier and donned a new one from the supply closet; this one had a button missing and she picked at the dangle of loose threads absently. "I know what I saw, and I'm telling you—for at least the hundredth time: He was alive. He got up. He left. And that's that." Well, she thought unwillingly, not quite.

"Excuse me," a familiar voice said. Both she and Officer Leggitt looked up to see Detective Jude Ewing standing at the end of their table. "Sorry I'm late." Evelyn and the detective stared at each other for a moment, and if the plainclothesman was shocked at her appearance, he hid it well as his expression smoothed and he nodded politely at her.

Leggitt dropped the clipboard on the tabletop and stood, looking relieved. "Thank God. She's all yours. I got absolutely nothing that makes sense."

"*Excuse* me?"

The uniformed cop jammed his hat on his head, then gave it a belated tip in Evelyn's direction. "Nothing personal, ma'am. The detective will take it from here—and be sure to sign the report at the bottom of page two. Have a pleasant night."

"Oh, I'm *sure*," she said sarcastically. Not that it mattered; she was already speaking to his back as he got the hell out of there.

Ewing took the vacated seat across from her but ignored the clipboard and the notes that Leggitt had spent nearly two hours taking. "Not a happy camper, I take it," he said companionably. "So what happened?"

Evelyn groaned. "Don't you guys ever stop? I've been talking to that guy for the past two hours and he hasn't listened to anything I've said. Now I have to start all over again? Don't you guys have lives, for crying out loud? Why do you have to spend so much time in *mine*?"

"You're lucky this week, I guess." Ewing's voice was mild. "Unfortunately," he peered at the notes, "I can't read Leggitt's writing—"

"Oh, I don't believe this!"

"—so yes, I will have to ask you a few questions before you sign off on it. I do have some idea of what's going on here though, and I'm sure the occurrence has been pretty well documented all around." He gazed at her steadily, unperturbed by her impatience. "By both you and the other staff members." When she sat there in stubborn silence, he finally leaned forward and gave her his most reassuring smile. "I know you've been through a lot over the past week, Evelyn—may I call you by your first name?" If she remembered him asking her the same question the night of her attack, she gave no indication of it. "I'm not hinting that your ordeal last Friday has anything to do with tonight," he continued, "but I have to ask you this, Evelyn, from one adult to another. Are we talking about the same patient here? Everyone in the emergency room—you included—swears this man was gutted like a field-dressed deer and he couldn't possibly be alive. So how can you sit here and say otherwise?"

Evelyn stared at him, trying to sort through the sudden surge of anger and frustration. The detective, she knew, had access to all the details of the report the two responding officers had filed on her attack, had probably read the thing cover to cover at least a dozen times. What the hell, she thought with a sudden and uncharacteristic nastiness. These people think they're so damned smart, let's really dig them in deep.

Her return smile was cold and thin, and not at all agreeable.

"Because *I* did it, Detective Ewing. *I* brought him back from the dead."

21

"All right, Mrs. Pelagi, Mr. Spiro. Keep in mind at all times that the men on the other side of the glass can't see either of you, or into this room. I want you to look at each man in turn, very carefully, and take your time. We will be instructing them to turn to the left and the right, and if you wish we can order a specific one to step forward so you can see better. All you have to do is say so."

Jason had never seen Detective Wilfred before, the tall, sharply dressed woman who was talking, although she had introduced herself as Ewing's partner. He didn't really care who or what she was, and a cursory glimpse at the seven men being spread out and numbered was enough to make him immediately certain that the jogger he'd seen last Friday evening wasn't among them—not one of them had the right athletic build. He wasn't about to say that, not yet, because he wanted all the time he could get to sit here and stare at Evelyn Pelagi.

So that was her name. Evelyn—like the biblical Eve, born of Adam's rib, his wife, the mother of all creation. It had to be divine providence that had caused him to arrive at the station a half hour earlier than a bleary-sounding Detective Ewing had told him on the telephone this morning. Now that he thought about it, Ewing probably meant it to happen the other way, no doubt thinking his partner could hustle Evelyn in and out before Jason got there. Surely God had intervened on his behalf, and he had to force his face to keep its bland look; the more the idea went around in his head, the more he wanted to grin.

Evelyn Pelagi. She was a beautiful woman, even after obviously working all night and being tired, and despite the injuries from the attack superimposed over her face and throat, a ghostly overlap that Jason knew only he—and probably Evelyn—could see. He was the same way, he knew: six puncture wounds, each surrounded by a virulent rainbow of bruises, dotted his face, neck, chest and one forearm. Five of those were clearly visible to Evelyn—he saw that much in the shock that had danced across her face at her first sight of him. But her recovery had been instantaneous—so fast, in fact, that he would never believe she didn't realize she was in the midst of a holy miracle, *his* holy miracle. As far as he was concerned, her eyes, such a delicate shade of light hazel, said it *all.*

"Mr. Spiro? Mr. Spiro, pay attention, please."

"What?" Jason jerked and found Detective Wilfred looking at him. She reminded him of a teacher, except she had a sense of possessing a lot more *power* with her short, efficiently styled blond hair and deeply piercing blue eyes; being pinned under that gaze made him want to squirm like a misbehaving schoolboy. Her strong voice had a way of reverberating in the mind. "Sorry," he muttered. "I missed the question."

"Then I'll repeat it. I asked if any of the men you're viewing look familiar, Mr. Spiro. Could any one of these men possibly be the man you saw jogging late last Friday night?"

Jason forced his gaze back to the one-way glass, although he already knew the answer. He waited, letting what he guessed was a reasonable length of time go by, before he shook his head. "No, he's not in there."

The obligatory question—

"You're positive?"

Followed by the expected confirmation—

"Yes."

If he hadn't been positive, he thought scornfully, he wouldn't have said so in the first place. His fingers wanted to tap, to reach over and touch Evelyn Pelagi to see if her skin still felt as warm as it had when he'd resurrected her. An odd thought, since his hands were mostly numb; he shoved them in the pockets of his jeans to keep them still.

"And you, Mrs. Pelagi? Does anyone in the lineup look familiar to you? Let me remind you to think not only of your attacker but about the jogger that this young man says he saw. That person could be the attacker, or he could be a witness."

Evelyn, too, shook her head. "No, he's not in there. I distinctly remember telling Detective Ewing that I scratched the man across the face. Unless someone in there's wearing makeup—"

"No."

"Then he's not in there." Evelyn's tone of voice teetered on the edge of cranky, her question unvoiced but evident. *Why did you bring me here when you knew that to begin with?*

Divine providence, Jason thought, that's why. Nevertheless, he couldn't resist adding to it. "The man I saw had something across his face. It could have been scratches. Didn't that other cop tell you that?"

"Yes," Detective Wilfred said evenly, "he did." Her expression remained the same. "We do, however, have reason to believe that one of the men in the lineup was in the vicinity of Mrs. Pelagi's attack at the time it occurred. That person has a known record of sex offenses. We're just covering all bases." Jason could offer no response to that, and the detective turned, flipped a switch and spoke into an intercom. "Move them out," she said simply, then shut it off. "Thank you both for your time, and I'm sorry we weren't successful. As I said, we have to investigate any lead, no matter how small it might seem. The next time might pay off." She sounded like she was reciting a memorized speech as she opened the door. "I'll show you the way to the front entrance."

Foster Avenue was extremely busy in the morning, more than Jason had expected for a two-lane street that ran east and west all the way through Chicago. Detective Wilfred had left them outside the entrance to the police station and disappeared back inside and away from the noise and rush of cars and the more offensive roar of the No. 92 CTA buses. No doubt Ewing was already home and done with the business of Evelyn Pelagi's attack for the time being. The morning light had made it suddenly evident how tired Detective Wilfred looked; apparently she'd stretched her shift to show them the lineup of suspects. Jason and Evelyn walked out the door side by side in silence, and Jason thought privately that they seemed to be quietly in step with each other, even if they didn't have anything to say right now.

When they reached the sidewalk, Evelyn finally spoke, a little embarrassed. "I—I want to thank you for helping me last Friday," she said awkwardly. The hot sunlight made her skin look ghastly white and swirled the dark bruises across the freckled planes of her face like unstable ink. "That was, uh, very brave of you. Most people wouldn't have bothered."

"I'm not most people," Jason said, staring at her; he thought she looked beautiful. "I think you know that."

Evelyn's eyes scanned his face and neck and she winced visibly, then shuddered. "I—I don't think you—"

"Come with me," Jason said suddenly. Before she could react, he faced her and stepped close, grabbed her hands and held them up between them. "We belong together. Look at us, at our fingers," he ordered. *"Look."* His fingertips, dead and dried and flat, made a grotesque clacking sound against hers.

She turned her head away. "No!"

"You see me, don't you?" he demanded. "The *real* me, like I see the real you. You *know* what we are."

"I don't know any such thing!" she choked out. "Let me go."

Jason didn't relinquish his grip. He pushed his face close to hers. "I brought you back to life," he said in a low voice. "You are my Eve. No one else could have done that."

This time Evelyn managed to snatch her hands free. "You're not the only one!" she blurted. "I can do it, too!"

Jason froze, too flabbergasted to speak for a moment. Then, "That's *wonderful!*" He tried to take her hands again, but she would have none of it. "Don't you see? I *gave* it to you, and you . . ." His expression went slack, then lit up. "You've given it to someone *else*! It's a gift, a divine inheritance. From God to me, from me to you, from you to . . ." He looked suddenly puzzled. "Who did *you* give it to?"

Evelyn's mouth dropped open in horror. "Oh my *God*," she whispered. She twisted, then stumbled in the other direction.

"Wait!" Jason called. "We have to stay together! Don't you realize, we can give life to the dead—and those we bring back can do the same! We've been *chosen*—"

"*Stay away from me!*" she cried. Jason stopped short when she thrust out one hand at him, and if she'd been from down home he would've expected her to do something utterly stupid like make the sign of the evil eye. "Sweet Jesus, what have I *done?*"

"I'll walk you home," Jason said desperately, starting after her. He couldn't let her out of his sight, now that he knew he'd graced her with the same gift that had been given to him. He didn't even know where she lived. "Please—hey, be careful!" At first he thought she was so crazed that she'd darted into traffic recklessly, then saw that she'd succeeded in hailing a Yellow Taxi. "Mrs. Pelagi—*Evelyn!*"

Too late. Dismayed, Jason had time to do nothing but watch as she jumped inside the cab and it sped away.

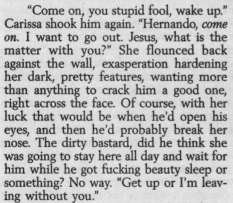

22

"Come on, you stupid fool, wake up." Carissa shook him again. "Hernando, *come on*. I want to go out. Jesus, what is the matter with you?" She flounced back against the wall, exasperation hardening her dark, pretty features, wanting more than anything to crack him a good one, right across the face. Of course, with her luck that would be when he'd open his eyes, and then he'd probably break her nose. The dirty bastard, did he think she was going to stay here all day and wait for him while he got fucking beauty sleep or something? No way. "Get up or I'm leaving without you."

Her words might not have been heard but the threat was far from empty, and she got off the bed and started pulling on her clothes. He didn't look right anyway, like he was sick. Probably some aftereffect of being shot, shock or something. She believed his story, though she wondered if he'd dropped a hit or two of acid and dreamed up the part about the woman bringing him back to life. More than likely the bullet or the buckshot had caught him at the right angle and messed up his shirt; they were always talking about technical stuff like angles on the TV cop shows.

He'd been sleeping for how long now? They'd gone to bed right about when the sun had started to come up yesterday, so that meant nearly thirty-six hours—not that she'd stayed in here with him the whole time. She was pregnant, after all, which meant she got hungry a lot, and had to use the bathroom twice as often as a normal person. She'd watched a few television soaps with Tho and his new girlfriend, listened to Adelpho and his wife make the bedsprings scream in the next room for what seemed like hours last night, at last flipped through a bunch of fashion magazines she'd managed to lift last weekend from the Jewel Food Store on Clark and Gregory. She'd crawled back into bed with Hernando at three o'clock, thinking it was about time he woke up and they could fool around a little, but no dice. It was almost five o'clock, the bastard was still fast asleep, and she was finally bored out of her skull.

"What to wear?" she muttered. There wasn't much around that could make the body look attractive these days, and while all the yuppie women seemed to revel in pregnancy, Carissa hated it. She felt like someone had taken her once trim body and jammed it inside a balloon filled with congealed chicken fat, and if she looked the way she felt, Carissa was surprised people didn't openly point at her on the street. Still, there were certain advantages to being knocked up—take the grocery stores, for example. No one paid two shits' worth of attention to a pregnant woman flipping through maternity stuff at the magazine rack, and she'd walked out with countless copies of her favorite 'zines over the last four months. If she felt like working, that was a breeze, too; it was much easier to use her mouth than be flat on her back. As usual, this lazy piece of garbage was on *his* back while she was going to be out earning money. What the hell else was new?

She finally found a red top that wasn't too wrinkled and was still long enough to cover her blue jeans and the front zipper that was open all the way and tucked in on itself—no way was she going to spend good money on so-called maternity pants. They were nothing but jeans with a forty-dollar piece of wide elastic in place of a zipper anyway. She slipped her feet into sandals and slammed the bedroom door behind her as she left, one last chance for Hernando to wake up. Nothing but wasted effort.

In the bathroom, Carissa looked in the mirror critically. She had a good tan for a change, and her color was a rich, dusky olive. The hair was wild, as usual, and she spritzed it with water and patted it in a few places, but not much else. No more makeup than a small amount of black mascara and deep red lipstick. She made a face and checked her teeth; no food stuck between them, so she wouldn't bother to brush. She gave her neck and wrists a generous dose of Chantilly cologne and decided she'd do fine for the type of jobs she was after.

One last glance in the bedroom told her Hernando was still out. That was fine with her; he could sleep for another thirty-six hours for all she cared. All that meant was that whatever money she earned tonight he wouldn't know about, and she wouldn't have to share. Carissa eyed the sidewalk out front warily from the front porch in case that asshole Neilson was hanging around again, but it was clear. Apparently the beating Hernando had given him was still keeping him away, though it was a wonder the old man hadn't called the cops. That would've put them all in a fine mess, but why waste energy thinking about something that hadn't happened?

Another hot, humid night, with the temperature stuck in the low nineties. As she headed toward Montrose Avenue a southbound Ravenswood train rumbled by on the elevated tracks above her. The noise swelled to a roar for a moment, then faded, leaving her ears tingling in time to the heat pulse of blood in her temples. After a block Carissa could feel the sweat running down the small of her back and circling her breasts, making dark, scarlet smudges in the loose-fitting cotton top; all this extra weight wasn't helping the cooling factor in her body. One stupid accident with Hernando—too much marijuana and wine, and a forgotten condom—and look where she was, trying to earn spending money with her belly leading the way down the street. What were they going to do with a baby? Her imagination was already supplying her with ample pictures of the future: crying all night, non-stop dirty diapers, puke stains on the shoulders of all her clothes. Maybe it was time to get friendly with her mother again. Sometimes grandmothers made the best moms of all.

There was a neighborhood bar on the corner of Montrose and Ashland, a joint whose owners had changed so often they didn't bother with a sign anymore. Carissa checked the cheap watch on her wrist and figured her timing was just right. At five-thirty the place would be nearly full of construction workers, a sizeable portion of whom would be well on their way to being soused. The odds were good she'd get at least one, maybe two or three, to fork over some cash for a quick pleasure trip out back. It was a fairly well-patrolled area, but this corner wasn't too much of a risk as far as standing since she could always act like she was waiting for the eastbound Montrose bus. To complete the picture, she'd tucked a *Mademoiselle* magazine into her canvas tote bag and had a bus token in the watch pocket of her jeans.

It didn't take long, maybe five minutes, before a guy with overly long blond hair and a beefy build wobbled out of the door and leaned against the front of the building. Carissa saw him glance at her and look away; she gave it a full minute before she started a conversation.

"Hi," she said. "You look a little woozy. You okay?"

He seemed surprised that she'd spoken, then recovered and nodded. "Sure, I'm fine." He glanced back inside. "It's the smoke," he explained. "After a while the stink gets to me and I need fresh air."

"Oh, yeah," Carissa agreed. "I'm the same way. I can't stand it." He looked her up and down and Carissa studied him narrowly; this was where things sometimes got tricky. If he turned out to be a Bible Belt boy, she'd be in for an earful of trouble. Still, you never knew until you tried. "So," she said casually, "you having a good time in there?" She gave him her prettiest smile.

He shrugged. "It's an okay place for a beer after work."

"Just okay, huh?" Again, a noncommittal shrug. "My name's Désirée," she said. She never gave her real name to a customer. "What's yours?"

He hesitated, but only for a second. "Quinn."

"Well . . . Quinn," Carissa said, stepping closer, drawing him within perfume range. The guy was an easy target; she could see his nostrils flare as he breathed in. "If you're looking for something more interesting, I know where to find it."

He darted a glance over his shoulder and into the bar, checking to see if anyone had noticed him talking to her, then turned his attention back on Carissa. "I don't know," he said doubtfully. "You seem, you know, sorta big for that kind of thing—"

"We don't have to worry about *me*," she said smoothly. She was almost touching him, close enough to run the tip of one fingernail up his denim-clad hip. "We'll just think about *you*, okay?" She smiled again, wider this time, and let her tongue run across the front of her teeth. "I've got a really nice . . . touch." He swallowed visibly, mesmerized by the red of her lips. "Tell you what," she said softly. "I'll walk around by the back door. There's a spot there where we could have some privacy if you, you know, decide there's something I can do that might suit you. All right?" She moved her hand as if she were going to dig in her purse and succeeded in brushing against the front of his jeans.

"How much?" His voice had gone hoarse.

"Twenty-five, firm." Carissa eyeballed him, waiting.

"Give me, say, five minutes."

The heat and anticipation were getting to the guy, and Carissa couldn't help but chuckle. "I won't wait long." She turned and walked away without hurrying, knowing that at least from the rear she still had a semblance of a waistline; an optical illusion but one she used successfully.

The area behind the bar was dirtier than Carissa remembered from the last time, more evidence of another change of ownership. Either business was good or the guy hadn't paid his trash bill; the Dumpster was overflowing with cut-up boxes and bottles, but at least the place didn't serve food, so there wasn't much in the way of a stench. Thank God for that, she thought in disgust as she checked the alcove; all she needed was some rotted bag of fish and vegetables to make her puke in this heat. She did manage to kick the worst of the excess cardboard out of the way before Quinn eased open the back door and poked his head out like a terrified deer.

"Uh, Désirée?"

Carissa motioned at him to step outside and join her in the small hideaway created by the odd-shaped back of the main building and the side of a neighboring building. With the Dumpster blocking the gangway that led to the alley, she and Quinn were virtually guaranteed the seclusion they'd need. He stood there awkwardly, shuffling his feet and looking anywhere but her face; finally, she sighed. "I'm sorry to sound callous, Quinn, but a girl's got to look out for her livelihood." When he still seemed perplexed, she said it outright. "The money?"

His face went red. "Oh, right! Here, right here." He thrust a twenty and a five at her and she took them and expertly tucked them away, her hands moving too quickly for Quinn to see where.

"Now," Carissa said, her smile returning. "You relax and enjoy the fun, okay? If you like it, you tell a few of your friends in there that I'm around tonight." Her hands went to his belt buckle and he twitched.

"Can I, uh, you know, touch you, uh, during—"

She tossed her shaggy mane of curls. "You can touch my hair, as long as you don't pull. In fact, I *like* having my hair touched." Carissa bent her knees until she was in a crouch in front of him; when she looked up she could see his Adam's apple working. He reached cautiously for her hair.

"*Quinn Pallaton, I don't believe my eyes!*"

Carissa's john yanked himself out of her reach and plastered his back against the opposite wall of the alcove; his face had gone crimson. "Theresa! Honey, this is not what you think! She just—"

"Oh, I *see* what the little whore's doing, all right!" The southern voice was followed by a hefty woman who barreled into the tiny space. Carissa had enough time to think that it was no wonder the guy looked elsewhere for sex when his woman's hand whipped out and jabbed her in the shoulder. She lost her balance and fell onto one elbow, deep in the shadows cast by the two buildings. "And *you!*" the woman spat. Carissa couldn't believe it; Quinn had to be close to two hundred pounds, yet his lady punched him a good one, really put some weight into it, smack in the middle of his chest. He yelped and tried to scramble away, but the woman was too fast and grabbed him by the belt before he could escape. He damn near ended up on the ground next to Carissa.

"Hussy! You're messing with my *husband*!" Her voice was almost a scream, and she followed the name-calling with a hard kick that Carissa was far too ungainly to avoid. The woman's foot, clad in a ridiculously pointed cowboy boot, caught her deep in the lower abdomen and Carissa couldn't keep from crying out at the ice pick of pain that rocketed up her belly. She folded over and got kicked again, this time in the side but not as bad, before Quinn managed to drag his wife backward and out of toe range.

"Leave her be, Theresa! Can't you see she's pregnant? No harm done—we didn't do nothing, I swear!" He tried to take her in his arms, but she cracked him again.

"Well, ain't that just a prize," she sneered. "Get back in there, you jackass." Theresa glowered at Carissa's hunched figure over her shoulder. "I guess you'll think twice about coming 'round here again, won'tcha? Slut." She twisted back to her husband and shoved him forward. "Go on!"

And it was only Carissa, and the lancing pain in her gut, in the hidden alcove off the alley.

Carissa made it back to the apartment thanks to the twenty-five bucks and the Checker Taxi that pulled over for her when she'd hailed him despite the Not for Hire sign flipped down on the visor. The guy was Pakistani and to Carissa's pain-racked mind he sounded like a fucking broken record—

"You okay lady? You okay? To hospital instead? No? You okay lady? You okay?"

—until she was ready to scream as much from the sound of his high-pitched accent as from the agony engulfing the lower half of her body. If she could get upstairs and get rid of these tight jeans, get out of this fucking bumpy *cab*, for Christ's sake, she knew she'd be all right. When he finally pulled up to her address on Ravenswood, she threw the twenty-dollar bill at him and practically fell out of the car and onto the street. So much for the illusion of wanting to help; the guy sped away like the ass end of his cab was on fire.

Getting upstairs was the hardest thing she'd ever had to do, at least that she could remember right now. The second-floor landing might as well have been Mars, but she made it, step-by-step, and fuck *no*, she would *not* pass out in the stairwell for that greasy Vietnamese bastard or Hernando's smiley-faced, teenybopper sister-in-law to find. They'd do something supremely stupid like call an ambulance or a doctor or someone else she didn't have the bread to pay, and screw them all anyway, she didn't need anyone's help.

She pushed open the door, unlocked as always—they had nothing worth stealing—and went inside. At last, the apartment, mercifully quiet with no one home or maybe Hernando was still sleeping. The pain was bad but she could bear it—a bruise, that's all, a bad one. Stupid bitch probably struck a hipbone with the toe of her boot and Carissa hoped desperately that the woman would someday end up with one of those boots up her ass.

The wood floor was mercifully cool against her face, and with a start Carissa realized that she'd come into the apartment crawling and had fogged out in the middle of the dining room. Her jeans felt nasty and wet, and somehow she managed to haul herself up and stagger into the hallway, finally rolling around the door frame that led into the bathroom. She kicked her sandals away and tried to sit on the bath mat on the edge of the bathtub so she could pull her jeans off. But it was one of those ancient claw-footed things with a rounded edge and she and the mat kept sliding forward, each time bringing her a more vicious jolt of pain. Finally she just slipped down, feeling the cool ceramic bump against the vertebrae of her back as her blouse rode up on the lip of the tub and hung there. Her hands were resting on her thighs and they seemed far away, though she could look down and see how very, very red they were. Red and wet, like the fabric of her blue jeans and the old bath mat that had come off the side of the tub with her and was now bunched underneath her butt.

"Uh-oh," she said out loud. Her voice sounded little, though she knew she'd spoken at normal volume. She *felt* little, tiny and insignificant and shrinking more with each passing second. "I need to get up, and maybe call an ambulance." She could have sworn she said the words but she couldn't *hear* them, then decided that things were better now because the pain had lessened a bit, at least enough to become bearable. She thought again about standing and instead rolled her eyes heavenward. The ceiling wasn't there anymore, or if it was, it now extended so far up that Carissa couldn't see it. Instead there was nothing but a big blob of bright white, like a blinding cloud swirling where the old electrical fixture should have been.

Don't be stupid, she told herself and closed her eyes against the painful brightness.

It's nothing but the lightbulb.

23

"I am not nervous," Jude Ewing told his steering wheel. "I am *not*. I am a grown man, and I've been on a thousand dates. This is no big deal." He heard a giggle off to his left and turned his head to see two young girls, probably about twelve years old, staring at him and whispering as they walked by. His face gained a little heat when he realized they'd heard him talking to himself in his car. He checked his watch again, then pulled a comb from his back pocket and ran it through his hair, which he was sure had gotten messed up from when he'd combed it five minutes ago. His stomach was doing a lazy set of anxiety rolls, like one of those little balls with a lead weight hidden inside; he resisted the urge to pop a cherry-flavored Maalox tablet, afraid his teeth would be full of chalky pink grains. He supposed he was lucky; most guys would have been drenched by now, between the nerves and the humid, hot air.

The long June days would let full sunlight bake the city until after eight-thirty, but the heat seldom bothered him—in fact, he *liked* hot weather. Even so, he hated summers as much as any other cop because the high temperatures made tempers snap and the crime rate skyrocket.

"Time to go up," Jude muttered, then peered around belatedly. The two girls were gone, thank God; he didn't need any more embarrassment before he got to Karla's damned front door. He rolled up the window and climbed out of his car, a freshly washed '94 dark green Saturn—he refused to drive an unmarked cop car unless he was working—then locked it. For a minute he stood beside the driver's door and fingered his collar. Should he have worn a tie with his jacket? He'd gone for a casual sport shirt, but now that he thought about it, they hadn't talked about where they were going—

"You going to stand down there all day or are you coming up?" Karla's voice floated down from one of the windows and he looked up guiltily. Finding a spot right in front of her building had disadvantages, too.

"Hi," he called. By the time he crossed the sidewalk she'd come down the stairwell and opened the door for him; the air in the dim hallway felt cool and slightly damp after the bright sunshine outside, not exactly pleasant. "Cooler in here, isn't it?"

Echoing his thoughts, Karla made a face. "Bleh. Hold on a sec." She paused at the top turn of the stairs to unlock the small window facing west and slide it open a few inches. "That ought to help." She reached down and tugged briefly on his hand. "Come on in, Evie's here. She told me what happened at the hospital." She glanced furtively toward the open door to her apartment. "Strange stuff, Jude. Plus . . . she looks awful."

"Oh?" He searched her face but she shook her head.

"Never mind, you'll see for yourself."

"Where's the dog?" he asked automatically.

"I shut her in the other room."

Surprised, Jude followed her through the door and into the kitchen, and when he thought about it later he was damned proud of the speed with which he slammed an invisible mask over his expression when he saw Evelyn. The word *awful* was an understatement; why, he'd seen her less than a day ago at Illinois Masonic—and by God, he'd remember that interview for a damned long time to come—but it might as well have been three years. Three *bad* years. "Mrs. Pelagi—Evelyn," he managed. "How are you?"

Evelyn Pelagi stared at him without answering, long enough to make both him and Karla uncomfortable. From the corner of his eye Jude thought he saw Karla shudder slightly, and beneath the affable smile on his face he had to grit his teeth at the sudden flash of aggravation he felt. What the hell was Evelyn thinking, to put Karla in an awkward position like this?

"Evelyn?" Karla asked uncertainly. "Is something wrong?"

The other woman stood suddenly, her chair scraping backward with an unexpected screech across the linoleum. "I have to go," she said woodenly. "Thanks for having me."

"I'll walk you downstairs." Karla stepped toward her friend, but Evelyn held up her hand. Ewing blinked and started to say something, but Evelyn snatched it away, spun and pulled open the back door.

"No need." Evelyn's head swiveled back toward Ewing and he got the absurd impression that her head and neck were two separate pieces, resting on each other and rotating unwillingly on rusty ball bearings. Another moment of her staring at him, then she finally nodded. "Nice to see you again, Detective." She stepped out and pulled the door closed.

Karla rubbed at her forehead shakily. "Is there something I missed?" She was having a difficult time keeping her voice light.

"No, I don't think so." Ewing looked around the kitchen. "I'm sure with everything that's gone on these past few days, she's probably had it up to here with me and my questions. Sorry about that." He spied Evelyn's colorful coffee mug on the table, its contents apparently untouched.

Karla followed his gaze and picked up the mug, frowned, then dumped the coffee into the sink without saying anything for a moment. "Well," she said at last, "let's not think about it right now." From somewhere, she managed a strained grin. "Where are we going for food?"

"I clearly remember leaving that decision to you," he

pointed out. He was still burned by Evelyn's rudeness, but he purposely pushed the thought away.

"And I clearly remember deciding to give it *back*," she responded primly. "So I'll ask you again. Where are we going?"

Ah, the all-important question. Ewing leaned back against the counter and tapped his fingers against one leg thoughtfully. "What do you like?"

"Anything," she answered promptly. "*Every*thing. I'm not a picky eater, though I don't like slimy stuff or sushi." She motioned to the outfit she was wearing, a long-sleeved cotton dress printed with huge intertwined white-and-gold flowers that Ewing thought contrasted exquisitely with her complexion. "Not too fancy, though. I'd rather not have to change. I'll be right back." Thirty seconds and she returned, Creature stepping happily at her heels. At the sight of Ewing, the animal spread her mouth in that toothy, custom-to-Creature grin.

"Why wasn't she out?" He had to ask, though he thought he knew the answer already.

Karla looked troubled. "It's the weirdest thing—Creature doesn't seem to like Evelyn anymore. She won't stop barking at her. Evelyn can't even walk her for me when I work late now."

So his hunch was correct. Back to the food situation, and a flash idea. "How about Reza over on Clark?"

"I don't think I've heard of it. I'm starved—let's go." She grabbed her pocketbook.

Ewing laughed, delighted. "Just like that? No questions? Not even what kind of food they serve?"

Karla flicked her hand at him. "I'll find out when we get there. I'd rather have an adventure than an answered question, wouldn't you?" She smiled and stepped over the dog, which had settled crossways across the doorway into the dining room and thumped her tail agreeably at the both of them. "Come *on*, let's go."

"I'm not so sure about that," Ewing answered softly.

But only the dog seemed to hear him.

Reza Restaurant turned out to be a Persian place, a huge establishment that stretched a quarter block deep and took up nearly the same amount of space in width. Rough-cut oak beams crossed the fifteen-foot ceilings, while lower to the floor softly polished wood fashioned in elaborately carved scrolls and wide arcs surrounded the customers. Plenty of dangling lamps bounced light off the oak tables and onto the brass-and-glass-framed travel posters of Iran that dotted the walls at regular intervals. It was packed, even on a Wednesday night.

"Wow," Karla said. "Looks like we just missed a waiting line. Persian food?"

Jude steered her toward a dark-skinned man holding menus. "Two, please," he told him. As they followed the host, Jude told her there was an entire lower level filled with more tables. "Persian food is Middle Eastern, though they do things a bit more elaborately here. They've been open for years, despite the trouble between the United States and Iran. I guess they figured it made a lot more business sense to call it Persian cuisine than Iranian, and if they can feed you once, you'll probably be back." The host found them a table and they settled themselves and opened the menus.

When a waiter returned, Jude asked for a Guinness and Karla promptly ordered a glass of pomegranate juice. Jude made a few suggestions and they finally decided on two platters of joujeh kabob, the house specialty of tasty roasted chicken wings and heavily dilled rice. The meal started with a plate of standard appetizers—large chunks of fresh onion, feta cheese, parsley and radishes accompanied by quarters of hot pita bread. If that wasn't enough, the waiter set two bowls of heavily spiced soup in front of them.

"This is delicious," Karla said after she tasted it. "But I can't figure out what's in it." She studied a spoonful. "Tomato base, parsley, something else—"

"Ground up Iraqis," Jude said without missing a beat.

Karla's mouth fell open, then she giggled. "You're evil, Jude. What a thing to say."

"Fine. Then *you* figure out what's in there, Miss I-Can't-Cook."

"Well, I . . ." She giggled again. "Stop that." He grinned and they ate in silence for a while; she must have gotten tired of the quiet when she finally decided to throw the opening question. At least she did it prettily, pushing her soup bowl aside and balancing her chin on her fingers. "So, tell me about you."

"About me?"

Karla tilted her head. "Well, I'm not asking about the fellow at the next table."

"Who?" He craned his head around.

"Silly. Stop trying to change the subject. Why are you a cop?"

An interesting way to ask, he thought with amusement. Not *what made you* but *why are you*. Abrupt, too. "It's in my blood," he said simply. "My dad's a cop, my brother's a cop, my grandfather—my mom's dad—was a cop. I never wanted to be anything else."

"No 'I'm going to save the world' syndrome?" she inquired with a wry smile.

Jude chuckled. "Afraid not. With three generations in the family, things have gotten more realistic. It's a job and I try to do it decently. Nothing more complicated than that."

"You can take it?"

He knew what she meant, and wished the conversation would take a different turn, something beyond the obligatory personal histories. He didn't like talking about the job much, and would have preferred to avoid his family altogether. But doing so was unlikely, and he knew it. He didn't want Karla to feel shut out, which was exactly what would happen if she had to force the information from him. "I do all right," he offered after a moment. "Ups and down, like anything else." He nodded at his beer, still three quarters full. "I've seen a lot of good guys try to douse the day's work in booze and have the liquor end up dousing the work. So I keep the booze at the lower end of the scale, though I suppose I slip up as much as anyone else when the times get ugly." He picked at the edge of the table for a moment. "It's not that easy, I guess. But it's me." He looked at her, his gaze frank. "I do all right," he repeated.

"How about your brother?" Karla asked. "How does he handle it?"

"He does okay, I suppose." She was watching him closely, but he couldn't make himself meet her eyes. If she noticed, she didn't say so.

"What's your brother like? Are you close?"

His expression soured for a moment, then he willed the lines of his face to smooth out. "He's . . . a lot like my dad," he finally said. "But not much like me."

Karla studied him without comment, and when he didn't say more the silence began to get uncomfortable. "I'm sorry," she said at last. "Was I out of line? I didn't mean to pry—"

Jude shook his head. "No, *I'm* the one who should apologize." He tapped a finger nervously against the tabletop, stopped when he realized what he was doing. "I . . . don't deal much with my brother. We don't think alike, and the truth is we don't get along very well."

"That's very sad," Karla said softly.

"Yeah," Jude said. "It is." He stared into space for a few seconds, then his eyes cleared and focused on her. His smile was genuine when the waiter appeared, standing at the side of the table and holding two platters of hot, aromatic food. Silence fell again, the agreeable kind, as they picked up the silverware and dug in. Winding down eventually and feeling for all the world like they could happily slip into food comas, then Karla looked up from her meal.

"Your mother must be one tough woman," she said. Her eyes were unreadable.

Jude pushed the remaining food around his plate thoughtfully. "I think she lives behind a wall," he said after a moment. "I don't think we have any idea. But she's steady as a rock most of the time, and you couldn't move her with a bulldozer if she didn't want to go."

"I'll bet."

"What about you?" He sat back, hoping the waiter would come and take the rest of the food away before he exploded.

"Trying to change the subject again?"

She smiled and he spread his hands. "Life's a compromise. I told you something, now it's your turn. I know where you work but nothing else. Not if you're originally from Chicago, how old you are, or anything."

Karla folded her hands neatly on the table. "Well, let's see. I *am* from Chicago, as a matter of fact. I grew up in the Cabrini Green projects, where my mother still lives."

Jude could help frowning. "Why does she stay there?"

"Because she won't move out," Karla told him levelly. "She works as a cleaning woman in a nursing home and she lives in the projects because that's all she can afford on her salary." Her grip on her juice glass tightened. "Pride makes her call my offers of help 'charity.' It's the most frustrating thing in my life." He nodded but said nothing, and could have sworn she looked relieved that he didn't start spewing out a bunch of unwanted advice. "Anyway," she continued, "that's where I grew up. I got out of Cabrini on a scholarship to Harold Washington College—back then it was still Loop College—and a student loan. I never went back." For the first time she broke the gaze and looked down. "I haven't been there since I started working at Burnett."

"You don't see your mother?"

"She visits occasionally, but I don't go to her. I don't . . . *fit*. The people who hang out there think I'm too successful, too *white*. They'd sooner tear me apart than look at me." Karla touched her fingers to her shoulders. "I'm not white, I'm just me. I got where I am by doing things differently from the way they're done in the 'hood. In Cabrini successful means cars, money and drugs, and if you're a woman, it's who you get to keep you or how much money you can make without getting stuck with too many babies. I saw all that when I was growing up and I thought, no way was I going to grow old like that, not stranded in a place where you were afraid to go to the grocery store or close your eyes at night." She stopped and looked a little embarrassed.

"So you went to Loop," Jude prompted. She nodded and looked relieved at the direction his question would take the conversation.

"That's where I met Evelyn—we had a few classes together. We hit it off well, and I'd discovered a roommate to split the rent on a ratty loft apartment off Milwaukee Avenue. She got someone to help her with the art classes she was stuck with, and I got a nurse."

"Oh?"

Karla smiled vaguely. "Just a quip."

"So you roomed together for four years?"

"Most of it. Evelyn didn't move in until the second semester of my first year—her second, but once she was in, she stayed. After that she went on to nursing school and met

Warren right after she graduated, during her training period in Cook County ER. He . . . filled something in her life. There's no reason for you to know, of course, but Evelyn had a . . . difficult childhood." Her gray eyes met his steadily. "Her mother was a borderline drug addict and alcoholic the entire time Evelyn was in high school, eating Benzedrine and amphetamines by the handful and washing the whole mess down with booze. Evelyn spent every spare moment trying to help her mom kick the habits, but she failed, something for which I don't think Evelyn can forgive herself."

Jude winced. "Did her mother overdose?"

Karla shook her head. "No, though I suspect the woman's lucky to be alive today. Evelyn and her father forced her into a rehab center, out of state and away from her drinking-and-partying buddies. The program worked, for a while, then she fell back into her old ways. By then Evelyn was in nursing school and her mom cleaned up her act on her own this time, then demanded a divorce from her dad. It wasn't a happy time for Evelyn, but then she met Warren. Like I said, he seemed to fit something in her that she needed very badly. They were married about six months later and she moved out, of course. I found another place—where I'm living now, actually—and I've been there ever since. I don't move around much." She flashed him a self-conscious smile. "I'm sorry. I'm rattling."

"Not at all." Jude looked at her quizzically. "You said you've been living there awhile. Do you own the place?"

"What? Oh, I see—no, I'm a tenant. Warren and Evelyn bought the building when it went up for sale about five years ago, before property got expensive in the area. I told them about it. I knew they'd find the location perfect—both of them can get to work within twenty minutes."

"Good call on the building," Jude commented, then hesitated. "Speaking of Evelyn, she looks pretty bad, doesn't she? Is she sick?"

"I don't know, to tell you the truth. The attack Friday night did a pretty bad job on her mind—"

"Of course."

"—and she's saying some wild stuff." Distracted, Karla peered into the bottom of her juice, then swirled the melting ice cubes a few times. "I think we'll give it another day or so, and see how she is then. Okay?"

" 'Nuff said," Jude agreed, though he had to wonder if Evelyn had told the same fantastic tale to Karla as he'd heard in the hospital. "By the way, how'd your presentation at work go?"

"It's finished." Karla's voice was clearly relieved, then she laughed ruefully. "Now we move on to the next one. *Ad infinitum*."

"Dessert?" The waiter slid the question smoothly into the conversation at the tail end of her sentence and looked at them both expectantly. "We have fine pastries, made here and honey-dipped."

Karla groaned and motioned to Jude. "Tempting, but I couldn't eat another bite. You go ahead."

Jude patted his stomach and shook his head. "No thanks. Got to watch my girlish figure. We'll have the check, please." The waiter nodded and moved away.

"May I pitch in?" Karla asked when the man returned with their bill and placed it discreetly on the table. "At least let me leave the tip."

"Not this time. How about a trade instead? I'd like to try some of that terrible cooking you bragged about. I can be adventuresome." He dropped a pile of bills on the table and tucked his wallet into his back pocket.

Karla rolled her eyes as they stood and made their way out of the restaurant. "Oh boy, and would you be sorry, too. I *hate* cooking and believe me when I say it shows in the end product. How about if I treat next time and I really do pick the place?"

Jude grinned. "Nothing beats a woman who says what she thinks."

"And do you?"

"What? Say what I think? On the job, no. But in my personal life, honesty saves a whole lot of grief. I hate playing games with people's heads." He held the door open for her, then followed her out. The sun had set while they ate and the front of the restaurant was awash in the soft light spilling through the plate-glass window from its interior. Karla was, he thought, an extraordinarily beautiful woman and he enjoyed the chance to admire the candle-soft glow accenting the blond streaks in the darker, reddish brown of her curly hair. She stood tolerantly, staring back at him for a second or two, then finally smiled uncomfortably.

"Something on your mind, Detective?"

That schoolboy nervousness again; it had faded during their comfortable conversation but returned now with a healthy twirl in the pit of his full stomach. "Yes, now that you mention it. I was thinking about your invitation to treat me to dinner, and wondering when this was going to take place."

"Well, my schedule is fairly predictable, nine to five weekdays with lots of overtime." She tossed her hair back. "But I make room for food, and I've always thought sleep was a supreme waste of time anyway. You're the one with odd hours—up all night, sleep all day, and probably staggered workdays to boot. When's *your* next night off?"

"Tomorrow," he said promptly. "And I'm free."

Karla looked positively delighted.

24

"Isman, wake up. Wake up *now*." Lillith Jerusha shook her husband's broad shoulder again, harder this time, and he finally mumbled something into his pillowcase. "I can't *hear* you with your mouth full of goose feathers," she said testily. "Will you take your face out of the pillow and get the *fuck up*?"

"What—!"

That did it, she noted with some satisfaction. What was he doing in bed at nine o'clock anyway? He should be downstairs with her, watching some silly television show, sharing a bottle of sweet Hungarian merlot, sharing her *life*, for God's sake. Maybe then none of this mess would have happened.

"What's wrong?" he managed to croak as he struggled upright. That was another thing: Isman was a big man but not overweight, healthy and strong—like Cecil, she thought with a hint of melancholy—and more than capable of making her feel loved. She didn't need sex for that, just his company. His hair was rumpled and thinning on the top and the back, but that didn't matter either. She hadn't married him twenty-five years ago for his hair.

Now Lillith stood at the side of their king-size bed and she might as well have been staring down at a stranger, that's how much they'd talked in the last two months. Looking back, it was amazing that she'd ended the relationship with Cecil on force of will. She'd certainly gotten no impetus to do it on the homefront.

"Tell me something," she demanded. She imagined what she must look like from above, her lithe body all decked out in a pink-and-gold silk peignoir set and her puny fists bunched at her sides, trying to look threatening at a man half lying on a huge, square bed. Nothing to do now but keep going. "What were you *doing* all those nights that you left me alone?"

"I don't understand," Isman said. His voice was getting that spoiled "go away you're bothering me" crankiness with which she'd become familiar very early in their marriage. "You woke me up for this?"

Lillith jabbed him in the right shoulder with a knuckle, hard—

"Hey!"

—and bent closer. "I asked you what the hell you've been doing all these months—screw it, all these *years*, almost every damned evening. I want to know. I want to know if it's been worth it." Fear in his eyes then, a little. Did he still care about her, about their marriage? It was time to find out.

"What are you talking about, Lillith?" He was starting to pay attention now. "I've been working, working *hard*. For us. I—"

"Is that all?"

"Yes!" he snapped, suddenly *very* wide-awake. "I haven't been keeping a mistress, if that's what you're aiming at. I've never been unfaithful to you."

Lillith straightened up again and stared at him. "Really?" She lifted her chin. "That's wonderful, Isman. I'm so proud of you. Now would you like to know what *I've* been doing? Especially over the past year? *Because that's how long it's been since you bothered to ask, damn you!*" She couldn't help it, she screamed the last words right into his shocked face.

He grabbed at the covers and started to pull them aside, intent on standing up. Maybe he was, finally, going to take her in an embrace; ironically, she didn't want him to touch her, not right now. "Lillith, honey, I'm sorry—"

It was amazing how much strength she found in her arms, more than enough to shove him back down; she supposed it was the boring aerobics classes she faithfully attended, three times a week, every week, keep that youthful waistline and your husband's attention. What a joke. "Then let me tell you what's been on *my* agenda, Mr. Aspiring CEO." To her ears, her voice had never sounded so cold. "While you've been making love to your corporate loan applications and your mergers and your acquisitions and your projects, I've been lonely. While you've been pushing me back to my edge of the bed every time I accidentally touch you in the middle of the night, I've been *crying*. So I've been *fucking* another man." Isman's face went ghost white, but Lillith felt no regrets, no sir, at least not about telling the truth. If she was going to wipe the blackboard clean, she was going to beat out the damned eraser, too.

"And now my ex-*lover* is killing women *who look like me!*"

"It was the news broadcast that did it," Lillith said woodenly. She was sitting at the mahogany table in the formal dining room, the polished wood stretching away to seat twelve easily and when was the last time it'd been used? "They said they had a suspect, and I thought oh good, it's over, and then they said the police let him go. That it was the wrong man." She turned her head and looked at her husband. "Do you know what day it is, Isman?"

"Wednesday."

Lillith faced away from him again. She wasn't crying right now, not yet, but soon; she could feel the same old tears of bewildered frustration that were always so near the surface every time she looked at this man whom she idolized, but who had been so blissfully *careless* with her love for so long. "Yes. It's Wednesday. He's killed someone four out of the last five weekends, did you know that? The woman last weekend survived, but the police say it was a fluke, that she should have been dead. I've seen all their pictures," she continued. Her voice sounded low and dull, like someone droning into a microphone. "Just a glimpse on television, but enough to know it's me he thinks he's killing over and over." Her head dropped forward and she covered her face with her hands, but she still didn't cry.

"You have to call the police," Isman said. He hadn't bothered changing out of his heavy satin pajamas, and the two of them looked like some ridiculously romantic couple from the pages of a Victoria's Secret catalog. "You have to tell them everything."

"When should I leave?" she asked suddenly, raising her head. "How long do I have?" The air-conditioning was turned down and the house was warm—she'd never been able to sleep in the cold—but Lillith felt like she was sitting in a refrigerator as she waited for her husband's answer. Beneath her gown, her legs were shaking.

Isman stared at her, his face rigid except for his eyes, still lake blue and clear, but slightly misty. "I . . . don't believe you should go at all, Lillith. Unless you want to, of course. Then I wouldn't stop you." He dropped his gaze and focused on the floor. "I wish you would stay," he said softly. "I love you. I'm so sorry that it's come to this before I was smart enough to tell you."

Lillith's first impulse was to laugh, but it faded as quickly as it had come. "You mean you don't want a divorce?"

Isman scowled. "No, I don't want a divorce." He pulled his chair around until he faced her. "That's not what marriage is about. It's for keeps, remember? In good times and bad? We've had our share of good times, I think, and maybe it's time we learned to weather the bad as well."

"But this—"

"Is perhaps more than most people could take, but we're not weaklings, Lillith. *I'm* not. I'm here for you, and I swear to God I'll never let you down again."

She felt her shoulders start to shake the same as her legs and fought it desperately. "Isman, I'm *so* sorry. I never intended this to happen, I never planned on having an affair, or looked for it or tried to start one. Please—" Tears then, and why fight it after all? Her heart was breaking under its load of guilt and shame and deadly knowledge. She found her hands gripping the cool blue satin of his pajamas at each shoulder, holding on for dear life as if she would drown if she let go. "Please, just . . . try to forgive me. We'll try again, and I promise on my soul, on our *son*, that it will never happen again."

God love him, Isman was crying, crying and smiling and holding her in his arms for the first time in months.

"You don't have to do it this way, Lillith. I'm not sure you should even try. I'll stand by you no matter what happens." Isman kept his voice low but his face might as well have glowed for the sincerity beaming from it. Lillith couldn't help smiling, though she knew her lips, and probably her voice, were trembling.

"We'll do it like this at first and hope it's enough," she said stubbornly. "There's no sense tearing down everything you've worked for—your reputation, your career, our privacy—if we don't have to." She pulled her gaze away from her husband's, almost afraid of the strength and the love she saw there. God, if only she'd seen it, *asked* for it, years ago. Her shabby liaison with Cecil Gideon wasn't Isman's fault, it was her own; she'd let boredom blind her to the real wealth in her own home and in her husband's heart.

"Please, God," she whispered so softly that Isman, standing right next to her, couldn't hear. "Please let this be enough." Lillith's palms were slick with perspiration and she rubbed them against the sides of her slacks absently, then curled and uncurled her fingers. "Please," she repeated. They were in suburban Lincolnwood, parked at a drive-up phone booth at the corner of Devon and something-or-the-other, she had no idea what the name of the cross street was. She could feel Isman's gaze boring into her as she picked up the receiver of the pay telephone.

Lillith's fingers were cold, like long, white icicles, but they felt like they were touching live coals as she carefully punched in the number of the Foster Avenue Police Station.

Cecil knew it was a mistake the minute he decided to do it, but he called Lillith's house anyway, just to hear her voice but half hoping she wouldn't be home so he wouldn't have to suffer the agony. He got his wish and the housekeeper or maid or whatever the hell she was told him in a stuffy voice that "*The missus and mister have gone out for the evening.*" He thought for a second that he'd go nuts, right there on the telephone, reach right through the fucking line and squeeze that snotty voice clean out of the puny mouth that was uttering it. He slammed the receiver down instead and it broke, infuriating him further. Before he knew it his new Ameritech Touch-Tone was strewn in about sixteen pieces across the living-room couch and carpet, and he was holding nothing but the coiled cord he'd used to swing it around and around and . . .

"Christ," he said. "Maybe that's the smartest move you've made all week, Cecil Old Boy. Damn, but that woman makes me angry." He got up and went to get the broom and dustpan, then headed for the bedroom instead, not caring about the crushed plastic on the floor in the other room. He'd go for a run, he decided. He was reaching for fresh shorts and a clean tee before he realized that it was way too late, damn near midnight and he had to go to work in the morning. Lately though, these urges to run at odd times had started to get the best of him and he was giving in more often because he liked the feel of pounding the pavement so much. Still, it was good to know that in a pinch common sense could take over and talk him out of it.

This time.

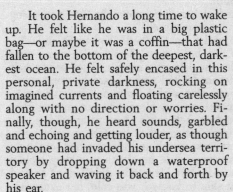

25

It took Hernando a long time to wake up. He felt like he was in a big plastic bag—or maybe it was a coffin—that had fallen to the bottom of the deepest, darkest ocean. He felt safely encased in this personal, private darkness, rocking on imagined currents and floating carelessly along with no direction or worries. Finally, though, he heard sounds, garbled and echoing and getting louder, as though someone had invaded his undersea territory by dropping down a waterproof speaker and waving it back and forth by his ear.

"Hernando, man, you'd better get up. Come *on*!" Tho's voice, hissing and close, as if to talk any louder might attract unwanted attention. Struggling to sit up, Hernando realized he couldn't feel his hands or feet, but Tho didn't give him any time to think about it. The wiry man pulled him out of the bed with deceptively strong arms. "Get your ass in the bathroom," Tho ordered. "Your woman's on the floor and it don't look good."

"What—Carissa? Did she pass out?"

"You better hope it's that simple," Tho said grimly. Hernando pushed by him and stumbled to the bathroom, mentally cursing his feet when they dragged instead of working properly. He made it to the door but couldn't see past the other three people crowded around Carissa's prone body.

"Get the fuck out of the way!" he barked. Maralina was crying and whining and trying to shake Carissa's shoulder, and if his brother hadn't been there, Hernando would have slapped her and *given* the silly bitch something to cry about. Adelpho looked at him with frightened eyes and grabbed his wife by the hand; he had to pull hard before she'd move. Tho's nameless new girlfriend stood her ground and glared at him, her face rigid.

"She's dead," she said. "While you were sleeping she died in this bathroom."

Hernando stared at her dispassionately. "Are you going to move or do I move you myself?"

"You heartless prick," she sneered. "You try it and—"

"Get your ass out here, *now*." Tho's voice came over Hernando's shoulder; he'd known his friend for nearly half his lifetime, but Hernando had never heard his tone so vicious. The broad, bony planes of the woman's face twisted in anger, but she stepped around Hernando without another word. Finally, he had enough room to move around.

"Carissa?" He knelt and touched her face, a useless gesture since his fingers were numb and the tips had somehow sunken in on themselves while he slept; now they looked like mini–emery boards. But Hernando didn't need to feel Carissa's grayed-out skin to know it was cold; her eyes were open and dull, moistureless, and her lips were a fine shade of purplish blue. "Oh, fuck," he muttered. Had she taken something, coke, downers, what? He glanced down at the swell of Carissa's belly, then saw the darker stain mapped on the fabric of her thighs; when he tugged on the bath mat beneath her hips, the section that slid from underneath her was scarlet with still-wet blood.

She was dead all right, as dead as he'd been in the emergency room of Illinois Masonic the other night. Crouched next to her corpse with the memory of his own reawakening filling his mind, a sudden thought bloomed in Hernando. On the heels of that, instant, fierce *need*.

Everything around the two of them faded, the bathroom, his companions still babbling and arguing outside the door, the floor underneath his feet. There was only him, and Carissa, and a vibrant, escalating song of desperation in his head, that question that *must* be answered:

What that nurse had done to him . . .

Could he do the same to Carissa?

Hernando didn't care if she came back to life or not; all he wanted in the world was to quell the dark, undeniable hunger that was roaring through every pore in his body.

With his back to the door, Hernando buried his nerveless fingers within the dark curls of Carissa's hair and pulled her head back until her face was tilted up, then crushed his mouth over her bloodless lips. Vague memories of the times they'd been together bobbed unbidden in his brain. The skin of her mouth was dry, then went unexpectedly *hot*, a strange, instant transformation from frigid to hot that sent rapture rocketing through his body, bunching his muscles and making him nearly lift her limp body off the floor by her hair and neck alone. A faint burn on his eyelids—the slits of Carissa's half-opened eyes were glowing a deep, lava red—was followed instantly by a mind-numbing roaring in his ears. Kneeling with his girlfriend's body in the cold puddle of her blood, he let a frenzied hurricane of sound sweep him along, surge his senses up and up and then drop him. Again it swelled and ebbed, and again, and under it all his deep, keening sound as feeling returned momentarily to his hands and feet, and he felt, ultimately—

Carissa's arms, wrapping themselves around his neck of their own volition as she returned his fierce kiss.

"I'm telling you she was *dead*." The Vietnamese woman's expression was obstinate and obviously ready for an argument.

"Bullshit," Hernando said. "She passed out. Didn't you, baby?"

"Well, I'm obviously not dead now, am I?" Carissa sat calmly on the edge of the tub, surveying the bunch of them like some queen holding court. Hernando kept wondering how long it would be before somebody noticed the bloody bath mat tangled between Carissa's feet, or the deep red stains on her lap. But no one did. Then again, Hernando was shirtless and none of his roommates seemed to notice that his chest was carrying the ever-so-faint image of shotgun holes and a huge surgical incision either. He had no idea what the fuck was going on here, but he could play along with anything if he had to. The only sad thing was his hands and feet had already lost all feeling again.

"Carissa?" Maralina slipped around Hernando and went to her friend's side. "Do you feel okay? With the baby, I mean?" Hernando watched, his face carefully expressionless, as his young sister-in-law stepped next to Carissa, then bent and picked up the scarlet-soaked bath mat with her bare hands. "We can, you know, get you a doctor or take you to one if you want. It don't matter about the money. We can find a way." Folding the bloody square of fabric now and draping it over the end of the tub, it was a miracle none of it smeared onto her skin. How could she—or any of the others—*not* see the blood?

Carissa stared at Maralina, then her expression melted into forced warmth. "That's okay, I'm fine. Really." She gave the younger woman a reassuring smile and a pat on the arm, and Hernando caught a flash of her surprise as Carissa first realized something odd was happening to her fingers. "You go on out," she added. "I have to use the bathroom."

Maralina nodded and rose, shooting Hernando an embarrassed glance when he made no move to follow her. Instead, he pushed the door closed and stood with his back against it, watching his pregnant girlfriend. "So," he finally said, waiting.

Carissa flexed her fingers thoughtfully, then looked up at him. When she spoke, her voice was calm and completely emotionless.

"I can see the holes in your chest, Hernando."

26

Thursday—Late Afternoon

I must have been out of my mind to agree to this, Evelyn thought. On the other hand, she really hadn't been able to say no; the woman for whom she was covering this afternoon had pulled a graveyard shift on Warren's birthday several weeks ago so that Evelyn could have that night off. While they had originally planned to trade off during the same week, some sort of scheduling situation had made her friend want her night later than expected.

So here Evelyn was, working the ER at five in the afternoon and struggling with an uncooperative pen as she tried to fill out a referral form. She should've just been getting up, if only to wander around like a zombie and puzzle about what exactly was wrong with her. She'd been in the medical profession for more than a decade; she might not be a doctor but she knew the symptoms for nearly every common disease, and a few of the rarer ones as well. But this . . .

She felt *tainted*, as if the rapist murderer who'd attacked her nearly a week ago had been the springboard for something that teenager had given her—yet she couldn't bear to ask for help. ER people, the technicians, trauma nurses, doctors—they didn't *get* sick, or get attacked or violated, or become involved in anything that put them on the other side of the stainless-steel carts the paramedics rolled into the emergency room every night. They didn't play with guns, share needles, or flirt with someone else's girlfriend in a bar filled with leather-jacketed bikers—

Though sometimes they walked alone too late at night.

Damn this pen, Evelyn thought irritably. And double-damn this stupid chart and all the nosy questions it asks. Writing had become more of a struggle with each passing day. For an hour or so after she'd . . . been in *contact* with that criminal in the ER on Tuesday night, her hands and feet had been normal again. That was ridiculous, of course, because if the tips of a person's fingers and toes were dehydrated and dead, there wasn't a thing you could do to restore the damaged flesh. It was *dead*, and it stayed that way; pretty much the way her fingers and toes looked now, as a matter of fact. Thank God for disposable plastic gloves and lots of baby powder. Her feet were encased in shoes, of course, but her hands . . . well, she hadn't worked without these gloves on all week. She'd been telling people her hands were so badly chapped that the skin had cracked open and bled, and no one asked beyond that. Another constant challenge was the matter of maintaining her balance when she couldn't feel her feet.

"Crap," she murmured. It was hard enough to hang on to the small stuff—pens, syringes, those tiny paper cups that held medication—without this idiot pen skipping like this. Twice she tried shaking it; the third time she dropped it on the floor. Cursing under her breath, she bent to retrieve it; her hand snagged the pen as a wheelchair came rolling into her field of vision. She pushed backward and straightened up in time to get out of the way. "Excuse me," she said automatically to the orderly and the patient he was wheeling down the hall. "Didn't mean to block traffic." As she stepped aside the orderly nodded mechanically and started to keep going, but when the elderly man seated in the chair glanced up at Evelyn, he gave a cry of shock.

"Good God! What happened to your face?"

She should have stayed where she was, turned her back to the guy and ignored him, or better, headed down the hall in the opposite direction as though it was assumed he wasn't talking to her. While Evelyn's thoughts were much too sluggish for that kind of reasoning, her reflexes were still about the same: instinctively, she whirled to face the speaker. Her bruises had disappeared Tuesday night, then returned after a couple of hours. She knew also that her color wasn't very good—more a grayish brown than the former healthy tan— and that the bruises from the attack were fairly visible. But were they so apparent that a stranger would forget his manners and have an outburst like this?

Unless what he saw wasn't what everyone else did . . .

Unless it was what *she* saw when she looked in the mirror.

" 'Scuse me," Evelyn mumbled to the bewildered orderly. "I'm needed, uh—somewhere else." She clutched the pen and chart and got the hell out of there, the orderly's words of reassurance to the patient following her down the hall until she ducked onto an elevator headed . . . which way? Up; that was enough to get her away from the guy in the wheelchair. As the bell indicating the top floor rang and she punched the button to return to the first floor, Evelyn finally focused on her surroundings. There was no one else in the mirrored elevator with her.

Except her own beaten and bloody reflection.

"So, like, did you know that guy or something?"

Evelyn looked up from her untouched dinner plate and saw the young orderly from a couple of hours ago standing on the other side of the cafeteria table. His ID card wasn't pinned on his smock, a flagrant violation of hospital policy, but she didn't care; she didn't want to know his name. "No."

"I was wondering, you know, since he acted like he knew you or something. I mean, everybody around here knows what happened to you and all."

She felt a flash of anger that immediately faded to apathy. She hoped this guy didn't decide to sit across from her and yap; she wasn't in the mood, and she certainly wasn't fond of the idea of discussing with a pimply-faced stranger how she'd been raped and strangled, and how she didn't remember or care about who'd done it. Her indifference did not make for a good reputation with her female coworkers, and in all honesty she didn't understand it herself. "I don't know him."

The orderly shrugged. "It don't matter. Guy went home, though it's a freakin' miracle. Acting like he did when he seen you, he could've gone right back into cardiac arrest. People just don't know when to chill, you know?" He shrugged again and turned to go. "I'll see ya around."

"Wait a second," Evelyn said. The young man paused and looked at her expectantly. "That man, do you remember his name?"

"Sure, only 'cause it's kinda weird, not like Joe or Bob or something. It's Anstice Corwin—C-O-R-W-I-N." He peered at her. "Why?"

"I—just wondering, that's all. Thanks."

"Anytime." He looked around the room, then headed for the Pepsi machine in the corner.

Evelyn rose and dumped her full plate of food on the bus tray, her mind shying away from the question of when she'd last eaten or drunk liquids—the answer was easy but way too disturbing to think about. The orderly had mentioned that Anstice Corwin had experienced a cardiac arrest, and it was easy to make a small stop at one of the computer terminals in a private staff office and call up his records.

> Anstice Corwin, age 69, Admitted 03 June by accelerated transport. Arrived in cardiac arrest, bp 0/0, flatline heart monitor, pupils unreactive, 0 respirations . . .

More data, scrawled microfiche notes, medications. Obviously the man was very much alive now, though he'd certainly been in defib when the paramedics had brought him

in. Evelyn found the answer to her curiosity on page two of
Mr. Corwin's chart:

Total cardiac arrest time 32 minutes.

Dead, like she'd been, but probably longer. Unlike her
own immediate dark resurrection, the trauma team had kept
Anstice Corwin's body full of circulating oxygenated blood,
then brought him back via the miracles of modern medicine.
But his journey had still given him the ability to see her brutal injuries as if he'd been there on the night she'd gotten
them.

Evelyn signed off the computer and thought of Jason
Spiro, and the snakebites that pocked his face and neck.

Somewhere in the city tonight walked a murderous
young man with a yawning hole where his chest should be.

27

"Hernando, was I really dead?"

Carissa's voice floated somewhere in the deep shadows over him; the ceiling lightbulb was off and he'd blacked out the one window to prevent the starlight from seeping inside. He liked it better in the dark. "Yeah."

"And you were dead too, that night after you hit the liquor store." A statement, not a question; nevertheless, he answered.

"Yeah."

She shifted and her hip brushed against his leg. Their sex had been clammy and perverse, dry tongues exploring skin that was too cool to be normal. Both moved away now that it was over, not wanting to touch. Silence again, the slow, annoying tick of the second hand in the old electric clock on the chest of drawers. Finally, the crucial question.

"How did you *know* you could bring me back to life?"

Despite the absence of light, Hernando could still see her silhouette, face turned slightly toward him, heavy breasts, the high mound of her belly. A tiny light leak somewhere, just enough ... or maybe his night vision had become enhanced. He didn't know. "I did, that's all. Like I told you. That nurse did it to me, and I knew I could do it to you." His mouth stretched in a grin. "I bet you could do it now, too."

"Why should I?"

He pushed up on one elbow, leaned over her to be sure she was paying attention. "Don't you feel hungry yet? *Empty?* You do it because it feels *good*, Carissa. Like nothing else you've ever done, *nothing*. Not dope or acid, not even crack." Hernando flopped onto his back again and laughed. "You wait, you'll see. Give it time, and you'll *want* it."

"Really?"

Hernando didn't bother to answer. He didn't have to.

"Across the street," Hernando said. "See her? Coming out of the courtyard building."

Carissa followed the direction of her boyfriend's pointing finger. Squinting in the darkness, she could barely make out the small woman across the four-lane width of Ashland Avenue, her view interrupted by the occasional swiftly passing car. It wasn't all that late, barely ten o'clock, but this babe must live in a building full of old folks. Almost every window on all three sides of the deep rectangle of space splitting the building was darkened; the soft yellow lighting at ground level was romantic but cheap and spread much too far apart to be of any use. The woman wasn't that big and she was walking one of those long, tan dogs with tiny legs, the kind that looked like they ought to be roasted and stuffed into a bun. The thought made Carissa giggle out loud.

Hernando didn't notice, but his grip on her wrist tightened and he pulled her with him as he crossed the street, weaving between the sparse traffic. "We'll take her when she comes back."

"How?"

"With this." He pulled something long and thin from the pocket of his blue jeans, a bundle of stainless-steel wires, hand-twisted into a homemade garrote. "She won't be able to make a sound."

For the first time Carissa felt a stirring of nervousness, a fleeting twinge of guilt. "I don't know, Hernando. I never killed nobody before. What if we get caught? I mean . . . murder? They can execute you for that."

He snickered and guided her quickly down the walkway leading into the courtyard of the woman's building, then off to the side. "Don't be stupid, Carissa. How can it be murder if we bring her back to life? What's she gonna say to the cops if we *do* get pinched? 'Arrest these two, they killed me.' " His mirth started to grow into a full laugh and he muffled it with effort. "I don't think so. We'll stay behind her the whole time—she'll never see us."

Carissa's face, the skin already much more pale than before this afternoon, seemed to float above the thick bushes behind which they lingered. "But what if I can't do it like you? What if I try to bring her back but it doesn't work?"

"It'll *work*," Hernando said impatiently. "Now shut up or she'll hear us. Stop worrying—you're bitching about nothing."

Carissa looked like she was going to say something else, then closed her mouth and settled down to wait.

Alysson Lane tugged on Coco's collar and tried to pull him down the walkway leading to her building. "Come on, boy. What's the matter with you?" She couldn't understand his reluctance to go home—he *never* pulled against his leash. It was almost as if he knew it was useless to pit his nine pounds against her weight and besides, she'd owned Coco for almost seven years. After a while you learned who was boss, even if you were only a spoiled wiener dog. But this time her sharp tone of voice went over his head, another indication that something was seriously off-kilter. "Oh, for Pete's sake," she finally said. She bent and scooped his struggling body into her arms, letting the strap of her purse slide down her shoulder and rest in the crook of her elbow. She didn't want to drag him—he'd end up scraping his legs and then she'd feel guilty. Still, he should have quieted once he was in her hold, but he was fighting harder, actually growling now. "Coco, what on earth is the matter with you?" she repeated, bewilderment creasing her forehead. "I don't—"

Her air was *gone.*

No warning, unless she could count the brief hiss as something thin and cold whistled past her face from above and buried itself deep in the flesh of her neck. With no way to breathe, there was no way to scream. The dog in her embrace, hardly heavier than a large bag of potatoes, went completely crazy as he clawed and snapped his way out of his mistress's suddenly too tight grip; she never felt it. When her hands opened and she dropped him, the dog landed hard on his hind end. He yelped once, then ran like hell for the deeper recesses of the courtyard and away from the two dead-smelling things that had frightened him so badly to begin with.

Alysson's thin fingers instinctively and uselessly clawed at her throat. The last thing she saw was the winking out of the stars, far overhead.

Hernando and Carissa stood over the woman's stilled body, two black figures moving within the darker shadows of the landscaping. It hadn't taken long to kill her, two minutes of Hernando's muscular arms holding the garrote tight while their victim put up a feeble struggle. Carissa hadn't had to lift a finger. Now the woman lay at her feet like a primitive sacrifice, blond hair tangled around eyes that were open and staring into a realm Carissa had visited but of which she retained no memory.

Carissa knelt next to the body as Hernando pocketed his weapon. She was fascinated by the stillness of this woman who had been moving only a few minutes before, at her peaceful face and those open eyes. There was enough of a reflection from somewhere to see that they were dark blue. "What do I do?" she whispered; her skin felt odd, numb and twitchy at the same time, a disturbing sensation that was growing stronger as each second passed.

"Kiss her," Hernando instructed in a low, shaking voice. Carissa glanced quickly up at him; for an instant she'd thought he was just being kinky and was about to tell him this was a stupid time to try and get his rocks off. But his face looked pinched and hollow, *strained*, like a junkie standing over a double score of crack he knows he can't have. Sudden knowledge bloomed in her mind, a cold, physically felt greed following on its heels—*She's mine!*—and she ducked her head and covered the woman's lips with her own.

Liquid fire swept through her, exploding within her mouth and stealing her oxygen, spiraling down the nerve endings and hitting her heart, lungs, the baby in her womb, her groin, all the way down to her toes. Burning her, consuming her until she felt like she could curl into a fetal position, like the crisped corpses hauled out of fiery buildings or airplane crashes. All the narcotics in a lifetime would never feel like this, and in the blurred semiconsciousness of this most secret and corrupt form of bliss, as she felt the woman's mouth open beneath hers and draw in air, Carissa knew she was bound to this sensation as she had been to no other drug in her life. . . .

Carissa came to her senses when Hernando hauled her rudely to her feet. "Get up, stupid," he hissed. "She's coming back, like I told you—let's get out of here!" Carissa shuddered and hugged herself, feeling the last tingles dart away as she stared at their victim. Her neck was sparkling—no, glowing, a rich orange red yellow, like the end of a blown-out match. Next to her, Hernando had the woman's purse in his other hand and by the time Carissa had found some sort of balance, he had rummaged through it and taken her money, just for the hell of it.

And they booked, and left a woman named Alysson Lane to open her eyes in the darkness and wonder what in the hell had happened to her.

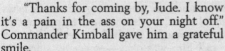

28

"Thanks for coming by, Jude. I know it's a pain in the ass on your night off." Commander Kimball gave him a grateful smile.

Jude Ewing was sitting on the stiff wooden chair across from Renny Kimball, a huge and rumpled pile of papers making a barrier between them that he was certain was supported somewhere by a desktop. Nobody could have a pile of papers that high; he hoped to God none of his own paperwork or the evidence on any of his cases was buried in the mounds tipping in at least five different directions, each one more precarious than the last. Ewing put the disturbing thought out of his mind and shrugged. "It's not like I live on the other side of the city, you know." He scraped a hand over his face and felt the healthy stubble of a light-colored beard trying to take root there; he'd showered but hadn't had a chance to shave yet, and if he didn't, he'd look like

some kind of baby Viking when it was time to pick Karla up
for their date.

"Yeah, and that's a piece of trivia I wouldn't be too generous with, if I were you."

"Little too late for that, Commander. I've been in this
neighborhood for most of my life." As he watched, his senior
officer pulled together a pile of papers to make a surface on
which to write rather than clear a spot on the desktop. The
desk was so disorganized it was frightening.

Kimball stared at him a moment, his eyebrows raised.
"Well, if you want to spend your free time running in and
out of here, it's not my business. That's why I thought you'd
probably want to hear the tape of this call while it's still
somewhat hot. I ran it by your partner early this morning,
and she said as long as she knew about it not to wake you
up. That's why we waited until now to call you in to hear it."

"That's fine." At four in the afternoon, Ewing was still
groggy—not enough caffeine yet, he supposed—and he sti-
fled the semisarcastic *thanks for not waking me up in what
constitutes my middle of the night* that wanted to pop out of
his mouth. He liked Commander Kimball, he really did, and
the decision not to call him was okay—especially since it'd
been Sandra's rather than Kimball's. Who better than his
longtime partner to know what was hot enough to warrant
calling him at home? Still, Kimball was always trying to
make decisions about what the cops at the station house
should or shouldn't do on their personal time. That trait
flickered between annoying and intolerable on Ewing's mental list of pet peeves depending on how bad his day was going, like a piece of gravel in his shoe that never stayed in one
place and therefore didn't bother him all the time.

"The call came in at ten-oh-three last night, and we did
try to call you then, but there was no answer. We're guessing
the call was timed perfectly with the ten o'clock broadcasts
about the Ravenswood Strangler. Listen to this." Kimball
pushed the play button on a reel-to-reel shoved among the
piles on his desk and the eerie static of dead air momentarily
filled the room, followed by the voice of the desk sergeant
who'd been on duty downstairs that evening.

"*Foster Avenue Station, Sergeant Lance speaking. Can I
help you?*"

"I . . . I know who the Ravenswood Strangler is. His name is Cecil Gideon and he lives at 2943 Pine Grove."

"Would you hold on, ma'am? I'll connect you to one of the detectives and he'll take all the information."

"No! I—I mean, I'm not going to tell you my name anyway, so it doesn't matter who I talk to. Just listen, okay? And if you put me on hold, I'll hang up. Is that clear?"

There wasn't a pause in Lance's voice here, and Ewing could imagine the man's training kicking in as he must have motioned to another cop to ID the phone number and get a car to its location.

"Yes, ma'am, completely. You said his name is Gideon? How do you spell that?"

"G-I-D-E-O-N. He's tall, about six-two, with brown hair and brown eyes. He's got a very athletic build. He works at an accounting firm downtown."

"Which one?"

"Coopers & Lybrand."

"All right. What makes you think this Gideon fellow is the Ravenswood Strangler?"

"Because the killings started right after Cecil and I broke up. We . . . had an affair, you see, and I broke it off. You have to understand, all these women who've died—I've seen their photographs on the television. Black hair, green eyes . . . they all look like me."

"I see."

"You can't tell it from the news or the papers, of course, but I'll bet they're all fairly tall, too. Over five-seven, anyway, and built slender, aren't they?"

"I'm sorry, I can't disclose that information. Why—"

"I have to go. I've been on the telephone too long as it is—I know you've got a police car on the way here right now. Please, just—stop him, all right? Before he does it again."

"That's all of it." Kimball abruptly punched the stop button. "You can tell she was starting to panic at the end, probably afraid a patrol car was to show. The call was made from a pay phone on the corner of Devon and St. Louis. The Lincolnwood PD had a car there within three minutes of the woman hanging up, but no one was around. A complete dead end."

"Did you expect anything else?" Ewing asked dryly.

"Anyone who watches television knows the cops always trace calls and they'd have to be an idiot not to realize we have an industrial version of Caller ID. It's obvious she's intelligent, probably upper-class suburban purposely going to a different suburb to make the call. Sure, we know—or we *think* we know what she looks like, but unless this Cecil Gideon guy turns out to be our man—or she calls again and decides to tell us—we'll probably never know who she is. What's being done about Gideon?"

Kimball sat back. "The usual routine. Can't do much based on a telephone call. He's under surveillance, of course, and we did discreetly check Coopers & Lybrand. He's an employee, all right. Junior partner; he's been there for six years. You know the drill: solid citizen, lived at the same address for a decade, dependable at work, same checking and savings accounts since he graduated college, et cetera, et cetera. All of which means nothing when something goes haywire upstairs." He tapped his forehead for emphasis. "The woman's claim that as his ex-lover she looks like all the murder victims means nothing unless we see her in person and can verify this. At this point we don't have enough to pull him in for interrogation. There are certain things that seem questionable, obviously."

Ewing leaned forward on his chair. "Oh?"

"Well, his address is close in proximity to the murders—"

"Along with about thirty thousand others," Ewing retorted.

"—and he does fit the physical description given by the Pelagi woman of her attacker, and also by Jason Spiro of the jogger he saw on the night of her attack."

"Like I said, him and about thirty thousand others."

Kimball gave him a smug smile and crossed his arms behind his head. "But I've saved the best for last, Jude."

"What's that?"

Kimball's face turned serious and he uncrossed his arms, placing his palms flat on the top of the desk. "You know we can't get too close given what info we have, not yet. But Jude, all the reports indicate that Cecil Gideon has two good-sized scratches right across his face."

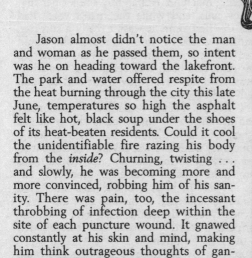

29

Jason almost didn't notice the man and woman as he passed them, so intent was he on heading toward the lakefront. The park and water offered respite from the heat burning through the city this late June, temperatures so high the asphalt felt like hot, black soup under the shoes of its heat-beaten residents. Could it cool the unidentifiable fire razing his body from the *inside*? Churning, twisting . . . and slowly, he was becoming more and more convinced, robbing him of his sanity. There was pain, too, the incessant throbbing of infection deep within the site of each puncture wound. It gnawed constantly at his skin and mind, making him think outrageous thoughts of gangrene and dying from ghostly wounds that no one else could see.

Nearly a week—six nights, to be exact—had passed since he'd resurrected Evelyn Pelagi and she had yet to seek him out. She could easily find him by going to

Detective Ewing and asking, but still . . . silence. Cold and bleak and infuriating. Could he have been so wrong all this time in his thinking, in his *convictions*? If *he* had been brought back from the dead by a living, breathing person— and not God Himself, as had undeniably been the case— Jason could imagine nothing but the desire to find that person, know him or her, be *like* them. Didn't Evelyn Pelagi wonder about him, who he was as a person, what he was like . . . damn it all, *where* he was? Although she wasn't listed in the phone book, learning her last name had enabled him to get her telephone number from Ameritech's information line, but Jason had tried without success to talk three different directory assistance operators into telling him her address. He'd thought the telephone number was a prize, too, until repeated tries had gotten him nothing but a man's voice on the answering machine. Apparently she let her machine screen all her calls, and while the man's voice had made him hesitate the first time, it wasn't really a surprise. Evelyn was a beautiful woman; it stood to reason she would have been married before her resurrection. What mattered, however, was *now*. As it had been with Jesus, *now* was when her every hour was precious, every movement and decision sacred. How much had she wasted already?

But still . . . Evelyn Pelagi remained intentionally clueless. Immersed in purposeful ignorance of the great gift Jason had given her, God alone knew what she was doing, whom she was touching, what she was saying. He'd spent so much of this past week believing that she needed him and that together they could do such wonderful, practically unimaginable things. . . . Had he been wrong all this time? Had only his resurrection been likened to the one that the Savior had experienced nearly two thousand years ago? Like the faithless apostles, perhaps earthly worries and fears blinded Evelyn Pelagi to the gifts he offered.

And now, those two. By the time Jason's eyes and brain processed the sight, they had turned the corner nearly a half block away and disappeared. He dismissed the idea of Lincoln Park and its lush greenery and sprinted after them, but it was useless. When Jason was finally able to slew around the turn onto Hutchinson, they were long gone. He was left with nothing but an empty street and the startled face of an old man trying to shove his key into a door lock. The guy looked at him so fearfully that Jason knew it'd be ridiculous to ask if he'd seen the slender young man and his lovely girlfriend. The details—the man's chest sporting the ghostly overcoat of a gunshot wound and the woman's bloodstain-smeared ankles and feet—would terrify the old man more.

Had he really seen them? Or was his mind playing some new trick, teasing him with bloody images to go along with the hungry sensations that constantly crowded his mind? Stumbling along in whatever direction, another possibility occurred to Jason, one that stopped him on the sidewalk like a video image frozen by a remote's pause button.

Those two he had passed . . . *were they like him?* The wounds he had seen on their flesh were a *mirage*—the same divine covering that graced Evelyn Pelagi's body and his and made their mortal wounds visible only to those he had pre-viously believed were special, *chosen.* But all this time . . .

He was *not* so special, *not* that divine.

But still, he *was* alone.

Suddenly aware of how ludicrous he must appear, Jason began walking again. Lit by the unflattering light of blue-white sodiums, Montrose stretched to the west, two lonely pothole-eaten lanes of concrete. Cars lined both sides, some parked so tightly that Jason couldn't have squeezed through if he'd tried, others still sending heat shimmers into the air from earlier use. If he tapped his fingertips against their doors as he passed, Jason guessed they would make the tiny, dead *thunks* a worn-out toy drum might make when whacked with a piece of flatware. The same dead sounds be-cause *he* was dead, and he was alone.

It wasn't fair, damn it. He, Jason Spiro, had started it all. *He* was the first one to be resurrected. The young man and woman he'd seen—surely they were his offspring, just as Evelyn was. Perhaps they were *Evelyn's* children—hers, thus his? An entire generation already reaching out—

Then how had he ended up like this? Full of unan-swered longings, alone and frustrated—he had to make Evelyn Pelagi see that she should be at his side. Especially if she had truly begun to resurrect others using the power he had instilled in her.

A split-second decision accompanied by an awkward

change of direction sent Jason veering north along Marshfield. Illinois Masonic—that's where he would find her. Why hadn't he thought of it before? She was an emergency-room nurse there—that much he remembered from the night he'd found her in the alley off Lakewood. It'd been late, after eleven, and he heard her tell the police she'd been on her way to work, which meant she worked nights. He couldn't risk going into the emergency room now; after the scene outside the police station, she might have security toss him out—or worse, call the police and he'd end up with Ewing hounding him again. No, better to duck into a discreet spot close to the ER and wait for her, and while it was tempting to rehearse all the things he'd have to say, Jason knew it was much better to bide his time and simply follow her home.

30

"I'll never eat again," Jude groaned and sat back. "This place is great." They were in a brightly lit restaurant called the Zephyr on Wilson. From their table beside the west window, they could see the Metra tracks and hear the trains roar by every now and then.

Karla grinned at him impishly. "You think so? You haven't eaten my cooking yet. Why do you think I'm so thin?"

"Well, it's sure not from eating at this place." His mouth turned up in a mischievous smile. "Come here often?"

It was Karla's turn to groan. "God, I thought I'd heard the last of that line years ago in a Rush Street bar."

"Greatness never goes out of style, my dear."

"True," she replied. "But someone forgot to tell you that they filed that line under 'cornball.' " She pushed her half-empty dish of ice cream in front of his empty one and waved at it with her spoon. "Here, have some dessert."

"No way am I going to eat that," Jude protested. "Besides, what do you call the banana split I polished off?"

Karla giggled. "The appetizer for your dessert?"

"I don't think so," he said sternly. "Finish your own artery-clogger. I've had mine."

"Fine." She pouted at him. "You have no idea what you're missing."

"I think after my dessert, I sure do. I bet I've gained five pounds since I walked in the door tonight, and it's your fault for bringing me here. I've got all night, and to get even I'm going to sit here and watch you eat until you blow up."

"I'll make a mess," she warned.

"I've seen worse."

Karla twirled her spoon around the dish, then set it down. "Okay, you win. You can eat more than me." The tables around them were nearly empty and she pushed her chair back and stood, letting the muscles in her legs stretch momentarily. "I'm going to make a visit to the ladies' room, then shall we go? I feel like we've been sitting here for hours."

"We have. I'll get the check while you're gone and meet you at the door."

"Oh, no you don't." Karla snatched up the bill the waitress had left them a few minutes earlier before Jude could pick it up. "I told you this was my treat."

"But—"

"—nothing," Karla finished for him. "I'll only be a second."

"That's good." Jude rubbed his hands together lightly. "I can't wait to get out in the heat. Between the air-conditioning and the ice cream, I'm freezing from the inside out."

Karla's nod was sympathetic. "Me, too. Back in a flash."

Five more minutes and they were standing in front of the restaurant, letting the warm night air envelope them and chase away the slight chill they'd picked up. Tonight the humidity was down and the air was not as heavy as it had been the previous week. Jude gave her a lopsided grin.

"Feels good, doesn't it? Kind of like climbing into a dryer after a cold wash."

Karla laughed. "I have to admit I hadn't thought of it in quite that way. I'll have to try it sometime."

"Works wonders on the hairdo."

"I'm sure." She smiled at him as they started toward her car. The lot across the street from the Zephyr had been full, and finding a parking spot earlier had resulted in a two-block walk; despite the hike she certainly felt safe being escorted by Jude. He wasn't that big a man, about a half foot taller than her five-foot-seven, but the way he moved reminded her of a trained grizzly bear, with all that power carefully packed into one place, moving with an odd sense of controlled grace. He must be a handful when he got angry.

"Penny for your thoughts."

Karla turned her head to see him smiling at her, the streetlights barely lighting his face. Nothing moved around them, on either the sidewalk or street. Quiet, dark, and hot, the city seemed to have packed everything away for the night, leaving only the brightly lit windows of the Zephyr a block and a half behind them. She felt him take her hand, his warm and dry and causing a mild shock of attraction to tingle in her palm. *My goodness*, she thought in surprise. *Down girl.* "I was thinking I'd better drive you home and call it a night," she said aloud. "It's almost eleven-thirty."

"I was hoping for a nightcap," he said lightly. "I know a great place on Lincoln close to Fullerton called the Red Lion Pub. It's supposed to be haunted." He gave her hand a light squeeze. "I'll protect you, of course."

She chuckled. "I'm sure you would. But *I* have to get up in the morning—you don't. Remember?"

"I thought you said sleep was a waste of time."

"I did, but it's still a necessity. Going into work with three or four hours' sleep would be hard enough for someone with a normal job. For me it'd be downright suicide—I'd never be able to deal with the stress. Also, Friday's the day I work out at the Sports and Fitness Center instead of having lunch. I'll need my strength."

"It's nice to have a health club close by that you can go to during work hours," Jude commented.

"No kidding," she agreed. "I don't even have to go outside. My building is connected to several others. To the east is the Stouffer Hotel, a great place to take clients for lunch, and to the west is the R. R. Donnelly Building and the Fitness Center. Beyond that is the Transportation Building."

"Transportation Building?"

"It's called that because quite a few of the airlines have offices and ticket counters on its mezzanine level. But it's got tenants too—Rudnick & Wolfe, a large real-estate law firm, and Coopers & Lybrand, one of the big accounting firms in the city."

"Ah." For a second Jude looked thoughtful, like he was filing something away mentally. "How come you know so much about that building when you don't work there?"

At her car, a late-model bright yellow Miata, she unlocked the door for Jude and smiled as she watched him work his way into the small front seat. "I'm in and out of it all the time," she finally answered as she settled behind the wheel and started the engine. "I've got a friend who works at that law firm; sometimes we meet for lunch at the restaurant in her building. Are you comfy yet?"

"Sure. I love having my legs shoved under my chin. In fact, I look forward to it." He reached over his right shoulder and pulled the seat belt into place. "Actually, it's not that bad. I probably wouldn't want to use this thing to do a cross-country jaunt, but it's a neat little car."

Karla grinned as she pulled smoothly out of the parking spot. "I'm rather partial to it."

"Where to?"

"Time to take you home, Detective." She couldn't stop the slight note of regret that crept into her voice, and wasn't sure she wanted to anyway. Would it be so bad for Jude to know she liked him? Maybe not ... but maybe so. There were a whole lot of things the handsome policeman didn't know about this woman to whom he'd taken such a liking, but would he feel the same way when all her cards were on the table? Time would tell, of course, but she wasn't ready to lay everything out just yet.

"Too bad," he said mildly.

Nothing Karla could think of seemed like the right response, so she lapsed into silence and drove, the Miata gliding smoothly north on the wide, mostly empty expanse of

Ashland Avenue. She'd always thought Ashland was an especially pretty street at night. Lined with trees on both sides and brightly lit, the streetlights sent a broken golden glow through the leaves rather than dumping harsh white light on the cars parked at the curb. The brownstones and turn-of-the-century apartment buildings were fairly well kept in this part of the city, and they reminded her of the smaller two- and three-unit apartment buildings of the farther northwest neighborhoods. Like those, they were quiet and clean, and the front lawns were carefully trimmed. The areas might be interchangeable if it weren't for the noticeable difference in the crime rate, which rose dramatically farther east. Ahead and on the right, as if to remind her where they were in the scheme of city life, the blue lights of at least three police cars strobed, tinny voices crackling over radio speakers as they eased past.

"Wait," Jude said suddenly. "Would you mind pulling over?"

Karla opened her mouth to ask why, then thought better of it as she guided the car to the right and put on the vehicle's hazard lights, one more pulse to add to the menagerie of flickering lights in this quarter of a block. She'd never been this close to a crime scene before—it couldn't be anything else—and it made her nervous. Her job as an advertising account executive ranked one of the worst in the employment industry for stress, but she couldn't imagine dealing with the level of pressure that must hang over Jude every day. "Where are you going?" she managed as her date opened the passenger door and started to climb out. For a second he looked at her as though he'd forgotten there was anyone else in the car with him, then his expression went sheepish.

"I . . . see someone I know. Just want to ask a few questions, that's all. Be right back, okay?"

Karla nodded and thought briefly about going with him rather than waiting in the car, even went so far as to turn the engine off before reconsidering. If there was a body or someone hurt, she didn't want to see it; let the police and the trained people, like Evelyn, handle situations like that. She'd only be in the way, a distraction. She turned on the radio instead, then shut it off almost immediately when the music sounded inane and out of place, surrounded as she was by the police lights and cars, all those uniformed and plain-clothes officers. She could see Jude in her rearview mirror. His face was earnest as he talked first to a tall woman with short blond hair, then leaned inside a squad car to speak with two uniformed officers who were bent over paperwork within the lighted interior of their patrol vehicle. It didn't seem that long before she saw him start back toward the car, although when she glanced at the dashboard clock Karla realized almost twenty minutes had passed. Seeing the clock say twelve twenty-five made weariness abruptly settle in and she had already started the engine by the time Jude pulled open the passenger door and climbed inside.

"Hi," he said. He looked contrite. "I'm sorry—I didn't re-alize I'd be gone so long."

"It's all right," she said, and meant it. "But I do need to get you home. By the time I take Creature out and get my stuff together for tomorrow, it'll be one-thirty. I'll be a zom-bie in the morning."

"I don't like the idea of you on the street this late at night. There's a killer still on the loose, remember?"

Karla gave him a small smile. "I'm used to walking the dog at all hours." He opened his mouth to protest, but she held up a hand. "I'm no fool, Jude. I'll look out the window to make sure the gate's latched, then just let the dog into the backyard. Are you ready?"

"Sure." The seat belt went into place again and Karla pulled back onto Ashland.

"So what was that all about?" When Karla finally asked the question, it was more to make conversation than out of morbid curiosity. She felt uncomfortable driving with Jude staring out the window, and quite frankly, she wanted to hear the sound of his voice.

"What?" He looked up in surprise, and again Karla had the unsettling feeling that he'd forgotten she was there. Not that she could complain about someone who became im-mersed in his job—look at her, and the hours she sometimes piled into Burnett. "I'm sorry," he said suddenly. "That was rude, wasn't it? The whole thing, I mean—making you wait in the car like that, then staring into space." He chuckled self-consciously. "I make a hell of a date, don't I?"

Karla had to laugh. "Yes, you do," she said sincerely. "But I wouldn't worry about making me wait for a few minutes. You haven't been around me enough times to realize how late I can sometimes be." She turned off Ashland and steered east on Grace Street; Jude's apartment was only a few minutes away, on the corner of Grace and Wayne.

"That wasn't much," he said abruptly.

"What?"

"The scene back there. A mugging, they think. The woman's purse was rifled."

"You thought it might be something else?"

Jude shrugged. "Doesn't hurt to check, and as you can see by the response there's a lot of manpower coming out because of the Ravenswood Strangler." He lapsed into silence again, but Karla had the funny feeling he was staring at her. Still, when she peeked at him from the corner of her eye, he was looking straight ahead, gazing at the street unfolding beneath the car. "But there is something else."

"What?" she asked again.

"The victim remembers almost nothing."

Karla jerked, recalling Evelyn's postattack blankness. "Nothing at all?"

"Just about, although that could be attributed to shock. She knows she was walking her dog one moment and the next she was on the ground with a bunch of her neighbors staring down at her and waiting for the cops."

"Did they see anyone?"

"Yeah. One of them—the one who called the police—says she saw a man and a woman running away. She described them both as being slender."

"So," Karla said thoughtfully, "although she doesn't remember anything—like Evelyn—it obviously isn't the same attacker. Which is what you were thinking, isn't it?"

"The possibility was bouncing around in my brain," he admitted, watching as Karla pulled the Miata over to the curb in front of his small apartment building. He lowered his voice. "Funny thing, though." Jude turned to look at her, and something in his eyes gave her a sudden, deep chill.

"The woman's dog won't have anything to do with her now."

31

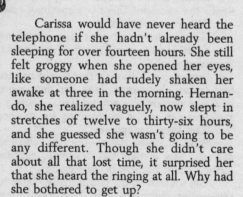

Carissa would have never heard the telephone if she hadn't already been sleeping for over fourteen hours. She still felt groggy when she opened her eyes, like someone had rudely shaken her awake at three in the morning. Hernando, she realized vaguely, now slept in stretches of twelve to thirty-six hours, and she guessed she wasn't going to be any different. Though she didn't care about all that lost time, it surprised her that she heard the ringing at all. Why had she bothered to get up?

" 'Lo."

"Carissa? Is that you? You sound sick."

Her mother's voice got things going a little faster in her head, though not necessarily in a pleasant direction. If she hung up, the woman would call back; take it a step further and leave the phone off the hook, and her mother would be pounding on the front door in an hour, probably

with Carissa's father in tow, and wouldn't that just suck?
"I'm fine."

"You don't sound good, Carissa. You live there with that
boy and he doesn't take care of you, doesn't work—"

Carissa tuned out for a minute or two, letting her
mother ramble on with the usual recital of complaints about
Hernando. The same old shitty story, and did the woman
ever look at her other children, Carissa's two brothers and
older sister? It wasn't as though they were prizes.

"Carissa, are you there? *Carissa!*"

"What!" Jesus!

"Don't use that tone with me, young lady. I *said*, do you
want me to pick you up or can you get there yourself?"

"Get where?" Carissa looked idly at her fingertips, then
tapped them experimentally on the wall next to the telephone. She didn't feel a thing, even when she kept beating
on the dirty wallboard hard enough to sound like that stupid
cartoon woodpecker.

"You haven't heard anything I've said at all, have you?"
her mother asked irritably. "Carissa, what in the world is that
noise? Never mind. I'll repeat what I said about going to
your Aunt Imalda's. The one who has cancer, in case you
don't remember? She's been asking for you for weeks, and
you haven't bothered to visit. You've almost waited too
long."

"I . . . don't have time," Carissa said. "It's—"

"You make time, young woman, or I'll send your father
over there to get you. The woman is *dying*, for God's sake,
and you were always her favorite. The very least you can do
is go to her house for one last visit."

Carissa was silent for a moment. Aunt Imalda, dying?
Yes—she remembered that. Stomach and intestinal cancer, a
particularly agonizing way to go, untreatable and not much
to be done about the pain, either. It seemed to Carissa that
she had liked the old woman at one time, when she'd been
younger. She recalled something about playing with dolls
and cookies and make-believe tea parties, babyish shit like
that, left behind for the more tempting attractions of teenage boys and money—and drugs, of course.

"Hello? Hello?"

"I'm here." She sighed and hoped Hernando's car was

running and had enough gas to get them there and back. There was no question that he would go with her—she wasn't traveling alone anywhere feeling like this, though she couldn't describe what *this* actually was. Plus there was the matter of her father, a big, beefy man who worked in an auto repair shop and who would be incredibly pissed if they didn't show up. Aunt Imalda was his closest sister, and Carissa didn't want to risk getting on her father's bad side, not over something stupid like visiting a dying old woman. "All right, we'll go. But don't pick us up. We'll take our car."

"I'd like to say that's good, but since you're taking that death trap, I'll wait to see if you two make it to her house in one piece."

"Fine." At another time—*in a previous life?*—Carissa would have jumped at the argument bait her mother dangled in front of her, but now, in this new and . . . faded-out version of herself, she simply didn't care. "We'll be there later."

"How much later?" her mother demanded.

"Later." Carissa hung up, knowing she would pay for her insolence this afternoon when she'd be forced to listen to her mother and father preach, but again—she didn't care. All she felt was . . . *faded.*

The thought returned to her as she made her way into the dirty kitchen and sat at the table, staring dully at the walls. Nothing seemed important now, not money, Hernando, the baby, or drugs—they were *things*, unimportant trinkets in a life that meant zilch and paled in comparison to the new need raging within her. She knew, somewhere deep within the recesses of her mind, that the child within her belly hadn't moved since . . . when? Wednesday, of course. It was difficult to remember, but Carissa thought that she'd felt the last kick from the previously vigorous mound of her stomach while she'd been talking to that construction worker whose name she couldn't remember, not long before she'd met him behind the bar and his wife had come outside and made things go ugly. She couldn't recollect much after that beyond the bright fire of pain in her abdomen, not even what had caused that pain, but that didn't matter either. All that mattered, of course, was the all-consuming . . . *spin* she'd felt, first when Hernando had resurrected her, and

again when she had brought the woman Hernando murdered back from the dead. So intense, nearly blinding, like a
hot, dark orgasm of the soul. She couldn't wait to do it
again.

A few minutes later—or maybe it was an hour—her
gaze drifted to the wall clock and she watched the second
hand jerk around a couple of times before she finally focused
on the actual time. She had to get Hernando up and get herself dressed, find out if the car would start. Maybe they
could work something to eat into the schedule—God, she
hated having to keep a timetable, the vague one implied by
her mother or anyone else. That's why she could never work
someplace where you had to punch a time clock; more than
likely she'd tell them where to stick that clock before the
first day ended.

Carissa started toward the bedroom to wake Hernando,
then stopped at the refrigerator instead and pulled open the
door. There wasn't much to see inside, though the package
of lunch meat looked fairly new—maybe bought by
Maralina—and there was probably bread stuffed into one of
the cabinets somewhere. She remembered the idea of eating
and spent a full five minutes considering a sandwich, standing there with the fridge door open and the cool air from its
interior washing around her, although she couldn't feel much
of it anyway. Ultimately she shut the door and walked away;
she had absolutely no desire to put anything into her mouth.

Her aunt's house was on the south side, a small two-story on
Artesian and 45th, a block west of Western Boulevard. If
nothing else, it was easy to reach and she and Hernando
drove there in silence. Hernando guided the car in a straight,
simple line along the right lane of Western without passing
or trying to push through the traffic lights that always
seemed to turn yellow as they approached. It seemed like
forever since Carissa had visited her aunt's home. Had it
taken this long to make the trip in the past? It didn't make
any difference; she sat quietly on the passenger side and said
nothing.

The house was old and worn, a ramshackle structure on
the corner that looked like it'd been leeched of life, much
like its owner. Carissa remembered it from her girlhood as

being white and well cared for, but time and age, not to mention a vicious disease, had weighed hard on her Aunt Imalda. Now the little clapboard house with the peaked second-floor attic in which Carissa had once played was dingy and seeped with an insidious sense of sickness, all the way down to the pavement. The small walkway leading to the front porch stairs was cracked and pitted, dotted with weeds and cigarette butts from the teenagers who hung out at the intersection in the evenings.

The boards of the porch creaked beneath their weight and Carissa and Hernando fidgeted and waited after ringing the bell, then finally heard the sound of footsteps as someone came to answer the door. When it opened, Carissa was greeted by the grim face of her mother, the older woman's lips pressed in a tight, unforgiving line above the sharply edged collar of a harsh black dress. Her father's sister wasn't even dead yet, Carissa thought wryly, and already the family was wearing funeral black. Carissa's jeans and oversized maternity shirt hardly fit in, but beyond an unfocused preoccupation with the bloodshadows that appeared on everything she wore, clothes were one more thing about which Carissa didn't particularly give a royal damn. To prove it, standing right next to her was Hernando, yet she couldn't have told anyone what he was wearing without looking over at him first.

"I was starting to think you two weren't coming." Her mother's voice was harsher than it needed to be. "You're almost too late."

Carissa pushed past her and left Hernando to make his own way inside. "I told you we'd be here. Where is she?"

"The back bedroom." Her mother looked at her pointedly. "If you'd have come here more often, you'd know the way."

"Just tell her which way, would you? Bitchin' ain't gonna get anything done." Hernando looked at them both impatiently.

Carissa's mother frowned at him. "I don't think I like your attitude very much," she finally said.

"I don't *care*," he retorted.

She shook her head in disgust. "It's the bedroom three doors down the hall on the right." For a moment the anger disappeared from her expression, making her seem younger, sadder. "I'm the only one here right now, but your father will be here as soon as he gets off work. No one else has been in to see her today. Do you want me to go with you?"

"No," Carissa said. "We'll be fine." She motioned to Hernando. "This way." She threw a nasty look at her mother. "And I do remember the way to her room." She started down the hallway with Hernando following, both silent, listening to the quiet, shadowy squeaks that filled the house. The hall was longer than Carissa recalled, stretching the depth of the small house and making it seem unaccountably large, as if the wood and plasterboard and ratty gray carpeting under their feet had warped and pulled into a bigger size out of desire alone. The door to her aunt's room was closed but not latched, and the two of them slipped inside and pushed it shut behind them, letting their eyes adjust to the feeble light of a single dim dresser lamp.

Hernando, Carissa knew, had been here once before, last summer before she'd gotten pregnant. Aunt Imalda had had cancer then, but had not been so emaciated; in fact, she'd just been told of her illness. At the time of the family gathering for a dinner of homemade tamales and chicken with molé sauce, the thin, pretty woman who was not much older than Carissa's mother still hoped that the doctors would find a way to put her into remission. But the cancer was dark and hungry and all-consuming; what neither she nor the doctors had known at that early date was that it had already spread voraciously throughout her body. Despite the medicines and the chemo and all the other kinds of therapy they could try, the disease was unstoppable. From the perplexed look on her boyfriend's face now, Carissa realized that he didn't quite recognize the skeletal form wrapped, despite the heat, within the rumpled sheets and faded, hand-crocheted afghans on the bed. For that matter, neither did Carissa. If she had passed this woman on the street, she would have walked right by her, her only second thought being *Jesus, she looks like a mummy*. How in God's name had her father's sister come to look like this in only a year?

Aunt Imalda did, as much as any living person could, resemble something out of one of those Discovery Channel shows, the ones about Egypt and its pyramids and all the dried-up things they found inside. Except, of course, that she was still breathing, and still moving, though not with any strength. Carissa stood by the side of the bed indecisively, staring down at her. What should they do now?

"Aunt Imalda?" she whispered at last. "Tía?" She reached out a dried-up finger that looked very much like the skin on the sick woman's face, touching her aunt's frail cheek and marveling that someone could deteriorate so drastically and so quickly. Her aunt's skin was soft and dry and cool, as though her body was no longer able to maintain the proper temperature, despite the heavy pile of bed linens.

That tiny touch—

—such a *small* thing, really—

—made Carissa's breath lock in her throat with a sudden, ferocious *need*.

She heard Hernando make a strangled sound next to her, knew suddenly that he was feeling the same thing. The rush again, urgency blasting through the both of them and steering their hands toward the pitiful, helpless woman on the bed. It was so easy, completely conscience-free, to snatch the pillow from beneath that onionskin-covered skull and use it to still the feathery and disease-tainted breath coming from their victim.

They fought, the two of them, silent and hard, for the right to take the unseen charge screaming out to them from the dry circle of Aunt Imalda's open mouth. Carissa somehow reached her first, her desperation lending her uncanny speed in spite of the pregnancy that made her waddle through everyday tasks. She clamped her mouth over the dead woman's and tasted medicine, then the start of ecstasy, building and building—

—until Hernando grabbed her by the hair and yanked her away, tossed her behind him with no thought of where she might land or how much noise she might make. No consideration at all of the danger of her mother and God knew which other relatives who might now be guzzling coffee and eating *churros* in the kitchen, a room separated from them only by the thin plaster wall behind the bed. Carissa landed with a grunt and came up again instantly, her face white and twisted and looking like that ridiculous evil doll-thing come to life in the movies. Hernando was already feeding on the old woman, and it was as simple to bury both of her clawed hands into the thick curls of his hair and haul him backward as it had been for him to do it to her.

"Get away—she's mine!" Carissa's voice, despite her rage, was a soft, controlled hiss.

"Fuck you! You had the last one. It's my turn—"

Carissa twisted around him, using her belly's bulk to force him aside. "She's my blood relative, not yours! Now back off." She bent back to her aunt, and it was so good and sweet and hot all at once, it must be like the street Ice she'd been too afraid to try, even her, knowing its deadly addiction. Heat filled her, spinning her insides, her soul, in an accelerating circle, pulling her toward a spasm of pleasure—

—and that bastard Hernando, again he wrenched her away, *again*, an instant before culmination of the roaring sensation, struggling with her and finally in frustration drawing back his fist when she tried to claw at his eyes—

"Carissa? What's going on in there?"

Her mother's demanding voice, followed by the *click* of the doorknob as it turned, a tiny sound turned explosively huge because of the situation. They froze for an instant, then Hernando's fist opened, dropped, and wrapped around her upper arm. He pulled her to his side an instant before Carissa's mother pushed open the door and stepped into the room. Before the older woman could move around them and see, Hernando had leaned over and tucked the pillow neatly behind Aunt Imalda's skull; a deft pat spread the wispy strands of the dead woman's hair around her peaceful face like a lacy halo.

"Mama." Carissa turned imploringly. "Mama, I think Aunt Imalda is—is dead. She just . . . *went*, just like that!"

Her mother's face turned ashen and her hand covered her mouth. "Oh, God in heaven—why didn't you come and get me?" She stepped to the side of the bed and gazed down uncertainly, then cautiously touched the side of the old woman's face.

"It just happened," Hernando insisted. "Now, right before you walked in."

Mrs. Novia didn't question them any further. "Poor Imalda," Carissa's mother murmured. Her eyes filled with tears. "So much pain at the end, and nothing to do for it.

She's at peace now, finally gone on to a place where the pain can't follow." Hands shaking, she drew the topmost sheet up and over her sister-in-law's face.

The older woman picked up the bedside telephone and made the first of a series of calls that would fill the small house with people. All Carissa and Hernando could do was stare helplessly at the covered corpse on the bed as the molten light of its fulfillment winked out of reach.

32

The bathroom again, huddled inside the small dark room, where much to Warren's dismay Evelyn had replaced the white ruffled curtains with blue ones so dark they looked almost black, despite full daylight coming through the fabric. It wasn't so much that she wanted to be in the dark as she wanted to be *alone*, and it was that sense of aloneness that she got from sequestering herself in the lightless room. Then again, maybe she wasn't alone at all.

Just look in the mirror.

There was a stranger in the bathroom with her, someone whose reflection had replaced her own, or perhaps stolen it. The woman who stared back hardly resembled the Evelyn Pelagi of . . . how long ago? A week? No, it was more than that, much more: it was an *eternity*. An eternity of trying to coexist with a never-ending, screaming call of *I WANT!* from deep within that sent her mentally ranting and reeling around inside herself. It wasn't just in her head and her blood, but in her *soul*, with nowhere to flee or to escape. That impotent rage again, staring at her dead hands and dead feet but feeling nothing, *nothing*, flailing her hands at each other and the wall, the sink, lunging over her feet and trying uselessly to find the floor with the nerves that used to be present in the cold flesh of the bottoms of her feet.

Always, *always*, that craving, that dark thing inside her that was yanking her apart, cell by cell, stretching her skin toward something unattainable and driving her insane as she struggled not to listen to it. It would have been so easy to fill, too—the county morgue could provide ready access to more dead and bruised lips than a hospital. God, it was so *hard* to resist, so much more difficult than Karla, her sweet best friend, realized, even from her point of view and first-hand experience. And it didn't go away if she resisted. That was the evil of this craving inside her that gained more strength as time went on, like some sort of perpetual scorpion in her gut, stinging and stinging and living on, staying forever on the defensive and determined to win its war of need. How much easier it would have been to fight the sweet and vicious call of crack or heroin, and know that someone, somewhere, could help. Ultimately, if she desired to be free of a drug habit badly enough and she withstood it, the chemical craving would fade to the occasional hot pulse over which she could at least, with enough gritting of teeth and force of will, continue to triumph.

Plus that farce during the last few hours of her double shift in the ER yesterday . . .

Calm again as she remembered it, Evelyn accepted her fate because there was no alternative. "Jesus," she finally whispered to the woman in the mirror. "What are you?"

Narrowly missing unspeakable surrender, she was discovered as she bent over the corpse of an overdose victim, a thin man dressed in filthy clothes, dirt caked on his face and within the bloody cracks of his lips. Still she would have resurrected this walking piece of human garbage, not giving him a chance at a better life but introducing him to a new and improved addiction, a rush that a man like him would kill to feed. Forced to explain to a dubious Phia Holey that

she had merely been examining the cadaver's face for signs
of tattooing deep beneath the layers of grime, she had seen
the *I've-never-heard-such-a-crock* expression on the other
woman's face. Evelyn, shaking and chattering in frustration
in her mind, finalized the dead man's death packet while her
supervisor waited inside the curtained cubicle with her.
Again, a forced reprieve masqueraded in a work schedule re-
vised by Phia: suddenly Evelyn was off the schedule for the
next two days, then temporarily reassigned to the more pop-
ulated second shift. And this time Evelyn was glad, because,
God forgive her, how much longer could she continue to resist?

Now the afternoon was gone and Warren would soon be
home. He would want to turn on the lights and the television, fill the apartment with the sights and sounds of the living, the life sounds of those with whom Evelyn no longer
believed she could exist. Then he would fix something to
eat, because Evelyn hadn't bothered to, easy sloppy joes or
an omelette, or he might get fancy and make spaghetti with
meatballs in an attempt to perk up her appetite. Then he
would expect her to eat it, or drink the iced glass of diet
Pepsi that he would set out for her on the table while he
cooked. What could she say? *Sorry honey, I haven't felt hungry, and I'm not thirsty either.* She was not so fucked up that
she couldn't see herself through the eyes of her husband, not
so much the fool she didn't think he'd noticed that she
hadn't eaten or drunk in front of him since the attack a full
week ago. The excuse that she'd eaten before he'd come
home would only get her so far.

And her skin—now wasn't *that* attractive? Bless Warren
for his tactful avoidance of the subject, although how much
longer could he hold out before he insisted she see one of
her colleagues at the hospital? She was a new and different
shade of white, undercut with layers of gray and a vague,
unhealthy-looking pink where her watery blood traveled
close to the surface of her skin. In all her years as a nurse,
Evelyn had never witnessed this coloring on another living
person, and God knows she wouldn't want to climb into bed
with someone who looked as downright *dead* as she did.

She turned on the light and held her fingers up to the
faintly buzzing fluorescent tube. The dark, curled ends

twitched in response to her mental instructions, proving that although she couldn't feel the appendages she could still tell them what to do. Likewise with her feet: her toes were flat and seemingly dead, and she thought it was a miracle that they were still able to function and help keep her balanced upright.

"What did you do to me?" she whispered. If that boy, Jason whatever, was here, with her in the room this second, she thought she might very much like to kill him. Because he certainly had done *something*, hadn't he? Some great and monstrous fundamental change had passed from him to her—and from the way he'd acted and the things he'd said, he'd done it on *purpose*. No, she decided abruptly, it hadn't been passed to her, because that implied she had asked for it, or at the very least accepted the offering. That wasn't the way it had happened at all. He had . . . *infected* her somehow, with something hideous and corrupt that she couldn't escape. Her eyes, so bright and clear a week ago, were now dull green, leeched of vitality, the color of dying leaves on a plant deprived of water—

—and too far gone to save.

Evelyn lowered her eyelids then, but it wasn't that easy to hide the ugliness inside her. After a moment the lids flicked open and she faced the mirror again: emotionless eyes, lifeless face and flesh. Why, she wondered with bitter black humor, couldn't she find the *deadrush* her body sought by tonguing her own fouled reflection in the bathroom mirror?

33

At eight in the evening, Jason had been slipping through the sanitized hallways of Illinois Masonic for over five hours. Finding Evelyn Pelagi had turned out to be the most frustrating task in his life, and layered atop that was a mounting sense of hopelessness. What if he *never* found her? What if she'd transferred to a different hospital somewhere in this sprawling city, or just flat *quit*? Neither possibility was unthinkable after being attacked by a murderer. Maybe she didn't want to live around here anymore, maybe—

Jason's eyes widened. He'd lost track of exactly where he was in the hospital, although he knew he was still on the first floor and somewhere to the rear north of the ER. Down the empty hallway stretching in front of him, facing the other way and too far to clearly see, a tall, dark-haired nurse with her hair in a French braid came through an office doorway and stepped onto a waiting elevator.

"Wait!" Jason cried. He sprinted for the elevator, feet slipping on the waxed linoleum and the soles of his sneakers leaving black marks on the speckled white pattern. "Wait!" he cried again. "Hold that elevator!" The woman gave no indication that she heard and the doors slid shut long before he could get a good look at her face.

He jerked to a stop in front of the closed doors and spun in indecision. The elevator was in the middle of another long hallway, one that crossed the first, and a quick scan in either direction showed no stairwell entrance. Jason had no choice but to punch at the elevator call button and wait for the car to return. He clearly remembered that the red arrow had been lit, thus the elevator had been going to one of the several levels below. When the empty car finally returned and he leaped inside, Jason could only guess at the nurse's destination. While it could have been his impatience, it had seemed like a long wait. He pressed the button marked L-3 and the elevator started with a soft jerk. He'd never been anywhere in the hospital but the first floor, since he'd reasoned that an emergency-room nurse would logically spend most of her time in or around the ER. Now his thinking seemed faulty—there were laboratories and departments everywhere in this sprawling complex. He should have checked them all.

The elevator lobbies—there were several—on the first floor were decorated in a visitor-pleasing natural color scheme, executed in curving abstract patterns on the walls that had gone out of style several decades ago. The lobby in which he stood when he came off the elevator couldn't even be called such; it was just another part of the hallway, sterile white with no paintings or any other wall decorations. The only break in the eye-blistering whiteness in either direction were the aluminum rails that were bolted at gurney height between the unevenly spaced doors. There was no sign of the nurse.

Uncertain, Jason turned to his right and wandered down the hall. The doors on this level had frosted glass in their upper halves and used numbers as identification, none of which meant anything to him although occasionally the number was followed by a department title in bold black letters. At a door marked PATHOLOGY—FORENSIC MEDICINE he paused and almost went inside, drawn by nothing more than curiosity. Instead, he shook his head and kept going; he wasn't down there to explore. There was only one more door, marked HOLDING, directly in front of him, then the hallway took a right turn.

Jason bypassed the last door and turned the corner, stopped short when the hallway dead-ended in another door, a gray one with the words SUPPLY CLOSET stenciled across it. He turned back, disgusted, then halted when he heard noises from around the corner—voices, two, maybe three guys headed in his direction. It wouldn't be good to get caught down here, and no excuse in the world would explain why he'd come this way instead of taking the elevator back to the main floor. He fumbled a hand behind him and found the closet's doorknob; too late he registered that above the knob was a dead bolt. The door wouldn't open; apparently the hospital was tired of giving its employees free boxes of tissues and cleaning liquids.

Grinding his teeth, Jason inched forward. The door marked HOLDING was right here, its lock side closest to him and just to the left of the hallway it faced, the corridor wall still shielding Jason from view. It opened easily and he slipped inside and eased the door shut, then crouched and crab-walked along a wall until he came to a desk that had nothing on it but a clipboard and a pen. He crawled quietly behind it and waited, listening carefully. The voices grew louder as the speakers passed the door and Jason heard keys jingle. He tensed, but the door that opened wasn't the one to the room in which he hid. Then he heard things clanking and laughter, and smiled to himself. If the door to the supply closet *had* been unlocked and he had hidden there, he would have been discovered.

The door outside slammed shut and the voices faded and finally disappeared, and for the first time Jason became aware that it was quite a bit cooler in here, almost *refrigerated*. He stood cautiously and looked around; the lights in the room were off but the glow from the door's frosted window still provided a muted white shine that made the walls look soft gray instead of white. He could see quite well that he wasn't the only one in the room, and now he knew what HOLDING stood for; three sheet-covered bodies rested on side-by-side metal gurneys not ten feet away.

Jason considered leaving, then decided to wait a few more minutes and give the guys in the hall time to catch their elevator and go elsewhere. Having the corpses nearby didn't bother him at first, but as he watched the seconds tick by on a big industrial-style clock over the door, his gaze kept going back to the secretive white mounds again and again. The only dead body he'd ever seen was Evelyn Pelagi, and now she wasn't dead at all. What did these look like?

He walked to the door and pressed his ear against the glass. Nothing, not even the sound of the elevator doors opening and closing. Come to think of it, he hadn't heard the double *ting!* of the elevator bell, and he wondered if those men might not still be on this level, mopping the floor or washing the glass on the doors. Best to stay put for a while.

Jason turned back to the interior of the room, then walked to the closest gurney. The body atop it was the largest and when Jason drew the sheet back from its head, he found a hefty but well-wrinkled old woman, eyes closed and face peaceful beneath a short, unruly crown of iron-colored hair. He blinked and had the sudden impression that he was disturbing her sleep; quickly re-covering her, he stepped a little more hesitantly to the next cart. When he peeked beneath its sheet, he discovered a man whose age he couldn't tell. His skin was marble white and smooth where it wasn't pocked by large, painful-looking red sores. The crease-free skin made Jason decide the man had probably been young, though his cheeks and eyelids were so sunken into his face he couldn't have weighed more than ninety pounds. The corpse's limbs looked like tissue-covered twigs and his skull was totally hairless. Looking at him made Jason think instantly of cancer, or AIDS and all its terrible complications. Careful not to jar the body, he covered the man's face slowly and turned to the last gurney.

The shrouded cadaver on this cart was less than a third the size of the woman Jason had looked at first. He frowned and glanced at the clock again; plenty of time had passed, and he really should get out of here. But another minute wouldn't make any difference, and he *was* curious. The decision made, he peeled back the sheet to reveal—

A small child, a boy. His hair made him look Afro-American but his skin was light gray, almost white. Jason wondered if that was his natural color and he pulled the sheet back farther, until he exposed tiny hands that still retained a slight pinkish coloring. The child's eyes were only half-closed and Jason leaned closer, peering at them. They were a dull light green, much the same as the enormous bruises that peppered the child's skin, and Jason couldn't stop himself from finally pulling the sheet away altogether. The dead child was emaciated, underfed, a tiny angel whose face was swollen and split and bore a four-inch wide swatch of scorched skin in the wedge shape of an iron on its left side. One skinny shoulder was misshapen, obviously dislocated, and the little fingers were loosely curled under each other, as if the boy had become so used to clenching his fists against pain in life that he couldn't stop in death. The toddler's face had been washed but dried blood still crusted the inside of the tiny nostrils and one corner of his mouth. Beneath the mat of fine, curly hair, there were lumps along the small skull the likes of which Jason had never seen on human flesh.

Hanging from the end of the cart was a white plastic bag with a drawstring on it—personal belongings. Jason recovered the undersized body, then glanced through the bag, wanting to know more about this miniature casualty. He found a T-shirt that was a permanent dirty gray and stained blue shorts at least four sizes too big, probably leftovers from an older brother—and what had happened to *him*? Last was the smallest, saddest pair of toddler tennis shoes Jason had ever seen. He put the things back and lifted the other plastic bag, the clear one clipped around the boy's ankle which contained the hospital's forms. Jason could read the top one without opening the bag:

Name: *Junius Drury*
Month and Day of Birth: *0407*
Weight: *19 pounds 2 ounces*
Cause of Death: *Traumatic blow to the head with*

*blunt instrument, subdural hematoma. Extensive in-
dication of physical abuse; malnutrition.*
Name and Address of Parent(s) or Guardian(s):
*Mother: Minerva Hackett—currently being held at
Cook County Jail, 12th and State.*

Then, stamped in large, smeary red letters: AUTOPSY RE-
QUIRED; DO NOT RELEASE CADAVER EXCEPT TO COOK COUNTY
MORGUE.

The form went on to say that the child had been dead
on arrival and his father's whereabouts were unknown.
There was more, but Jason didn't bother to read it. What
good would it do?

Knowing that this little boy had turned three years
old only a couple of months ago made Jason shake his head
in bewilderment. How much had the boy suffered during
his short life? He wondered what Junius had been like—
unhappy, no doubt, terrified all the time.

Suddenly Jason felt death pressing all around him, calling to him. Evelyn Pelagi had been just like this, hadn't she?
He remembered the way she'd lain in the alley, broken and
mangled, bearing her own marks of Chicago's savagery. But
he had brought her back to the land of the living, had giv-
en her another opportunity to live. A woman with a mind of
her own, an intelligence that wouldn't let her accept the
miracle of rebirth without questioning it, without refusal.

What if he did the same for tiny, brutalized Junius
Drury?

Once it was in his head, Jason couldn't rid himself of
the idea. He thought he could suddenly *feel* the toddler calling out to him, begging him for a second chance. And Jason
could do it for him, so very *easily*. There were others in the
room, but he would leave them to meet their Maker—the
withered old woman, the tormented young man whose body
was already destroyed from the inside out. It wasn't that he
thought those two had deserved to die, not at all—that
wasn't for him to judge. But to bring someone back—that
was his decision, his *gift*. And he chose to give it to Junius
Drury.

Jason bent over the cart and carefully pulled the sheet
back again. Despite the corpse's invisible pull, nothing

showed in the half-open slits of the boy's green eyes, just
that flat, dead color, no sparkle at all. How long had the boy
been dead? Jason had forgotten to look and his skin had a
cold, grayish cast, but it couldn't be *that* long or the body
wouldn't still be here. He longed to see the shine of life start
to burn in those eyes, feel the small chest rise again as it took
in air. Senses spinning, Jason started to lower his mouth to
the boy's.

From far off, he heard the elevator bell—

ting! ting!

He jerked upright and froze.

Five seconds, six, seven, and he'd almost decided to
keep going. Then voices filled the corridor, grew louder until
they stopped directly outside the door. By then Jason had
dropped the sheet over the small corpse and silently scurried
back to his hiding place beneath the desk. As he heard the
door open, he realized too late that this was the worst possible hiding place, because the desk, with its clipboard of
forms, was the first place the visitors would probably go. He
wasn't disappointed.

Scrunched as small as he could make himself and sitting
very still, Jason could do nothing more than hope that neither of the two men who'd entered the room would sit on
the chair that was stationed a few feet away. If either did and
rolled it forward to work at the desktop, someone's foot was
bound to connect with Jason.

"Cold in here, huh?" A young voice betraying an edge of
nervousness came from overhead, at the outside edge of the
desk. Whatever had to be marked on the clipboard, the guy
had thankfully decided to do it standing up.

"What did you expect?" The question came from someone older, although it sounded humorous rather than sarcastic. "Here he is." Jason heard retreating footsteps, then the
rustle of material followed by a sharp hiss of breath.

"Jesus," said the younger guy.

"Yeah. The wonders of the Department of Children and
Family Services at work again." This time the older man's
voice was clearly bitter. "According to the file, they kept
sending social workers over there but for some reason they
never took the boy out of the home. Bureaucratic judgment
at its finest."

There was silence for a few moments, then Jason heard a series of dull squeaks from the wheels of the cart as it began to move. "So now what, Dr. Amasa?"

"Now we do the autopsy," the older man answered in a flat voice. "We get enough evidence to send his mother away for fifty years but watch her walk out in two."

"What!"

"That's the way it always works. Let's go."

More soft squeals and the door opened; a louder click, then silence. Jason was alone again, with only the two older corpses for company.

He crawled jerkily out from beneath the desk and stood, frowning and staring around at the room, with its ghostly gray walls and cold, silent occupants. He had no compulsion to revive either of the other two; only the boy had drawn him. But why? There hadn't been a good reason, only an urge to satisfy a hunger inside him, an illicit *temptation*. All of a sudden Jason was convinced that he could recall that same craving, right now, just by bending as close to the dead woman or man as he had to Junius Drury. It hadn't been the *child* crying out—death itself had been the lure. He was surrounded by it, *drowning* in the bestiality of this enormous and degenerate city with its voracious appetite for human life.

"It's time to go home," Jason said out loud. In a way the echoing words were an admission of defeat, a surrendering of his dream of establishing some kind of following here. But now, after his brush with the pathetic remains of Junius Drury, Jason needed more than anything to return to Harmony and a cleaner, safer life.

He checked the hallway, then let himself out of the room and closed the door quietly behind him. Heading toward the elevators, he knew the only thing in Chicago that remained incomplete for him was to find Evelyn Pelagi and take her with him.

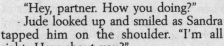

Late Friday/Early Saturday

34

"Hey, partner. How you doing?"

Jude looked up and smiled as Sandra tapped him on the shoulder. "I'm all right. How about you?"

She returned the smile but it didn't reach her eyes. "Fine. Are you ready to roll or do you have more paperwork?" She looked around the station house and Jude caught a tinge of impatience in the movement.

"I've gone about as far on this as I can," he responded as he pushed together a stack of papers, bounced the edges a few times, and placed them in the lower of the two wire baskets on the desk's front corner. "You look edgy. What's the matter?" He lifted the lightweight jacket slung over the back of his chair but didn't put it on; he'd caught the weather on the radio a few minutes ago, and as much as he liked the heat, he could do without the jacket when it was still nearly a hundred degrees outside. The sun had set several hours ago but the heat remained blistering; there had to be some miserable people cooking in all those un-air-conditioned apartments across the city.

"Nothing."

He followed Sandra in silence, watching her fire up a cigarette and knowing he'd have to be an imbecile to believe anything she said in that tone of voice. In the meantime he decided to shut up and wait for her to say what was on her mind. He'd worked with her for almost five years and knew it wouldn't be long; she was a true professional and a consummate actress when the job called for it, but with her colleagues, Sandra Wilfred was honest and overly blunt most of the time. If it was in her head, odds were it would come out of her mouth pretty soon. That was fine with Jude; he liked having a partner who was forthright and with whom he could communicate. It made it easier for him to trust the person who sometimes had to save his butt, and vice versa.

The disc jockey on the radio hadn't been joking about the temperature. When they stepped out the front doors of the police station, the heat wrapped them like a big, steamy blanket. The humidity sat solidly at ninety-five percent and the air crawling into Jude's lungs was like a hot wad of wet cotton, sticking in his throat and heating up the inside of his mouth. For a moment he almost believed that even paperwork was better than this, as long as he could do it inside the building.

Sandra grinned at him, her normal cheer returning for a second. "So, Mr. I-Like-It-When-It's-Hot, how does tonight grab you? Maybe you'd like to knock it up a few more degrees, go for that hundred-and-five mark."

Jude groaned. "You're out of your mind. I might like the heat, but you know I can't stand this freakin' humidity. I should move to Arizona, where it's hot but nice and dry, almost all the time."

"Yeah? I saw a comic on the tube once who was pointedly sarcastic about all the people who think Arizona's so great because it's hot and dry. If I remember correctly, his response was 'So's an oven, but you don't stick your head in it.' " She smirked. "Maybe you could let me out of your oven before you crank it up next time, bud."

He chuckled as they reached the unmarked police car.

"Trust me. My hand's not on the temperature control today. I would have turned it down a little."

Sandra pulled open the passenger side door and started to climb in, then pulled back. "Christ, I think I spoke too soon when I told you to turn it up. Has this thing been sitting in the sun all day?"

Jude lifted an eyebrow as he opened the door on his side and left it that way, letting the first blast of heated air escape. "Excuse me, but there seems to be a shortage of shade trees in the wooded parking lot here."

She mumbled something in response, scowled and settled atop the hot vinyl of the passenger seat with a small hiss of disgust.

"What was that?" Jude asked mildly.

"I said next time let me park the damned car. I'll find a spot somewhere that's not in full sun!" she barked.

"Anytime, Sandy."

"San*dra*," she snapped.

He grinned. "What's the matter? Heat getting to you? Or you got another thorn in your side? Come on, spill it—I'm tired of taking your shots and not knowing why. What'd I do?" He tossed his jacket onto the backseat and started the engine, but made no move to pull the car into the late-night flow of traffic on Foster Avenue. "We'll sit here and cook until you tell me what's on your mind."

Sandra was quiet for a few moments, then she sighed. "Let's get going so we can at least turn on the air conditioner—assuming, that is, that you *are* willing to do something other than roll down the windows, right?" She shifted on the seat, grumbling and pulling at the fabric of her jeans when it stuck to the back of her legs. "Damned heat. Drops everybody into a lousy mood."

"I see."

She shot Jude a glance. "Point taken, and I apologize." She sighed again. "I don't mean to pick on you, buddy. I just . . . got a load dumped on me earlier, and I guess I'm passing it on to you. That's not fair."

"What or who dumped on you?" Jude asked.

"Your brother."

Jude stiffened visibly behind the steering wheel. "What's his problem?" he finally asked. "I'm sure there's something

that he's not up-front enough to come straight to me about."
He steered the car southward, unconsciously heading toward
Evelyn Pelagi's neighborhood, the last place where they believed the Ravenswood Strangler had tried to strike. Now it
was Friday night, a full week since Evelyn's attack and time
for the guy to hit—if he planned to kill at all. Sometimes
these wackos dropped out of sight and were never heard
from again. There were thousands of unsolved murders in
this city. Jude figured that a lot of the perpetrators, the ones
who planned what they did with great deliberation and efficiency, simply changed their MOs so drastically that the cops
and computers never made a connection. As if this murderer
on the loose wasn't enough of a problem, Brandon had to
poke his nose into things and start screwing them up. And
Jude knew, without it being said, what his brother was going
to focus on this time.

Sandra didn't waste words. In her mind, out her mouth.
"I'm sure you know that the problem is Karla. What else?
Someone saw the two of you in the Zephyr last night and
told him."

"Why'd he call you and not me?" Jude demanded. They
cruised up Belmont, past Ann Sather's Restaurant and the
CTA elevated train station, another dozen restaurants dot-
ting the crowded sidewalks between shops that filled their
windows with cheap imported merchandise. Farther up and
on the left, he passed a neighborhood bookstore that sold
science fiction, horror and fantasy, a place called *Stars Our
Destination*, in which Jude loved to spend a few hours every
now and then. He thought Karla might like the place; he'd
have to bring her over.

Beside him, Sandra stared out the window and
shrugged. "Why does he do anything the way he does? I
know he's a relative and everything, but in case you haven't
noticed he's not exactly the most well-liked guy at the station. We've got some old-time hard-asses there, but he
seems to put off even those guys. Hasn't he been talked to
a couple of times by people in Command?"

"Yeah," Jude said grimly as he turned south onto Sheffield
and eased past a couple of double-parked cars, automatically
checking the drivers and gauging what they were doing. "Plus,
I think IA's had him in their sights once or twice for God

knows what, but he always manages to squirm out of it." He passed the parked cars and looked up the width of Sheffield as he crawled toward Wellington and the majestic towers of St. Alphonsus Catholic Church, noting that on the right was the German bakery next door to the building in which Jason Spiro lived. "So what'd he have to say?"

"A bunch, most of which I don't care to repeat to a stranger, much less a friend."

"I wouldn't have doubted it for a minute."

Sandra turned her head and gave him a frank look. "You'd better talk to him, Jude. Honest to Christ, he's already on the edge of what the Department will tolerate and doesn't have the common sense to keep things under wraps. But you and Karla . . . you should've heard him. I could swear he's totally flipped out this time."

Jude frowned. "Well, I'm sure the fact that Karla is black pissed him off no end, but he didn't outright threaten to do anything to her, did he?"

"Not in so many words, though he made some less than complimentary claims you ought to know about. He wasn't particularly kind about what he thought of you, either. Apparently being family makes it okay in his eyes to rant about a younger brother and swear to beat some sense into him."

"That'll be the day," Jude retorted, but it was an automatic response, a verbal defense he didn't think about or mean and Sandra knew it.

"I'm telling you again, you better talk to him. Especially if you plan to keep seeing Karla—"

"I do."

"Then you need to at least try to calm him down before he explodes and does something stupid or humiliating. He's never going to be happy about this relationship."

"I'm not asking him to sing songs," Jude said, his voice harsh. "I don't care if he's happy about it or not.

"He just has to accept it."

" 'Morning, beautiful."

Karla groaned aloud. There he was on her doorstep, big and handsome, with a mischievous grin that warmed her heart though it didn't wake her up. She felt like a foolish little girl, standing at the bottom of the stairs in plaid cotton pajamas, even if they were styled like a man's and extra roomy. "You big dumb cop," she said with a smile. "Do you have any *idea* what time it is?"

Jude shoved his hands into his pockets, purposely ignoring the look she shot toward the watch on his wrist. "Time for coffee, I'd bet." His grin widened. "Unless of course you already have company."

She wrapped a hand around one of his arms, letting her fingernails sink in slightly. "You're getting dumber by the minute. It must be the heat—you'd better come inside."

"My brain does appear to be melting under all this sun. You can see it's already washed all the color out of my hair." Jude followed her up the steps, peering around her to see Creature's long snout poking through the partially closed door. Something whacked the other side of the door a couple of times—the dog's tail, swinging in welcome.

"Everybody has an excuse," Karla retorted.

Jude winced good-naturedly. "Good comeback, though maybe a bit on the sharp side, my dear."

She led the way into her apartment, then folded her arms and faced him. "You deserve it for waking me up. And don't think *I'm* making the coffee either, buster. You make me lose sleep, so you buy breakfast."

"I'll keep that in mind," he said warmly.

She flushed and struggled not to laugh. "Pushing your luck this morning, aren't you?"

His blue eyes sparkled. "I'll make up for it with eggs and bacon at Loree's, and plenty of coffee. If you're still hungry, you can top it off with one of their specialties—a triple chocolate ice-cream sundae."

"At eight in the morning?" Karla asked, incredulous.

Jude reached down and scratched at Creature's ears where she was butting his legs to get his attention. "It's not unheard of. I've had them earlier."

"You keep strange hours to begin with," she said. "I'll get dressed."

"Why? Those are cute."

"These are pajamas!"

"So who will know?"

"You *are* out of your mind—heatstroke, no doubt, from running around all night in that hot car without using the air-conditioning. What does your partner have to say about your penchant for high temperatures?" Karla demanded. "Or did you manage to cook her out of riding with you again? I'm changing my clothes."

"I'll help."

She couldn't believe it; he actually started to follow her out of the dining room. "Down boy," she warned, amused. She pushed him backward with a hand against his chest. "You stay here."

Jude caught her wrist in one big hand. "Condemned to stay with the dogs?"

"Just the one." Karla nodded toward the greyhound still trying to lean against Jude's leg and started to step away. He surprised her by pulling her forward and into an easy hug instead. Her mouth opened to protest but the words were lost behind a soft kiss, only a few seconds long but enough to make her senses float.

"Okay, but don't be long," he said.

His face was inches from hers, and she saw his eyes as she never had before; the familiar light blues had a faint golden ring around each iris. They were incredible. The touch of his lips had made her overly warm and suddenly the long sleeves and baggy pants of the pajamas were too much. "I'll be out in a minute," she promised. "Two at the most." He nodded and released her.

Surprisingly, the small bathroom was cooler. Karla hadn't really been asleep when he'd rung the bell, though she'd only been up long enough to muddle her way through a decision about what to wear and hang the outfit over the shower-curtain rod. She *had* been hungry and thinking about breakfast, although the concept of food had suddenly faded from priority. What had prompted the kiss? Oh, there was no denying that there was an attraction between her and Jude—the air practically crackled whenever they got within two feet of one another. Still, to *kiss* her . . .

She wasn't the romance-of-the-month type and felt certain Jude knew that without being told; if she was going to fall for someone—no, not just someone, but *Jude*—she'd likely do it big time. So here she was, shut in the bathroom, wavering between her heart, which was pounding out *Go for it!* and her mind, which was saying *Wake up, fool. You're opening a box full of trouble.*

"I've carried heavy boxes before," Karla said softly.

She heard the sound of Jude walking across the wooden floor in the kitchen and the click of Creature's nails following him. Jude said something to the dog and, from the sound of things, opened the refrigerator door. She hoped he had the sense not to feed the animal whatever goodies he found in the fridge. A full-length mirror hung on the back of the bathroom door and she slipped out of her pajamas and stood naked, looking critically at her reflection. Her body was in good shape thanks to the workouts; trim and lean, her skin was a smooth, uniform color because of the long sleeves she wore year-round. She looked at her arms and realized that it'd been years since they'd been bare except for here in the bathroom or, much more rarely, in a darkened bedroom, and what would Jude say to that? *Especially* Jude? If she didn't stop this relationship right now, it was a good bet she was on her way to finding out.

Karla filled the sink and rinsed her face with cold water, but it didn't help her make a decision. Jude's short knock at the door nearly caused her to bang her nose against the faucet as she bent over the sink to rinse again. "Hey," he called amiably. "There are people and animals starving out here and we can't find the dog food. Aren't you supposed to be in charge?"

She smiled as she slipped into a pair of denim jeans, then donned a lightweight cotton poet's shirt with long sleeves held at the wrist with elastic. "Always."

"Well, if you don't come out of there pretty soon, Creature and I are going to split the old pizza we found in the fridge, and elect someone else to take command. Don't say I didn't warn you."

Karla heard him return to the kitchen as she dried her face and hands, then picked up a wide-toothed comb and ran it through the streaked brown curls that fell to her shoulders. After deliberating for a moment, she finally pulled the soft mass into a ponytail and secured it with a hair band, ignoring the shorter strays that fell against the back of her neck and here and there along her forehead. A touch of powder on her face and she was ready.

Well, almost.

When Karla walked out of the bathroom and into the kitchen, she still had no idea what she was going to do.

Loree's Ice Cream Shoppe was a brightly lit restaurant on the corner of Foster and Sawyer, furnished like a thousand others in the Chicagoland area. Karla and Jude followed the waitress to a booth by a window overlooking Foster and close to the entrance of the restaurant. The location gave them a warm wash of the heavy outside air every time a customer came in or left, but neither minded; it was a break from the air-conditioning, which seemed to be operating at high efficiency.

"Nice place," Karla commented. The ceiling had a wide tray shape built into the middle, its outer edges finished in a band of imitation stained glass boasting a pattern of green-and-gold fall leaves. Tulip-shaped light fixtures with amber shades hung over every booth and gave the large, rectangular room a golden glow, despite full daylight.

"It's all right. Pretty ordinary as far as the way it looks, but they make great ice cream. And coffee." The window at their table faced south and they had a full view of Albany Park College across the street; sharp, hot sunbeams already striped Foster Avenue from the east. The light coming from Jude's right turned his blond hair silver white, softening the faint wrinkles on his face and deepening the more prominent ones. The bright blue of his right eye was nearly washed away by the sunlight and gave Karla a brief, uncanny glimpse of what he would look like in thirty years. He was, she realized with a pang of envy, still going to be as handsome in that sort of well-preserved way that happened to men who took very good care of themselves. How would she look that far in the future, her body with its history of ups and downs and—

"Hey," Jude said. He waved a stainless-steel spoon playfully in front of her eyes and Karla blinked, embarrassed. "Is my company that dismal or are you still asleep?"

"Sorry." Flustered, she plucked the paper napkin from the table and smoothed it onto her lap. "I guess you're right. I'm not awake yet."

"Then we're even," Jude said lightly. He handed her a menu and turned their coffee cups upright so the waitress would fill them on her next pass. "It's early on a Saturday, you're not awake yet, and I haven't been to sleep. Isn't equality between the sexes a wonderful thing?"

Karla grinned, unable to pass up such an opportunity. "Who said you were equal to me?"

Jude's eyebrows raised. "Well, I—"

"He's not," said a cold voice from behind her. "He's *better* than you."

Startled, Karla twisted on the booth's seat as Jude's gaze shifted to a spot over her right shoulder and his eyes went hard. She caught a glimpse of Jude's white, furious face in the corner of her eye before her sight settled on the man who'd spoken. There was no time for anything but a glance and the realization that the brittle, vaguely threatening words were coming from a uniformed cop. "Excuse me?"

"I guess you didn't hear me," the man said flatly. He raised his voice. "So I'll repeat myself—"

"No, you *won't*." Jude was already out of the booth and standing by her side of the table. As he faced the stranger, his big hands were rolled into fists and he looked angrier than Karla had ever seen him. "You're way out of line, Brandon."

"What are you going to do, Jude? Lose that famous temper of yours and punch me out?" The man Jude had called Brandon stood and Karla saw with a jolt that he was slightly taller than Jude, with the same build and sun-washed blond hair, those crystalline blue eyes—

"I take it you two know each other?" Karla managed. Her voice sounded small and she cursed her cowardice, wanting to sound large and cool and confident despite the feeling of complete doom that had settled in her stomach at seeing these two, so very *alike*, scowling at each other in this brightly lit restaurant.

"Well, I guess so," the stranger sneered.

"Karla, this is my brother, Brandon," Jude said tersely. "I'd hoped to introduce you under better circumstances but I see that's not going to be possible. I was probably a fool for thinking otherwise."

"What'd you expect me to do, say 'pleased to meetcha" and offer my hand?" Brandon laughed. "I don't think so."

"You folks want to sit together?" The waitress, oblivious to the tension between the three people, thrust a coffeepot in front of Karla and started to pour. She nodded at Brandon and indicated Jude and Karla's booth with her head. "It'd be easier if you moved over here—"

"Don't pour that," Brandon said sharply. "The black woman was just leaving."

The waitress froze and her eyes, wide and suddenly very frightened, met Karla's steady gray ones. Karla felt sorry for the woman—girl, actually. Still a teenager, without a clue about what to do; showing her age was a childish plastic pin on her left breast pocket that said LOIS in primary colors.

"Pour the coffee. We're not going anywhere." Jude glared at the waitress and she nodded dumbly, her hand trembling as she tried to regulate the stream of coffee.

"You got insurance for that old beater you're driving, Lois?" Brandon's voice was suddenly soft and filled with false concern. "It's a five-hundred-dollar fine if you don't, you know."

"This is ridiculous," Karla said firmly. Poor Lois looked like she was ready to erupt in hysterical tears, and it wasn't hard to imagine that these two men might start swinging at each other. She didn't want to be here if that happened, and the fact that they were relatives made the whole sordid thing even more horrifying. "I've lost my appetite anyway." She tried to slide out of the booth but Jude, incredibly, refused to step aside. She stared up at him, aghast, as the waitress retreated gratefully. Karla hoped to God that Lois was going straight for the manager. "Jude? Let me out, please."

"I believe *Brandon* was just leaving," Jude said obstinately, staring at his brother. "Weren't you?" In the midst of the angry, rigid faces, Karla could clearly see the family resemblance, so clearly, in fact, she was amazed she hadn't made the connection instantly. "You didn't want to eat here anyway."

Silence then, stretching as if it were some great and tangible thing that could go on forever. Brandon's eyes flicked to her and narrowed; the glint in their depths made Karla go cold. He shrugged suddenly, glancing down at his table and its load of empty plates, the movement reminding her of a name her mother had for a certain kind of dog.

A sneak biter.

"You got that right," Brandon said easily. "I'm done, and I don't much care for the clientele anyway. Still, I want you to see something before I go." His tone of voice turned

agreeable, friendly, the type of *we've-been-buddies-all-our-lives*
banter Karla would've expected to hear between brothers
rather than the acid-laden words spoken so far. His next
move, however, was harsh and accurate, and way too fast for
her to stop. Before she could protest, Brandon grabbed her
right wrist in one hand and yanked the elasticized sleeve of
her poet's blouse up past her elbow, exposing the flesh of
her wrist and inner forearm with a righteous jeer at his
younger brother. No evasive action in the world could have
helped her, and fighting his hold would have only demeaned
her further in Jude's eyes. Karla's heart felt like it had thundered its way right out of the customary spot in her chest
and plummeted to the bile-filled bottom of her stomach.
How long had it been since those pale pink scars had been
exposed to the judging eyes of someone else?

"Aren't they pretty, Jude?" Brandon hissed with a smile
that turned his rugged face ugly. "Call me when you bring
this babe home to Mom and Dad. Your colored girlfriend's
a *junkie*, brother."

"Not anymore," Jude shot back. He didn't miss a beat in
his answer or in the way he slapped Brandon's hand away
from Karla's wrist and tugged the sleeve of her blouse back
into place. His brother's smug look wavered, then disintegrated altogether with Jude's next words. "Besides, I'm not
an idiot, okay? I already knew about it."

Brandon scowled. "Then your standards are sinking."

"No, they've gone up." Jude's face was so stiff with anger
he seemed barely able to form the words.

His brother chuckled suddenly. "Oh, *please*. Where'd
you dig up that line of crap—Public Relations One-Oh-One?
Or maybe you've been rehearsing it." Frustration darkened
Brandon's eyes. "Christ, Jude. You belong with a woman of
your own kind, and you *know* it. Maybe you can lie to her,
but not me. Not *family*." Brandon snatched his hat off the table. "I'll see you around."

"Not if I can help it," was Jude's heated reply, but
Brandon, his face twisted with growing hostility, was already
out of earshot and pushing through the revolving door that
led onto Foster and Sawyer. "Whoever said people get better
as they get older either lied or never met Brandon." Jude
turned and slid back into his side of the booth. "I can't be-

lieve I didn't notice him when we came in. He must have been in the rest room."

"Mister?" The waitress stood timidly by their table. "That guy, uh—I guess he was your brother? He didn't pay his bill." She looked helpless.

"I'll take care of it." Jude sounded thoroughly disgusted. "Combine it with ours. We'll start with coffee."

"So we're staying," Karla said after Lois had disappeared again. She ran her tongue around the inside of her cheek thoughtfully. "Despite what your brother told you about me."

Jude's gaze didn't waver. "Like I said, I already knew."

Karla sat back and crossed her arms in an unconscious gesture of self-protection. She wasn't sure how she felt about that, but in reality that wasn't the focal point here, not right now. "Well, then what are you doing here?"

"What does it look like I'm doing?" he shot back. "Getting ready to order breakfast on a Saturday morning and sharing a table with a woman whom I would very much like to know better."

"Why?" Karla asked bluntly. "You're sharing a table with a junkie." She held up a hand to stop him from interrupting. Her menu, as well as the coffee the waitress had finally poured, sat untouched in front of her. "And I think your brother was right in at least one respect." Her eyes were hard. "So tell me in your own words what exactly he saw in your eyes."

"I'm not like my brother!" Jude said heatedly. His face had gone scarlet.

"Oh? How about your father, then? Or even your rock-steady mother?" She was so outraged her voice was starting to shake. "I'm not your damned *experiment*, Jude Ewing, someone with whom you can test yourself to see if you've conquered the family bigotry."

"But—"

"Shut up," she said. "I'm not finished talking. I'm a person, and I live and breathe, and just like you, I *hurt* when someone drops a line of shit on me. Like now." She grabbed her purse and started to stand; she'd be damned if she'd let him see her cry.

"Karla, wait. *Please*." Jude snatched at her arm and managed to get a handful of the poet's blouse.

"Let go!" she snapped. Everything about the stupid blouse was elastic and when she pulled against his grip, the neckline started to stretch.

"No," he said firmly. "I won't. I listened to what you had to say, now you have to do the same."

"Go to hell!"

"No way. Brandon'll get there first." His attempt at a quip failed terribly, but he still hung on to her sleeve. Now he was steering her back down, and the maddening stretch of the blouse's neckline gave her no choice but to follow, and finally sit. "Karla, listen. I know you hurt, and I never meant to do that to you. If I close my eyes, you're just like anyone else—"

"That's the stupidest thing I've ever heard you say," she said bitterly. "You can't keep them closed all the time."

"I don't want to," he retorted. "I don't care what color your skin is."

"And that's the biggest *lie* you've ever told yourself!"

"Then I don't *want* to care," he snapped. "It's ridiculous to let skin pigment come between two people who care about each other. And I care about you."

She snorted. "Be realistic. People don't change."

"Now who's being stupid? Of course they do, if they want to badly enough." He leaned toward her. "I despise my brother, Karla, and I don't think very much of my old man, either. I might've been raised to think like Brandon, but everything in me fights it, every day. Because I know it's just not *fair*. And nothing Brandon or my dad can ever say will make it right with me." He leaned back. "I don't have to change, Karla. I just have to resist the stuff I was raised with, the old habits. *Of all people, you know that can be done.*"

Karla stared at him, wanting to be but not knowing if she was truly convinced. "How did you know I'm a junkie?" she finally asked.

"An ex-junkie." Jude shrugged. "I'm a detective. Curiosity is in my blood. While it wasn't something I would've done under normal guy-meets-girl circumstances, you were connected to Evelyn Pelagi, so I ran a check on you. All that stuff is still in the records, though it's years old, of course."

"You don't understand, Jude." Karla's hands gripped the edge of the table. "I am not an ex-junkie, I am a *junkie*. Despite your persuasive little speech, I will *always* be a junkie, like an alcoholic will *always* be an alcoholic. I live with it every day, and I think about it every time I go to the doctor for a sore throat and he gives me antibiotics, then offers me a prescription for painkillers. It will never, *ever*, go away." In a nearly savage move, she pushed both sleeves up to her elbows and thrust the small, pale knots of scar tissue toward him, inescapable testimony to past abuse. "Sure, I have a handle on it, but that's entirely because of Evelyn, not me. *She* was the one who yanked me out of the trash, Jude, and believe me, I kicked and screamed all the way. If you've got some romantic notion about how strong and determined I must have been to change, or how I took a good hard look at myself and didn't like what I saw—well, you can kiss those off right now. I got hooked on cocaine in college and when that wasn't enough of a rush, I went to crack and heroin and speedballs. And I liked it, oh did I ever." Her mouth tightened into a grim line. "I probably still would, if I sunk a needle into my arm again. *That's* the thing that's never going to go away—that's the thing that's *never* going to change!"

"But you can live with it," Jude said stubbornly. His bright blue eyes were frank and unnerving. "Don't you see? Lots of shit in the world never goes away, Karla. That's what I'm telling you—we both have our situations, and we do the best we can to deal with them. Sure, the effects might never totally disappear, but Christ!" He slapped the table for emphasis, making her jump. "We're adults here, not screwed-up adolescents. We can *learn* from our mistakes, and our lives—isn't that what you've done? At least you've got a handle on the skeleton in your closet." Jude's face had returned to its normal color, but now his eyes clouded. "Hell, you just met the skeleton in mine."

The waitress's arrival to take their order postponed Karla's response for a few minutes but didn't stop it. After Lois had gone to turn in the food ticket, Karla folded her hands school style in front of her and frowned at her breakfast companion. "I have to admit I didn't understand why you avoided talking about Brandon when we were in Reza's. He's awfully . . . I don't know. I suppose *vehement* might be a good word. He sounds dangerous."

"Well," Jude said reluctantly, "to be honest, I don't know if he is or not—dangerous, I mean. Maybe. I know I can't do anything about him. Or my dad, for that matter. It all comes down to that 'wanting to change' thing." He met her gaze, his expression hopeful. "But my mom's a good, decent person, and I've got an older sister who's one of the nicest people you'd ever want to meet." Jude toyed with his coffee cup, then opened a creamer into it. "Brandon and my dad both . . . well, they're hard to live with."

Karla fell silent for a few moments, watching Jude as he in turn watched the cream swirl on the surface of his coffee and waited for Lois to come back and top off the brew from a fresh pot. When the plates of food arrived a couple of minutes later they still hadn't spoken, and their appetites seemed to have gone the way of their words for a while. They picked at cheese and bacon omelets without much enthusiasm and left enough food so that when the plates were cleared the young woman who'd served them asked nervously if something was wrong with the food. Finally, though, they had enough in their stomachs to cushion the acrid aftertaste of the surprise encounter with Brandon.

"Jude," Karla said at last, "why did you ask me out?" He opened his mouth but she held up one hand. "Wait, I'm not finished." Her hand wavered in midair for a moment, then she placed it palm down on the table next to his lighter one. "I mean, look at the big picture, Detective. Do I have to spell out all the differences here? You don't seem like you'd be the rebellious type, yet I keep going back to that experiment theory." Her eyes fixed on his, but to his credit he neither blinked nor lowered his gaze. "I mean, really. What on earth were you thinking?"

Unexpectedly, Jude smiled. "The same thing you were. You're so smart, but you're obviously so *blind*, too. Remember what made you *not* say no? It was something . . . indefinable." He looked flustered for a second, but plunged on. "I looked at you and saw someone beautiful and intriguing, someone I wanted more than anything to get closer to. And I haven't changed my mind."

His hands, strong and warm and so pale next to her darker skin, closed over hers. "Tell me you've changed yours," he said softly, "and I'll drive you home right now, and not bother you again. But I hope you haven't."

But Karla could only sit wordlessly across the table.

35

Saturday Afternoon

"Why do we have to go? Why bother? She was an old woman, and sick. Who—"

"Jesus, Hernando, stop *whining*. You sound like an old woman! We're going, fool, because she was my father's sister and if we don't show up he'll be pissed like you wouldn't believe." Carissa stood indecisively before the cramped closet, trying to remember the last time they'd done laundry and wondering if there was anything clean enough in the piles of clothes wadded on the floor to wear to Aunt Imalda's wake. What would get her past the critical eyes of her relatives? She had no intention of going to the funeral, and if it was good for nothing else, being seven months' pregnant would give her the excuse she'd need to get her and Hernando out of that part.

"So what?" Hernando asked petulantly. His arms were draped over the bed's edge, and he looked a lot like a mound of dirty clothes. His face was grimy, and God knew when he'd last changed his shirt and jeans. Not that she was much better—although at least she was willing to change for the wake and check her face for dirt.

"You think Neilson gave you a hard time, wait till you fuck with my dad," she retorted. "You should know better by now." She didn't have any maternity dresses—what she'd always called tents—but she saw the edge of something promising sticking up and pulled on it: out came a navy-blue maternity top with white buttons. Inspecting it, she gave it a shake and thought she might be able to get by without digging out the iron. God, she hadn't felt good since last Thursday, when Hernando had killed that woman with the little dog on Ashland and let Carissa bring her back. Thinking about that night made Carissa wonder briefly what had happened when the woman woke up, what she'd said, or done— was she still alive today and feeling the way Carissa was? And the thing with her aunt, it had been so fucking *close* that it pained her to think about it. Now her stomach always hurt, and the pain tripled every time she remembered how close she'd come to getting another spin. Plus the bloodstains on her legs were getting more focused every day, like the mangled holes in Hernando's chest which were becoming more visible. Not just to her—she didn't give a shit anyway. Each day that went by made it more dangerous for them to be seen by other people, and this morning that stupid, high-cheekboned, no-name bitch who'd latched onto Tho had commented snidely that Carissa's legs looked dirty. Next time the woman might be able to make out the shape of the bloodstains, and after that . . . who knew? Nervousness had made Carissa throw out the bath mat two days ago, but what would they tell people when the blood splattered all over them both began to take on that nice, telltale red color?

"Your old man doesn't scare me," Hernando said, but all the interest had gone out of his voice and when Carissa glanced over at him he was lying back on the rumpled covers and staring at the ceiling. At least *he* seemed able to push the problem from his mind—or maybe he was in too much pain or too far gone to care. It was certainly a tempting idea. . . .

"I'll be ready in five minutes," she said. Her tone of voice was sharp more for herself than for him, to bring her thoughts back to the here and now. "What about you?"

"I'm ready now," he answered. "I'm not changing." His voice was dull, his eyes glazed, and despite the sweltering heat in and outside the apartment, he still wore the leather jacket over a T-shirt. If it was an attempt to hide his wounds, then he was showing his stupidity; the jacket's ripped leather did nothing to conceal the injuries that were becoming more and more apparent. Carissa shrugged and turned away. He was, she suspected, as dead as she felt, and the bottom line was that she didn't much care. She just hoped the heat didn't make him rot.

Ramon Valdez slid the cassette of his choice into his boom box and turned up the volume. Not too loud, or Mr. Lucanowicz would come stomping down the stairs demanding to know if Ramon was trying to wake the dead, and he'd be completely serious. Still, as long as he kept the volume reasonably low, Ramon could whistle along—he couldn't sing worth shit—while he worked. His job at Restmoor Funeral Home wasn't the most pleasant in the world and he appreciated the music because it helped make the time go faster, helped turn his mind away from what he was doing. All the cassettes he brought to work were compilations of his favorite tunes, and he was always working on a selection tape, building another one from the new CDs that he bought regularly. At thirty-four, he still lived at home but his parents didn't complain about the noise or his choice of tunes, and he knew they were happy he was into music instead of beer or bar whores like some of the other guys his age.

"Okay," he said to the naked old woman lying on the aluminum table, "let's get this over with." He checked to make sure the drains were clear, then pulled his rubber gloves back on and added a fiber face mask to cut down the smell before picking up a scalpel. The other guy who worked here, a part-timer, never wore a mask but Ramon still hadn't mastered the trick of completely closing off his nose and breathing through his mouth. Besides, who knew what kinds of germs came off these corpses? Ramon didn't even smoke, and he wasn't going to take any chances about what went into his lungs, no way. This poor old bird looked eaten up, and he'd seen plenty of cancer victims before. The Big C might not be contagious, but Ramon was smart enough to know a person that sick had hardly any resistance to the viruses and bacteria floating around. *That* was why he never bathed or embalmed a cadaver without first donning gloves.

It was a nasty job but the pay was decent and he'd been licensed to do it for almost ten years. It beat the hell out of loading lumber at some Builders Square or stocking shelves at a hardware store. After all this time he knew what he was doing and could at least feel proud that Mr. Lucanowicz no longer bothered to check his work.

Ramon bent to his task, cannulating the femoral artery in the woman's neck and adjusting the fluid pump to the right pressure, checking now and then to make sure the embalming fluid wasn't going so fast it'd make her weakened arteries blow in the postdeath version of an aneurysm. The enema was mucky but no big deal. Before working here, Ramon had worked as an orderly in a nursing home and helped the aides do the "backside tube tasks," as they'd called them, plenty of times. By far the worse thing was cutting open the abdomen and using a tube to suck out the internal organs; they came up the tube in mushy, red chunks that made noises too awful to describe and that the hum from the vacuum couldn't disguise. And this one—what was her name? Curiosity made him check the clipboard while he threaded the big suture needle. Imalda Novia, and when he looked at her year of birth he nearly choked. Jesus—she was younger than his mother! So completely wasted away—in death her mouth had a bitter downward turn to it, as though she was still frowning about something she'd left undone.

For some reason, the thought made Ramon shudder and he made his fingers go faster as he worked to close the holes left by the embalming process.

Restmoor Funeral Home was a run-down building on the corner of Western and 53rd. The neighborhood was low-income Hispanic and clean in that well-scrubbed way that hard-earned money seems to indicate—worn around the edges and patched, but still bright and with a lot of life left in it. As Carissa and Hernando turned into the small parking lot at the building's rear, Carissa started to wonder why her father had chosen to have his sister waked and buried by a Polish rather than Puerto Rican outfit, but the question fizzled away before its completion when she got a good look at the funeral home. Obviously Papa had chosen Restmoor because of the money thing.

The inside of the home wasn't as bad as the outside, or perhaps the heavy red drapes obscured the wear. Neither of them bothered to sign in—Carissa knew her mother would do it for her later—and her aunt was the only person being waked on this broiling summer day. Most of the family was already there: Carissa's mother and father, brothers and sister, her father's other sister and a dozen more annoying relatives from her mother's side of the family—uncles and more aunts, too many cousins to count. Her mother had some nerve to say Carissa didn't keep in touch; shit, if she'd tried, she'd spend her time doing nothing but visiting family.

Standing beside her, Hernando looked . . . *empty*, as if all the emotion had been sucked out of him. His face was white and much worse than hers. At least she'd slapped some pink powder on her cheeks back at the apartment; his eyes were so sunken in shadows they looked like black depressions in white bread dough. Both of them had instinctively shoved their hands deep into the pockets of their clothes, Hernando into his jacket and her into the front pockets of the stupid tent-thing that passed for a maternity top. She hoped no one wanted to grasp her hand. They'd be pretty fucking surprised to see that the ends of her fingers were a flat, dried brown nearly all the way to the first knuckle. Hernando's were more advanced than that; on the way here, she'd watched him do a bored drumbeat on the car seat every time they stopped at a traffic light. She couldn't help the snide smile that pulled at her mouth when she imagined herself and Hernando getting railroaded into going to some cousin or another's house for food after the wake. The looks that would appear on the faces of the family as she and Hernando poked among the cream-cheese-wrapped pickles and mini-quesadillas with their twiggy fingers might be a hoot that was almost worth the aggravation.

They stayed away from the coffin as long as they could. Then Carissa's father began glowering across the room in their direction and she knew that if she and her boyfriend—the father of her *bastardo* child in her father's eyes—didn't go pay their respects, her father would start raising hell. While she didn't care what he thought in general, she was up for anything at all that would lessen the general aggravation of being here to begin with. She'd much rather be home with her feet up, in the hopes it would lessen the steady, pounding ache in her side as well as the swelling in her ankles. Plus she and Hernando needed to figure out some way to get another buzz. It wasn't hard to guess that if they didn't come up with something soon, the pain for both of them might become so bad they'd end up lying on the floor and screaming. Hernando had finally admitted that the holes in his chest felt like torches on which the flames were getting bigger, and the more visible their original injuries became, the more her nerves jangled. What if they got so bad they couldn't function—couldn't even walk in public? Then what—insanity? Eventual death?

Or a private existence of agony?

Carissa shuddered inside. Better to die than that.

"Go pay your respects, girl. Now."

Her father's voice seethed in her ear, its normally grating pitch low and furious. She nodded quickly and surreptitiously tucked her hand into the folds along one elbow of Hernando's jacket, steering him toward the far back of the room and the waiting coffin. The cheap, polished wood gleamed amid the stands and vases of carnations, flowers wilted from the outside heat before they'd been brought inside. The air around the casket was heavy and smothering, a blanket of sickly-sweet scent that crawled up Carissa's nose and into the creases of her clothing. God, she *hated* that smell—it would take days to get it out of her hair.

There was no getting around looking into the coffin and at the face of the old woman they'd killed yesterday, and knowing they could have brought her back, that they'd been so close, just made it worse. Looking down at the drawn face, aged far beyond what it should have been, it wasn't difficult to believe that Aunt Imalda was better off dead, freed of the pain from the cancer that had chewed its way through her body with deadly efficiency. Who wanted to live like that, and for how much longer, anyway? Still, it was a shame they hadn't been able to get a high off the body; at this point, what else would she have been good for?

"How much longer do we have to stand up here?" Hernando asked querulously. "I feel like an—what the hell?"

"What?" Something odd in her boyfriend's tone of voice caught Carissa's attention. Her thoughts had turned away from her dead relative to the just-as-dead ends of the fingers she'd been clicking together inside the pocket of her top. "What's the matter?"

"She *moved*," Hernando said in a low voice.

"You're so full of shit it's coming out of your mouth," she whispered back. "Are you out of your *mind*?" Carissa felt Hernando's fingers dig deeply into the flesh of her arm, then he pulled her backward abruptly, leading her between the small clusters of people here and there around the room, threading his way through the maze of cheap metal folding chairs with her in tow. "We can't leave yet," she protested. "If we don't say good-bye to my parents, they'll bitch at me for a month."

"Trust me, in a minute they won't care. We have to get out of here now," he insisted. "Or—shit, there's your father."

"Where the hell are you two going?" Mr. Novia's olive-skinned face was hard and broad, and his eyes were harsh as he looked at his daughter and her companion. "You're supposed to go to the funeral, then come to the house with everyone else."

Carissa nodded automatically, trying desperately to look ill enough to get out of the whole, dull situation. "I know, but I don't feel—"

Bedlam erupted behind them.

She and Hernando whirled at the same time, watching, stupefied, as Carissa's father spun, then dashed toward the far end of the room. A man whose voice she didn't recognize was yelling something they couldn't quite make out above the jumble of other voices that continued to escalate.

"What the devil is going on here?" Carissa heard her father demand. "What—*dear God in Heaven!*" Someone else, a woman, began to scream monotonously.

"*She's alive! She's alive! She's ali*—" The crisp sound of a slap cut the shrill repetitions off in midsyllable.

"I *told* you." Hernando, the bastard, had a big, snappy grin on his hideously white face, like some kind of sharp-toothed albino cat that had disemboweled a mouse. "Fuck it, we might as well get a closer look now."

"Fuck *you!*" Carissa spat. "I'm not going near her!"

"Sure you are." His hand was around her arm again, the dried ends of his fingers digging painfully into muscle; it felt like he was trying to cut her with a dull butter knife but the more she resisted, the deeper he pushed his fingers and the harder he pulled on her arm. "Come on."

"Stop it, you asshole!" She tried to pull away and nearly got yanked off her feet for the effort. "All right!" she yelled. "We'll go satisfy your shitty curiosity!" If anyone noticed the volume of her voice or the name she'd called Hernando, they didn't show it. All eyes were turned toward the dark wood coffin and its occupant, and Carissa's mouth dropped open at what she saw.

Aunt Imalda was sitting up.

No mortuary excuse about muscle spasms or electrical synapses was going to explain why this woman who was filled with embalming fluid was *moving*, flailing her hands and beating at her body. Her long-nailed fingers went up and into the folds of loose skin showing above the lace collar of her dress and she began tearing at her flesh, going for the meatier parts underneath. All the while she made a sound, a keening that floated somewhere between a strangle and a moan.

"Oh, this is *too* cool," Hernando said in awe. Carissa forgot to resist as he led her closer to the coffin, pushing against the flow of people frantically climbing around the overturned chairs and purses scattered along the floor. Most of the floral arrangements at the end of the room had gotten knocked aside and trampled. Now the coffin was rocking dangerously, its movement dislodging the folds of cheap black velvet Velcroed around its base and showing the frame of the not-very-stable aluminum cart on which it rested.

"We already knew this could happen, stupid," Carissa breathed. "We should get out of here." But Hernando was too fascinated and didn't hear her, just kept edging toward the convulsing semicorpse and pulling her along with him. Why didn't the nosy jerk let her *go?* They were within a few feet of the coffin now, and Carissa wanted to gag when the dead woman turned her face and her eyelids opened, a slow-motion *pulling* that made Carissa realize the embalmer had sewn her aunt's eyelids closed . . . but not tightly enough. A disjointed forcing of the neck muscles and Aunt Imalda focused on them, the dry eyes behind the torn lids bulging with recognition and a feeble sort of spotty gray fire. Her lips began to work more furiously but they didn't part, and Carissa wondered suddenly if funeral homes still sewed the mouths of corpses shut. What exactly would Aunt Imalda say if that lipsticked, brutal slash of a mouth suddenly opened?

Murderers! You killed me and were supposed to bring me back—but you didn't finish the job and now LOOK WHAT'S HAPPENED TO ME!

"Hernando," she whispered in desperation. "Stop—I don't think we should go any closer." Inexplicably he finally did halt and Carissa nearly sighed with relief. His reason was quickly apparent; the funeral director, the elderly Mr. Lucanowicz himself, had stepped between them and the casket. He's brave, Carissa thought with a vague sense of admiration, or maybe crazy. No matter what Hernando would have said or tried to do, no way would she have gotten within reaching distance of the dead woman, much less stepped to the side of the coffin to steady it like Lucanowicz was doing now. He paid for his courage, too, as Aunt Imalda turned her attention in his direction and grabbed at him, then literally went into his outstretched arms. To her horror, Carissa saw that whoever had dressed the body hadn't bothered to zip up the black dress in the back; now it flapped open, sliding almost all the way around to the front. The exposed rib cage looked like it belonged on a starvation victim, and Carissa and the appalled onlookers caught a glimpse of the oversized abdominal stitches. Abruptly, Aunt Imalda went limp, sagging into Lucanowicz's arms and hanging there, dress askew and sleeves bunched around her dangling arms as her head lolled slowly to one side and was still at last.

Dead, finally, as she was supposed to be.

Carissa managed to turn Hernando toward the door and hurry him out. The voice of Carissa's father was already rising above the babble and confusion. It boomed across the scrape of chairs and the hysterical crying of children who would have nightmares for years, making the old funeral director cringe and shake his head in passionate denial,

no—no—no—

"You embalmed my sister when she was still alive!"

36

"Well," Jude Ewing said. "Here we are."

Sandra Wilfred smiled slightly from the passenger side of Jude's car but didn't turn her head from her study of Cecil Gideon's apartment building. "Yes."

"You ever seen this guy?" Jude tapped his fingers idly against the steering wheel and Sandra did turn then, looking pointedly at him until he stopped. "Sorry."

She turned her gaze back in the direction of the street. "Not in person, only the photos Kimball showed us. Taken from what—a good thirty or forty yards off."

Jude checked the rear and side mirrors automatically. "So what do you think about the scratches across his face?"

"What's to think about?" she retorted. "Obviously someone put them there."

"He could have a cat."

"Stretching it a bit, aren't you?"

Jude shrugged. "Just trying to look at it from all the angles. I'm not screwing up our work shifts on a lark, you know. Frankly, I think we should haul him in and rattle his cage until something shakes out. He fits everything—build, scratches, and especially the description given by the survivor of the last attack. Plus—"

"—there's that anonymous tip."

"Exactly."

"What makes you think he'll crack? We haven't got squat and you know it. Both your 'star' witnesses have admitted they can't pick the guy out of a lineup."

Jude rubbed his chin thoughtfully. "I don't know if this is our guy or not," he said. "I *do* know that it's the weekend, and if the Strangler's going to whack someone again, odds are he'll do it tonight. If there's a remote chance that we can prevent that by pulling in this Gideon guy, I think we ought to go for it."

Suddenly Sandra sat up straight, then ducked. "Well, if that's your decision, you'd better get ready to act on it. Not only did he just get home, but he made us."

Jude scowled and slouched down, peering through the windshield; across the street, Cecil Gideon was staring at Jude's car, then his gaze shifted to another spot down the street. "Shit," the detective growled. "He must have seen Waring. I told that meathead not to use the station car."

"He said he was out of gas," Sandra reminded him.

"He's not." Jude sounded profoundly annoyed. "He's too damned cheap to use a few bucks' worth for the department, or too lazy to fill out a reimbursement form for what he does use."

"Whatever," Sandra said. She'd slid down on the seat until the top of her cropped blond hair barely showed above the line of the passenger door. "Well, he's not running."

"What's he doing? The damned light post's blocking my view."

"Looks like he's going inside anyway—yeah, he's checking his mail." Upright on the seat again, Sandra raised an eyebrow. "So, Mr. Inspector-In-Charge-Of-The-Scene, what now?"

Jude pulled his revolver out of his underarm holster and

checked its ammunition. When he looked at his partner, his eyes were a cold, sharp blue. "How long've we been here? Two, three hours? I've had enough waiting around.

"We're going up."

Cecil couldn't believe it. The *police*, of all things, were sitting out there, watching his building. Were they watching him? He pulled a handful of envelopes out of his mailbox and closed it, then flipped through the bundle without seeing it so he would seem normal to the prying eyes of the men and the one woman in the two cars out front. Did they think he hadn't seen the big gray sedan with the spotlights and extra antennae sprouting from its trunk lid like skinny branches? Did they think he was *blind*, for God's sake?

Cecil dug out his keys and went through the foyer door. Then, in case they could see inside the building, he climbed the stairs at a slower-than-normal pace. Maybe they'd planted more people inside the neighbors' apartments, spies who were now staring at him through the peepholes as he passed. No way would they consider his everyday two- to three-step stride up the stairs normal. They'd think he was . . . what? Running, or something, though God knew there was nothing and no one from whom he had to run.

Except Lillith, of course.

By the time he reached his apartment, the expression on his face had gone from anger to cold calculation. That's what this was all about, wasn't it? Lillith. What had she done? He hadn't talked to her since . . . well, he couldn't remember *exactly* when, but he did remember her saying something cryptic and insinuating that pissed him off so much that he'd hung up on her. Then he'd gone for a run, always the best way to purge his anger and cleanse the mind and body. He'd been running several times since then, at the Fitness Center where it wasn't as satisfying because the best they could do for joggers like him was plant him on a heavy-duty treadmill. He hated those kinds of runs because they made him feel like he was going nowhere, was stranded in one place and fighting to go forward like some noisy little dog choking at the end of a taut leash. The best runs were the hard ones done in the neighborhood, like the one he'd had after his last conversation with Lillith. Generally he got those only on the weekends, but ... there was something funny about those. Thinking about them made a puzzled frown appear on his forehead, because though he felt tired and exhilarated afterward, like he'd pounded the pavement for a good forty-five minutes—

Every time he checked his watch, it told him that the neighborhood runs took over an hour and he just couldn't account for those missing fifteen-minute spans.

Inside his apartment, Cecil looked around blankly. There wasn't much to see—spacious and neat, clear, bright white walls and lots of clean, polished oak floors. No clutter atop the occasional piece of furniture, a minimum of things that needed dusting and maintaining. Even the comforter set on the bed was chosen so that he could simply shake it out and cover the whole bed every morning. He kept his life sparse and economical and, except for the year that he had invested in the lovely Lillith Jerusha, devoted himself mostly to his work. The past year—Lillith's year—had in retrospect been insignificant, a physically pleasurable waste of time. Now, devastated by losing her, he still went into the office on Saturdays to go the extra mile when most people, especially the ones who were less organized, worked weekends to keep up with the load. He didn't keep up, he surpassed—he worked his ass off, all the time. And look what he got in return.

Four plainclothes police officers, sitting outside his building and staring at him as he came around the corner from the bus stop.

"Christ," he said out loud, "I am so *tired.*" When it was only him in the apartment, sounds had a tendency to echo slightly. That's what happened now, and it was another reminder of his last phone call with Lillith, of a time when his angry words had seemed to bounce from one wall of the dining room to the other. He had no furniture in the dining room, preferring to use the room for weight workouts, though he kept his equipment neatly stowed away in the front closet. A workout would be good now, he thought. Stretch in front of the big mirror in the bedroom, then get out the barbells and floor pad and start with a thousand crunches—

Cecil shook his head to straighten out his thoughts and

the scratches across his nose and cheeks throbbed in protest—another frightening gift of the blank spot from that last
post-conversation-with-Lillith run. No, he couldn't start a
workout now, that was ridiculous. He couldn't get rid of the
notion that there were people outside, cops, watching his
apartment, watching *him*. Did they think he'd done something? Surely not. Well, maybe—though he couldn't fathom
what. Couldn't, in fact, think of anything beyond the sudden, overpowering feeling that he had to get *away* from the
apartment, and he had to do it without them seeing him. He
had no worries about leaving anything behind that would in-
criminate him in . . .

He shook his head; for a second it seemed he'd almost
remembered something, almost had a mental finger on
whatever it was that had turned their unwanted attention on
him. Instead, his thoughts veered toward his landlady; she
was a nosy old Slavic woman with no grandchildren and
therefore nothing to take up her time but meddling in the
private business of her tenants. Cecil knew she came into the
apartment when he wasn't here but he didn't care; he'd
been living here so long she'd gotten tired of poking into his
stuff—it was always the same, and he kept it that way
purposely—but she'd probably invite the cops inside without
a warrant. She lived on the first floor and if they managed to
get past the locked foyer door, she was likely sitting in the
old recliner near her front door, waiting for the creak of footsteps to tattle on who came home next. Still, it didn't matter; there was nothing in here to indicate he was anything
but a model citizen.

Abruptly Cecil headed for the back door and let himself
quietly onto the porch. Did they have people watching the
back, too? Of course they would, and he stuck to the shadows to compensate for it. This was easy to do since the way
the back of the building was constructed, the apartments in
his section had deep, narrow porches rather than decklike
things protruding off its backside. He peeked around the corner of the building and saw two stiff men sitting in a normal-
looking car, almost walked out in front of it until he saw one
of the guys lift a small walkie-talkie to his mouth and speak.
When they both turned their gazes upward to Cecil's third-
floor apartment, Cecil ducked around the corner and into

the stairwell leading to the basement. It was, he decided, a good place to wait. It didn't take long for the men—and they had to be cops—to get out of the car and walk cautiously to the backstairs, glance around, then quickly start climbing. Cecil eased out the stairwell and was already out of sight before they'd come around to the first landing.

Cecil's car was ready, waiting, and untraceable to him with its present vehicle registration. The kid he'd bought it from had signed the title over a good six weeks ago. Cecil simply hadn't had time to get over to the Department of Motor Vehicles in the basement of the State of Illinois Building and formally transfer the title to his own name. What extra time he did manage downtown, he liked to invest in one of his workouts at the Fitness Center. The car was still sitting there with the old, expired license plates on it, but Cecil didn't drive much anyway and he would have gotten around to registering the automobile sooner or later. Now he was glad he hadn't, since the police would never know he actually had a vehicle.

The leather seats felt good beneath his thighs, hot and steamy from sitting in the sun all day. The car had been an impulse purchase ... well, not really. He *had* been in the market for one, though he'd planned on buying something late-model—maybe a Toyota or a Mazda—and a lot more sensible than the black '69 Olds 442. He'd seen the 442 around the neighborhood plenty of times, as well as the teenager who drove and babied it constantly, always waxing and rubbing it down. Then the Olds was gone for a while, and Cecil learned later that the young man had joined the army and stored the car in his parents' garage for a few months, until he finished boot camp and received his orders. When the boy learned he was stationed in Germany, he decided to put the car up for sale and Cecil had jumped at the opportunity. Owning the car, sitting behind the wheel and gazing at the well-cared-for interior ... it all made him feel like a high-school student again. Free of worries and work, like when his main concern had been which girl to ask to the senior prom. The feeling didn't hold now, though, with the blank spots in his mind from his runs, the black spot burned into his heart by Lillith, and the police on the way up the stairs to his home.

The engine started with a quiet, powerful hum, louder than normal but not overdone. Thank God the 442's former owner was more into preservation than hot-rodding, or the Olds could have come fitted with Glass Pak mufflers that would've screamed for attention. Instead Cecil was able to pull the automobile out of the small back lot and into the alley with barely a rumble; he turned north with one eye on the road and the other practically stuck to the rearview mirror to see if they were following.

His first thought was to go to Lillith's and confront her, demand to know exactly *why* she'd set the police on him. One of the papers he had put together in college had been on the Ku Klux Klan and its operations in the southern parts of the country during the 1930s and 1940s. He imagined this was what so many black men then had felt, running through the forests and bayous, terrified of the hounds and unable to understand exactly why the men pursuing them cared so much about doing so. But going to Lillith's presented too many problems—what if her husband was there, or the police waited with her, or if she simply wasn't home? She had staff, neighbors, a grown son who might be home from college right now. Wasn't her school out for the semester? He thought he remembered her saying the boy was taking summer courses to shorten his school time, but the mysterious blank spots made Cecil unsure about his memory and the things it suggested.

Where to go, then? His mom and dad's? Cecil dismissed the notion as soon it occurred to him. There was politeness and tolerance between him and the now elderly couple who had raised him—his birth mother was an unwed teenager who'd given him up for adoption—but not much else. His childhood had been pleasant but uneventful, with little to distinguish his home life from a boarding school with patient and attentive teachers who nonetheless remained emotionally detached. He hadn't been lonely, but he hadn't been especially cherished either.

Finally, driving around and unable to come up with a better solution, he settled for the Diplomat Motel on Lincoln Avenue. Cecil checked in and glowered at the clerk when the man asked him if he planned on staying all night, disliking the idea that the scummy, skinny fart behind the

counter thought he had a prostitute waiting in his car or
planned on hiring one for later. He took his room key, then
reparked the 442 in a space in the back where it couldn't be
seen from Lincoln Avenue before going into the motel. The
room was dingy but fairly large, with a worn bedspread and
heavy drapes in what some decorator had incorrectly decided was a tasteful color scheme. He stood in the middle of
it, looking at the bed and the cheap furniture, amazed that
his formerly efficient if not exactly fulfilling life had come to
this: no suitcase, change of clothes, *anything*. He had his car
in the lot and, of course, his wallet, filled with credit cards
and some cash, the American fantasy of being able to come
up with more at the touch of a few electronic buttons on a
cash machine. All his basic dreams, the ones that counted,
were probably gone: no house in the 'burbs, no wife, no 2.5
kids on the demographer's statistical scale. Lillith had done
that, taken it all away, and left him, an empty, oversized and
unloved man.

So it was just him and his messed-up, angry mind, stuck
in a musty motel room filled with a depressing olive-green,
black and red scroll pattern reminiscent of the late sixties.
All pretty damned indicative that today was the end of life
as he'd known it.

"Nothing noteworthy in the kitchen." One of the young detectives who'd provided backup poked his head out of the
doorway that joined the kitchen directly to the nearly bare
dining room. "It's practically empty, like the rest of the
place. Guy doesn't have much in the way of furniture, but I
thought his landlady said he's been here for almost ten
years."

"At least you remembered that much," Jude snapped.
Sandra raised an eyebrow and Jude turned his back on both
of them and scowled at the floor. He might be snappish but
the kid was lucky he didn't have the senior detective all the
way in his face, after he and his partner had let their suspect
slip out the back without a glance. With Gideon gone, they'd
knocked on every door in this section of the apartment
building, six in all, but only the landlady and one other tenant were home. The other tenant had been napping and
heard nothing, but the woman who owned the building was

an old foreigner, Czechoslovakian or something, and she'd offered to let them in Gideon's apartment without question. They didn't have a search warrant but there was no way Ewing was foolish enough to pass up a golden chance like this; if they saw anything it'd be a piece of cake to keep the old woman there while they called and legalized the warrant situation. In the end, however, it'd been fruitless: the place was spacious and well lit, cleaner than any bachelor's apartment had a right to be, and utterly free of the most remote scrap of anything that could be considered evidence. They *searched*, too—closets, drawers, everything. While the young cops who had screwed up and let Gideon slip past might not have a talent for keeping an eye on someone, they certainly could talk. They managed to keep the elderly landlady gossiping in the kitchen far longer than was needed to go through Gideon's well-organized belongings. The search, however, didn't even turn up the telephone number of a girlfriend, and thus died the possibility of identifying the anonymous female caller.

"This is useless," Jude told Sandra. "He probably keeps everything in his desk at work." She shrugged in agreement and ducked into the kitchen to talk to the landlady one last time; Jude smirked when the woman asked Sandra in broken English why she'd decided to become a cop instead of marrying and having "nice babies." He glanced around again, checking to make sure they'd left no indication of their presence in case Gideon decided to come back, although it wasn't likely he'd make it through the front door before getting nabbed. Doing all this simply on the accusation, the *speculation*, of some unknown woman was going to rankle some suits in the Public Defender's Office if this guy turned out to be clean.

"You ready?" Sandra asked. She nodded toward the landlady, who watched them both with a sharper eye than Jude would have expected. "She wants to lock up. She also made a point of saying that we couldn't take anything from the apartment."

Jude nodded. "Understood. We're through here anyway." He turned toward the landlady. "Thank you, ma'am, for letting us into the apartment. It was a big help."

"You're welcome," the old woman responded. Her accent was thick, nearly guttural, and it reminded Jude of a waiter at a long-gone food joint on Lincoln Avenue called the Transylvania Restaurant. He wondered if the meals she made were as heavy and delicious as the food that used to be served in that old converted 7-Eleven Food Store. "I show you *all* out now, yes?" She put the emphasis on the word *all* and he nodded again.

Standing outside on the sidewalk with his partner, frustrated at this latest and greatest of police blunders, Detective Ewing watched the other unmarked car pull away and disappear. He couldn't stop wondering where Cecil Gideon had gone, and if he was indeed the Ravenswood Strangler. Children raced by on the sidewalk, barely a foot in front of the two police officers and calling out "You're it! You're it!" A moment of breathless silence, then one of the kids fell and let out a shriek of pain from two doors down.

To Jude it sounded like the scream of a young woman.

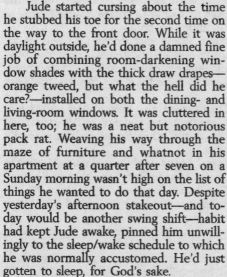

Jude started cursing about the time he stubbed his toe for the second time on the way to the front door. While it was daylight outside, he'd done a damned fine job of combining room-darkening window shades with the thick draw drapes—orange tweed, but what the hell did he care?—installed on both the dining- and living-room windows. It was cluttered in here, too; he was a neat but notorious pack rat. Weaving his way through the maze of furniture and whatnot in his apartment at a quarter after seven on a Sunday morning wasn't high on the list of things he wanted to do that day. Despite yesterday's afternoon stakeout—and today would be another swing shift—habit had kept Jude awake, pinned him unwillingly to the sleep/wake schedule to which he was normally accustomed. He'd just gotten to sleep, for God's sake.

"What?" he snapped into the intercom. "Who the hell is it?"

"Bite my head off, why don't you?" Karla's voice sounded metalicized and much farther away than one floor down in the hallway. "Ring us in."

Jude started to ask who *us* was, then waved the question away and pushed the buzzer. It wasn't as though he wouldn't let her in if he didn't like who she'd brought with her. Less than a minute later he heard movement on the other side of his front door and opened it before anyone could knock; as a reward for his cooperation, Creature nearly knocked him over as she scrambled through the doorway.

"Down, Creature, knock it off." Jude didn't know whether to groan or grin. "What's the matter? Your mother lose control of your leash?"

"Yeah, and she ran right over here," Karla said dryly. "Speaking of things going wrong, Detective, you look a bit 'peaked,' as *my* mother would say."

"What do you expect after fifteen minutes' sleep?" he retorted. He gestured toward the living room and pulled the door shut behind Karla. "Come in, make yourself right at home. I'll be back in about six hours."

"Oh no, you don't." Karla snagged him by one sleeve, then smiled and looked him up and down. "Hey, nice pj's."

"Don't start ridiculing my clothes so early in the morning," Jude said. "I couldn't stand the stress. Besides, that's my line."

"Poor baby." Karla turned him around and pulled him toward the kitchen, barely giving a glance at the greyhound as she nosed curiously in the other direction. "Come on, I'll make you some coffee."

"I don't want *coffee*," Jude said. "Are you crazy? I want to go to sleep, not bounce off the walls for the next two hours."

"Decaf then. I want to talk to you."

"Fine," Jude grumbled. "Wait and see what I look like if I don't get my beauty sleep."

"Didn't I say something to that effect just . . . gee," Karla tilted her head coquettishly, "could it have been *yesterday*?"

"Sure, but you were going to work anyway," Jude pointed out. "Don't forget all the facts."

"You've been a cop too long," Karla replied. "Where's the coffeepot?"

"Right in front of you, Miss Efficiency. I thought I was the one asleep here."

"Unfamiliar surroundings. It's not like it's the only thing on the countertop."

"Touché."

"What is all this stuff? God, no wonder I can't find the coffee." After scanning the canisters, bowls and spice jars all over the counters, Karla had opened three cabinets with no success. Although she managed to find the filters for the black Braun coffeemaker, the actual coffee was nowhere to be found.

"The freezer," Jude instructed her. "It keeps it fresh. Be sure to get the decaf kind."

"Ah."

While he welcomed her company, even at this ungodly hour of his somewhat altered day, Jude noted with something less than good humor that Karla loaded the filter with enough coffee to make a full pot. "What did you want to talk to me about?" he asked when she finally finished with the coffee preparations and settled across the table from him.

Karla looked back toward the coffeemaker. "How long will that take?"

"A few minutes. Now quit stalling and tell me what's on your mind."

"Evelyn," Karla answered. "What else?" She cupped her hands and ran them over her hair, smoothing it back from her forehead. "She's not . . ." Karla hesitated, then plunged on. "She's not *Evelyn* anymore. I guess what I'm trying to say is that she's changed, so drastically, and so *quickly*, that there's got to be something wrong somewhere. Something much more . . . I don't know. Much *worse* than we think. This change, it started right after she was attacked."

"Well, what's different about her?" Jude asked cautiously. From his dealings with the woman, he could have named a half-dozen things that weren't normal, but he'd only known Evelyn as a result of the attack. How would he know if some of the things he'd seen weren't representative of the way Evelyn Pelagi was every day? He'd seen so many things during his time on the force that his definition of *normal* would probably cover a lot more than someone else's.

Karla leaned forward, her voice low but still audible above the bubbling of the brewing coffee. "Oh, there's lots of things that have changed, Jude, and it would be very convenient to pin it all on psychological trauma caused by the attack. A handwriting analyst could probably build a dissertation based on the before-and-after versions of Evelyn. Look at this." She pulled a piece of paper from her back pocket and placed it on the table. "It's the name and number of an old friend of ours that Evelyn wrote down for me. Do you have any *idea* how her handwriting has changed?"

"Yes," Jude said. "I think I do." He got up and went into the other room, was back in a moment with the crumpled note Warren had given him. Side by side, the difference was dramatic. "Doesn't exactly take a magnifying glass, does it?" he finally asked.

Karla shook her head. "No, not at all. You should *see* her, Jude! She looks—well, she looks like some kind of a damned *zombie* out of a horror movie, for God's sake. Her face is paste white, her eyes are all sunk in, and she must've lost twenty pounds. Her hands are hideous, plus the things she tells Warren and me—" She broke off and sat there, shaking her head. "You wouldn't believe them, I'm sure."

"Well, I don't know what she's been saying, of course, but from a completely objective point of view, Evelyn sounds *ill*," Jude said carefully. "Has she seen a doctor?"

Karla looked at him severely. "Now it's my turn to say 'Earth to Jude.' Silly, she works with doctors all day, remember? Maybe she's wearing lots of makeup or they figure she's smart enough to get medical attention if she needs it. Because as far as I know, no one has said a word to her."

"At least that she's told *you*."

"Yes."

Jude yawned. "So what has she been saying?" Like he didn't already know; he got up and headed for the coffeemaker, wishing now that he'd opted for the real coffee instead of the decaf. His mind was pretty bleary and nothing happening so far had done anything to sweep aside the cobwebs. Karla waited, first while he poured two mugs and brought them back to the table, then again as he went back for the sugar and creamer and a couple of spoons.

"Are you finished puttering yet?"

He'd never seen Karla get irritable over something trivial and it surprised him; these things about Evelyn must be really starting to scare her. "Sure," he said mildly. "Just getting everything together so we don't have to get up again. Now tell me what's on your mind."

Karla's expression turned sheepish. "Sorry. I shouldn't have snapped at you like that. Here I got you out of bed and I'm bitchy on top of it."

Jude raised one eyebrow. "There's a big gap between you and bitchy. Now, we were talking about Evelyn and the things she's been saying?"

"Well, she's . . ." Now that the conversation had finally been geared to it, Karla seemed reluctant to squeeze out the words. After a few seconds she entwined her fingers and looked at him, her jaw set. "She told me—us, though at different times—that her attacker *did* rape her, but that's not all."

"Oh?"

"Evelyn says the man who attacked her actually killed her after raping her. That he strangled her."

Jude's eyes were suddenly sharp; there was no question in his mind that he needed some sleep, but there was also no doubt that it could wait for a while. So Evelyn was *telling* other people about this "bringing people back from the dead" thing, though this was the first he'd heard of Evelyn claiming the experience happened to her. "There's no evidence to support that," he said. It was a statement that wasn't quite true: in reality, there *was* written support. Officer Fremont's report would back up at least the claim about the injuries. He didn't want to have to think about the rest of the man's statement, not yet.

Karla didn't let him have that choice.

"Evelyn says that she was dead, really *dead*. She didn't see any great white light or angel or anything, but says that the teenager who found her brought her back to life. And healed her of all her injuries besides."

"She had no injuries." At least none the rest of us saw, Jude mentally added. Officer Fremont's report, again, claimed that Evelyn had been seriously—if not *fatally*—injured for a short period of time.

"Yes, because the boy healed them," Karla said patiently.

"Look, I know this sounds insane, but bear with me while I tell you all of it. It gets better, and I say that without a bit of humor because I'm way beyond thinking anything that Evelyn says about this is funny."

"I never thought it was."

Karla's mouth turned up at the corner, but it wasn't a happy expression. "I know that, but I could see how somebody on the outside looking in, or more appropriately, *listening* in, would start to think 'Hey, this lady's left the briefcase with her brains in it on the train.' Or something to that general effect."

"What else has she said?" Jude prompted.

Karla looked at her fingernails for a moment, then raised her gaze to his. "She says that she did the same thing to a man the paramedics brought into the emergency room, a Latino guy who'd been shot in the chest." When Jude's eyes narrowed and he sat forward, Karla swallowed and continued. "She says she brought him back to life the same way it was done to her—brought him back to life and healed him of his gunshot wounds. She claims he got up and walked out of the ER. Just came back to life, got off the cart and yanked out the tubes and whatever else was hooked up to him, and took off." She looked at him questioningly. "Do you know about this?"

"Of course I know about it," Jude replied. He scraped a hand across his chin and felt the prickly stubble there. "They called Sandra and me in when the body turned up missing because the guy was considered a homicide, even though he'd been killed in a robbery attempt. The dispatcher's computer showed that we'd worked with Evelyn a few days previous, so we got the call. Beyond that, I know the dead man's body disappeared and that everyone who was in that ER cubicle except Evelyn says there's no way that guy could've gotten up and left."

"Why not?"

"Because he wasn't just shot," Jude answered. "His chest was wide-open and had a rib splitter in it. Karla, the doctor had cut him open and tried manual heart massage. Not only was the guy filleted, but he had a big piece of aluminum holding his rib cage *apart*."

"But she says she *healed* him," Karla pointed out. "Thus

none of that stuff mattered because there wasn't a thing in the world wrong with the guy by the time he went out that door."

Jude shook his head. "I'm sorry, but I can't buy that. Too many people saw him dead—"

"There was no blood on the cart. Evelyn says it all disappeared, and that's why she and the rest of the hospital staff had such a difficult time explaining why all the hospital papers pronounced him dead."

"So he wiped it off," Jude said.

"Oh, please," Karla said in exasperation. "That's crap and you know it."

All Jude could do was shrug helplessly. "No, I don't. I wasn't there, remember? All I have is the word of a nurse who now claims to have returned from the dead—no, wait." He held up his hand. "I know she's your friend and all that, but again, looking at it from an objective point of view, it doesn't look like she's been very stable since her attack."

Karla looked at him earnestly. "Then we have to help her, Jude. I don't know a more steadfast, dependable person in the world than Evelyn. She'd do anything to help any*one*, and I can testify to that from personal experience. She didn't have to do what she did for me in college—she didn't owe me anything, didn't even know me that well. You know what?"

"What?"

"She's acting like I did back then, like she's on drugs. And that's unthinkable."

"Karla, drugs happen to a lot of people, and a lot of *those* are much stronger-willed than Evelyn. I'll bet you have no inkling how many people who work in hospitals and doctors' offices are into drugs," Jude declared. "The stuff is way too easy to get in those environments."

"Not Evelyn," Karla said firmly. "I'd know if she was. Jude, she'd *tell* me."

"So you think."

"I *know*."

Jude raised his hands in defeat. "Then I don't know what to say."

For a moment Karla said nothing. Then she met his eyes again. "How long since you've *seen* Evelyn?" she asked.

Jude frowned, trying to organize his sleep-shorted thoughts. "A couple of days or so, I guess. The last time was at your place."

"About four days, then. Well, let me tell you something—she's a treat for the eyes, all right. Like I said, her face and neck are covered in these . . ." For a second Karla faltered, as if she wasn't sure of the word she sought. "Vague is a good description, I guess. Vague bruises."

Jude's expression was puzzled. "Vague? What the heck does that mean?"

Karla shrugged. "It means that they sort of, I don't know, look like they're there, but not really. They come and go, change from hour to hour."

"You're not making any sense." He couldn't suppress the yawn that found its way out. "Or maybe I'm not processing the information right. Either you're bruised or you're not."

"Not in Evelyn's case." For a moment Karla picked at the tabletop with one fingernail, seemingly transfixed by the sight of her own finger. "Did you know that Evelyn's fingertips are *flat?*" she asked softly.

"Flat?"

"Like little boards. She can hardly pick anything up. But that's not the worst of it."

"I'd say she's right up there on the shock charts so far," Jude said. "Go on."

"She says that bringing people back from the dead is an addiction, like drugs—"

"Ah, so that's where you got that analogy."

"—and that doing it gives her a rush. She calls it a *deadrush* because she claims it comes from resurrecting—her word, not mine—dead people. And that it's getting almost impossible for her to fight the impulse that makes her do it."

Jude frowned. "It's hard for me to swallow that," he said eventually. "Say that it's true—say it *is* some kind of addiction thing. So far she'd been able to resist it, right? Since that guy in the ER?"

Karla nodded. "Yes, but she almost caved in the other night and got sent home by her supervisor, who didn't buy her story that she was inspecting the cadaver's face. The supervisor moved her to second shift where she'd be watched by more people. Evelyn has to go in at three today." Karla looked at the table. "She told me she was nearly caught in the act of . . . doing it. She says it's done by kissing the dead person."

Jude's face twisted. "You're joking."

Karla shook her head. "No, and she wasn't either, Jude. Look, I can't sit back and wait this out. I have to *help* her, in any way I can. There's got to be something I can do beyond just be there for her—that's just not enough. I owe her that much—no, *more* than that. I'd be dead now if it wasn't for her, and I can't watch her deteriorate like this and do nothing. She means too much to me, and to Warren, too. He's going as crazy as I am."

Jude tapped his fingers on the table thoughtfully. "What can I do?" he asked finally. "I'm not her favorite person—too many questions, too many unpleasant memories associated with my being a cop and which probably go back to the initial attack. I'm assuming that's why she walked out of your place when I got there last Wednesday."

"Well, I . . ." Karla sat back on the chair and stared at him. "I guess I don't know *what* you can do," she admitted. "I suppose I thought you'd be able to offer me some great bit of advice that would steer me down the right road to solving this whole nasty mess."

Jude gave her a tired smile. "Sorry, it seems I'm all out of great advice this morning. You'll have to ask again later."

"Listen, will you at least try to talk to her?"

He shrugged. "Sure, but I don't know that what I have to say would make any difference."

"Maybe," Karla suggested, "you can convince her to get some help, or at least talk to someone at the hospital about her injuries."

Jude was still perplexed. "*What* injuries?"

Karla's eyes widened. "I guess you didn't understand me, or maybe I should've put it in more detail. Each day that goes by, she looks worse. More bruised, more swollen, more . . . I don't know. Bloodless, maybe. Her face is a mess. And, Jude—

"You can *see* the ring of fingerprints around her neck now!"

38

"This has gone far enough."

Evelyn said the words aloud but didn't mean them, just as she'd never really meant to eat the meal she'd prepared—chicken salad on a rice cake topped with alfalfa sprouts—and which now sat slowly drying out in the hot air of the apartment. She'd opened the curtains in the front room to purposely let in the early-afternoon light, outright defying the barbs of pain the sunbeams streaked into her eyeballs and brain. For a while she'd toyed with the notion of dragging a lawn chair into the middle of their small backyard. She thought about dousing her white, white skin with Bain de Soleil and baking under the summer sun, living out her desperate attempt at regaining the golden tan she'd owned ten days ago. But stepping outside at high noon had proven too much and she'd been forced to retreat, back into the safe, darker haven of the apartment.

Normalcy, that was the key, the goal for which she reached. This apartment, with its cheerful white-and-blue country flowers and comfortable clutter should have given her a rock to cling to when Warren was at work—after all, he couldn't baby-sit her all the time. Since the attack he'd been at her side almost constantly outside of working hours. Now, though, he'd landed the Falconer & Dixon portfolio and was busier than ever before, had at last realized his dream of expanding his small office. Evelyn should have been happy for him, should have been able to share his joy . . . but she couldn't. That happiness, that well-deserved sense of elation, it wasn't *there*, and try as she might, Evelyn couldn't force it. Ultimately Warren's joy made her hate herself more because she knew she was ruining one of the highest points so far in his career.

Karla was right in telling her to get help. Over the phone she had refused Karla's plea that she talk to Detective Ewing—after all, no matter how much he wanted to help, what could he really *do*? She had agreed, finally, to go to someone at the hospital she trusted and let him or her perform tests and pseudo-miracles, fix whatever dark thing that boy had somehow injected into her body. Find it, heal it, clear it *out*, for God's sake.

Free her.

Blackness showed at the edge of her vision, the tiny sparkly black sequins that were coming more often now and that she dreaded so much, knowing that they meant another few moments of total loss of control—

Reeling, whirling, spinning, how many synonyms exist for the centrifugal force of herSELF that propels her senses around and around and nearly drives her mad in the process? The presence of others teetering on unbearable now, their soft pink skin and fleshy fingertips, the sight of everyone a drawing out to her, a yearning, a DARE for her to wrap her sharp-fingered claws around their throats and squeeze. Tighter and tighter, until the lifeforce is gone, stop its rich beat simply so she can start it again with her own dirty kiss of life. Her hunger always there and growing beyond confinement, so far gone . . . is it addiction or obsession? Only the dead could love her now, only they would tolerate the true touch of her swollen and soiled mouth.

Sounds, now, adding to her misery, pounding and crying and pounding—

The door! Evelyn screamed in her mind. *It's just someone knocking on the door! Answer it!*

It was a struggle to pull back, to *find* the mental commands that would translate from her muddled brain and travel to her sensation-deprived limbs. She forced her legs forward despite their near rebellion, make her head turn and look, finally steered her torso toward the light-filled front room and her insistent visitor. There at last, reaching out and watching in horrific fascination as her hands, the fingers looking like so much dried fruit wrapped around fragile sticks, found the doorknob and managed to grasp and turn it. It was a struggle to muster enough strength to pull it open and past the weather seal of felt Warren had installed around the doorjamb last winter to cut the drafts.

Breezing inside, almost painful in the intensity of feeling and light and life that she brought with her: Karla, her friend of all friends, who grasped her by the hand and never said a word about the disgusting resemblance it bore to a poor taxidermy job. Karla, shutting the door behind them and pulling Evelyn back toward the kitchen and reality.

"You've screwed around with this long enough, girlfriend." Karla sat across the table from her in the darkened kitchen, the remains of Evelyn's uneaten lunch withered and sitting accusingly between them, a flag that waved and screamed for attention. It wasn't long in coming. "Why didn't you eat this?" Karla demanded. "How long has it *been* since you ate?"

"I . . . don't know," Evelyn whispered.

"You're lying to me," Karla said grimly. "After all these years, after everything we've been through—" She reached across the table and grabbed Evelyn's arm, forced it up until the scrawny, senseless hand attached to it came into view. "Don't dirty our friendship, Evie. You're sick, in a big, *big* way, and no amount of denial is going to fix that. Now, how long has it been since you ate, damn it?"

"I . . ." Evelyn frowned and tried to concentrate, but it was so hard to distinguish between eating, in which she had lost all interest anyway, and the physical act of fixing a meal, which she had actually done quite a few times. But Karla wanted to know when she'd last eaten, not cooked, and hadn't that been—

"Friday, I think." Evelyn's voice was a rasp, as if the air in her lungs was sliding over sandpaper instead of vocal cords. "The day of the attack. Warren and I ate dinner before I left for work . . . I think."

For once her best friend was speechless. Finally, she started to sputter. "Evie, honey, that's over a *week* ago, nine days!" Karla looked at her expectantly but Evelyn had no explanation to offer. Somehow she didn't think *I wasn't hungry* was going to cut it. Karla's amazement had propelled her from the chair and now she stood in the center of the room, staring at her helplessly. Amazed, Evelyn knew, at how effective she'd been at bullshitting Warren for the past week and a half. In any case, deceiving Warren wasn't the issue here. There were things that needed taking care of, and she didn't have to wait long for Karla to shift gears. In a way that was good, exactly what she'd needed all along—someone else to take over and make the important decisions for her. The ones like—

"I'm going with you to the hospital like we talked about today, Evelyn. Not tomorrow, or next Friday. *Today*." Evelyn started to say something, give some autopilot excuse or another, but the look on Karla's face clearly said it would neither matter nor change her friend's decision to accompany her to Illinois Masonic. "I'm not just walking you to work, either. We're leaving early enough for you to have someone there examine you. Pick someone you know," Karla's expression was grim, "or not. I don't care which, but *someone's* going to take a look at you."

All Evelyn could do was nod and rise, find her clothes and dress in stoic silence as she waited for the world to fall apart this afternoon.

The hospital during the day reminded Evelyn of Karla: all light and sound and unbearable life, a hot whirlwind spinning in the midst of the cold chasm that had become her existence. Illinois Masonic Medical Center had given her a way to make a living for years now, and although she'd worked at two other hospitals before settling in this neighborhood, neither had compared with IMMC's people in the warmth and genuine caring Evelyn believed they felt. She remembered coming here as a child, when she and her mother were on better terms and her mother was sick with some sort of mysterious female thing that Evelyn now knew had been endometriosis. Barr Pavilion and the parking garage were under construction then, hardly more than a huge hole in the ground awaiting pilings and concrete and steel. Looking back, Evelyn was slightly stunned that she had walked across the span of that slash in the ground, balancing on the heavy metal beams that had been the skeleton of the lower-level ceiling. It had seemed such a logical thing to do at the time: her mother was sick and Evelyn wanted to visit her, no matter what hour it was. Their apartment had been only a block over, on Oakdale, so travel to and from the hospital was next to nothing. Evelyn had spent quite a few late night evenings watching television with her mother in the hospital room. As long as she could get past the front information desk, the nurses on her mother's floor would turn a blind eye and allow the little girl to visit.

The Pavilion was the hub of things now, the main entrance to the hospital and the first thing everyone saw when they entered via the normal route. The way to the information desk was down a long hallway lined with huge sketches of donors and influential doctors who had contributed to the original concept and financing of the Pavilion. Personally, Evelyn couldn't imagine a more frightening walk to confront if you were a newly arrived visitor or patient. The whole, echoing length was like a gauntlet of faces bigger than human beings, all staring and smiling and totally unnatural.

"Where?" Karla demanded. "Not the ER, either. You'd be lucky to get a five-minute slice of someone's attention there."

"Maybe not. It's still early; there's probably not much going on."

Karla looked dubious. "I don't want to go in there and have you get involved in some accident that comes in. You're not due to go on shift for another two hours. Isn't there anyone in Private Staff?"

For a moment Evelyn's mind went blank, as if it were having difficulty getting to that special place in her brain that contained the memories of who worked where in the hospital. *Necrotic brain cells*, she thought ruefully. *Parts of the inside of my head are long dead*. Finally, though, the synapses fired and caught, kicked in a name that she could grab. "Barry Josiah," she offered. "He doesn't usually have office hours on Sunday, but I think I remember him saying he was going to be looking over some files today."

"Well, let's go check." Karla tucked her arm in the bend of Evelyn's elbow and with a mild shock Evelyn felt warm skin and realized Karla was wearing short sleeves. She couldn't remember her friend ever doing that, misfiring memories or not. The old scars from college were still there, though the edges were softer now, blurring into the darker surrounding skin. She wondered if the drugs Karla had taken so enthusiastically during her time as an addict had given her anything near the pleasure Evelyn got now from the *deadrush*. She had the sudden impulse to just ask, blurt out the question and bare her soul—

Was it that good for you then?

Of course, that was unthinkable.

"Here we go," Karla said cheerfully. She guided Evelyn to a chair and gently pushed her onto it. "Stay here. I'll check with the security guard and find out where he is, have him told we're here."

"*If* he's in."

"Right."

"Wait." Karla paused and looked at Evelyn expectantly. "I . . . you don't have to hang around, you know. I can take care of this." She met Karla's eyes reluctantly, got trapped by her best friend's steel-gray stare.

"Not this time, Evie. You stay *put*, you understand? Unless you want to be embarrassed when I search this place from top to bottom until I find you." Evelyn shook her head.

A quick call from the woman seated beyond the combination desk and nurses' station guarding the entrance to the Private Staff was all it took. From the look on the young doctor's face when he hurried out to greet them, Karla knew immediately that this man was someone who dealt with Evelyn often in the course of hospital work. It was also apparent he'd been keeping a surreptitious eye on the strange things that seemed to be manifesting themselves in Evelyn's body and slowly destroying her in the process. He shook

Karla's hand automatically but his bright eyes were trained on Evelyn as he led her back into the examining-room area, motioning for Karla to follow when she hesitated.

"Please," he said when the three of them had entered a small white-walled room and he'd closed the door behind them. "I'm Dr. Josiah," he said to Karla. His gaze turned back to Evelyn. "I'm guessing you've finally decided to, ah—"

"She needs help," Karla interrupted firmly. "To be honest, I made her come here." She looked at Evelyn, but her friend stood there, silent.

"Evelyn." Dr. Josiah touched her arm. "Step up and sit on the edge of the examining table, all right? Let's take a look at you." When she obeyed but didn't say anything, the young doctor frowned, then started addressing his questions to Karla. "These problems, the ones I've been noticing at least, they all started after her recent attack. Isn't that true?"

"Yes," Karla agreed. "She told me earlier today that she hasn't eaten since then."

"What?" His mouth dropped open, then compressed into a thin line as he slipped on a transparent pair of gloves and began probing the area under Evelyn's chin. "These bruises," he murmured. "I don't recall seeing them last week—"

"They weren't there." Evelyn's voice was that same rasp that Karla had heard an hour earlier in the apartment. "They get more visible every day."

"What caused them?" the young physician asked.

For the first time, Evelyn lifted her face and looked him in the eye. "The attack, of course."

"That was well over a week ago. Any bruises suffered that night would be starting to fade by now, not manifest. Unless we're talking about internal injuries or a slow undiagnosed hematoma."

Evelyn laughed suddenly, and the sound of it, harsh, loud, *humorless*, made both Barry Josiah and Karla jump. "This is a waste of time. I—"

"I'll decide that." Josiah's tone had regained its authority. "And you can bet that decision won't be based on sixty seconds in this room. Now stop fighting and sit, quietly, while I conduct an exam."

"This is confidential," Evelyn said suddenly. "Neither one

of you has my permission to repeat anything you see or hear in this room to anyone. *Anyone*, understand? Otherwise I'm out of here, right now."

Karla didn't hesitate, though she squashed the momentary reluctance she felt when she thought of Warren. The doctor seemed to have a more difficult time of agreeing, and Karla could imagine his thoughts: review boards, medical ethics, the opinions and advice of his peers. All that help was being cut off here by Evelyn's curt demand. In the end it seemed he would rather agree to the situation than see Evelyn leave without any hope of treatment for her mysterious ailment. "All right."

Evelyn seemed to relax then, and if she didn't exactly cooperate, at least she didn't resist. Almost two hours— blood tests that the young physician assured her he could get looked at by a confidential contact in the lab, respiratory tests, endless questions. Dr. Josiah's expression went to mixed disbelief and fascination when he saw the compressed sticks of dried flesh and bone that now made up Evelyn's fingers and toes.

But he had absolutely no answers.

Finally, Karla and the physician, both utterly perplexed as they looked at Evelyn. Her expression was almost smug as she told them both, with simple, utter sincerity . . .

"I've been brought back from the dead. And I can do the same to other people."

39

I shouldn't be here, Lillith Jerusha thought as she parked the Mercedes 350SL in a spot not far from Cecil's apartment building. *The police get paid to handle things like this and I'm no Angie Dickinson.*

Still, they hadn't handled things, had they? Here it was, nearing the end of another weekend with no one in custody for the murders that had been committed—specifically, without *Cecil* in custody. And while there had not been another killing so far this weekend, the time bomb was ticking away, wasn't it?

Tick, tick, tick.

God, how she hated that sound, and now, because of Cecil, she felt like it was in her *head*.

Sitting indecisively in her car gave Lillith a chance to study Cecil's building. It was a nice one, built in the neo-Tudor style of nearly a hundred years ago, and it reminded her of the fancier places on Chicago Avenue south of the heart of

Evanston. Cecil's third-floor apartment, too, was above average; she had admired the way he kept it clean and free of clutter, with wide expanses of golden oak floor and picture-free walls that made the place look three times bigger than it was. It was a neat decorating trick that she wasn't sure Cecil was aware he was using. Lots of light, lots of air, everything modern with crisp lines and a nearly brutal efficiency that the rambling Victorian house in Wilmette didn't have, despite its large rooms and overly generous windows.

It was Sunday afternoon and Isman was playing golf with an old friend at the Medinah Country Club in the namesake suburb west of the city. He'd offered to cancel his plans, and Lillith had known he was sincere . . . but why should he? He loved the game, and she detested it, simply couldn't understand how he could stand on the green in the broiling heat and smack at a little white ball until it went into a hole. And Lillith certainly didn't expect him to sit home and be miserable about her ex-lover with her, at least not in the minute-by-minute scheme of things. Besides, seeing him climb into his Lexus and drive away had given her the chance, albeit impulsive, to come over here alone, sit in the sunshine, and think about what she should—or *could*—do about the problem she had come to bitterly call Cecil-On-The-Rampage.

On the table at home, the one at which she sat in the morning and looked out on the backyard, was a small white porcelain pot a friend had given her. In it were planted three paper-white narcissus bulbs, and if she tended to them carefully, using the directions so thoughtfully written on the card accompanying the gift, they would grow and bloom, actually *flower.* Her attentiveness had been quite successful, and the bulbs now had stems, and each stem also had a cluster of delicate white flowers bursting at its tip. This was the thing that disturbed Lillith the most. Not the idea that the stems were flowering—of course not. It was the concept that she could so easily *stop* it; by virtue of her size and strength alone, she could halt that flowering right now, before it had a chance to continue. Simply because she had the power to kill it.

Like Cecil had done to all those women.

Younger than her, too, every one of them. Some married, some not, and how many had or would have had children had Cecil not blasted uninvited into their lives and ended everything in one unforgivable, *unchangeable* act? What would he do right now if she got out of her car and went upstairs—presuming, of course, that he was home? Perhaps he would do what he'd intended, or believed, he'd been doing all these times. Perhaps he would kill her.

I shouldn't be here, she thought again. This had to be undoubtedly the most foolish thing she'd ever done short of having the affair with Cecil to begin with. What had she been thinking? The police were probably watching her right now, although they had no way of knowing who it was she'd come to see. Thinking that she might be under surveillance almost made her start the car and leave, but then again, how *could* they know, after all? She would go in, she decided, and ring the bell. If Cecil was home, she wouldn't go up to his apartment or be alone with him—damn it, she would not be *bait.* Surely she could get him to come downstairs, and after all, it was broad daylight on a Sunday afternoon. What could he do, especially if he was being watched? She—*they*—would be discovered, but she could deal with that if it meant peace of mind, if it meant that another woman somewhere in the city could *flower.* Right now she felt so responsible, so *guilty* about all those dead women, all those snuffed-out blooms, gone forever. If stopping him meant discovery, then so be it; Isman had made it clear the other night and several times since that he would stand by her if she admitted her identity to the police. Cecil . . . would he listen to her? Lillith had always been able to talk him into anything, but this was the biggest challenge of all.

Could she convince him to turn himself in?

It was an effort to get out of the car. She hadn't realized how long she'd been sitting there, feeling the warmth of the sun through the windshield as it competed with the cool breeze slipping from the Mercedes's air conditioner. She was stiff, frightened, out of place before this monumental task, an ant frozen beneath the foot of a petulant child. Would he crush her as he had the others?

There was one way to find out.

The foyer of the building was dim and stuffy, no central air in here beyond the window units of the individual tenants. The list of names for this entrance of the building was deceptively normal—Reynolds, Gideon, Keating, Mc-Namara, Olmstead, Doolittle, Newsham, McFarland, Wold. Three to a floor, and who would've guessed that the second from the top of the list was a murderer?

Cecil wasn't home, or if he was, he wouldn't answer her buzz. Belatedly she realized he could probably see her car from his living-room window, and she wasn't so stupid she planned on ringing someone else to get inside. Nor would she do something as ridiculous as go around to the shadowed back-porch entrance. "A waste of time," Lillith said out loud. Her voice echoed back at her in the dark, spacious foyer as a small bead of perspiration began working its way down the valley between her breasts—such a short time out of the car and already she was sweating. As she went back outside and unlocked her car door, she decided she wouldn't blame the police at all if they didn't want to sit in the blistering heat and watch an empty apartment. What was there to see, anyway?

Detectives Wilfred and Ewing were, indeed, again sitting in a car outside, although they had at least managed to park it under the shade of one of the old oak trees about two buildings down. As they watched a tall and attractive woman with dark hair climb into a pearl-colored Mercedes 350SL, the flip phone in Jude's hand gave a small bleep and he answered it, his eyes still trained on the Mercedes. "It's Waring," he finally told Sandra. "He says he heard the doorbell ringing in Gideon's apartment. I'd bet you my next paycheck that this is our woman."

Sandra watched through the windshield thoughtfully. "I don't think we should grab her," she said after a moment. Jude's eyebrows raised. "Let's follow her instead. If we stop her now and she won't admit to anything, we'll waste hours detaining her and probably get our asses in a sling with some high-priced private lawyer."

"What'll we gain by following her around all day?" Jude asked. "She obviously doesn't know where he is—if she did, she wouldn't be here." Still, it only took a minute for him to instruct the undercover car assigned to watch the rear of the building to call for another unit to cover Jude and Sandra's spot.

This time they were in Sandra's automobile, a blue 1965 Corvair Corsa with a body that had seen better days. The vehicle was deceptive, though, and the rust streaks edging down the fenders and the roofline had nothing to do with the car's performance. Sandra's husband Henry kept the 140 horsepower engine meticulously tuned, a feat Jude thought was nothing short of a miracle considering the Corsa had four carburetors; if they weren't synchronized, the auto might as well be parked. Although Sandra constantly goaded him, Jude refused to admit that this old rust bucket might actually outrun his '94 Saturn. Not only did it look like crap, the Corvair was almost thirty years old, for crying out loud—an antique.

"She might have other places to check." Sandra pulled smoothly out of the parking space and followed the pearl-white Mercedes, staying far enough back so that she wouldn't draw the woman's glance. When their subject turned north onto Lincoln, Sandra occasionally allowed a car—never more than one, though—to slip between her and the Mercedes, letting the semiheavy afternoon traffic mask their movement. "We'll keep on her until we hit the first suburb-city limit, then we'll call the station and have Lance contact the local cop shop and have someone tail her so we can go back to Gideon's building," Sandra decided.

"Not that there's anything to see there," Jude said dryly. He grinned. "Guy doesn't even have any plants."

Sandra smiled a little. "It is a pretty bare place—hey, look at this!"

"What's she doing?" Jude twisted on his seat as the woman they were following suddenly threw on her turn signal and took an abrupt left into the circular driveway of an apartment building, then pulled back onto Lincoln Avenue.

"Watch her," Sandra commanded as she jerked the wheel and stomped on the accelerator. The Corsa leaped across Lincoln, darting into the narrow opening between two oncoming cars, the drivers of both too stunned to blow their horns. They bounced hard and stopped, then Sandra threw it into reverse and backed out of the alley into which she'd driven, taking the Corvair in a reverse turn tight enough to keep it against the curb and out of the southbound traffic. "Is she still there?"

Jude suddenly chuckled. "I don't think there's any hurry, partner. Our lady has apparently decided to go to the International House of Pancakes for lunch."

"Well, what the hell?" Sandra said crankily. "She sure did it in a *hurry*."

"It's their fabulous coffee."

"We're going to sit in the parking lot for a while." Sandra steered into the left lane, then turned into the IHOP lot.

"There," Jude said and pointed. "Guy's pulling out."

"Good catch." She put the car in reverse and backed into the slot, giving them both a clear view into the main dining room of the restaurant. "Couldn't ask for a better seat to watch the action."

"What action? She's probably going to have pancakes. Maybe we should have lunch."

"Oh, for crying out loud. We've been on duty an hour!"

"So?"

"So nothing. Get your stomach under control and sit back and wait."

Cecil's car was in the parking lot of the IHOP restaurant on Lincoln Avenue, and belatedly Lillith realized she had forgotten to tell the police that Cecil even had a car—because, of course, he'd never registered the Olds or given her a ride in it. She couldn't believe it, and the nearly reckless left-hand swing that put the sports car into the driveway on the west side of Lincoln was mere reflex—she had no plan of action and didn't know what she was going to say to him. *Hi, how are you? By the way, are you going to kill me now?*

If she'd thought getting out of the Mercedes at his apartment was difficult, that was nothing compared with the fear she felt now when there was no question he was here. Wherever he was sitting, he was out of sight of the windows, but that didn't mean he wouldn't see her as she walked in. At least there were lots of people around, with a good half of the parking spaces in the lot taken. It was as public a place as she was likely to get. But . . . was it *safe*?

Lillith smoothed her hair nervously and got out of the

Mercedes, letting the driver's door close but not lock, the vague thought that she could run to her car if she needed to floating somewhere in the recesses of her head. She took three steps, then got disgusted and went back and locked it. There was no sense in fouling up the day more by coming back to the car and finding the dashboard ripped apart and the CD player stolen. She sucked in a lungful of the hot summer air and strode to the restaurant's entrance.

The inside was noisier and busier than she had expected; it seemed that half the parking lot outside meant nearly a full house inside. She didn't see Cecil right away, then her eyes picked up the familiar broad shoulders and carefully trimmed light brown hair. Seated at an inside booth in the smaller back section, he hadn't bothered to look up when the door had opened. Apparently the bustle of the place had lulled him into believing he could blend in with the crowd. Lillith's mouth twisted; such a foolish thought from someone who was normally so intelligent.

She nearly jumped out of her shoes when a sprightly voice over her left shoulder said, "Welcome to IHOP, one for lunch?" The young woman's smile faltered at the frozen-rabbit expression on Lillith's face, then returned when Lillith managed to say, "I'm joining someone, thanks." She gestured vaguely toward the back section and the hostess nodded and looked at her strangely before stepping away.

To say her heart was hammering when she walked over to Cecil's booth and slid onto the seat across from him would be an understatement; she felt as if someone had sewn the organ to the shoulder strap of a firing machine gun. "Hello," she managed. Lillith tried on a tremulous smile but it didn't work and she gave up at the look on his face when he raised his gaze to hers. "May I join you?"

"Doesn't seem as though I have much choice."

He looked . . . different. *Dangerous.* What had she expected? The all-American boy? Still, Lillith had never seen him quite like this, with bluish shadows under his eyes and his jaw slightly unshaven. The shirt he wore was package-creased and obviously new, taken right from its wrapper. With a start she realized why: he was in *hiding*, for God's sake—he had no electric razor and no change of clothes, nothing. *Of course* the police were watching his apartment. . . .

And she'd led them right to him.

The smile she sent his way was genuine this time. "Cecil," she said gently, "the police are outside." It was a guesstimate, but she felt it was probably accurate. "Don't you think it would make things a lot easier if you turned yourself in? They have people who can help you."

"I don't know what you're talking about." He looked at her sullenly. There was a plate of picked-over Harvest Grain pancakes in front of him and Cecil pushed his fork halfheartedly through the syrup.

Somewhere in the line of her right peripheral vision, Lillith saw a waitress step up to the table. "Hi, can I get you coffee?" she asked.

"Go away," Lillith said without taking her eyes off Cecil. "And don't come back."

"Well, I never!" The waitress spun and stomped off.

"I wanted coffee," Cecil said petulantly.

"I'm not here to talk about coffee, Cecil." Lillith studied him for a moment. Her heart had stopped its frantic thumping and now faithfully did its job, giving one steady beat after another in her chest. In some detached mental mode, she was rather surprised at its efficiency, considering the amount of stress she still felt. "Cecil, I'm *sorry* I hurt you." She lowered her voice and leaned forward, knowing the waitress was staring at them and no doubt doing everything in her power to eavesdrop. "But you can't . . . you know." Lillith's mouth closed; despite her resolve, she was finding it impossible to say the words to his face.

"Can't what?" Cecil shoved the plate away roughly, purposely letting it bang into his empty coffee cup and the sugar container. "Who are you to tell me I can or can't do anything?" he demanded. "The only thing you *can* tell me is that I *can't* have you. So get out of my life, lady."

His face was starting to flush with anger and Lillith's gut did a lazy flip. Still she had to keep going. Why else had she come? "All right," she said calmly, barely able to hear herself above the roaring pulse of fear in her head. Her eyesight was throbbing, as though she had a head-blasting migraine, and she took a deep breath. "I won't tell you that you can't do anything. But I will tell you what you *shouldn't* have done, and that's go out and kill four women who looked like me." There, the words were out and hanging in the air between them, ugly and huge and unavoidable. Something indefinable in his eyes went oddly . . . hazy. Then his gaze cleared, as if a light had suddenly turned itself on inside his brain, and Cecil laughed at her—*laughed*, for God's sake.

"You're right, of course. How stupid of me." He waved a hand carelessly in the air. "All this time, I've been confusing them with *YOU!*"

Cecil lunged at her then, and his speed was incredible. Maybe it was her sluggish reflexes or the simple inability to believe he was really coming after her that prevented Lillith from jerking out of his range. She wouldn't have made it anyway; his forward motion pushed the edge of the table into her stomach and pinned her against the back of the booth like a baby in a car seat; all she could do was flail helplessly at him as his big hands locked heavily around her throat. She didn't even have time to *scream*. No wonder no one had heard a cry from all his victims. He was too damned fast.

Above and beyond the pain in her throat, though, she did have an advantage that Cecil's other victims hadn't had.

Other people were screaming for her.

The woman they'd followed to the restaurant had gone inside and turned to the right rather than to the left, thus the great view that Jude and Sandra had into the IHOP's main dining room was useless. They'd both been inside the building before and knew the layout; while the smaller dining section on the east side of the building had its share of windows, the front entrance jutted out and effectively blocked the view from Sandra's car. They were discussing the merits of moving the car to a more advantageous spot when a man careened out of the front entrance, stopped short, then spun indecisively.

"What's he looking for?" Sandra asked, suddenly suspicious.

"Damned if I know. He's in a helluva hurry, though."

"Let's find out." Sandra opened the car door and stepped out. "Hey!" she called. "What's going on?"

The man stared at her for a second, then rushed toward the Corsa. By the time he got to the front bumper, Jude was out of the passenger side and on the defensive. "Hold it right there," he ordered. "What—"

"There's a guy in there attacking a woman!" the man said excitedly. "I have to find the police!" He whirled again, as if his sense of direction had gone haywire in all the commotion.

"You've found them," Sandra snapped. Jude ran for the restaurant entrance as her badge appeared. "Now stay out of the way."

"Backup!" Jude yelled over his shoulder as he grabbed for the door handle, but the flip phone was already in her hand and she was talking rapidly into it from a few steps behind him. To the right of the front door people were yelling around a huddle of figures; Jude could see several men struggling uselessly with someone, hear someone else, a woman, screaming in a shrill voice, *"He's gonna kill her! He's gonna kill her!"*

"Move *ASIDE!*" Jude bellowed. *"NOW!"* His revolver was out but it was a useless weapon in a situation like this—too many bodies, too much hysteria. He was plowing through people like a linebacker trying to get to the center of the fray, and some dim part of his brain was not at all surprised to find that the cause of everything was Gideon and the woman who was probably his ex-girlfriend. Who was going to die if they didn't get to her fast.

"Get the hell out of the *way!*" Sandra was snarling at people behind him and he felt her hands on his shoulder blades, felt her give him a good push that sent him forward through the last two fools who were pounding ineffectively on Gideon in an attempt to get him to release his hold on the dark-haired woman's throat. Gideon was literally on *top* of the table, knees planted wide and firm, as he proceeded to throttle his victim.

"Police!" Jude yelled. "Let go of her and get your hands up! *Now*, damn it!" The woman's two would-be rescuers jumped ship then, throwing themselves backward in a move so synchronized it might have been rehearsed. For a moment Gideon didn't seem to notice the two police officers any more than he'd paid attention to the people pulling and beating on him a moment earlier. Then he twisted off of the table and gave a bellow, yanking his victim out of her side of the booth and hauling her up until her torso was between himself and Jude. The woman was still conscious, still clawing ineffectively at the massive hands locked around her slender neck, totally incapable of making a sound until Gideon threw her bodily into Jude's arms.

Jude's gun went flying as he raised his arms in an instinctive attempt to catch her. The sharp knob of her shoulder caught him full in the chest and nearly knocked the wind out of him, then they both toppled backward amid the sounds of screaming and Sandra demanding at the top of her lungs that Gideon halt. The woman splayed atop Jude was retching and trying to suck air into her lungs at the same time, and Jude was still trying to get untangled from her when Gideon jumped from his table to another, and leaped through the plate-glass window across the aisle.

The glass exploded. Jude let his reflexes take over and he embraced Gideon's victim and spun her, ended up on top of *her* and used his back as a shield against the sharp fragments raining on everyone. Sandra cursed from somewhere above him, then whirled and leaped over the other people crouching between her and the entrance to the restaurant. "Freeze, Gideon—I said *freeze!*"

Jude struggled upright, and this time the woman came with him under her own power. "You okay?" he demanded.

"Yes—*yes.*" She looked frantically at the remains of the window. "Don't let him get away. I'm fine—go on!" Hands were already reaching to help her.

He didn't need to be told a second time, nor was he going to bother with the door. Jude clambered onto the booth between him and the window, placed one foot on the glass-crusted edge of the frame and was out of the restaurant. A one-second scan and he saw Sandra chasing Gideon along the side of the building toward Lincoln Avenue. When Gideon veered back into the lot, Jude realized he was on his way to one of the cars, and he had a sudden mental image of this bear of a man grabbing some clueless man or woman as a hostage. The ugly possibility jolted him into action and he ran then, legs pumping at full power to try and cut the man off. Neither he nor Sandra would be able to catch Gideon if the man's objective was the side street at the south side of the IHOP's parking lot.

"Hold it, Gideon—you're under arrest!" Jude yelled uselessly. Gideon ignored him, of course, weaving through the cars, flitting in and out of view. When the large man skidded to a stop beside a black 442 with an out-of-date license plate below its back bumper, Jude suddenly understood why they hadn't been able to link their suspect to a vehicle—the damned car wasn't registered to him. Jude was still four cars away and Gideon already had the driver's door open and was climbing in. "Don't get in the car!" Not surprisingly, he didn't listen. He was already inside and reaching down to the floor, looking for something. What? Keys? A tire iron?

Then Sandra's voice overrode Jude's and she was *there*, five feet from Gideon, too close to be safe but stuck with it because of the surrounding autos. "Hold it, mister. No, no— don't move, not an *inch*." Her voice had shifted from its frenzied pitch of a few moments ago to something that was almost a monotone. Something in her tone must've finally reached Gideon and he went still, staring at both detectives with his mouth twisted in rage and his brown eyes wild and dark despite the bright afternoon.

When he came out of the car and leaped at Sandra, Jude saw that his last mental question had been correct: gripped in Gideon's right hand was a newly chromed tire iron, a bright and shiny weapon.

He was a big man and Sandra had no choice but to fire.

She had loaded her .38 with Glaser Blues, and Gideon took her first shot in his upper left shoulder, where it damned near blew his arm off. He spun and kept coming, the tire iron still gripped in his other hand. Whether it was madness or momentum that propelled him, personal safety demanded that the policewoman fire again, at point-blank range. When he lurched at her the last time, it was in a spiraling, almost graceful fall.

There was someone behind Jude, one person—no, two— trying to peer over his shoulder. "Call 911," Jude snapped. "Tell them to send a *trauma* unit, not an ambulance, understand?" Both people nodded furiously and ducked back into the restaurant.

Three feet away, Sandra reached out with catlike swift-
ness and kicked the tire iron out of Gideon's hand; the fingers didn't move, didn't even *twitch*. His chest looked like
someone had thrown a container of crimson paint on it. Sandra grimaced and reluctantly probed Gideon's neck for a
pulse while Jude watched, his revolver still drawn in case the
guy pulled a flash recovery. But that only happened in the B
movies; real life was a whole different game.

"Jesus, he's still alive!" Sandra said in amazement.

"Not for long," Jude replied matter-of-factly. "Unless we
get a trauma unit here fast."

"Did someone—"

"Yeah." There were sirens already wailing from the south
end of Lincoln Avenue, but it was too early to tell if it was
the backup they'd radioed for or an answer to the 911 call
from the restaurant.

"Oh, *no*," a voice rasped from behind them. "Oh, *Cecil*."
The woman from the restaurant, who would've been Gideon's next victim, stood with one knuckle pressed against her
teeth. Tears were running down her face and jaw, enough to
wet her neck and the splotchy purple fingerprints the man
on the ground had put there less than a minute earlier. Already it seemed like an hour.

"I take it you know this man," Jude said. She nodded,
eyes sparkling with moisture. "In that case you have some
questions to answer, ma'am. We'll also take you to the hospital and have your throat checked out, make sure the swelling doesn't get dangerous." She nodded again, then covered
her face with her hands and began to cry in earnest, shoulders shaking but still not making a sound as Jude patted her
shoulder awkwardly. Was it shock? Or grief? This was a new
one to him and he didn't know what else to do; not many
victims cried when the man who had without a doubt meant
to murder them was shot. The sirens increased appreciably,
as did the number of people crowding out of the restaurant
and edging forward, vultures come to peek at the kill. "You
folks get back and stay out of the way," he ordered harshly.
"Anyone who gets in the way of the medical personnel will
get cited for obstructing an investigation." They backed off
with the usual murmur of discontent, squelched by the sight
of a CFD trauma transporter and two squad cars squealing

into the parking lot. People were gathering on the sidewalk along Lincoln Avenue as well, staring toward the restaurant and the small group clustered out front. Jude hoped to hell he and Sandra could get out of there before they had to deal with any of the reporters who were bound to pick up the lead from the police scanners.

The back doors of the ambulance flew open and two trauma specialists hurried toward them, hands laden with supplies. They crouched next to Gideon without bothering to wait for instructions or a go-ahead, assuming from the stance of the two officers that the victim would not fight. It wasn't until their routine was already rolling that the senior of the two, a man who looked to be in his early forties, glanced over his shoulder at Sandra and asked for details. While his partner was occupied with that, Jude learned the name of woman they'd followed to the restaurant, Lillith Jerusha, and jotted down notes as she admitted to making the telephone call. Off to one side, Sandra gave the paramedics a quick rundown of the events leading to the shooting.

"How's it look?" Sandra finally asked, and Jude, whose hand was on Mrs. Jerusha's elbow, felt her stiffen.

"Not good," answered the younger paramedic, a woman whose grim expression had already answered Sandra's question. "This guy is—" She stopped abruptly when her gaze locked with the dark-haired woman's. After a second she shook her head. "Not good," she repeated, then bent back to her work.

Jude put enough pressure on Mrs. Jerusha's arm to turn her away from the paramedics and their patient. "Let's go over here," he suggested. "They'll be transporting him any minute now, and we'll be in the way."

"Where will they take him?" she asked. Her eyes were a deep green and still filled with tears; they looked like wet emeralds in the late-afternoon sunlight. "Can we go there? Please?" She touched a hand to her forehead. "God, this is all my fault. I can't believe he's been shot, or that he'd really do those things—"

"Swedish Covenant is closest," Sandra cut in to answer the woman's question, "but Illinois Masonic has a trauma team and the extra distance will be worth it. They probably can't do much more for him at Swedish than they can in the mobile unit anyway."

"She needs to have her throat checked out." Jude waved at a uniformed officer and he came over. "This officer will take you over to the IM emergency room. One of the doctors will give you a quick exam, make sure there's no serious damage. My partner and I will meet you over there in . . . oh, say half an hour." It didn't take a brain surgeon to know that his thirty-minute estimate would likely include wrapping up the case of the Ravenswood Strangler permanently. The reason the Jerusha woman had tried to hide her identity was pretty obvious, too: there was a three-carat wedding set on her left hand. "This officer will stay with you during that time. You do understand you won't be able to leave?" He looked at her pointedly and she nodded, casting a final, miserable glance in the direction of Gideon's body and the scurrying paramedics.

"Say," Jude said to Sandra as they watched Mrs. Jerusha climb into a waiting squad, "you doing okay?"

Sandra nodded, then grimaced. "It's not like it's the first time I've shot somebody, though he's probably going to die."

Jude nodded. "It's weird, isn't it? A classy woman like her tied up with a murderer—"

"Or maybe the *cause* of it all," Sandra interrupted. She motioned toward the Corsa. "Come on. Kimball will be here in a few minutes, and the uniforms can hold it together until he arrives. Let's leave the witnesses in the restaurant to him and the Deputy Chief and go on over to the hospital. It's not like we're looking for fingerprints here. Maybe the guy will tell us something before he's gone for good."

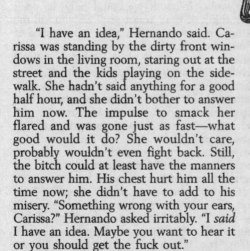

40

"I have an idea," Hernando said. Carissa was standing by the dirty front windows in the living room, staring out at the street and the kids playing on the sidewalk. She hadn't said anything for a good half hour, and she didn't bother to answer him now. The impulse to smack her flared and was gone just as fast—what good would it do? She wouldn't care, probably wouldn't even fight back. Still, the bitch could at least have the manners to answer him. His chest hurt him all the time now; she didn't have to add to his misery. "Something wrong with your ears, Carissa?" Hernando asked irritably. "I *said* I have an idea. Maybe you want to hear it or you should get the fuck out."

That woke her up, but not much. "What?" she asked dully. She didn't bother to turn toward him, but at least she could still speak. Carissa's body was a silhouette against the brighter light outside the window, and with a guilty start

Hernando realized he hadn't thought about the bulge in her belly—the baby—since . . . when? His thoughts of the unborn child disintegrated just as quickly as had the impulse to backhand his girlfriend, simply . . . flew away, like the friendly family parakeet whizzing through the window so stupidly left open.

"We'll take out each other," he suggested in a low voice. "Then bring each other back. That way we get our buzz but we don't have to worry about the cops or getting buried under some murder rap."

Carissa laughed unexpectedly, a strange sound that cut nastily along his already raw nerve endings and reminded him of banging two old pots together. Another resisted impulse, this one to clap his hand over her mouth and stop that awful noise. "You're crazy," she said, her humor abruptly gone, "if you think I'm going to try something like that. What if it doesn't work? What if we could only die *once*, huh? Did you ever think of that, smart guy? So you kill me and that's it, no holy resurrection this time." She stared at him grimly. Her once beautiful face was sunken and so very, very white, a walking nightmare of shadowed hollows and deeply bruised crevices above a still-lipsticked slit that was supposed to be her mouth and that still fascinated him. "No fucking way, Hernando." She turned back to the window and Hernando wondered briefly what she saw out there. If she was like him, and he was so sure she was, every warm body moving below was . . . *potential*.

"You can do me first," he suggested slyly. "Come on, baby. See how much I trust you?" He stepped up beside her and stroked the cooled flesh of her arm with his hand, careful to use the side of his palm where there was still a little fleshy padding left. "I know you're hurtin'," he wheedled. "I know your *need*—why fight it?" He gestured at himself and smiled, wondering briefly what that stretching of his mouth actually looked like. "It's right here, in front of you, in *me*. Safe, at home, and best of all, *free*. What do you say?"

Carissa glanced sideways at him and for the first time since they'd ducked out of the funeral home he saw a spark of interest in her eyes. Nothing had livened her up since then. Not the telephone that rang every hour—probably her parents trying to reach her and give her the all-too-livid final details of what had happened at Restmoor, nor the invitation of their friends to climb in a "borrowed" car and zoom up to Milwaukee for a few days to crash Maurilla's cousin's wedding. But now . . .

"What if it hurts?" Carissa sounded like a petulant kid. "I don't want to hurt you. What if it *doesn't* work, and you don't come back?"

Hernando laughed. "Hell, you know I ain't afraid of a little pain. And baby"—he tilted her face up until her eyes met his—"remember your aunt? If *she* can come back like she did, after so long and being filled up with that embalming shit . . .

"What's going to stop *us*?"

Darker afternoon shadows, as if time were stretching the daylight in its fingers, trying desperately to keep it at its most intense before giving it up. Outside the sun was still hot and vicious, no relief for the climbing temperatures, not yet. Inside the building, the apartment reeked of dirty bodies, death and impatience.

"Come *on*, Carissa—"

"I *can't*." They were sitting on the bed, legs twisted amid the rank sheets, and Carissa threw the switchblade aside. It hit the wall and fell to the floor with a dull thump, as if the old blood—evidence of someone else's forgotten wound—that had crusted on the blade's edge had stolen its metallic sound.

"Give me the damned thing," Hernando spat. He pushed her and she slid awkwardly off the bed and onto the floor. "Go on—get it. I'll do it myself."

"I'm *sorry*, okay?" Carissa grabbed at the handle of the blade, then cursed in frustration. It was like trying to pick up a toothpick while wearing knit gloves. "Damn it!" Finally she managed a grip using both hands.

Hernando yanked it out of her fingers, nearly succeeded in dropping it all over again. "You shouldn't have thrown it to start with." He fumbled with the switchblade, trying to jockey it into a position he could hold for more than a moment, fighting to keep it stable.

"Hernando, isn't it going to *hurt*?"

He grinned at her, his anger already forgotten. "So what?

A touch of pain for a lot of gain, Carissa. That's how you have to think about it, remember?" He lowered the blade and leaned over, pushed his lips against hers in a bizarre mockery of a kiss; his mouth was dried out and cold, like refrigerated plastic. "I know you remember . . . you can't help it." His grin widened, pulled into a smile that showed brownish, unbrushed teeth. "Can you?"

She looked away and closed her eyes. God, he was *so* right. That need, the roller-coaster-like *demand*, rose without command, surging up and beyond the constant pain in her lower belly, deepening the bloodshadows that streaked her legs. Their bedroom was dark, on the north side of the apartment, but to Carissa's eyes the ruin of her boyfriend's chest looked almost neon red, sweet and bright despite the cracked and dull gray walls that surrounded them.

"I can't *kill* you," she said plaintively. "I just . . . can't."

"It's all right." Hernando's voice was soothing. "I can do that part. It's not like it's suicide or anything, not when I know I can come back. Right?" He waited patiently; finally, she nodded. "Besides," that horrific smile again, "I always thought a scar around my neck would make me look cool."

Without another word, ear to ear—

One long cut.

"What a gyp."

Hernando was sleeping peacefully now, his face turned toward the wall amid the same dirty sheets, though now the cheap cotton bore the newer stains from the blood that had spewed from the cavernous gash he'd opened in his throat an hour earlier. Even those red splotches weren't right, weren't real *stains*. More like illusions of the splashes of blood Carissa knew had been there in the aftermath of Hernando's second death. Almost disappeared now, as if they had fled when his lungs had drawn breath again, but left a ghost of themselves to wait and see if he really was alive. Watching his throat sew itself back together had been cool, but like the weird green shine that had leaked from his mouth and throat and the high itself, it'd been over far too fast to truly appreciate. Not at all like the full-body buzz she'd gained from their night victim on Ashland, who was probably walking around Chicago with a nifty red necklace just like Carissa's boyfriend's.

But *was* Hernando alive? Really?

Bullshit; he was as dead as she was.

Speaking of dead, the baby hadn't moved in days, not so much as a nudge. Surely it too must be dead, lifeless and rotting inside her, taking her with it from the inside out like a big, nasty tick. How long before it had to be cut free of her body?

Or did it matter?

Already the heat and high she'd gotten from Hernando's corpse was fading to nothing but a memory, a lost and longed-for feeling that left her lying cold next to him, staring at the ceiling and wishing idly that she had the guts to kill him all over again before he woke.

41

Pay dirt! Jason felt like a spy in one of those Sean Connery movies, creeping around for days while he tried to spot his intended target, constantly formulating answers to questions he imagined the hospital's security guards would ask him if they stopped him.

No thank you, I've already been helped.

I'm waiting for my sister.

I'm here with my dad but he went to get something out of the car.

My doctor won't be here for another hour, and I'll wait.

None of that had happened, no one had bothered with him. His mind was functioning well enough to realize that was probably because he'd become adept at avoiding the areas that were obviously restricted. These were easy to tell, guarded as they usually were by reception desks or nurses' stations, but the emergency room might as well have had a sign

that read ANYONE CAN COME IN painted over every doorway—and there were several—that led into its depths. Jason
had erroneously thought that Sunday would be a quiet day
in the ER, *dead* quiet as a matter of fact, but he couldn't
have been more off the mark. At 3:15 in the afternoon the
hallways and waiting rooms were filled with people, most of
the victims recipients of summer weekend accidents. Everywhere he saw scrapes from skateboards and bicycles, overex-
posure to the sun that was again blistering Chicago, fender
benders and domestic fights fueled by the unrelenting heat.
Despite his corpselike appearance, blatantly out of place
among the sun-kissed and Latino complexions so prevalent
in this neighborhood, Jason felt invisible, one more little fish
in a huge school swarming through a section of the ocean.

And finally, *finally*, there was Evelyn Pelagi. Fully uniformed, she must have come in a different entrance, or perhaps she'd simply arrived earlier than he for reasons he
would never know. None of that mattered; what was important now was to get close enough to talk to her again, try and
get her to see how important it was for them to be together.
He'd been skulking around the waiting room of the Barr Pavilion at all hours, trying to catch a glimpse of her or figure
out if she'd changed shifts. During that time Jason had for-
mulated a hundred speeches, reasons, unarguable logic. Now
that he finally saw her, this woman about whom he dreamed
and thought of every waking moment of the day, he could
remember none of those repeatedly rehearsed words. All
that floated in his memory were fragments of the last, futile
conversation he and Evelyn had managed on Foster Avenue,
when she'd jumped inside a cab rather than stay and listen to
what he had to say.

Now that she was here, within reach, Jason's immediate
impulse was to run to her, take her by the hand and *leave*,
simply drag her out and forget wasting any more time in this
dirty, death-filled city. The days and nights of waiting for
Evelyn and watching the activity at IMMC—and especially
after what he'd nearly done to that child's corpse Friday
evening—had reinforced his change of mind about staying in
Chicago. Thinking about it since then had made him certain
that it was better to return to Georgia and a simpler life,
start small and let things grow to their own full potential. At

least his stay in Chicago had made him realize the danger that existed in the gift he possessed, that sweet, dark calling that had made him resurrect Evelyn Pelagi and now doubtlessly spoke to her in the same way. If it did the same for each of its children . . . and Jason was finally ready to accept that it was not *his* gift but it's own . . . what? Presence, manifestation, the earthly existence and implementation of the same magnificent power that had brought Jesus Christ back to this earth from eternal sleep. But this great power, this ability that came from God, was the new and improved version, one that could spread from person to person, neighborhood to neighborhood in the wink of God's eye. What if it just . . . went out of control? All those crazy people—no, he couldn't let that happen. He wasn't ready to share it with *everyone* yet, and besides, he was the First of God's chosen; thus he was the one who would have to guard the power, and keep it safe.

And Evelyn Pelagi was the second.

There she was now, headed toward the emergency room and looking so much like him and so *miserable* that it made his heart cry just to see her. He took a step in that direction, then stopped when he realized that the black woman walking beside Evelyn was talking to her, going *with* her. He didn't want to confront Evelyn in front of someone else who would interfere and help weigh against him any decision Evelyn made. It would be better to talk to her when it was just the two of them, two souls joined as one by God's divine gift—without the misunderstanding and meddling of those not touched as they were. Uncertain now, he followed the two women at a distance, finally stopping in the hallway outside the ER and blending smoothly into the throng of people going in, out and simply lingering. There were too many cops around to get away with hanging out for very long; sooner or later one of them would start asking him questions. Jason walked the length of the hall cautiously, then almost grinned when he reached the men's room a short distance away from the main entrance to the ER. It was a great place to hide—nobody else would stay in there long enough to pay him any mind as long as he ducked into a stall and didn't come out. An odd place to wait, but handy nonetheless.

Jason passed a policeman on his way inside, almost did a double take at the resemblance between this older man and Detective Ewing, the homicide cop who'd given him such a hard time over Evelyn. Brothers? Quite possibly. It was hard to miss the fact that the neighborhood police were in and out of the ER so much they knew everyone on a first-name basis. In any case, there were other, more important things for him to think about right now. Like how best to approach Evelyn this time, how to word his proposal so she could accept it without being afraid and viewing it as the curse she apparently did. When the way to do it popped into his head, he almost staggered, it was so ridiculously obvious.

Perhaps she still couldn't accept that she was not the only one. Did she not realize that Jason had given her this wonderful ability and that it could be passed on to others? Maybe, he pondered as he stared at his ghoulish reflection in the mirror hanging on the men's-room wall, it would be worth one more resurrection just to give her a bit of proof.

He settled down to wait, smiling slightly.

"What are you doing here? Leave, or I'll call security." Evelyn stared at that teenager, Jason Spiro, who was standing not five feet away from her and had seemingly materialized right out of the air. He looked awful, ten times worse than the last time she'd seen him, as if the puncture marks that dotted his skin were infected, or worse. His movements were wrong, palsied, as though he'd ingested something poisonous that was affecting his central nervous system. For a second Evelyn looked around wildly, but Karla was already gone around the corner to the lounge and its cache of vending machines in search of a cup of brew. If there'd been a guard close by Evelyn would've motioned to him. But no such luck, and as her glance skimmed by the men's-room door, she finally realized where the boy had come from. Then another thought struck her: was it only *today* that he'd been lying in wait for her? Or had he been nearby all this time, watching her, feeding that general awful feeling of lassitude that had taken over her life?

"Get out," she repeated, but fear and doubt made her voice weak and ineffective, and of the two dozen or so people milling around the main corridor outside the emergency room, no one paid any mind to Jason as long as he kept his head down. He was just one more piece of humanity among the hodgepodge crowd.

"Can I talk to you for a minute?" Jason asked. He was being careful, Evelyn saw, not to come any closer or reach out to her, and suddenly she wondered exactly how long he'd been following her. God, did he know where she *lived*? Here he was on his best behavior; if she screamed now, all his efforts would be wasted and they both knew it. "I won't hurt you, I promise."

"Hurt me?" The words wanted to boil out of Evelyn's mouth but she kept them low, barely audibly. "You've done much, *much* worse than that. I should be dead, and *you brought me back to life*!"

Jason suddenly looked immensely pleased with himself and with Evelyn. "Yes! You *do* understand—and here I was starting to think you didn't realize what a wonderful gift you'd received—"

"Gift?" Evelyn stared at Jason, her mouth open; she felt like spitting at him. "You call this a *gift*?" she whispered. "Look at me—no, look at *us*. Or haven't you been near a mirror lately?"

"These bodies are shells," Jason argued. "Vessels of the Lord, his tools. What do we care what they look like? Vanity is a sin, anyway." He looked at her expectantly.

Evelyn took an involuntary step toward him, then cringed guiltily as a passing orderly gave them a curious glance, paused, then kept going. "This isn't vanity, you idiot," she hissed when the orderly was out of earshot. "This is *dead*." She held up her hands. Encased in milk-colored plastic gloves heavily dusted with powder on the inside, the leathery ends of her fingers—flat halfway to the second knuckle now—were faintly visible. "Another day at the most and I won't be able to work anymore. That's what you've done to me, you monster." Her mouth worked furiously, barely able to form her next words. *"You should have left me dead!"*

"You're *wrong* about this," he argued. Impulsively, Jason tried to grasp her arm but she yanked it out of his reach, unwilling to be touched by hands that so closely resembled her own. "We can give this—"

"TRAUMA TEAM TO THE EMERGENCY ROOM, STAT. TRAUMA TEAM TO THE EMERGENCY ROOM, STAT."

Autopilot kicked in, years of training taking over as she turned her back on him and started away. "Wait!" he called. "I have other things to tell you, to *show* you."

"Not now," Evelyn snapped over her shoulder. "Go home or wherever else it is that you belong. It isn't *here*."

Face twisted in anger, Jason watched helplessly as Evelyn Pelagi responded to the PA announcement and ducked through the double swinging door marked EMERGENCY ROOM, just hurried away and left him standing in the corridor like he was nothing more than a bratty kid she simply didn't want to talk to. How could he explain all these wonderful things, all these possibilities, if she wouldn't stay and listen? He didn't care that this was a hospital, or an emergency room, or that someone might be dying a room away. That was an easy thing to fix, to change, and—

That was it.

It was one thing to be tempted, to actually lose control as he almost had with the Drury boy; it was another to *choose*, to teach by way of example. Evelyn still didn't believe, despite all his efforts and her personal experience, still hadn't made the connection in her head that it wasn't just her he'd brought back from the dead, but it could be *anybody*. Did she think it was a onetime thing?

Well, Jason could fix that.

Evelyn wasn't simply groaning inside, she was *screaming*. It was that addiction again, that dark cry to feed the *deadrush*, welling inside her head and heart and clamoring for the fulfillment that was so within reach in the body of the man they'd brought into the ER. And that wasn't the truly scary part: what terrified Evelyn was that something deep inside· her had recognized him instantly. Even before she saw Detectives Ewing and Wilfred watching her closely from the entrance, she knew without a doubt that this was the man who'd attacked her.

And here he was, dead—or as close as he could probably

get without dropping into that abyss—not five feet away. She felt no desire or need for vengeance.

She wanted something far more profound.

But there were too many people around him, a melee of doctors, nurses, and technicians. Other people, too, moving swiftly through the routine of trying to save a man who was undergoing increasing hemorrhaging in his chest, the efforts useless despite the actions of the two trauma specialists who'd transported the guy. Wasted O-negative blood, wasted IVs, wasted time—no way was this man going to open his eyes again.

Or so the rest of them thought.

Evelyn performed her duties in a dreamlike state that was somewhere between anticipation and absolute certainty. Her normal supervisor was not on the second-shift schedule, of course. Her new supervisor had no doubt glanced at Phia's notes regarding Evelyn's last shift, but if she'd picked up anything unusual, she hadn't said so.

Once this man died, he would become Evelyn's responsibility. She planned to take care of him well, because after all, hadn't he started the whole thing, the entire downward spiraling of her existence? Sure, she could blame it on Jason Spiro, who was probably still lurking about the hallway outside like some sort of misplaced farm boy playing James Bond. But what Jason had done would never have been possible had this man, this *beast*, not attacked her to begin with, mauled and murdered her minutes from her home.

It should have ended, right there. It hadn't and here she was, alive but not alive, dead but not dead, like some ridiculous zombie except she didn't exactly want to *eat* human flesh. A memory sparked in her mind and Evelyn almost grinned, stopped because she realized how bad the expression would make her look in the midst of trying to save a patient's life. Hadn't there been a zombie in a nurse's uniform in that gore-filled movie *Dawn of the Dead*? Wandering around a mall with a cap on her head cocked at a jaunty angle, looking for the next bite to be chewed. That was Evelyn, all right, all the way down to the nice white uniform and the stethoscope dangling from her neck.

They were losing the victim already, and somehow Evelyn had managed to steer clear of the whole procedure.

At least a half-dozen cops crowded together outside the entrance, reluctant to come in and get another look at the bloody victim no matter how famous he was; they saw enough butchery on the job. Other things kept happening outside the partially opened curtains surrounding the cubicle in which the murderer rested on a metal cart. A different doctor examined a woman who'd come in shortly after this man and who was still guarded by a policeman, looking closely at the heavy bruises on her neck while she peered in Evelyn's direction. Still others, Saturday-afternoon trivia, nothing more; there must have been at least twenty people rushing purposefully around the emergency room.

The man lying on the cart could not be saved. It was as simple as that.

Too much blood loss, two plastic-tipped bullets that plowed through bone and soft tissue and were designed with muscle-ridden madmen like him specifically in mind. The medical personnel filed away without comment; there were other cases to treat and other things to be done, and they took off in all directions quickly, like cats at the sight of a vicious dog. It wasn't long before Evelyn finally got her first look at the chart and discovered her killer's name was Cecil Gideon. As she gazed at what was left of the man on the table, she decided there wasn't much difference between him, as huge as he was, and the young Latino man she'd resurrected last week. His chest was opened wide in the same way, a rib splitter firmly in place, and tubes and wires trailed everywhere—blood, glucose, lines for the heart monitor and urine, a feed line for oxygen. She went around and dutifully shut everything down, careful not to miss anything, careful not to touch his cooling skin.

By the time she twisted the final knob to off, Evelyn's entire body was shaking so badly she almost couldn't hang on to the chart.

The dead man was . . . *calling* to her. Not in words, but in impulses, dark images that flitted behind her eyes and in the deepest spaces of her brain, indefinable pictures with twisted promises all their own. All those unspoken things sang in her nerve endings and enticed her, pulled her, taunted her with past memories of sweet flashes of orgasmic pleasure experienced only in her last moment of—

deadrush.

She slapped herself viciously, then thanked whatever God still looked over her that no one else was in the cubicle to see. The pen in her left hand dug along her cheekbone but didn't break the skin. Not much pain from the blow—hardly any—but enough to pull her away from the dirty lure of the *deadrush* and back to the cold, sterile reality of the emergency room. She felt fortunate for a second: the pen in her hand could just as easily have been the surgical scissors she always kept in the pocket of her uniform.

Water, that's what she needed. She might not be able to drink the stuff but she could still splash it on her face, gain another thirty seconds in which to plant her feet firmly on physical and mental ground before she came back and finished Gideon's death pack. No matter what lies her addiction tried to tell her brain, she didn't *want* to resurrect this man, this *murderer*. This wasn't some holy man wrongfully crucified and lying on the cart. This guy would rise and kill again, and again—and maybe the Latino man she'd brought back to life last week had already done just that. No way— Cecil Gideon *needed* to stay in oblivion, and she hoped fiercely it was his own private hell.

Evelyn dropped the pen into her pocket and tucked the clipboard with Gideon's chart on it beneath his leg, sliding it partway between the heavy flesh and the cart. She stepped outside the cubicle and took a couple of deep breaths, finally had to look to find the foot lever to get water running in the washbasin; she just couldn't feel the metal beneath the sole of her shoe. Evelyn wished she could have thought that the water felt good on her face, cold and refreshing, but the truth was she couldn't feel that either. Since there was no reason to hang a mirror in the ER, someone had tacked a piece of some kind of mirrored paper at eye level above the sink, nothing more than the means for the occasional ego check of lipstick or hair. Evelyn peered at her reflection on the paper now, then regretted it. The image was distorted and mesmerizing, pulled sideways by a flaw in the paper like a child's image in a funhouse mirror. It warped her fish-white paleness and steadily increasing bruises into a view more hideous than she'd thought possible. The reflection was a silly thing that froze her in place and let time slide by unnoticed until she heard a noise. Something fell—the chart—and she yanked her thoughts free and backed away from the sink without looking behind her.

Straight into Cecil Gideon's arms.

Evelyn backpedaled and tried to scream, but it was a useless attempt; the sight of the murderer come back to life had sucked all the sound from her body, from her *soul*. The night she died came back in all its forgotten, homicidal glory. All the details she'd been unable to tell Detective Ewing reasserted themselves in her memory slots with a malicious glee. It was like someone was riffling a deck of cards inside her head, only the cards were pocked with long straight pins and each one jabbed her as deeply as it could in passing. Her mouth opened but nothing came out except a tiny noise that sounded as if she were trying to clear a piece of popcorn from deep in her throat.

"Isn't he beautiful?"

Evelyn jerked her head to the left and saw Jason Spiro standing there, a bloody, faraway smile spread across a face that was inexplicably healthier looking than a short while ago. Gideon was upright and standing, yes, but not quite . . . *there* yet, as if coherency were slower to return to someone so large. He seemed confounded by all the tubes and needles embedded in his flesh, puzzled at the sight of the wide metal grid of the rib splitter buried within his rib cage. His exposed bones were glowing, *throbbing* with a hideous luminescence that Evelyn had never seen before, not even on the Latino man she'd brought back.

"Look," Jason continued, his eyes wide and shining, the only thing alive in the gaunt expanse of his face, "I—*we* can do what modern medicine can't. This man was dead, gone beyond mankind's reach like Jesus Christ Himself, but now he walks. Don't you see?"

"I don't know what you're talking about," Evelyn whispered.

Jason shook his head sadly. "Deception," he chided. "It will give you nothing. What I gave you—and him"—he inclined his head at the still blank-faced Gideon—"you can give to others." He looked at her closely. "I think you already have."

"Oh my God." Evelyn's gaze was transfixed by Gideon,

by his mere vertical position in the physical universe. Then again, why *was* she surprised? Jason had nailed her down, all right. Was this not merely a repeat of the young Latino man of last week? Only another—

Gideon looked up suddenly and saw her. His eyes were brown and blank, but something in his head must have clicked at the sight of Evelyn, and those dull brown orbs abruptly began to glitter, to show a startling depth of hatred.

Oh no—not a repeat at all.

Gideon shook his head, glanced over at Spiro and dismissed him immediately, as if the teenager were nothing more than a speck of dirt on the floor. The boy didn't notice, just kept talking to, *at* Evelyn, his words rolling around her and not making any more sense now than they ever had. Would he never shut up?

A minor miracle then, or at least a tiny triumph within the ugliness that had become her life: Evelyn found her voice and screamed as loud as she could.

Response was almost immediate but still not fast enough. Gideon had his hands around her throat before the first group of cops and doctors launched themselves through the emergency room's main entrance. Already he was squeezing and the garbled thought ran through Evelyn's head that she *still* had it all wrong, it *was* a repeat after all— but of her murder rather than of the resurrection in the ER last week. Here was the teenager again, the same as on that hot summer night when she'd first encountered Cecil Gideon, though this time he tried desperately to keep her life going rather than bring it back. Still, what could a skinny teenager do against someone Gideon's size?

A cacophony of shocked words and shouted demands for which there was no time amid the chaos her cry had caused, all of the words meaningless faced with the phenomenon that stood before them.

"Let her go, Gideon! Let her go and no one gets hurt!"

Evelyn recognized Detective Ewing's voice, but she felt like a rag doll dressed in a nurse's uniform. Gideon suddenly dragged her around in front of him to use as a human shield; absurdly Evelyn could feel the cold metal edges of the surgical instrument protruding from his chest against her back. Her vision was skewed, as if she were trying to see the room from a twisted position on one of the ER carts. She blinked and there was Jason Spiro, trying his best to pry at the massive fingers digging so effectively into her throat, felt more pressure as they forced deeper and located the fragile shell of her windpipe. So many voices—Ewing's, his partner's, even Karla's, her friend probably drawn from the lounge by the shouts and panic. All fading along with the oxygen to her brain, someone's faint demand that Jason move out of the way barely comprehensible, ignored by the teenager anyway. Her hands and arms were jellyfish, beginning to go numb as Gideon dragged her farther back and Jason followed. The rubber soles of her shoes pulled against the floor and gave resistance that seemed to infuriate her attacker even more. Her elbow hit one of the IV stands but there was no pain, then her hand flopped against her pocket and the lump of metal there. It took so *much* effort to get her fingers to obey her mental order to go into the pocket rather than simply flail uselessly at the outside fabric. But—finally—Evelyn had the surgical scissors tightly in her fingers, felt them cut into her hand as she yanked them from her pocket.

Her eyes were nearly closed, reduced to slits by agony and oxygen deprivation. She forced them open and glimpsed Jason Spiro—close, as though he were floating within a bubble above Gideon's crushing grip. Waiting. Speculating on her impending death like a crouching hyena, eager to do it to her all over again. Why wouldn't he just let her *die*?

There were choices, and there were choices, and like people always said, you do your best to make the right one. Usually it was the lesser of two evils.

This time it was the greater.

Jude Ewing had never had a hostage situation develop like this one, nor go from bad to worse this quickly. There were not enough cops around to handle it, no sharpshooters or bulletproof vests at all, no way to stall the perpetrator or keep everyone out of the area who shouldn't be there to begin with. Now that Cecil Gideon was not only alive, but *moving*, gawkers seemed to be coming out of every broom closet and supply room in this wing of the hospital like cockroaches. Drawn, certainly, not only by the fact that Gideon was strangling one of their own, but because Jude and all the rest of them would have to be blind not to see the aluminum bone splitter in Gideon's chest. The guy was a walking corpse—he just hadn't understood that yet.

Evelyn was dying in Gideon's hands and Jason Spiro—what the *fuck* was he doing here to begin with?—wouldn't get out of the way so Jude or someone else could try a shot at the killer.

Jude was far too close to the victims in this one. Somewhere in the action he'd lost the ability to distance himself and play cop. Every time he looked at Evelyn Pelagi he saw Karla instead, standing in her kitchen and holding Evelyn's coffee cup with fear and love shining from her face, instantly imagined the agony she and Warren Pelagi would feel if he didn't find a way to turn this thing around.

Unbelievably, it got worse.

Ewing didn't even realize the voice pleading with Gideon was his own when Evelyn's hand came out of her pocket. Clutched in her fingers was a pristine pair of surgical scissors, glinting under the harsh ER lights and razor sharp. Ewing had time for one grim thought—*Good for you! Ram it right in Gideon's eye!*—then Evelyn stabbed Jason Spiro deep in one side of his throat, finished the job by pulling the scissors sideways and gouging out a fatal five-inch furrow in his neck. Jason gave a surprised cry and his blood sprayed like hot water from a busted faucet.

Then Karla came charging thoughtlessly from behind the detective and launched herself at the struggling trio.

Jude hadn't known she was at the hospital, and it was the epitome of the things that had gone wrong with this situation. The sound that came from his own mouth was incomprehensible as Sandra shouted at Karla to stop and grabbed belatedly for her arm. Someone else—one of the doctors or a techy—reached out but was as unsuccessful as Sandra and, given the rapidly deteriorating circumstances, was clearly unwilling to do any more.

Karla howled at Gideon, oblivious to the blood splashing her and Evelyn, but Evelyn never heard her cries. Her eyes had rolled up and gone blank, and as Jason grabbed at the scissors in his throat and made a final, weak bleat, Karla lunged around him and clawed at Gideon's face, aiming for the madman's eyes, nose, anything to get him to release her best friend.

Shouts, the clatter of more falling equipment, and Jude finally lost it. Spurred by a terrible premonition of Karla looking the way Evelyn did now, he shoved his .38 back into his holster and dove for the cluster of scuffling bodies with a bellow, determined to get to Karla before Gideon did. Gideon's reflexive response at last set his hostage free, but before Jude's momentum could give him a linebacker tackle into Gideon's legs, Evelyn's body landed on top of him. A heartbeat later and the dead Jason Spiro fell gracefully into Evelyn's lifeless arms.

"*Jude!*"

Karla gave a panicked shriek and Jude rolled to the side and fought to get out from under the two bodies, then stopped with his eyes a few inches from Gideon's feet. His effort at standing was cut short when he strained his gaze upward and saw those massive hands on Karla this time, one digging deeply into her sun-streaked hair and pulling backward and the other . . . where else?

Tightly clenched around her slender throat.

"Don't move, mister." Gideon's voice wasn't right; there was an echoing, empty quality to it that sent a shudder down Jude's spine. "If you do, I'll kill her—and I swear I'll do it faster than any of you can shoot me. Now you back up, real easy, and keep your hands away from your gun. *Do it!*"

Something thick and sticky ran into Jude's eyes—Jason's blood—but he didn't dare reach a hand up to wipe it away. Blinking instead, refusing to let the image of Karla's frantic face sink into his mind, Jude scuttled backward, never breaking eye contact with Gideon while he forced his legs out from under the deadweight of the two bodies. Elsewhere in the room, the noise level had dropped to almost nothing; muted comments and questions, a doctor's bitter remark about Evelyn and his belief that the teenager had been the catalyst for it all. Gideon had a wall behind him, and the other entrance, the one that led directly to the circular drive outside, was a mere two feet to his right. It was ridiculous to think anyone might already be out there waiting when all the excitement had taken place *inside*, with no time to call for backup. One foot farther—two agonizing seconds that felt like sixty—and Gideon dragged Karla out the door with him.

"Get someone around front *now!*" Jude snapped at the nearest person as he yanked out his pistol. The trauma nurse who happened to be there was accustomed to jumping into immediate action and was already barking orders into the wall telephone by the time Jude slammed into the wall beside the door. When he stuck his face outside for a quick look, what he saw made his heart stutter.

Gideon, still maintaining his one-handed grip on the struggling Karla, reached into the driver's compartment of an idling automobile with his free hand and yanked out the driver, spilling the elderly man rudely onto the pavement before he tried to force Karla inside.

"Gideon, *stop!*" Jude yelled desperately. "Don't add kidnapping to the charges—"

"Like it really *matters*," Gideon snarled back. "I—shit! Be *still*, you little bitch! Stop right there, damn it—I see you sneaking around the car, lady!" Sandra froze at the outside west corner of the building and Gideon suddenly spun, reversing his direction with Karla's until he was half in and half out of the car, crouched behind Karla's figure. She was making hardly any noise now and Jude hoped to God she could still breathe.

"Tell you what," Gideon said almost conversationally, "you want her that bad, take her. She doesn't look anything like Lillith, anyway." He gave Karla a hard, abrupt shove that sent her stumbling forward on her hands and knees, planting his hands on her hips to propel his body the rest of the way backward into the driver's seat. Gasping for breath, Karla still managed to fling herself away from the car as Gideon's arm snaked out and yanked the driver's door closed. His pedal-to-the-floor acceleration sent the automobile careening around the concrete posts that supported the overhang and onto Wellington Avenue.

"Call it in!" Sandra was yelling to a uniformed officer who was shouting into his radio microphone. "Late-model blue Park Avenue, license number Frank Betty two—"

Karla scrambled to her feet, grabbed Jude's hand and pulled him back toward the emergency room. Sandra waved him on, already in charge of the upcoming pursuit. "Are you hurt?" he demanded as he tried to reach for her. She wouldn't stop to let him see. "How's your throat—can you breathe all right?"

"I'm fine—come *on*, Jude. I've got to get to Evelyn!"

Jude knew he couldn't let that happen, not . . .

. . . just yet.

He clasped the slender hand that held his and pulled back until her forward motion was cut short. Karla paused and shot him a look that was half bewilderment, half anger; then her eyes met his and she halted.

"Karla," he said gently. "No."

For a painful second Jude thought she was going to argue, then her expression crumbled. "It's not—she's not—" Her hands came up and fluttered, then fell to her sides. She simply couldn't finish. When he nodded, she folded up in his arms and cried.

42

"I knew that man," Karla remembered to tell Jude later, much later, after all the painful reports and all the terrible details were recorded. "Not personally, his name or anything, but I'd seen him before."

"Where?"

"At the Fitness Center downtown, working out on my lunch hour." Karla shook her head, her eyes dark and faraway. "All this time, and Evelyn's attacker was so *close* I could have literally touched him on the way to my locker." Her mouth twisted bitterly. "If only I'd done something."

Jude's eyebrows raised. "Sweetheart, I don't recall seeing a working crystal ball in your apartment. What you have now that you didn't have last week is hindsight, and we *all* have that at one time or another."

Karla looked down at her hands, turned them palm up and flexed the fingers, watching them work and remembering the way Cecil Gideon had looked, standing and walking and talking when he should have never been able. "Yeah, but this time—"

"Is one of the worst, it's true. Like I said, we all have those." Jude squeezed his eyes shut and rubbed the bridge of his nose. "I know someone who's going to have a much worse case of it than you," he said quietly.

Stricken, Karla stared up at him, flinching when Creature crept over and pushed her muzzle against Karla's knees. It was ridiculous to try to mask the tears running down her cheeks and Karla didn't bother. "We can't put it off any longer, can we?"

Jude shook his head and showed her the face of his wristwatch. "We just heard him come in and it's almost time for the six o'clock news," he said grimly. "We can't let Warren hear about his wife on channel five. We just can't."

Wordlessly, Karla stroked her pet on the head a few times, then rose and walked to the door. Through the old, thin walls of the building, she and Jude heard the muffled sound of voices from the first-floor apartment as Warren turned on the television set in the front room. They picked up their pace in unspoken agreement.

Some things were too devastating to hear from a total stranger.

Much later in the night, after Karla had held Warren while he cried, and after she had sat with him and grasped his hand as he made his telephone calls, Jude did the same for her.

43

Monday

That same dark motel room, the same sense and smell of years of dirt ground into the printed curtains and the green carpet, decades-old dust still ignored in its corners. For some reason, this time around Cecil Gideon didn't find the place nearly so offensive or depressing. He had way too many other things to think about.

To be depressed about.

To think about.

To be—

"Stop it!" Cecil said sharply. Sometimes he had to do that now, say something aloud to make his train of thought jump free of its loop, like hitting the break key on a computer keyboard to interrupt a program. His deep voice sounded odd in the room, flat and light, kind of hollow—as if he weren't here in the room at all but had thrown his voice through the keyhole like a ventriloquist.

Was he really here?

Cecil reached up with one hand and dug his fingers through his close-cropped hair, found a grip then pulled hard. Pain ran sluggishly through his scalp, but not nearly as much as he would have expected. Still, it was enough to convince Cecil about his place in this room, and in the space of the things that were happening right here and now. Enough to prove that a physical version of himself sat on the edge of a cheap mattress and stared down at the floor, too afraid to look at its own arm and chest. After all, wasn't there supposed to be *wounds* of some kind there, *gunshot* wounds to be exact?

Time to get back, Cecil decided, to the question at hand, to the reality check. *That* was the thing of which he had lost control, and some dim corner of his mind told him that things weren't getting any better in the mental filing cabinet. At least he was trying, and that effort was important in the scheme of things. Problem solving, the senior partners at work would call it, problem solving and initiative.

Cecil frowned and tried to concentrate. He'd definitely been lax in those two areas over these past five or six weeks, lax or perhaps outright incorrect. Lillith—or rather, the absence of Lillith—he now realized, had been The Problem. He had taken matters into hand—right there was the initiative thing—and tried to deal with it. Hence also, the problem-solving part. But he had gone about it all wrong and only created more problems, more situations, and now he had to deal with those as well. There was the matter of *himself*, too, and the way his body had . . . changed in various ways since yesterday afternoon's escape from the emergency room.

That memory turned his frown into an outright scowl. What a mess! Of course, he hadn't realized he was at Illinois Masonic until he'd jumped into that old man's Park Avenue and taken off. For a few minutes Cecil had driven in circles with his mind completely blank, like a chalkboard washed clean by the teacher. He'd very nearly followed a police cruiser right back to the hospital before he'd realized what he was doing and turned around; it was a damned good thing the cop driving that squad hadn't paid attention to the car in his rearview mirror. Cecil knew he couldn't pick up his 442—very likely it was already in the CPD pound, anyway—

316   *Yvonne Navarro*

and he certainly couldn't go back to his apartment. Would the police know about his rented motel room? His brain simply wouldn't function on a future more complex or far-reaching than Lincoln Avenue, and it was a risk he decided to take. With a bit of unintentional black humor, he'd left the stolen Buick in the back corner of the IHOP parking lot and walked to the motel from there.

Thus here he was, thinking—as usual—about Lillith. These thoughts were different, not so angry and not so clear either, muddled as they were with the memories and images of too *many* Lilliths, and the pictures his mind was feeding the projector behind his eyes weren't pleasant, either. The statement that had probably summed it all up and hit right to the heart had come not from some policeman, or even Lillith. Cecil's own damned words, spoken at the height of his escape from Illinois Masonic:

"You want her so bad, take her. She doesn't look anything like Lillith, anyway."

That was the whole thing right there, wasn't it? The attractive black woman he'd had in a stranglehold at the time didn't resemble Lillith any more than the woman he'd killed in the ER a few moments earlier. Sure, the nurse might have had a close feature here and there—nice dark hair and greenish eyes, the same shape face. Distant cousins maybe, but we weren't talking twins here.

He'd *killed* her, for God's sake.

It hadn't been the first time.

This was the part where things got confusing, where he usually ended up talking out loud to get a grip. It was that "first time" part that did it, because now that things were coming together in his mind and the blank spots were filling in with lurid details, he realized he'd killed before. Different women, all hapless victims of some tiny feature or mannerism that at some unfortunate moment had reminded him of Lillith. Now Cecil's hands opened and closed and he watched them for a few minutes in silent fascination, repeating the movement, again, and again. Such strong hands before the fingertips had gone so strangely flat, sturdy despite the fact that he'd worked in an office all his life. He'd never been afraid to get his hands dirty, no sir, pitch right in there and help do whatever nasty job needed doing—garbage, work on the car, stuff around the apartment, whatever. How unforgivable that these fine and capable hands had become so destructive, had been used as a murderous tool to steal human life.

Then again, there was that "different women" part, wasn't there? The woman in the emergency room tonight, the nurse . . . he'd killed her *before* tonight, too. Yet she'd been alive—

As he was now.

He shouldn't be. The sight of the policewoman shouting at him in Illinois Masonic had brought the images roaring back: charging straight at the barrel of the gun that same female detective had pointed at him, the belch of fire as she squeezed off the first shot and the resulting explosion of pain in his shoulder and arm. More—the sheer rage that carried him forward in utter defiance when Cecil knew, *knew* right then and there that if he didn't stop, he would die.

And he had.

Not right then, but soon after. There had been no great flash of holy light or sensation of sweet uplifting, and maybe, if one held those kinds of beliefs, such things were denied him because of the terrible crimes he had committed. The sound of the second gunshot had come instantaneously with an overwhelming agony in his chest, so fierce and enveloping it was unlike anything he'd ever experienced or imagined. His loss of consciousness had not been sudden; rather, it had sort of . . . faded away, as if his mind and the secret workings of his body had simply retreated from the outside world and this monstrous pain, gone into a hiding from which it had decided not to return.

Until something—or some*one*—changed its mind.

Fragments of sentences returned, phrases and words, bits and pieces of the conversation that had taken place in the ER as Cecil had slid cautiously off the hospital cart and jockeyed into a standing position. Someone else had been there besides the nurse he'd killed twice. Who? A teenager, that was it. The one that the *nurse* had killed soon after, stabbed in the neck with a pair of scissors after accusing the boy of bringing *her* back to life.

The nurse.

The teenager.

Himself.

It wasn't so hard to follow after all.

That boy had brought the nurse back to life after Cecil had raped and strangled her a week and a half ago, then had done the same for Cecil despite the massive damage done by the policewoman's bullets.

The next monumental jump in logic—if a person could call any of this logical—was again taken from the boy's words to the nurse.

Cecil had to think that he could do the same thing.

There was the problem-solving thing again, waving frantically in his mind and demanding to be heard. He'd killed how many times? Four? Five? Such terrible crimes. But it was okay; it didn't matter.

Because he still had the willing spirit and the tools—the motel telephone book was the best start of all—and it would be an easy thing, *now*, for him to undo what he had done. All it took was a little research.

Cecil pulled the battered telephone book out of the night stand and opened it to NEWSPAPERS.

"Come on, baby. It's my turn—I let you do me, remember?" Hernando gave Carissa his best smile, the one that he was always able to use to soften her up no matter how wildly they were arguing. The way his face was sinking in, it probably didn't look that great, but what the hell; she didn't look so hot either. Then again, getting the buzz off him had improved her looks a bit. For a second he wondered if either one of them could ever look normal again. He thought the potential might be there, but the means . . . well, that would be harder.

Right now Carissa looked anything but pleased, like the child who'd promised his prize baseball card for a bag of candy when he was hungry, then couldn't believe he had to pay up. In fact, she looked downright *suspicious*, as if suddenly she'd gotten the idea in her empty head that perhaps she shouldn't trust him. "Come on," he said again. "We had a deal. I did my part, now it's time to do yours."

"How do I know it'll work?" she asked sullenly. "I don't want to die like, you know, forever or anything."

"Of course it'll work," Hernando said smoothly. "I'm

standing here talking to you, right? Look right here." He raised his chin and pointed to his neck. "You saw me cut it open with your own eyes, right? Nothing there now."

"Sure there is." She peered at the shadowed area under his jawline.

"No one else can see it, right? If I couldn't come back a second time, would I be alive now?"

"You're not pregnant." She stared at him. "Maybe that makes some kind of difference or something. What's to say it'll bring the *baby* back?"

"Who said the baby died to begin with?" he retorted.

"Well . . . it sure doesn't move much."

"You're not hurting like you were last night, are you?" Hernando spread his hands. "See? So it's a give-and-take. I gotta tell you, I'm not too happy as to how I'm feeling right now, either. About the baby—I don't know what to tell you other than whatever's going to happen to it probably already did." He did his best to rearrange his face into something sad, find an expression that would touch Carissa's heart—assuming she had something in her chest other than a piece of ice to begin with. "Carissa, I'm in pain, too, you know? You could fix that. I did it for you. Hell—you *owe* me."

"Yeah, well, I'm not much on doing it to begin with." Her mouth was a purple line in the white, dried flesh of her face. "I don't know if I could, you know, let you cut my throat or shoot me or something. I've had enough pain lately. I don't need no more."

"We won't do it like that," Hernando said soothingly. "We'll do it easy. I know—you take a nice hot bath, get the circulation going, and we'll take a nip out of each wrist. A couple of stings and it's over. Plus when you wake up you won't have that shadowy blood stuff all over the outside of your clothes; it'll all go down the drain with the dirty water."

Finally she seemed interested. "You think?"

"Sure." Relief washed through his head, made him uncurl the fingers he hadn't realized had gone into fists in his lap. "What do you say?"

"Well . . . I guess so."

Hernando grinned. "Great." He got up and went into the bathroom, was briefly thankful that his brother and their friends were still gone on their Wisconsin trip. Carissa followed, dragging her feet, then seemed to perk up when he stuffed the drain plug into place and started filling up the old claw-foot tub with steamy water. "Hey." Hernando plucked a dusty bottle from the shelf over the radiator. "How about a bubble bath?" He gave himself a mental pat for thinking of it when she finally managed a small smile.

A few more minutes and the tub was filled the way he knew Carissa liked it, close to the top where the water would rise to her chin when she climbed in. Personally, he didn't give a damn if it went on the floor or not, or flooded the whole fucking apartment. He watched as she undressed carelessly and tossed her clothes over the edge of the washbasin, then checked to make sure there was a towel close by for when she climbed out. There was no easy way to describe how Carissa looked. Where her skin had once been smooth and white as china, now it held a gray-blue cast that robbed her cheeks of any blush and made her eyes sink so far back into her head that they looked like black stones. Despite the pregnancy, her body hadn't lost any of its firmness, and he supposed under normal circumstances she would have been beautiful. Now he thought she looked like a mildewed and knocked-up female version of that animated doughboy character in the baking commercials.

There was no question she'd get in the water; the warm liquid tempted even him, reminding him that he couldn't remember the last time he'd felt *warm*—wait, that was a lie. Sure he could: the last time he'd gotten a high, or a piece of one, which meant he'd been freezing from the inside out for days now. Carissa, the selfish bitch, could've helped him out at her aunt's house, could've easily let him take the buzz from the old woman and be done with it.

But all that was old shit. Right now Hernando wanted to grin with anticipation, because Carissa was climbing over the bathtub's edge and carefully sliding into the water with those slow, special and graceless movements that only women that far along in a pregnancy seemed to have.

Finally, she looked up at him with a grimace, her face and hair moist from the hot steam. "I'm ready."

"Cool," Hernando said and pulled his switchblade from the pocket of his jeans. "Me, too."

He didn't waste any more time, because experience had

taught him there was too much of a chance that Carissa
would change her mind yet again, and then they'd have to
start the whole thing all over—cajoling, promising, the same
"I did it for you now you do it for me." She was already starting to hesitate and Hernando had to snatch at her wrists
when she would have pulled them back to her breasts. Two
quick flashes of silver—down the length of blue veins on
each arm rather than across—and the deed was done. Fear
was rampant in Carissa's eyes as she stared in dismay at the
blood sheeting across her arms and staining the water around
her body a faded scarlet. Hernando patted her shoulder and
waited, expecting her to cry, but she didn't make a sound.

"It's all right," he said finally. He couldn't think of any
other words and Carissa's eyes were beginning to flutter unwillingly. "Don't worry. It'll be like going to sleep."

"I'm not tired," she whispered. "Not right now."

"You will be," he said gently.

Carissa didn't say anything else, and Hernando sat on
the edge of the tub and watched her quietly die.

She shuddered as she went and never quite closed her
eyes the rest of the way, as if she was reluctant to give up
that last glance at the cracked bathroom ceiling. Hernando
studied her for a long time afterward, making sure the up-
and-down motion of her chest had stopped, watching the
water until the tiny ripples caused by the movements of her
body had faded to total stillness. After a while he gave her
corpse an experimental push and she slid farther into the
water, until the slowly melting soap bubbles swirled and
crawled into her nostrils, then crept into the slightly open
space between her eyelids.

Finally, he let himself be drawn by the sight of her
mouth. It was a rigid gash across her face, but it beckoned to
him as if it were still moist and red and full, could still start
a streak of desire within him. As he lifted her face from the
water and his lips covered hers, Hernando felt like a tiny spider being sucked into the maw of a vacuum-cleaner tube,
spinning and powerless, completely disoriented. With the
fingers of one hand still tangled within her wet hair, his
other hand reached out, searching for something to grab as
the room began a wild rollicking motion around him. He
missed the edge of the tub and found the high curve of Ca-

rissa's belly instead, then clung to it as a thundering chorus began inside his head and sensation started to take him.

His heartbeat swelled and rammed within his chest—
once—
    twice—

Beneath the callused palm of his right hand, Hernando felt the baby kick, two hard jabs in time with the jackhammer throb in his rib cage.

The movement was like an ugly jolt of electricity. He threw himself backward and tore his mouth from Carissa's despite the agony of need roaring through his body. He landed awkwardly on his back and whacked his head against the side of the toilet hard enough to snap his teeth together, tasted old, thin blood as he bit his tongue. A faint orange glow underlit the soap bubbles floating on top of the bathwater around the lower half of Carissa's body, and Hernando ground his jaw and rubbed at his eyes to shut out the sight. When he looked again a few minutes later, the glow was gone and the water that had sloshed over the side of the tub when he'd let go of Carissa had stilled. Once again, she'd slid nearly all the way under the surface.

He sat on the toilet seat for a while to calm himself, panting and purposely focusing on the pattern of tiny ceramic tiles set sloppily into the bathroom floor. The memory of her mouth called to him the whole time, and it was such a hard thing to resist. But the down-and-dirty truth of it was, Hernando just wasn't the junkie that Carissa had been, and never would be. Sure, a good hit from some coke felt fine now and then, the sleepy high of a few joints, the slow-motion action of an occasional Quaalude if he happened to get his hands on one. The bottom line was he preferred an old-fashioned drunk to anything strictly chemical. He might yearn for the charge her body could give him, but Hernando could get that elsewhere. The world was full of potential sources and things would be a whole lot easier now that he was free of Carissa and the bellyful of responsibility he'd nearly forgotten about in his greed. He knew a couple of dudes who had a place on Kenmore, in a building where the landlord wasn't around and no one bothered with anyone else's business. The weed and gravel-filled empty lots scattered among the apartment buildings on Kenmore's west side were home to lots of folks, dealers, derelicts, scrawny kids who shouldn't be out so late to begin with. The pickings ought to be real good in the dark, when the glow from the streetlights didn't reach where the lots all backed up to the rear wall of Graceland Cemetery. Hernando had been over there often, hanging out at a friend's place, checking out the groups clustered around fires built in the metal garbage cans year-round. It was a good and dark place to start his hunt. Hell, once he got situated in a new place, Hernando thought he might go back and pay a visit to that asshole who owned that Halsted Street liquor store, the guy who'd shot him. Revenge? Nah; he just wanted to laugh at the expression that was sure to be on the man's face when he saw Hernando walk in.

One last look—Carissa really had been pretty once upon a time—and Hernando got up and walked out of the apartment.

All she could think about were the children.

Alysson Lane had called in sick again today, and that wasn't going to sit well at all when Mrs. Cannice, the owner of the day-care center where she worked, found out. The first time hadn't been a weekday, and that made the offense worse. Each employee had to work a Saturday every five or six weeks, and her absence the day before yesterday meant imposing upon someone else to do more than their share to cover for her. Saturday had been a *really* bad day, the one that marked the start of all these weird impulses inside her head. Her body had started seriously trying to get control of things then, plus Coco had actually *bit* her that day, for the first time in the seven years that she'd had him. At the time Alysson hadn't been able to decide what was worse: the incessant, nameless gnawing inside her head, the unexplainable seeping and semi-invisible line across her throat, or the fact that Coco, her constant, loyal companion and the only thing in the world that loved her, now hated her enough to hurt her.

The dog had started growling at her the same night she'd been mugged. As if the attack hadn't been the worst thing imaginable, she'd been faced with carrying him back inside and listening to his warning rasp the whole time, had finally put him in the bedroom so she could concentrate enough to talk to the police. Her neighbor, the one who'd seen the attack from the window and called the police, had said she'd been grabbed from behind by two people, a man and a woman, and dragged into the bushes. Had they done something to Coco, something he couldn't forget and which had permanently scarred him?

The answer, apparently, was a resounding yes. She'd had to use a broom to force the dog into a box yesterday morning so she could take him to McKillip Animal Hospital on Clark Street. They were as puzzled by her pet's sudden viciousness as she was, and in the end could recommend no solution other than euthanizing the once mild-mannered dog. Seven years, ended just like . . . *that*, as quick as the push of blue fluid from the syringe the veterinarian had plunged into Coco's right hip. It was over and done with so rapidly Alysson couldn't even get the strangled *I've changed my mind!* to come out of her mouth fast enough to stop it.

She could still see the dog's accusing, endless stare.

So here she was, alone. Just her . . .

And her dark new thoughts, of course.

Images of the children at the day-care center flitted about in her mind again, flickering in and out like the frames of an old silent movie on a roughly used television set. Cindy, with her fine platinum hair and sparkling blue eyes; Edward, shining red hair cut in a bowl shape above brown eyes in a face that was far too solemn for a boy his age; Anita, a pale two-year-old with dark eyes and black hair whose features and coloring looked more Oriental than Latino. And Kwasi, too, a prekindergartner with chocolate-colored skin and wide, intelligent eyes. So many colors and shapes and smells and sounds, all bright and good and *alive*.

Why, then, did she so badly want to hurt them?

The apartment was empty now that Coco was gone, and Alysson was beyond the point of caring if her neighbors heard her talking through the walls or floor. What did they matter, anyway? She'd always believed they listened—what else did a building full of elderly blue-collar retirees have to do?—and this time, by God, she'd give them something that would burn their busybody ears right off of their heads.

"I don't want to *hurt* them," she said loudly. On impulse,

she hugged the inside wall, the one that joined her apartment to that of the Bauers. "I want to *kill* them!" Her voice grew to a momentary scream that lost some of its impact in the press of her lips against the plaster. For an instant she considered pounding on the wall to emphasize her words, then she changed her mind and stumbled away, turning in time to drop clumsily onto the couch. Crocheted doilies and shabby bits of never-completed afghans surrounded her, placed so carefully in her three-room slice of the world.

Jesus, she thought in sudden disgust as she looked at one of the afghans, can't I finish *anything*?

Her thoughts spun back to the kids at the center, and the idea of facing them tomorrow morning was overwhelming, insurmountable. Did she really want to hurt them, to *kill* them? No, she didn't think so. The desire to hurt, to kill, all that was nothing more than the means to an end—which was the insane belief that she could bring them back, no matter what she did to them. But . . . why would she *want* to? That was the puzzle, the answer to which she couldn't figure out.

All her life she'd battled depression, and Alysson knew she should've sought help years ago, when the bouts had not been so huge and frequent. Be that as it may, she hadn't, and there was a whole slew of excuses she could bring to the fore as defenses. Not enough money, too much embarrassment, too busy at work, on and on—despite the fact that her black moods had driven away friends, cost her jobs, alienated her from her family by their choice. The only thing she could honestly believe hadn't deserted her because of her state of mind was Coco.

Instead, he'd simply turned on her.

Why didn't matter; *facts* did. Fact One: No more pet. Fact Two: No more job. No way could she go in to work and be around the kids there. How could she touch them, breathe their air, touch them some more, with these murderous thoughts ramming around in her mind? And Fact Three: Something was physically wrong with her now. Her body was changing, visibly *deteriorating* at startling speed, hurtling down some predetermined path toward . . .

What?

Jesus, she couldn't finish a *thought* anymore, not to mention a stupid afghan.

The children again, images creeping unbidden into her mind, followed by dangerous visions and ideas of the unspeakable things she might do.

Alysson got up and walked to the countertop where her purse was, her steps jerky. Her keys were inside, and it took a bit of fumbling to find them because of her newly nerveless fingertips. When she did, she kept them clutched carefully in one hand as she left her apartment and didn't bother to close the door behind her. All those nosy neighbors, especially the Bauers—now they could invite themselves right inside and go through her closets, if that was what they wanted.

Such a dark, hot night, so full of twisted possibilities and people, all unwilling candidates for her freshly born and perverted appetite. The idea of dealing with it, of dealing with *herself*, had grown huge, practically overnight.

She'd never been good at solving problems or finishing things, even the smaller ones. Judging from the size of the situation that faced her now, it was much safer for Alysson to slip into her rented garage. She did make sure to close and lock all the doors behind her before she started the engine of her old four-cylinder Chevette.

Sitting there and breathing deeply, she thought that this time she could finally finish something—

Simply by not opening the garage door.

Tuesday

44

"Let's move."

It could have been anyone speaking,
but after so many years Jude was attuned
to Sandra's voice; at the sound of it he
looked two desks over in the squad room
and saw her as she hung up the telephone
and stood. He tossed down his pen,
grabbed his jacket—he always carried it,
no matter what the temperature was—
and followed her outside without slowing
them up by asking questions. Whatever
was going on, she'd fill him in when they
were on the road. This time they headed
to a department unmarked car that Sandra had found a spot for near the front of
the parking lot. It was one of a whole
crew of autos the cops at the station
laughingly said the city issued in a nice,
camouflage gray with ornamental spotlights that no one would "notice." Sandra
started feeding him details before they'd
settled inside the gunmetal-colored Ford.

"A shooting at Rosehill Cemetery,"
she said grimly. "It went down about fifteen minutes ago."

"That's on Peterson." Jude looked puzzled. "Why are we going? I thought that was the 24th—Roger's Park."

His partner gave him a glance that seemed to last a very long time, though in reality she'd hardly taken her gaze off the road. Finally, she answered. "The woman was shot and killed by a Chicago Police Officer. Her name was Delta Arvel. Remember the name, Jude?

"She was Cecil Gideon's fourth victim."

Rosehill was fairly close and there wasn't much time to talk about it. Sandra didn't know much anyway, judging from the answers she gave to Jude's first explosion of questions. When they pulled up, Rosehill Cemetery was a riot of people—police from the local cop shop, paramedics, all clustered around the Medical Examiner's wagon. Off to the side was a small group of reporters, held at bay by a couple of uniformed officers. The victim's body, covered by a sheet to keep the press from snatching grisly telephoto shots, was crumpled across someone else's grave. It was wedged unceremoniously against the aged base of a tall, stately stone angel that was now splattered with the fluids caused by the bullet wounds. But the bits of flesh and discolored liquid dribbling down the robes and the tips of the angel's long, graceful wings had no resemblance to blood, nor did the stains on the sheet covering the body.

Jude and Sandra joined the knot of cops clustered around the dead woman. One guy in particular looked ill, his face as pale as the few clean spots still left on the corpse's cloth covering. "What happened?" Jude asked. "We got some garbled information at the station." He started to bend and pull back the sheet, but the man who looked so sick stopped him with a hand on his arm. Jude looked at him quizzically, noting that his name tag said LANDERS.

"I shot her," he said. "If you're going to take a look, you'd better be prepared."

Inexplicably, the humid early-evening air was heavy with the smell of decaying flesh and the young cop's words were strained as he tried to breathe through his mouth. Af-

ter a moment's hesitation, Jude decided he could wait to get
a look at the body after all.

"Got a call from the security guard about a trespasser,"
continued Landers, "and when we rolled up to the gate the
guy was so scared he wouldn't come out of the guardhouse.
All he'd do was shout out the window that a couple of visitors had stopped to tell him that something—not some*one*,
mind you—had chased them around the back section. They
hightailed it out of there before he could get any more information, so he trucked out to the back side of the cemetery
to see what was going on, figured it was a couple of kids
screwing off, maybe smoking a joint. Instead, he runs headfirst into this . . . thing, and she goes after him. He said she
was completely wild, like an animal, and once he got a good
look at her, he decided it wasn't worth trying to talk to her
about anything. Claims the only reason he was able to outrun her without a car is because he jogs regularly.

"So we cruise around the lots for a while and we finally
spot her, wandering up here in the northwest quarter. She's
going along the inside Peterson wall like she's trying to find
the way out but can't see very far, feeling her way across the
wall like a blind person. Can't see her face, but her clothes
are all messed up and weird, flapping open. Then we realize
that they're, you know, funeral clothes, from someplace
where they just cut 'em down the back and tuck the material under the corpse rather than dress the whole body.

"At first she didn't hear us and we didn't want to use the
speaker, didn't want to scare her." Landers ran a hand
through his hair, then rubbed at the perspiration beading on
his forehead. If there was birdsong in the old trees in this
part of Rosehill, it couldn't be heard above the static-filled
phrases being spewed from squad radios and the chatter of
conversation. One thing had already begun, though, and
they all noticed it: the buzzing of flies.

"We were thinking—I don't know, that maybe she was,
you know, buried alive or something. I know it sounds ridiculous now, but at the time it wasn't such a stretch. I mean,
here's this woman, and she's done up like a corpse and her
skin looks all beat to hell but she's up and walking around.
You could tell from the way she was moving that it wasn't
somebody playing a joke—it was too *awful*. Hell, maybe her

family was paranoid, or into that 'it's against my religion' shit and the family didn't have the woman embalmed when she died.

"So anyway, we get out of the car and start calling to her, trying to find out who she is, what's the problem, et cetera. She turns and sees us, and"—Landers snapped his fingers for emphasis—"just like that, she goes after my partner, Sancho."

"She attacked him?" Sandra's expression was starting to turn skeptical.

"With everything she had. He was on the side closest to her and happened to be the lucky one, I guess. There wasn't any doubt about what she was trying to do—this babe was going after his throat. The only question was *how* she planned on killing him."

"Where *is* your partner?" Jude asked suddenly. His head was starting to ache.

"At Swedish Covenant. They're patching up a whole mess of wounds on him, plus pumping him full of antibiotics just in case, with a tetanus shot to boot."

"Are you telling us she tried to bite him?" Jude demanded. Behind him he heard Sandra snicker and he resisted the urge to elbow her; she might have a macabre sense of humor but it was obvious this man wouldn't find it at all funny right now.

"No, of course not." The cop looked sharply at Jude and Sandra. "You think I'm trying to make this into some fucking zombie movie? I'm just telling you the way it was, okay?" Sandra cleared her throat and looked properly contrite, and Landers finally continued.

"So Sancho whales her a good one, right in the jaw. She doesn't *flinch*, doesn't even slow down. Now she's all over him, she's got her hands wrapped around his neck and, let's face it, she's got the upper hand. Sancho's trying to fight her off, and gagging at the same time, and he can't get to his revolver. So I grabbed her from behind and managed to get her off him, but honest to God, I don't think she felt a thing in the pain department."

"PCP?" Sandra wondered aloud.

Landers shook his head. "I don't think so, and you'll see why when you look at her body. So anyway, nothing I did to her fazed her, and I finally hauled her backward and shoved her away. She stumbled and went down, and by the time she got back up, my gun was out. Sancho was still on the ground, when I yelled at her—twice—to freeze. But I swear, she didn't care. And this time she was coming after me. So I shot her, and it took three rounds to take her out."

"Okay," Jude said. He took his notebook out and flipped back until he found what he wanted. "The dispatcher said that the woman was identified as Delta Arvel, but we know for a fact that the Arvel woman died a month ago. In fact, I was at the scene of her murder." He closed his notebook with a small snap. "How . . . ?" His voice trailed away.

Landers held up his hands. "Don't ask me. Talk to Amasa—he's the one who pegged her. I never saw the woman alive, but I'll tell you this." He shot a bewildered glance toward the stilled mound lying across the grave site. "When the security guard finally came out here after it was all over, he told us that the Arvel woman's grave was dug up and the burial vault and casket forced open. It was empty."

"Jude, how are you? I haven't seen you since . . . when? Hey, this is some coincidence, huh? It was at the scene of the Arvel murder." Trevor Amasa looked much the same as he had the night Delta Arvel had been killed and he'd been roused out of bed to come to the murder site. His hair was mussed, his clothes haphazard, eyes squinting behind his glasses. Now that Jude thought about it, he couldn't remember seeing Amasa when he *didn't* look rumpled. The back of the Medical Examiner's wagon was open and ready, waiting to receive Delta Arvel—if it really *was* her—for the second time.

"Got some funny stuff going on here, Trevor. We were hoping you could clear up some of the facts. Landers over there claims you identified this corpse as Delta Arvel. We've seen some crazy stuff recently, but . . . Delta Arvel died a while ago, and in this heat—well, this body is pretty decomposed. To be straight with you, I can't imagine it got up and attacked anyone."

Amasa sighed. "I don't know what the hell to tell you," he admitted as he pulled on a heavy pair of rubber gloves. "The evidence here is not strictly circumstantial—we're not simply looking at a grave that's been dug up. Jude, I supervised the Arvel woman's autopsy. Remember how those are done? All the body cavities are *emptied*, and this corpse"—he pointed toward the ground—"the one that was up and running around, has the autopsy incisions and sutures to prove it. This is Delta Arvel, all right. I got enough pictures of her the first time around to burn her face into my memory, and you can't tell me that you don't recognize her."

"Sure, we recognize her," Sandra said. "But you're saying it's true that a woman who was strangled and autopsied almost three weeks ago came back to life, broke open her casket and metal vault, then dug her way out of the grave?" Sandra looked incredulous. "Christ, this has *got* to be some kind of hoax!"

"Oh, there's definitely someone else involved in this. No doubt about that."

"What?" Jude's eyes narrowed.

Amasa smiled. "I saved the best tidbit for last, Detectives. Alive or dead, whatever, *she* didn't come out of that hole in the ground by herself. There's not a speck of dirt under her nails or a scrape on her hands. Oh no, someone else dug up the coffin and pulled her out." Amasa peered through his thick lenses at the two detectives. "There's a lot of weird shit in the reports that have been coming out of this case, Jude, and now you can add this to the paperwork. I went over it all last night, after that mess at Illinois Masonic. First,"—he began ticking off points on his fingers— "you got this teenager saying he brought Evelyn Pelagi back to life a week and a half ago, and swearing she was dead when he first found her. Now he's dead, and the Pelagi woman is dead—*after* she and that kid were alone in a hospital room with Cecil Gideon, who was also dead, but isn't anymore. And let's not forget that an unidentified man pulled the same stunt Gideon did, namely tooling on out of the ER after he'd been split like a chicken breast." Amasa was waving his hands around so much he was beginning to look like a conductor. "So Gideon can't be dead, because he's running loose somewhere, though he was damned near gutted by the trauma team. So now he's free and one of his *victims* seems to have come back to life. This looks to be turning into an interesting chain reaction, and if you want my unofficial opinion, I'd say you'd better get your asses over to—"

Jude and Sandra were already running for the unmarked car.

Graceland Cemetery on Clark Street was not as large as Rosehill, but somewhere in its depths it cradled another two of Gideon's victims, not hard to believe since all four—five, if Evelyn Pelagi was included—were women from the same neighborhood. Over the past ten years the area had slowly slid downhill. Hard times and a lousy economy had done a real number on the older buildings and the streets, cracking and weathering stone three- and six-flat apartment buildings that no one had the funds or desire to repair. The sidewalks were speckled with trash of both the paper and human kind. The Clark Street front wasn't so bad, but things got quite a bit seedier on the east side of Graceland where the train tracks ran overhead and the CTA el trains made enough noise to drive a person crazy if he lived too close. Here the outermost layers of the cemetery's concrete boundary walls were crumbling to powder and covered with drippy lines of spray-painted graffiti, and the tops were laden with shards of glass epoxied in place between erratically twisted strands of razor wire. Inside, however, it was still as pretty as had always been intended: green and peaceful despite the train noise, muted as it was by heavily leafed oaks and maples that were close to a century old and home to thousands of sweet-singing birds. As a kid, Jude and his friends had pulled relatively harmless practical jokes for the passersby involving ketchup and dead-body poses across the flat-topped grave markers inside the Clark Street entrance. That was before it had become necessary to build guardhouses and post security people at the gates to stop thieves from breaking the copper vases free and taking off with them. What had taken place in Graceland today went far beyond the petty thievery and resale of metal flower vases.

Two opened graves, no corpses.

"All right," Jude said to Sandra. His face was stony. "The bodies of Deirdre Windsor and Jayne Williamson have disappeared. We have to assume they've been stolen by Cecil Gideon."

"So you don't believe Gideon's bringing them back to life?" Sandra asked dryly.

"I don't *disbelieve* it either," Jude shot back. "*He's* alive, isn't he? Can you honestly tell me you think Gideon would be capable of walking around after you shot him and the hospital sawed his chest open?"

"I wouldn't think he could walk."

"Well, we both saw him do more than that. At this point we'd better start thinking about who's left on the victim list. That ought to tell us where he'll be headed next."

"Well," Sandra said, "as I recall, the first woman he killed was Celestina Francesco. He's not going to be digging her up anytime soon; her family had her cremated. That leaves Evelyn Pelagi, and to get to her body he'll have to find a way into the Cook County Morgue."

Jude rubbed his eyes. "So what this means is that we don't have any idea, do we?"

"Not a clue."

"Well, we've got a car posted at his apartment, and Evanston's PD has people watching the Jerusha house—all of which may be a colossal waste of time if his objective is to find his own victims. Then again, if Lillith Jerusha was his intended victim the whole time, it might be worth it. I tried to convince her to at least check into a hotel until he was caught, but she refused. Said she and her husband were going to get reacquainted with their life together, and she wasn't going to start it off by being forced out of their home." Jude looked thoughtful. "He might go to the place where the Francesco woman's ashes are interred, if he doesn't know she was cremated."

"No way," Sandra said. Her memory had always amazed Jude; faces, names, dates—she could remember it all. Something in her head organized facts and figures and tied them all together in a manner Jude and most of the rest of the cops at their station could only envy. In fact, as a test last week, he'd asked her if she knew the name of the restaurant where they'd eaten the first night they'd ridden as partners. After about ten seconds of thought she'd told him it was Little Budapest. She remembered, she'd said, because the next day was her mother's sixtieth birthday and though she'd scrubbed her teeth thoroughly, her mom had said she could still smell the garlic on Sandra's breath. "I've talked to the Francescos several times since Celestina's death," she said now. "The parents weren't from Chicago, and they had her daughter's ashes shipped back to New Mexico. Her father told me they're moving back as soon as the murderer is caught. They'd been here six months when his daughter was killed, and they're only sticking around to see the arrest. Gideon had to do a bit of research to find where these women were buried, and he probably went to the library or looked it up in the newspaper archives. It'd be right there that Celestina Francesco was cremated."

"Then the thing to do is set up a door-to-door canvass," Jude said. "He can't have—"

The radio Sandra had hung from the waistband of her slacks suddenly let out a squeal of static-filled words and Sandra yanked it free and held it up to her mouth. "Come again?" she demanded.

"We've got the perpetrator cornered by the mausoleum on the west side. He was trying to hail a *cab* at the entrance." The speaker's voice was loaded with sarcasm. "This guy is whacked out."

Jude snapped on his own radio. "Don't rush him," he ordered. "Stall until we get there. We don't want him hurt— remember what happened at Rosehill. If he gets killed, we may never find the missing bodies."

"Roger." The transmission died.

"Let's go," Sandra called as she ran for the car. "We'll be there in sixty seconds."

The ride was as brief as she'd predicted, and the scene that greeted them was ten times more crowded than the Rosehill situation an hour earlier. Squads and unmarked cars were lined up outside the Clark Street entrance as well as along the access roads leading to the guardhouse and the mausoleum. Cecil Gideon had backed into one corner of the deep doorway opening into the impressive stone building, but it was solidly locked. He was unarmed and it was only a matter of time before they'd simply go in and bring him out. There was more than enough manpower present to avoid a repeat of what had happened with Delta Arvel at Rosehill Cemetery, regardless of Gideon's size or physical strength.

A gray-haired man by the name of Ricker hurried up to

the car as Jude and Sandra climbed out, his expression disbelieving. A faint acrid scent filled the air, dissipating now but enough to sting their noses and make their eyes water. "We tried to gas him out," he told them. "It didn't *work*—he didn't even cough. What the hell is this guy, Superman?"

"Then we'll go in and get him. He's not armed, or he would have been blasting away by now." Jude turned to Sandra and she nodded in agreement.

"Four officers—no, make it six," Jude began, "then we—"

"He's coming out!" someone yelled. "Freeze right there, mister! Get your hands up—higher!"

Jude and Sandra dashed forward in time to see Gideon as he was tackled by a pile of uniformed and plainclothes cops. For one ludicrous moment it looked as if there was an impromptu football play happening in front of Graceland's mausoleum. It was over almost immediately; Gideon simply couldn't beat his way free of so many police officers, though he was still struggling mightily when he was dragged to a paddy wagon and forced inside. Locking it up tightly, the cops who had grabbed him backed away and brushed at their clothes in disgust; dirt and pieces of uprooted sod, as well as a generous amount of unidentifiable bits, were plastered all over them. One guy looked at his fingers and sniffed them curiously, then turned away and gagged.

"Bleh," Jude said, watching.

"Funny how these things build up so big, then they're over so fast," Sandra commented as they stood with another group of people behind the wagon.

"Judging from the racket coming out of there, I don't think we're going to be holding any meaningful conversations with this guy for quite some time," Jude said. In spite of the fact that Gideon was handcuffed to an iron railing inside the wagon—or maybe because of it—the vehicle was shuddering and rocking as its prisoner bellowed with rage and threw himself from side to side. "I'm surprised no one got hurt bringing him down."

"That's because there's something *wrong* with him." The gray-haired detective joined them again.

"Like what?" Sandra's eyes narrowed.

"It's odd," Ricker said. "The guys told me it's like he doesn't have any coordination left, which is unusual for

someone so athletically built. They also say he's acting like
he's high on something. He didn't feel a thing when he was
nabbed, not even the nightsticks, and it's a damned good
thing we had so many people or we'd have never been able
to overpower him. Wait'll you see his fingers."

"His fingers?" Jude's eyebrows raised.

"Yeah. Weirdest thing I ever saw. They're all *flat*."

"I got the scoop from one of the staff psychiatrists I know at
HCA Chicago Lakeshore," Sandra told Jude sometime after
they'd come back to the station.

Jude was buried up to the elbows in forms: arrest reports, transport reports, death reports—Jesus, he was starting
to think the department was going to come up with a report
that had to be filled out before you could file the *other*
forms. Sandra's interruption was welcome. "And?"

"Gideon's brain is toast," she said flatly. "They can't do
anything at all with him. He's in a straitjacket and a padded
cell, loaded up the whazoo with tranquilizers. And he's *still*
roaring and bouncing off the walls. Apparently the fact that
he's upright after all the junk they've pumped into him
makes him some kind of medical anomaly. He shows no
signs of letting up."

Jude put his pen down and leaned back on his chair.
"Isn't it kind of soon to make a diagnosis like that?"

Sandra shrugged. "Obviously they don't think so. They
did manage to get a blood sample for testing, but the results
were inconclusive. There's no evidence of any drug use or
chemical ingestion of any kind, although the guy I talked to
said the blood wasn't quite normal. Something about the
amount and way it was carrying oxygen."

"So what you're telling me," Jude said in exasperation,
"is that there's no way Gideon is going to be prosecuted. We
can tie him to the rapes and murders of four women through
skin and semen analysis, and we saw him murder Evelyn
Pelagi. Yet ten years down the line, he'll be 'all better' or
some bullshit like that and they'll turn him loose. In the
meantime we've got two missing corpses to find and he
can't—or won't—talk."

"Oh, I don't think they'll let Gideon out on the streets,

and you can bet if he gets enough sanity back in his head to form words, we'll put him up for trial," Sandra said wryly. Her expression clearly said *We knew this was going to happen.*

"The first thing he did when they took the cuffs off on the ward was try to strangle one of the other patients."

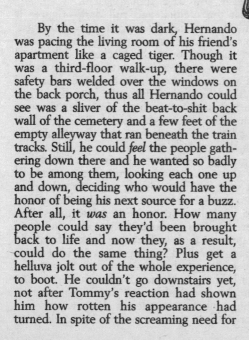

45

Wednesday

By the time it was dark, Hernando
was pacing the living room of his friend's
apartment like a caged tiger. Though it
was a third-floor walk-up, there were
safety bars welded over the windows on
the back porch, thus all Hernando could
see was a sliver of the beat-to-shit back
wall of the cemetery and a few feet of the
empty alleyway that ran beneath the train
tracks. Still, he could *feel* the people gathering down there and he wanted so badly
to be among them, looking each one up
and down, deciding who would have the
honor of being his next source for a buzz.
After all, it *was* an honor. How many
people could say they'd been brought
back to life and now they, as a result,
could do the same thing? Plus get a
helluva jolt out of the whole experience,
to boot. He couldn't go downstairs yet,
not after Tommy's reaction had shown
him how rotten his appearance had
turned. In spite of the screaming need for

a rush and the burgeoning pain in his chest and across his throat, common sense told him it was better to wait for darkness. Shadows did a lot for the appearance.

Hernando strode to the front room again and stepped out on the balcony, staring down at Kenmore and the cars parked along both sides of the street. There were plenty of choices down there, too; people coming home from work, kids playing and making noise out there all damned day—all of which remained off-limits because of the way he looked. Tommy had taken off, deserted his place after less than a half hour of looking at Hernando, tossing him the spare set of keys and saying he had "plans" that would take him out of town for a couple of days. That was followed by the "suggestion" that he was sure Hernando would have a place of his own lined up by the time he returned. Point taken, Hernando thought bitterly, and see if I put your happy ass up when you need it, you backstabbing bastard.

Finally, almost ten o'clock and full dark—figures it would be the end of June and the longest days of the year when Hernando's blood was crying out for the cover of night. He tossed the keys onto the kitchen counter and watched them slide into a corner and scatter the cockroaches clustered around a piece of pizza that'd been there for God knew how long. Then he slipped down the backstairs without bothering to lock the door behind him; after the way he'd treated Hernando, it'd serve that fucker Tommy right if everything he had ended up stolen—not that there was much of value in that rat hole anyway.

Hernando's journey down the backstairs and into the alleyway was less than quiet, and he cursed the lumps of numb flesh that were his feet, hissing in frustration when they whacked into the stairwell posts and dragged after him, making him lose his balance more than a few times. The wide, trash-littered spaces underneath the elevated train tracks were not quite as dark as they had looked from the tiny, wedge-shaped view he'd had upstairs. At least three barrels along the length of the cemetery wall already had full-strength fires burning in them. People—mostly men, a few low-priced hookers—milled around the flames, laughing harshly, taking long pulls from bottles of cheap wine before passing the liquor along to the next person. Hernando hung back despite his raging need, looking for someone smaller and scrawnier than most of the beer-gutted drifters and un-employment fans out this early. He'd never been a coward and he still wasn't. This was more a matter of making a smart choice than being afraid of a fight; a beefy ex–construction worker was bound to make too much noise when Hernando took him out. Better to target someone smaller and lighter, some fool already tanked from the booze or maybe one of the skeletal addicts sneaking around the backs of the buildings looking for an easy fix. Tucked in Hernando's pocket was his good old switchblade, and who-ever his victim turned out to be, he or she was going down the same way Hernando had done himself a couple of days ago. Messy perhaps, but quick and quiet. He needed a high so badly that he was starting to feel a new hurt, a physical pain deep *behind* the semitransparent wounds in his chest. Somehow he didn't think dropping a couple of aspirins was going to help matters, and he almost regretted not bringing Carissa back as he'd promised.

Nah . . . not really.

Sliding through the blackest of the shadows, smooth and easy like dark motor oil poured into the night, until he eased behind a decrepit old couch someone had dumped by the cemetery wall, watching the smallest of the groups from fif-teen feet away with slitted eyes. One man, accompanied by three women, maybe a pimp and his street-dirty harem; sooner or later the guy would turn his back, go take a whiz, or slip off to do junk or business. Given the darkness, Her-nando was confident he could look good enough to convince the youngest one, a bone-thin girl of about fifteen dressed in skintight hot pants and a fake leather bustier, to go party with him. Failing that, he still had a little cash that would make her take the trick.

Firelight danced off the rusty metal supports, spitting and crackling and growing stronger as bits of wood and pa-per were fed into it by the man and his skinny groupies. Hernando crouched in readiness, rocking on his haunches like a starving wolf as he waited for the right moment. Fi-nally, *finally*, the man began to move away, jiving and laugh-ing with men from other groups, a step here and there that slowly took him in the general direction of Kenmore and away from the back lot. Ready to make a move at last, Hernando ground his teeth in fury when he heard a noise behind him. He whipped his head around and saw the shape of a woman making her way along the cemetery wall in his direction, lurching like she was drunk. Not far behind, some-one else followed—another woman—moving with that same, strangely off-balance gait.

Shit. If it'd been just one, he would've taken her out in-stead of the skinny broad at the fire. Two would fuck every-thing up—whichever one he didn't grab was sure to start screaming her damned head off. "Hey!" he hissed. "Fuck off! Go on—get away." He risked waving his arms at the two of them, then realized all he'd done was get their attention. Now they were intentionally heading for him. The only way he'd salvage his hiding place was if he went to meet them in-stead and drew them back in the other direction.

His movements, Hernando discovered, were rotting away pretty fast. They were still okay, not as clunky as they'd been coming down the steps of Tommy's apartment now that he was on flat ground, but not as fluid as before he'd first hidden behind the couch, stuck somewhere at a lousy midpoint. But his well-used fighter's reflexes weren't for shit now, and when he hurried up to the two women they were on him before he could do anything but yell in surprise.

It wasn't the pain that made Hernando scream, but the shock. All hope of maintaining his prime hiding place be-hind that stupid couch disappeared with his first bellow, and he stopped worrying about the idea of getting a fix when one of the women began tearing at his face and the other tried to help her along. They snarled like dogs, sounding as if they were trying to form words but had lost the ability, or maybe couldn't quite grasp the concept anymore.

Hernando was strong, stronger than he'd been before he'd been shot and killed that night at the liquor store—but so were these women. He felt the hurt they were putting on him, but it was a secondary thing compared with the sud-denly imperative business of trying to stay alive. The firelight dancing wildly in his vision was showing him horrific glimpses of his attackers' waxy faces that made it real clear that these two babes hadn't sauntered over from Broadway. Kicking, gouging, punching, the three of them entangled in a rolling mass of arms and legs amid a smell that made Hernando want to vomit despite the fact that he hadn't ingested anything in over a week. No matter how hard he tried, he couldn't keep a grip on either one of them; something about their skin was slick and swollen and leathery all at the same time, and though he *knew* he hit the first one hard enough to split her lip and send a handful of teeth flying, the fluid that sprayed from her mouth at his blow wasn't blood. Instead it reminded him vaguely of alcohol and the sticky liquid in jars of maraschino cherries.

He was tiring, fading under the attack. Closer to the drum fire now, Hernando could see the crowd of onlookers that had gathered, hear them cheer on the fight—*Go, man! Come on, hit 'em again!*—without regard for who he was or why the three of them were battling in the first place, free entertainment on an otherwise dull Wednesday night. The people gathered around them were street-vicious and while it wasn't uppermost in his mind, Hernando knew in his gut that if he came out the victor, he'd be meat for the drifters and hoods waiting eagerly at the edge of the fray.

Staggering now, the weight of both women trying to pull him down as he dragged the two of them across the rubble-strewn clearing, trying to get somewhere, anywhere. Face twisted in rage, Hernando finally got a hand buried deep in the long brown hair of the tallest one. He yanked backward, at the same time giving the other one a hard kick that pitched her on her ass. The first one was howling incomprehensibly, still writhing and trying to hang on to the end of his arm when he spun and lifted her, then jammed her, screaming wildly, headfirst into the fire drum.

Hernando turned to meet the other one before she got to her feet, but not fast enough. She leaped on him, screeching at the top of her voice, rancid moisture from her mouth stinging his eyes as they both toppled sideways. There was an instant feeling of heat against the back of his spine and scalp, then the fire drum went over, spilling its contents of wood, paper, and the scorched, still-moving woman shoved inside it. The one splayed across him had grabbed Hernando by the hair and was pounding his head against the ground with everything she had. Sinking fast, his fingers digging into the rough broken pebbles on the ground, Hernando succeeded in snaring a burning piece of wood, then brought it around and cracked the woman in the side of the face with the end that was on fire. The flesh of her cheek ruptured and blistered, but Hernando saw with horror that she still did not bleed—it'd been like slicing open a piece of cold meat.

Desperate, he hit her again, felt agony above and beyond the impact of his head against the ground as the dried-out ends of his fingers began to smolder where they clutched the hot torch. The small crowd of street people egging them on applauded and roared their approval as the hair of the woman straddling him caught. But she didn't seem to care about the burning of her hair, her clothes, or even her face as the hungry fire spread. Hernando tried to lift the piece of wood again, but his brain was bouncing around inside his skull, his ears filled with increasingly loud thuds as the back of his head whacked the ground, again and again.

Another attempt, and this time he brought the torch up and under her chin. He jammed it in as hard and as deep as he could, and saw with bleary, pain-filled panic from the corner of his eye that the first woman was moving. She crawled quickly toward the two of them despite the fact that she was *burning*, for Christ's sake, he couldn't even see her face she was so covered in flames. The woman atop him spasmed as the front of her dress caught fire, but still she wouldn't let go, her fingers firmly entrenched in the tangles of his hair. Trying frantically to pull his body out from under her, Hernando's last thought was still a yearning for an unnameable thrill before the second one hurled herself at both of them.

The three of them went up in a bright ball of flame.

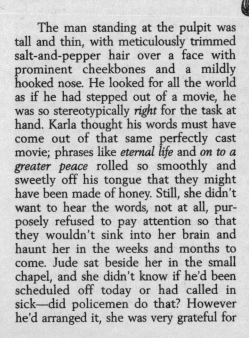

Thursday

46

The man standing at the pulpit was tall and thin, with meticulously trimmed salt-and-pepper hair over a face with prominent cheekbones and a mildly hooked nose. He looked for all the world as if he had stepped out of a movie, he was so stereotypically *right* for the task at hand. Karla thought his words must have come out of that same perfectly cast movie; phrases like *eternal life* and *on to a greater peace* rolled so smoothly and sweetly off his tongue that they might have been made of honey. Still, she didn't want to hear the words, not at all, purposely refused to pay attention so that they wouldn't sink into her brain and haunt her in the weeks and months to come. Jude sat beside her in the small chapel, and she didn't know if he'd been scheduled off today or had called in sick—did policemen do that? However he'd arranged it, she was very grateful for his presence and the quiet strength she felt radiating from him.

The pastor droned on, more talk about eternal life and God's glory, not much to be done about the people left behind. Warren sat to her left, his face ravaged by tears and grief, tidily dressed in a business suit, shirt and tie Karla had come downstairs to pick out for him early this morning, after he called her and said he simply wasn't able to figure out what matched what. Everything that was being said by the pastor was undoubtedly true—Warren *would* heal, given enough time, and the small problems he couldn't face today, he'd be able to solve tomorrow or next week. Big decisions were already being made solely on the basis of pain, as Karla expected they would be. In the car on the way here, Warren had given her advance notice that he was putting the building on the market next week. There were reminders and memories of Evelyn everywhere he turned when he was at home, and he felt that continuing to live there would be akin to mental suicide. It was a hurtful thing to face and one that would no doubt affect her place to live, but Karla could certainly sympathize. She felt the same way every time she sat at her kitchen table and remembered Evelyn perched across its width, her freckled hands wrapped around the mug Karla had gotten her for her birthday two years ago. The coffee mug, a huge thing covered with simple, childishly drawn women, had come from Starbucks. On the bottom was the artist's name, Kiki, and the title of the artwork— *Many Strong and Beautiful Women.* The mug, which Karla had chosen because it reminded her of Evelyn, was still in Karla's cabinet, and she couldn't bear to look at it. Not just yet. Later, when she was able, she would donate it to the Salvation Army resale shop.

The noise level around her increased and Karla lifted her gaze from the study of her hands to find that people were filing out. Somewhere between her thoughts about the building being sold and the memory of Evelyn's birthday mug, the pastor had concluded the memorial service. Now Jude was waiting patiently for her to stand and follow Warren and his in-laws outside. Picking up her purse, Karla realized for the first time how many people were packed into the place; nearly every seat was filled with those who had come to pay their respects rather than gape. There was nothing to gape at, since the Cook County Coroner had refused to release Evelyn's body for burial yet, and Warren and Evelyn's father had decided—another indication that things would work themselves out—to go on and hold the service so that Evelyn's mother could return to her home in San Antonio. When his wife's body was finally released, Warren would have a small graveside service for him and Evelyn's dad, and Evelyn would be laid to rest in St. Michael the Archangel Cemetery in Palatine. He had mentioned it to Karla, but she had declined; it was doubling the pain, pure and simple, and she simply couldn't watch as a wooden box was lowered into the ground and know that the best friend she'd ever had was inside. It was too much, coming as it was on top of the news that at the thirty-six-hour mark, some sort of rapid degeneration had taken place in both Evelyn's corpse and that of the teenager she had stabbed to death in the emergency room. The teen, Jude had told her, had snakebite wounds all over him plus postmortem symptoms of strychnine poisoning. While Jude knew the rest of the details about Evelyn, he hadn't shared them with her beyond adding that both of the bodies had begun to show signs of previous injuries, and the coroner had also refused to release Spiro's body to his mother and his aunt. The thumbnail sketch suited Karla fine; it wasn't hard to recall that young man's claims about Evelyn's condition when he'd first found her, and Karla didn't want a gory description to go with it.

The sun was harsh and overly bright after the low light inside Grove Memorial Chapel, but the air seemed sweeter, cleaner than it did back home in the city. While Warren talked with his in-laws and others who had come, Karla and Jude drifted to a stone bench and sat. They watched the people who left, their faces mirroring the same shock and sorrow so deeply embedded in Karla's heart. Startled, Karla realized that Brandon Ewing had also attended the service and was now climbing into a car; he saw her staring at him and his face darkened. Then he nodded, as if to say *I can still find my manners in public*. Karla hadn't realized he'd known Evelyn but after becoming acquainted with Jude, she wasn't really surprised. After all, the cops were constantly in and out of the hospitals along their beats and had lots of friends and spouses on the staff. The number of mourners here far outnumbered Evelyn's close friends, and it was easy to assume some were longtime but still casual acquaintances.

"It's nice out here, isn't it?" Jude was watching her watch his brother, but he didn't mar the moment's peacefulness by bringing it into the conversation. His blond hair looked platinum in the strong sunlight. "A lot different from the Chicago neighborhoods."

"Yes." Karla turned her face up to the sun, felt its heat on her skin. "I wouldn't mind living out here."

"Me neither, though of course I never could."

"Oh?"

"Cops, fireman, any kind of city employee—we're all required to live within the Chicago city limits," Jude explained.

"Really? I didn't know that."

He shrugged. "It's been that way for so long hardly anybody thinks twice about it. You live with it. I know a lot of cops who buy houses way out on the northwestern edges where the neighborhoods are quiet and clean and the schools aren't as bad. There's some nice places out by Harlem and Foster."

"Is that where you think you'll end up living someday?" Karla asked softly.

"Could be." His eyes were unreadable. "A lot of things could change my mind about working on the CPD until I retire. There's a police department in every suburb, you know."

Karla thought about this for a while, and about the night before, when insomnia had ruled and she had knocked on his door at three in the morning in tears. She'd ended up in his arms, moving so smoothly from friends to lovers that at the time she hadn't doubted for a minute that she was meant to be with this man right then, no matter her skin color or his. But now, in daylight . . . there were all sorts of problems. Family, friends, so many people who, willingly or unwillingly, still harbored the remnants of prejudice—Jude himself was the perfect example. To keep going, to move beyond a single sweet and passionate night . . . well, such a direction offered monumental family-oriented situations like Brandon and Jude's parents. Then again, problems could be solved, given enough patience and strength, and hadn't she

just been thinking about how strong Jude was? And she herself was no weakling.

She couldn't resist glancing at him. He met her eyes and
said nothing, but reached over and squeezed her hand.

Many strong and beautiful women.

Maybe, Karla thought, *I'll keep Evelyn's coffee mug after
all.*

Epilogue

Nothing moved in the apartment.

Over the past couple of days the surface of the water had gone through several transformations from the original soapy, heavy scarlet of blood. The first, after the heavier blood had settled to the bottom and only tinged the upper surfaces, had been two-toned, like a pink-and-red valentine parfait. Now it was mottled, a slight yellow undercut by brown, as if someone had slowly poured a bottle full of rotting vegetable oil into the bathtub water. Strangely, there was no smell of decay.

The shadows in the small bathroom changed around the dead young woman in the tub as the sun rose and set yet another time. Once beautiful, her mouth was slack and loose and filled with the filthy bathwater; the skin of her face and body had puckered hideously after lying underwater for so long. Still, her body did not decompose.

Three hours before the other occupants of the apartment were due to return, the unborn infant deep within Carissa Novia's womb turned sluggishly within its cold cradle. The fouled water in the bathtub began a slow, orange ripple that escalated in beat to the movement and pulses of need emanating from the baby still trapped inside its mother's body. The waves built and spread, until the glowing, polluted liquid sloshed over the edges of the porcelain and dirtied the floor, spreading in puddles that would permanently stain the tiles. The infant, a boychild, wanted—*demanded*—the soul-deep fulfillment of the fixes he had tasted at the hands of his mother.

A final, internal reaching out, child to mother—

Carissa shuddered, and opened her eyes.

She lifted herself from the tub awkwardly, stepped out and onto the floor. Then she simply stood with her head hanging and waited, rancid water dripping down her body and pooling around the puffed-up flesh of her feet. There was no cognizance or intelligence in the dark, wet splotches of her eyes, no specifically thought-out reasoning, only a compelling and all-encompassing instinct. After a few minutes, she began to laugh.

Sometime soon, the first dark child of the *deadrush* generation would be born.

About the Author

YVONNE NAVARRO is a dark fantasy writer and illustrator who lives in a western suburb of Chicago. Her first short story appeared in *The Horror Show* in 1984, and since then her short fiction and illustrations have appeared in over forty anthologies and small press magazines. She has also authored a reference book called *The First Name Reverse Dictionary* for writers and parents-to-be. She has written two previous novels for Bantam, *AfterAge* and *Species*.